Bob Stone was born in Liverp his wife and cat. He divides his time between running Write Blend, an independent bookshop and coffee shop and writing. He is the author of two children's books, A Bushy Tale and A Bushy Tale The Brush Off, a fantasy trilogy for young adults (Missing Beat, Beat Surrender and Perfect Beat) and a Faith's Fairy House, a children's picture book.

He spent many a happy day in his childhood wandering the beaches of Anglesey, beachcombing and looking in rock pools, and these memories are partly the inspiration for this book.

Letting the Stars Go

By Bob Stone

Wish on a Star,

[signature]

*To Estelle, with thanks
for believing*

Part One

1

Kate Wilde pulled down the shutters on the café and tried hard to ignore the way the muscles in the small of her back yelled at her when she bent and straightened up again. The yelling was becoming increasingly insistent these days, and more resistant to the ibuprofen Kate knew she shouldn't be taking as often as she did. Still, the warmer weather was due soon, possibly even next week if the forecasters were right, and her back was always better then. It was the damp that did it, but if you own a café located right next to the beach on the North Wales coast, damp was something you got used to.

As Kate stood upright, her balled fists pressed into the small of her back as if she could shove something back into place and make it right, she noticed a light shining through the gaps in the shutters and realised she had left the light on in one of the counters. *Sod it*, she thought, *I'm not going back in now.* One night wouldn't do much harm to the electricity bill. It was high enough as it was. She debated sitting for a minute on one of the benches outside the café before walking home but decided to press on instead. A misty drizzle was soaking everything, and the seat would be wet if nothing else. The dire warnings that her mother used to give her that sitting on a wet seat would give you piles were probably an old wives' tale, but it was probably best not to risk it. Piles were about the last thing she needed right now. No, home it was, back to her little cottage where she could shut herself in for the night and the only difficult decision would be whether to put the kettle on or finish the bottle of wine she had opened last night. In any case, she didn't fancy sitting outside in the gathering dark. The lights were off in

Gemma's workshop next door to the café and the security light, which was supposed to be motion activated, was in one of its moods whereby it was only activated by motion during the day. When it was really needed, it looked the other way and stayed resolutely off. Getting it sorted was one of the items on Kate's list of things to do at some point in the future.

There were seventeen stone steps up from the beach to the road, and Kate felt every one of them. It wasn't that long ago that she practically skipped up the steps, but now she had to risk splinters by using the wooden handrail, which hadn't been sanded or varnished in decades. Although it wasn't her responsibility—nobody knew whose responsibility it *was*—it was a job Kate had frequently meant to get around to. The weather and the time to do it had never coincided though, and now she'd probably never get around to it. She didn't want to pay someone to do it, not when the rail didn't belong to the café (she had checked), so it would have to stay like that for now, and she would have to get the occasional splinter. It was either that or move into the rooms above the café, and she didn't want to do that. The cottage was about all she had left of Al, and she had no intention of letting it go. It had been hard enough to let Al go.

She paused at the top of the steps to get her breath back (that was something else, she breathed like a twenty-a-day smoker, what was that all about?), zipped up her coat against the mizzle that was now making a determined effort to be proper rain, and started to make her way up the lane towards the cottage. She would grab something to eat when she got in (although right now she wasn't sure if there was anything worth eating in the fridge), have a bath to ease her muscles and then the wine was definitely calling.

It was getting dark now. It was still that time of year when the later nights were only a few weeks away but seemed like months off, but Kate had walked this stretch of lane so many times that she could do it with her eyes shut. She knew every pothole and dip in Chapel Bay (and there were many) and had, so far, never put a foot wrong. That was probably why she was so startled when something solid and furry brushed against her leg and nearly made her stumble.

'Gwyl!' a voice called out of the darkness, and Kate knew that old Huw's soggy and stupid border collie had just soaked her leg.

'Evening Kate,' Huw said, appearing out of the gloom. He was so engulfed in the oversized parka he was wearing that even if it had been daylight Kate probably wouldn't have been able to see his face. His voice sounded muffled as if he was speaking from inside a box, but there was no mistaking him. His shouts of 'Gwyl!' could often be heard around the lanes and heard by everyone except the dog, who took no notice whatsoever.

'You on your way home, then?' he asked.

'I am,' Kate replied, resisting any number of sarcastic answers she could have given. 'What are you doing out in this, Huw?'

'Got to take 'im for a walk, haven't I? I'd rather get a bit wet than find dog shit in my slippers.'

'On balance, I think you might have made the right choice.'

'No choice,' Huw replied, and Kate immediately regretted trying to be humorous, 'I've only got one pair of slippers.'

'I'd better let you go, Huw. You don't want Gwyl getting lost.'

'He won't go far. He can't find his way round without me.'

'See you, Huw,' Kate said and carried on up the lane, smiling to herself about how a dog could be so thick that it didn't know its way around lanes where it had lived all its life. Huw in his parka, and Gwyl the Idiot Dog, had been a fixture of the village for as long as Kate had lived there, and probably for many years before. Like most things in the village, they never changed. Kate had this vision that even if a nuclear war destroyed Chapel Bay, Huw would emerge from the debris looking for his dog. Kate sometimes found the constancy of the village reassuring, and sometimes she found it depressing. Tonight, in this weather and with the pain nagging at the small of her back, it was more on the depressing side. But Kate had been brought up to be an optimist. Tomorrow would be a better day, and you never know, something might happen.

As she pushed open the gate to her cottage, her sleeve snagged on the rosebush which was, little by little, taking over the path. Cutting it back was yet another thing on her list, but Al had loved that rosebush, loved its red velvet blooms and the fragrance with which it greeted you when you came home. Cutting it back felt like a betrayal, and Kate fully anticipated a time when she would no longer be able to use the front path to get to the cottage and would have to go in through the back door instead. All her life, she had never thought of herself as sentimental, but it was funny the things she clung on to these days. When Al had gone, so much else had gone too, that it made the things that were left so much more precious. There were CDs that Kate had never liked and would never listen to but stayed on the rack in the kitchen as if Al would suddenly come in, put some Happy Mondays on and do that stupid dance while cooking and drinking too much wine. There were DVD boxes under the television with no discs in them, action movies and thrillers—the films Al had tried to encourage Kate to watch, calling them 'classics'. Kate had no idea where the discs were but couldn't bring herself to throw the boxes away. Just like the disc of Die Hard, Kate didn't know where Al was right now. She hoped it was a better place.

Kate disentangled herself from the rose bush and finally got to her front door. She fumbled in her soggy pockets for the keys and let herself in. As she opened the door, The Cat shot out between her legs and disappeared into the night. She didn't own The Cat and wasn't even on close enough terms to give it a name. It was a cute tortoiseshell that had wandered in through her open back door one day and, although she had shooed it away that day, it kept coming back, yowling for food until she had succumbed and nipped out to the corner shop to buy some. Now it dropped in when it felt like it, mainly to relieve Kate of cat food rather than to supply any form of affection. It was a very one-sided relationship, but since Kate didn't want a cat and the cat didn't want an owner, it suited them both. She talked to it sometimes, and although it didn't reply, it seemed marginally better than talking to herself.

She scooped a couple of letters and a takeaway flier off the mat and tossed them onto the hall table. In the hall, she took off her wet coat, flicked the switch and turned on the immersion heater. While she waited for the water to heat up, she went into the kitchen and took the wine out of the fridge. It had been quite a nice Pinot Grigio, and there might be two glasses left in it. She wished now she had taken the time to drop in at Parry's corner shop to pick up another, but she wasn't going back out again now. It would have to do. She poured herself half a glass, figuring that it would feel better if she got three drinks out of the remains of the bottle and eased herself into one of the battered leather armchairs in her living room.

'Oh, Alison,' she said out loud. 'I do miss you.'

She said that a lot, but rarely meant it more than now

2

Frank Davies boarded the train in Liverpool, but nobody gave him a second glance. If anyone had bothered to look, they would have seen a tall (but not remarkably so), dark-haired, forty-something man, dressed in jeans, a black T-shirt with no slogan or logo and a brown leather jacket. They may have noticed that the leather jacket had seen better days, but who was to say whether this was age and wear or fashion? Similarly, who would know, if they noticed at all, whether the light stubble on this man's face was a deliberate attempt to appear casual and on-trend, or was simply because he hadn't bothered to shave for a few days? If the people around hadn't had their noses glued to their phones or their newspapers, they might have noticed that Frank was carrying a holdall that looked like it had seen as much life as the jacket. Perhaps the other passengers on the train might have assumed that he was on his way to the gym or to do his laundry. They might not have suspected that the bag contained everything he wanted to own or that he was leaving the city of his birth with no intention of ever coming back.

Unlike virtually everyone on the train, Frank didn't own a phone that gave him access to social media, the news and funny videos of cats. He had a very basic, pay-as-you-go phone tucked into the inside pocket of his jacket. He had put £10 of credit on it before he left, in case of emergencies. There was nobody he wanted to contact and nobody he wanted to hear from. When the phone was of no more use, it would go in the nearest bin. Instead of looking at a phone, he had bought a newspaper from a concession at the station and opened it. He had no real interest in the news but hoped it would act as an effective shield if anyone sat opposite him and wanted to engage him in conversation. There didn't seem much fear of that, though, because very few people on the train had any interest in talking to the people they had boarded with, let alone strangers. Frank, pretending to look at the paper, looked out of the window instead. The doors hissed shut, and with a slight lurch, the train moved off.

As the train emerged from the station into daylight, Frank watched the Liverpool skyline recede behind him. He could clearly remember returning home after holidays with his parents and the excitement he felt when, as his father navigated the last stretch of motorway, he could see the unmistakable and magnificent cathedrals in the distance and the Radio City tower standing sentinel over the city. It signified the end of the holiday and that they were nearly home. Now Frank watched as the buildings shrank and finally disappeared from view, and his throat tightened with the sadness of knowing he would never see that view again. He thought briefly of the old folk song that said, 'It's not the leaving of Liverpool that grieves me', but in his case, that was precisely what it was. He was leaving everything familiar behind and heading into an uncertain future, and it was all his own fault. He settled back into his seat, watched the scenery go by and tried not to think about it. For a while, nobody bothered him.

Frank got off at Chester to change to the Holyhead train. The illuminated signs told him he had a fifteen-minute wait, so he bought himself an insipid takeaway latte at the nearest coffee stand and crossed the station to what he hoped was the right platform. He didn't travel by train very often and always felt a pang of anxiety that he would accidentally end up on the wrong platform and watch his train pull out from somewhere else, with no time to catch it. He still felt that, even though he knew perfectly well he wasn't running to any kind of a schedule. It didn't matter if he missed a dozen trains because he was in no hurry at all, and it wasn't as though there would be anyone waiting anxiously at the other end. Luckily, the timetable hadn't lied to him, and five minutes ahead of time, the Holyhead train pulled into the station. Frank picked up his bag, and, making sure that the lid was firmly on his coffee, opened the door and got on board.

For a few minutes, Frank was the only person in the carriage. He picked a forward-facing seat and made himself comfortable. He had never seen a train as quiet as this. *Maybe everyone drives to Wales these days*, he thought. But with only a few seconds to go until departure, the carriage door opened, and a young man got on. As soon as he did so, Frank's heart sank. It wasn't because the man was dressed in a suit, so immaculate that it could have only been purchased recently, or that he was wearing a pink tie, which was fastened with an oversized knot, a style Frank had thought to be abandoned in the 1970s, but which had become inexplicably fashionable again. He also had no real objection to the young man's hipster beard, or the tattoos that emerged from his collar and snaked up the side of his neck, or the discs in his ear lobes that had holes so large a hamster could probably be trained to jump through them. All these things could be forgiven as the folly of fashion. What annoyed Frank most was the volume with which the young man was talking into his phone and the fact that, out of all the vacant seats in the carriage, he chose to sit in the seat directly behind Frank. Frank was immediately placed in the awkward position of either moving, which would give the young man a small victory, or stay where he was and be irritated. He elected to stay and to try and ignore his travelling companion. It didn't take long for him to realise that was the wrong decision.

The young man was talking to someone in his office, an assistant or something like that, and doing it without filters, self-awareness or volume control. Frank usually wouldn't listen in to someone else's private conversation, but because he had trapped himself in his seat, he was now given little choice.

'- And did you find the Richardson file?...The *Richardson* file. Fuck's sake, Becca, Richardson! You know, the one I asked you to get out before I left?...I did. It was the last thing I... No, I'm sorry. I *did*. As I was going out the door, I said... Sorry, is that my fault? Maybe if you got off your fucking phone and *listened* for once... Go and get it now... Yes, right now! I'll stay on the phone... No, actually, put me through to

Anthony while you go and do what I asked you.'

There was a long pause, and for a moment, Frank thought the call might have ended, but then the young man started up again, this time speaking to someone else.

'Jesus, Ant, where did you get her from?... She's fucking useless; that's the problem. She can't listen to simple instructions... Yes, I know she's got nice tits, but there's nothing between her ears. I think we should get rid... I don't know, get someone else. There must be someone else with nice tits *and* brains.'

Frank had heard enough. He listened to the voice come over the tannoy say that they were approaching the next station and stood up. He went around to the next bank of seats and stood over the young man.

'Excuse me,' he said.

'Hang on, Ant,' the young man said to his colleague. 'Yes?' he asked, looking up. 'What?'

'Sorry to interrupt,' Frank said, 'but I wanted a word.'

'Can it wait?'

'No,' Frank said, and before the young man could protest, he snatched the phone out of his hand. With his other hand, he pushed the young man back into his seat. 'Listen, Ant,' he said into the phone, 'do me a favour and get stuffed.'

The train started to slow into the next station, and Frank let go of the young man and went over to the carriage door. The young man was out of his seat and following, a furious look on his face.

'What the fuck do you think you're doing?' he demanded. 'Give that back.'

'The thing is, you need to learn to treat people with a bit of respect.'

'It's got nothing to do with you.'

'Then don't sit behind me shouting your business down my ear. It's simple, really. If you want your business to be private, *keep* it private.'

The train stopped at the station, and the doors slid open.

'You want your phone?' Frank asked. The young man made a lunge towards him, but Frank stepped to one side and tossed the phone out of the door onto the platform. It landed with a very satisfactory crack. 'There you go.'

The young man was caught in a moment of indecision, but Frank helped him along.

'Doors are going to shut,' he said. 'You need to be quick.'

The young man gave him a filthy look but said nothing as he pushed past Frank and stepped down onto the platform as the doors closed behind him. He was still yelling threats and curses as the train moved away from the station. Frank sat back down and picked up his newspaper. The only sound in the carriage was the soothing mechanical song of the train, and Frank remained undisturbed for the rest of that part of his journey.

3

From her small flat above the workshop, Gemma watched Kate close the café and make her way up the steps to the road. It seemed to take longer every day, and Gemma wondered how long it would be before Kate couldn't do it at all. She had, of course, suggested many times that the café owner should see a doctor about that back, but the reply was invariably 'I will when I have time', and that always closed the subject down. Gemma knew Kate would never find the time but didn't press it any further. Kate might be the nearest thing she had to a friend in Chapel Bay, but they had known each other for less than a year, so it wasn't Gemma's place to say. In any case, she had enough trouble organising her own life, so she wasn't really one to give advice to anyone else.

Purely out of routine, because she did it every evening after closing the workshop, Gemma unlocked the small, red cash box to count and record the day's sales. On days like today, there was no real point. After all, if you couldn't remember a solitary sale of ten pounds, then you shouldn't be in business at all. Ruth Prior, who came flying in to buy a birthday present for a friend, was the only customer she had seen all day. Were it not for the fact that Ruth's friend had made a snap decision to invite the girls out for birthday drinks, she might not have bought a present at all, and Gemma would have been the only person to set foot in her workshop all day. There was Ruth's slightly crumpled tenner in the cash box, along with the rest of the undisturbed float that Gemma kept. She shut the lid of the box and recorded the sale in the book she kept for that purpose, trying not to look at the records, which showed that this had, in fact, been one of the better days that week. In three days, she had taken nothing at all. The rent was due on the workshop at the end of that week, and it looked like she was going to have to dig into her savings again. The way they were going down, she might get another six months out of them, providing she didn't do anything too extravagant—like buying food, for example. Luckily the spring would start bringing the tourists, and things would pick up a bit. She hoped the weather would improve and the rain didn't keep everyone away.

The one thing Gemma had going in her favour was that, for the most part, her stock cost her nothing. Nature provided most of the things she needed, and her wholesaler was the beach. Everything else she needed had come with her from her old life. When the shop had closed down, she had packed several large boxes and thrown them into the back of her battered old Ford Fiesta. Consequently, she had bags of costume jewellery findings, thongs and necklace thread, and even a box of tubes full of jewellery cement. Nobody would miss them, but it saved her a lot of money, to say nothing of the hassle involved in setting up accounts with suppliers. With the cash she had ferreted away, and from selling the car, she had all she needed to start a new life and a new business. Everything else could be found lying around on the shore.

In some ways, it was the ideal life and one she had been prepared for since she was little. She had always been fascinated by the bounty that washed up on the beach, and that fascination had begun many years earlier, right here on the island of Anglesey. Her parents had brought her here on holiday for as long as she could remember. They had started out staying in various farmhouse bed and breakfast establishments, but when Gemma was about eight years old, her parents had taken the plunge and bought a static caravan. The site on which the caravan was situated was five minutes' walk from the nearest beach, a sheltered, sandy cove called Porth Dafarch, and from the moment she first set foot on it, she knew she would be spending a great deal of time there. Her parents were keen to let her explore, but her father, in particular, encouraged her to forage, to look at what was on the sand beneath her feet and to value its beauty. Her father could identify many of the shells they found—the periwinkles and razor clams, the whelks and the oysters. Most of the shells were in bits, smashed by the sea or by people walking on them, so it was a constant thrill to find intact examples. However, it was always a source of disappointment when Gemma spotted what looked like a complete whelk shell, for example, only to dig it out of the sand and find that the perfect visible part was all there was and that the rest was broken or missing altogether. When she found any complete shells, she carefully washed them out with seawater and collected them in her small, red bucket, ready to be taken back to the caravan at the end of the day. She had learned the value of washing the shells very early on after taking one haul back to the caravan without realising that one shell she had picked up contained a deceased whelk. It took several days for her mother to identify where the rancid fishy smell was coming from and an additional day, with all the caravan windows open, to get rid of it. After that, she was made to promise not to bring anything back without cleaning it thoroughly first. There was often an aroma of brine about that caravan, but at least it was preferable to the stench of rotting sea life.

Her father also taught her the joys of rock pooling, and how much pleasure could be had from sitting on damp seaweed, looking into the pools the sea had left behind and observing how much miniature life went on there, unnoticed by many. She was fascinated by the deep red anemones, like blood clots clinging to the rocks, their tiny tendrils swaying with the vague motion of the water. She was delighted to watch minute, transparent shrimp darting about as if they were going on the most urgent of errands. Her father taught her the value of lifting rocks to see what was hiding underneath, and she learned that there was as much life invisible to the naked eye as there was visible. He also gave her an instruction that stayed with her forever.

'If you lift a rock,' he said, doing just that and seeing Gemma beam as a small green crab scuttled out, 'always put it back and try and put it back exactly where you found it. Those rocks are somebody's home, remember. You wouldn't want someone to take your house away and put it somewhere else.'

Gemma took this advice to heart and always carefully replaced the rocks she moved, grateful that any life she had disturbed went straight back under the rock when she had done so. Even the strange worlds the rock pools contained had their own order, and she was proud to be able to maintain it.

When she had exhausted all the indigenous shells on her beach but still wanted to know more, her father bought her a book, and through its pictures, she discovered that there was a wealth of treasure still to find, not only on the beaches of Britain but everywhere. She was given a taste of this in a gift shop near Treaddur Bay, which had shelves of the most beautiful, large, polished shells, and she was delighted to learn that the world contained such things as spider conches and tiger cowries. She wanted to save up her pocket money to buy some for her own collection, but when you are that age and spending so much time at the seaside, there are too many other demands on your money, and she never managed it. She did enjoy going into the shop to look at them, though, and vowed that one day she would have a shop like this one, where she could look at the shells all day long. It was one of those childhood ambitions that tend to get overtaken by real life and forgotten about. In Gemma's case, due to a series of events, some of which were deeply unpleasant, that ambition had turned out to merely be postponed. In many ways, her current situation was a very good example of why one should be careful what one wishes for.

To some extent, Gemma wouldn't describe herself as unhappy. She was virtually broke, with little prospect of that ever changing, and alone, apart from the contact she had with Kate and the other residents of the village, but then money had never been that important to her and relationships, especially the last one, had done her very few favours so far. She had the workshop and the flat above it, both of which were, for the time being at least, affordable, and, most importantly, she had her freedom. She worked when she wanted and when there was demand. She would then spend the rest of her time roaming this and neighbouring beaches, doing what she had loved since she was a child. There were not many folk who could say that. How many people who passed their days cooped up in offices would be jealous of her? Life could be a lot worse. She tried hard not to think about her reasons for coming here and how much worse things could be if those reasons ever caught up with her.

4

Over the years, Kate had developed her morning routine down to a fine art. The alarm went off at seven (on the rare days when she hadn't already woken up before it went off), and she would get straight up, go into the kitchen and switch on the kettle, which she had filled the night before. Then she would quickly jump into the shower while the kettle boiled, towel her hair dry (it wasn't long enough to bother with a hairdryer) and get dressed. She didn't put any makeup on when she was in the café; that was for the nights out she didn't have any more, so by the time she had made herself a coffee and put some food down for The Cat, she was more or less ready to go. She drank the coffee quickly, partly because time was now getting short and partly because she drank it for the caffeine hit rather than the taste. It would have surprised many people that the owner of the café, which served some of the best coffee around, used a supermarket's budget coffee granules at home. But Kate knew only too well what a decent coffee machine cost and the money she allowed herself from the business didn't even justify buying a better brand of coffee for herself, not when its only real purpose was to wake her up.

Once she had finished her coffee, Kate would grab her keys, say goodbye to The Cat if he was around, and get to the café before eight. The milk delivery came at 8.30 and Dairy Dave ran to such a tight schedule that he was always bang on time and wouldn't wait. Kate had only ever been late once, just late enough to see Dairy Dave's van pulling away, and even though she ran after him, he wouldn't take the two minutes that was needed to come back. Kate had needed to rush home, get into her car and buy her milk for the day at the nearest supermarket, which was a couple of miles away.

She'd spent more on the milk than she usually would, been late opening the café, and Dairy Dave had a face on him for days. The whole experience had left Kate so paranoid that she considered getting to the café any time after 8.20 to be a failure.

It took five minutes to walk from the cottage to the café, but these days Kate had started to leave a bit earlier and allow herself a few minutes more. The lane was downhill all the way, and at one time, Kate would have used the momentum to speed down it to the café. These days, it was exactly the opposite. She had to force herself to slow down so that she didn't accidentally jar her back. It was far too easy to do, especially on the steps, and one tug on the aching muscles would slow her down for the rest of the day. She resented the hell out of having to be careful but had spent too many days in pain not to acknowledge the necessity. A thought popped into her head, a line from a film she had seen once (probably one of Al's), '*I'm getting too old for this shit*', and that seemed to sum up her life right now. Thirty-eight and too old for this shit. That wasn't the way Kate had expected her life to go.

She arrived at the café at 8.17 by the clock on her phone and had the door unlocked and the lights on by the time Dairy Dave's white van pulled up. She made sure she was at the foot of the steps waiting for him – there had been one occasion when she hadn't got around to putting the shutters up, and he had nearly turned around and left, even though the fact that the door shutter was up and the lights were on clearly demonstrated that someone was home. He had claimed he couldn't see it from the road, but Kate knew perfectly well you could. Dave climbed down from the driver's seat and opened the side door of the van. He was a small, grey, hairy man, barely five foot, and Kate had once decided that he could be Bilbo Baggins' grandfather. It was as well to have something funny to think about when you had to deal with Dave, because he was also one of the most miserable men Kate had ever met. Considering what a rigid timetable he ran to, he could always find time to complain about something.

'Cow shit all over the road by Tudor's farm again,' he said as he hauled the crates of milk out of the van and down the steps to the café. 'Have to clean my tyres when I get back and poke it out of the treads with a stick. Nobody wants a milk van that stinks of cow shit.'

'Bit of an occupational hazard on a country round,' Kate observed.

'Think I'll go back to the Mainland,' Dave replied, a promise he had consistently failed to keep for years. 'Dog shit's easier to clean. Though I did run over a cat once and that was a bugger to get off.'

He waited for Kate to sign the delivery note and hand the cash over, then, without another word, turned around and went back up the steps to his van.

'And a good morning to you too, Dave,' Kate said to his retreating back. She said that most mornings but never knew if he heard. He certainly never replied.

Back inside the café, she surveyed the milk Dave had left behind. It wasn't that long ago that she would have carried the four-pint bottles to the fridge four at a time, two in each hand. Now she forced herself to do it in twos, to be safe. It didn't take much longer, but it was better to be on the safe side. She still had time enough to do it before Briony arrived with the bread order. Dairy Dave and Briony the Bread. *Jesus*, she thought, *I'm living in a story from Ivor the Engine.*

Briony was slightly more fun than Dave. She had taken over the round a couple of years earlier when her father, Alf, had retired. Alf had, by all accounts, been delivering bread to the area approximately since the days the flour was milled by hand. He was a grizzled old-looking man with a lined face that was tanned by being outdoors so much—he always reminded Kate of a walnut. He must either have been younger than he looked, or had Briony very late in life because his daughter was only around Kate's age, cheery, blonder and way too glamorous to be delivering bread. Her visits were always the high spot of the early part of the morning. You could tell it was Briony's van pulling up by the sound of loud 1970s disco music coming from the cab. Briony had no respect for the peace at any time of the day. This morning, Kate heard the sound of a van and smiled as 'Rock The Boat' by a band whose name she could never remember floated down from the road. She smiled, recalling that Al always used to sing the wrong words to this song deliberately — 'I'd like to know where you got that nose from'. The smile froze on Kate's lips as she remembered that she would never hear her sing again. She pushed the thought from her head, and seconds later, Briony bounded into the café.

'Morning, my lovely,' she said, beaming and showing teeth so perfect that they had to be the work of an orthodontist. 'How's you today?'

'All the better for seeing you,' Kate replied and meant it.

'Thought so. Your usual?'

'Please. No, do you know what, can we make it three white, not four? It's been a bit quiet.'

'You'll put me out of business,' Briony said. 'And where will you be without me to brighten up your morning? Oh, go on then. Just this once and only because it's you.'

'Thanks, Bri. It should be back to normal soon.'

'Course it will. Back in a tick.'

Briony dashed out of the café to the van, taking the steps two at a time. Kate had no idea where she got her energy from. Maybe it was the disco soundtrack. While she waited, Kate put the kettle on. Unlike Dreary Dairy Dave, Briony was always happy to bring the bread into the café and didn't dump it inside the door.

'Got time for a cuppa?' Kate asked as Briony stacked the loaves on the counter.

'Is that all that's on offer?'

'Afraid so.'

'I'll pass then, my lovely. Got a bit of a full van this morning. If you'd offered sex, I'd have to think about it.'

Kate smiled. She never knew if Briony was serious when she said things like that, or even if she was gay at all, but it was rare that anyone flirted with her, so it always made her feel good, however it was meant.

'Not this time,' Kate said. 'Maybe next time.'

'I'll make a note in my diary,' Briony said. As she headed to the door, she stopped and turned, serious suddenly. 'Are you okay, Kate? You look – I don't know – tired.'

'Didn't sleep too well,' Kate said. 'Couple of foxes were either fighting or shagging outside. Kept me awake half the night.'

'They're getting more than me, then. As long as you're okay, lovely.'

'I'm fine, Bri, thanks.'

'You want to think about getting a bit of help in here, you know. You do a great job, Kate, but you can't do everything. I'll see you tomorrow then.' Briony flashed her a smile and scampered back up the steps to her disco bread van.

Kate watched her go and then turned her attention to getting the café ready for whatever trade the day brought. She didn't have much time to think about what Briony had said, but when she did, she had to laugh. *Get some help. That'll be the day.*

5

Frank had settled down to gaze at the North Wales coast through the window, when the train stopped at Colwyn Bay and more passengers got on. A young woman, dressed in full Goth garb, glanced at him with quite startling green eyes surrounded by heavy black mascara. She then sat down in the furthest seat away from him, put in a set of ear buds, opened a Stephen King paperback and shut herself away from the world. She was followed by a family, a mother leading a small boy by the hand and a harassed-looking father who struggled to haul a pushchair over the step into the carriage. The mother and the boy sat down a couple of seats away from Frank, and the father lifted an infant of indeterminate gender out of the pushchair and joined them. The mother took a tablet out of her bag and handed it to the boy, who immediately plugged himself into a game with a very irritating soundtrack. The father rocked the baby in his arms, and Frank thought it was quite sad that none of them was speaking to each other. Before the doors closed, a large, matronly woman carrying two large Tesco carrier bags hurried into the carriage. She plonked herself down in the seat opposite Frank, even though there were plenty of other seats available. She was breathing hard and had obviously rushed to catch the train. Frank hoped she wasn't going to expire on him. He knew a little first aid but had never done CPR and certainly didn't fancy getting his first experience now.

The train moved off and Frank moved his feet to try and find a bit of room. In doing so, his right foot snagged on one of the loaded carrier bags.

'Sorry,' the woman said and heaved the bags up onto the seat next to her. 'Bloody car's failed its MOT. I hate getting the train, but what can you do? Kids need feeding.'

'It's no problem,' Frank replied. 'Really.'

He hoped that might be the end of the conversation, but his fellow traveller had other ideas.

'Honest to God,' she said, 'they'll fail your car on anything these days. A new exhaust, they said. That's bollocks. I'm sorry, but it is. My Jack got a new exhaust done a couple of years ago and it can't have gone in that time. Bloody garage is trying to make money. Seventy quid it's going to cost *and* they're going to charge twice for the MOT because it failed. Robbing bastards. Still, you've got to have a car, haven't you? Can't be doing this all the time, not with these fares. You got a car?'

It took a second for Frank to realise that she had paused in her monologue and was now speaking to him.

'No,' he said. 'I haven't.'

'Probably a good idea. They eat money. If I didn't need it, I'd tell Jack to get rid. Trouble is, I need it for my job, see? I'm a carer, and I can't be going to see the old folk on the train all the time. Jack said get a bike, but can you see me on a bike?'

Frank didn't need to look to know that a bike probably wasn't a very good idea.

'Anyway, there's all the stuff I've got to take. They always need shopping, and you can't carry that on a bike. No, I'll have to pay it though I don't know where it's going to come from. Jack says we'll sort it out, but he always says that. It's not like it's going to be *his* problem, is it?'

Frank nodded, thinking it was probably the most appropriate response that didn't require saying anything, and snatched a quick glance to see if there was anywhere else in the carriage he could go and sit without appearing rude. The young family were still not talking to each other, and Goth Girl was immersed in whatever nightmare world Mr. King had conjured up, but wherever he chose to sit, the woman opposite would be able to see him. Frank wanted to be on his own but didn't want to be cruel. There wasn't anything wrong with the woman apart from her inability to shut up. The tannoy announcement that they were approaching the next station, Llandudno Junction, gave him an idea. He stood up and pulled his holdall down from the overhead rack.

'This is my stop,' he said, hoping that his travelling companion wouldn't suddenly announce it was hers too.

'Well, er, nice talking to you,' the woman replied, a definite note of disappointment in her voice. As the train slowed, Frank took out his wallet and removed three twenty-pound notes and a tenner. He held them out to the woman.

'Here,' he said. 'Get your car sorted out.'

'What? Are you sure?' she said, astonished by the offer but not too astonished to take the money. 'I'll pay you back...'

'I'll look out for you,' Frank said and got off the train before she could protest any further. He slung his holdall over his shoulder, watched the train pull away and crossed the platform to consult the timetable and find out when the next train to Holyhead was due. He had, it seemed, an hour to kill, and that would still give him plenty of time later.

He spent the first five minutes or so wondering if he had done the right thing. He hoped that the woman would put the money to the use for which it was intended. He also hoped that she wouldn't think he was being creepy, and that Jack wouldn't cause any trouble if she told him a stranger she had met on a train had given her the money for the car. Then he tried to put all such thoughts out of his head. There was very little chance that he would ever see her again, and so all those questions would remain unanswered. He had done a good thing, and, for the time being at least, could afford to do it, and when the royalties' cheque he had paid in yesterday cleared, he would be fine for quite some time. It was best to leave it there. Sometimes, if you were never going to find out the end of a story, it was better to believe it turned out for the best.

There was a small newsstand on his platform, and he decided to follow Goth Girl's example and buy something to read, something in which he could bury his head and shut everyone out. He was more than aware that the next train could be even busier and wanted to get himself a shield from any unwanted attention. The stand had a good array of newspapers and magazines, but Frank stood and stared at them; none of them caught his interest. He didn't want a newspaper because he had already read one and wanted to get away from the world, not take it with him. All the magazines seemed to shout at him with stories of minor celebrities he had never heard of and wouldn't be interested in if he did. Why would he want to know about the diet some soap star had embarked on, especially when the before and after photographs looked almost identical? He didn't want to read about the latest, fashionable eating disorder. At one time, his eyes would have been drawn to the music magazines, but that was a long time ago, and he didn't recognise anyone on the covers these days. It had been many years since Frank's own band, The Leisure Decree, had merited even a sidebar in one of these magazines. He wondered briefly what the other guys in the band were doing these days. The last thing he heard, Darren was still doing session work and gigging with a couple of other outfits, the same as Frank had done himself for a while. Shaun was putting out the occasional solo album, though Frank hadn't listened to any of them. Singer-songwriters would always be able to make music, and a good drummer was always in demand. Nobody remembered the bassist. Unable to decide what to buy and aware that the owner of the newsstand was starting to look at him with something that could have been irritation or suspicion, he bought a can of Coke and a sad looking tuna and sweetcorn sandwich and went to sit on a bench and wait for his train.

He opened the can and took a long swallow. The Coke was nearly cold and made him realise that he hadn't had any for a long time. On the road, he used to get through bottles of the stuff; Darren joked once that it was the only coke habit Frank had. Now, however, like so many things, it tasted so much better in his memory than in reality. He finished the can, put it on the bench next to him to find a bin later, and turned his attention to the sandwich. He was quite hungry, having not eaten anything that day apart from one piece of toast (the one slice in the arse-end of a loaf that didn't have scabs of mould on it), but the sandwich could hardly look less appealing. The tuna was anaemic-looking, almost grey, and the sweetcorn looked like it had come from a tin that had been opened for a day or so, but the need to eat took over. He tore the wrapper open and wolfed the sandwich down in a few bites. As soon as he had finished, he had that old familiar feeling of guilt and, even though nobody around had seen him eat the sandwich, he had an urge to dispose of the evidence. He crumpled the cardboard wrapper, and took it, and the can, to the nearest bin. He dropped his rubbish in the bin and looked around. There were a few people on the platform, but nobody noticed him, and he started to feel better immediately. He sat back down on the bench and looked up at the board. The Holyhead train was due in forty-six minutes. He began to do something he always used to do while waiting for trains but hadn't done for years. He waited until the illuminated sign changed to forty-five, then counted the seconds in his head to try and get the timing right so that he hit sixty at exactly the time the display changed again. It took him until the sign said that the train was due in thirty-three minutes to get it right. Then he got the next one wrong by two seconds and had to start again. It was a way of passing the time.

6

Gemma woke up late. The alarm clock on her bedside table said seven-thirty, which might not have been late for some people, but was a lie in for her. The alarm clock was a proper, old-fashioned Mickey Mouse clock, a red-painted tin case with Mickey's hands indicating the time and the two bells on the top. Gemma had picked it up in a car boot sale for a couple of pounds; she wondered, briefly, if it might have some collectable value to it, but bought it because it made her smile. She had never used the alarm, though. She usually woke up at the same time every morning without an alarm and being roused from her sleep by something that sounded like a fire alarm going off would not be the start to the day she needed.

She had no idea why she had overslept. She hadn't been particularly tired going to bed but had obviously needed the sleep. She shook off her duvet and went straight to the bathroom to navigate the cantankerous old shower she had inherited with the flat. It was a complete cliché, that shower. It had taken Gemma months to find the exact point on the temperature dial where the water was neither freezing cold, nor scalding hot. She had been so surprised when she found it that she had jumped out of the shower and grabbed a black Sharpie to mark the exact point on the dial. The mark had nearly washed away now and she could usually find the point without it. All the same, she still had mornings when she left the shower with bright red skin from icy or boiling water. This morning, she found the right temperature first time, had a quick shower and washed her hair with the dregs of the nearest shampoo bottle, making a mental note that she needed to do some shopping at some point. The tenner she had taken yesterday wouldn't go very far, so she was probably going to have to keep her shampoo bottles turned upside down to collect the remnants for a little while longer yet. She wound a towel around her long dark hair and got dressed. Normally she would go for a quick walk on the beach before opening the workshop to see if anything had been washed up during the night, but she would have to forego that this morning. She liked to open the workshop on time, even if she saw no one for hours. It was a psychological thing; she had standards to maintain, even if nobody was there to see it. She had her routine and stuck to it.

Her hair was mostly dry by the time she was ready to leave. It wasn't so dry that her mother wouldn't have told her she'd catch her death going out like that, but those days were long gone, and she could make her own decisions. Anyway, when you lived on the North Wales coast and spent quite a lot of time outdoors, you got used to the feeling of damp hair. Gemma didn't mind; she would rather have damp hair than being stuck indoors. She grabbed her phone and her keys, let herself out of the flat and went down the wrought iron fire escape to the passageway that separated her workshop from Kate's café next door. The morning dew made the steps slippery, and she held onto the handrail as she descended. She had slipped down the steps once, and the weeks she had spent with a Turner sunset on her backside had made her careful ever since. She could still recall the pain and embarrassment she had felt, sitting at the bottom of the steps while an elderly couple, who had come out of the café, hurried over to help her up, and she had no desire to do that again. With the usual sense of relief, she set foot on the concrete of the passageway and her forager's eyes were instinctively drawn to the ground. The passageway was never maintained, and the concrete was half-hidden by grass, but nearly every morning, Gemma found something discarded there, even though she never heard anyone go past. Empty beer bottles and takeaway cartons were by no means unusual, even though the nearest pub and chip shop were in the village, and this passage was on nobody's way back to anywhere. One morning, she had been surprised to find a pair of knickers tossed away amongst the grass. She didn't like to think what the story was there; they were the sort of novelty knickers with days of the week printed on the front, but what was worse was that this pair had Tuesday on them, and it was a Friday when she found them. This morning, she spotted something pink poking out from between the leaves of a thistle. She picked up a stick and hooked out the plastic arm of a doll. She picked it up, half tempted to give it a clean and keep it, but decided it was far too macabre a thing to have lying around, so put it in her pocket to bin it once she got into the workshop.

The lock on the workshop door turned easily first time, which was potentially a sign of a good day to come. Often it took a bit of jiggling before it engaged and one morning it had refused to do it at all for nearly half an hour. Gemma had been on the point of calling a locksmith when she had given it one more go, and it opened without any fuss. It had, she decided, been taking the piss. She opened the workshop door and let the morning sunlight in. By now, the café was open, so, as she did every morning, she popped next door to see Kate and get the first, much needed coffee of the day. She knew it would make much more sense financially to buy a jar of coffee and some milk – she already had a kettle in the workshop – but a cup of instant wasn't quite the same as a freshly brewed latte. In any case, sometimes Kate was the only person she spoke to in a day, and it helped remind her that her voice still worked.

Kate was getting herself organised for the day when Gemma went into the café, but she stopped what she was doing and greeted her with a smile.

'Morning, Gem,' she said, raising her voice a little so she could be heard above the noise of the coffee grinder. She always ground the beans for each customer and the place was filled with the delicious aroma of fresh coffee. 'Better day today.'

'At least that rain's gone off,' Gemma replied. 'I think we'll be mad busy today.'

Kate concentrated on frothing the milk. They said much

the same things to each other on many an occasion and both knew the truth. She ran the coffee into a takeaway cup, added a shot of hazelnut syrup and poured on the steaming milk, finishing it off with an approximation of a heart pattern. Kate always tried to do the elaborate latte art they did in the big chains but had somehow never quite acquired the knack. She put the lid on the cup and handed it over, and Gemma paid with the exact change.

'One of these days, I'll ask for something different,' she said.

'No you won't,' Kate laughed. 'I'd probably faint if you did.'

Gemma thanked her and went back to the workshop. That was the usual extent of their morning conversation. Kate had a café to set up and Gemma had an urgent appointment with the green and white striped deckchair she kept inside the workshop. She dragged it outside and sat down, sipping her coffee and surveying the view in front of her. There were worse lives than this. Everywhere else, people would be showing up for work in offices and call centres, but her office was a deckchair looking out onto a beach and an endless horizon. Her co-workers were the gulls that squawked overhead and the oystercatchers that stalked the shoreline. There were days when she felt lonely, missed having another human being to share it with, but wouldn't give it up for the world. All she had to do was find a way of making it pay a living wage, and she would be content to spend the rest of her days here.

7

The day had dragged. Even though the weather was a bit better than yesterday, it hadn't been reflected in the footfall at *Kate's*. It certainly didn't feel like a Friday. There was little sign that the weekend was approaching. Kate had seen some of her regulars; Gemma had been in for her morning coffee and again for a bite of lunch, and Geraint had occupied his seat by the window nursing first one flat white on its own and then another, accompanied by a toasted teacake. Geraint came in every couple of days and his orders were so predictable that Kate had his coffee ready on the counter as soon as she saw him coming down the steps. He was never any trouble, was always very polite but kept himself very much to himself. Kate would have loved to know what his story was; he was a well-known figure around the village and, although everyone knew his name, nobody knew who he was. He had lived in the cottage on the outskirts of the village for as long as anyone could remember; rumour had it that he had inherited the cottage from his parents, but nobody was sure. Although he had a house to live in, he always looked like his home was a hedgerow somewhere, and some days he smelt like it too. He always wore the same mismatched tweed suit jacket and trousers, and if the weather was bad, this was topped with a shabby raincoat. One day, Kate thought, she would make the breakthrough and encourage him to tell her all about himself, but he didn't. So for now, they exchanged pleasantries about the weather and maybe something in the news; he would then wander off somewhere else with his flat whites and teacake. Apart from Gemma and Geraint, there had been a few random customers but nothing much to speak of. The only way Kate could tell it was Friday was that shortly after three o'clock, Ruth Prior arrived, as she did every Friday.

Kate liked Ruth but didn't envy her life. Ruth's husband Phil worked away on the rigs or somewhere for a large part of the year, leaving Ruth at home running the village primary school. The school had, as far as Kate could tell, no more than thirty or so pupils, and Ruth was headteacher, class teacher and pretty much everything else. She had a couple of teaching assistants, parents of some of the children, who helped out part-time, but most of the burden fell on Ruth. Considering she had no children of her own, she was remarkably dedicated to the rest of the children of the village. She worked hard throughout the week but always came into the café at the end of school on a Friday for something to eat and a chat.

Sure enough, at ten past three, Kate saw her coming down the steps, her arms full of the files she always brought with her with the intention of doing a bit of work while she was there. As long as she had been coming in, Kate had never seen her open a file once. Ruth was, Kate guessed, in her forties somewhere, a short woman with braided hair usually tied back in a scrunchie. Considering that she was barely taller than some of her older pupils, the children were devoted to her and, when you passed the schoolyard, it was apparent that they hung on Ruth's every word. The parents loved her too, and despite the village community being predominantly white, nobody seemed at all bothered by the colour of Ruth's skin or lack of a Welsh accent. She was one of those rare, natural teachers who children would always grow up remembering. Kate knew that the responsibility Ruth bore weighed heavy on her at times, but she usually remained cheerful and good-humoured. She had, Kate couldn't help but notice, the prettiest green eyes, and when she laughed, the creases around them only added to her appeal. Today, however, her face was sombre when she came into the café.

'Isn't it time you got that alcohol licence, Kate?' she asked. She often asked this, but today she really seemed to mean it.

'Bad day, Ruthie?'

'Bad week,' Ruth replied and studied *Kate's* Specials board. 'What's the quiche?'

'Two cheese and leek. It's pretty lush, even if I say so

myself.'

'Go on. Let's go mad. I'll have some of that and a mocha, please, my love. I'll probably stick my face in a cake as well, but we'll see.'

Kate busied herself putting together the salad garnish for the quiche, while Ruth made herself comfortable at a table near the counter.

'So tell me all about it,' she said as she worked. 'What was up with this week?'

'Oh, money stuff. Dull dull dull. You don't want to know.'

'Ruth,' Kate said, placing a generous slice of quiche on the plate, 'tell me. Who else are you going to tell? Phil's not home at the moment, is he?'

'No, he isn't. I'll Skype him later. No, it's just that we had the Governors' finance review on Monday, and I've had Michael Tremaine on the phone pretty much every day. I could so do without having an accountant as Chairman of the Governors. I'll swear he's made up his own language to bewilder people like me.'

'Not good?'

'Not particularly. Ooh, thanks,' Ruth said, as Kate put a plate laden with quiche and salad and a steaming mocha in front of her. Ruth attacked the quiche for a moment. 'You're right, Kate, that *is* bloody lush. You'll have to give me the recipe. Not that I'll ever make it.'

'Trade secret. Go on. What did Moody Mike have to say?'

'Well, I thought at first it was going to be the usual crap about how much craft paper and copier toner I was buying, and how the cutbacks mean we'll have to go back to writing on slates and feeding the kids gruel, but it's a bit more serious than that. This time, it's the building.'

'What's wrong with it?'

'What's right with it? It's pretty much in the condition you'd expect for a school built in 1906 and hasn't seen much of a maintenance grant since World War Two. We've done our best with it, but it looks like there might be a problem with the roof. I'd noticed it for a while, of course, only a little trickle of water down the wall of the back classroom when there was really heavy rain, but I mopped it up and got on with it. Trouble is, there's a bit of mould at the top of the wall now, and I had to report that. I thought it was a question of getting someone in to sort it out with a spray or something, but it set all sorts of alarm bells ringing. Even though nobody's used the back classroom for years, the word 'damp' brings health issues with it. That means someone has to come and look at the roof and get it sorted properly. Which means money, and we haven't got any.'

'The LEA will have to sort it out, then, surely?'

'Well, there we have the problem,' Ruth said, taking a swig of her mocha and wiping the foam off her upper lip with a serviette. 'For a start, the LEA hasn't got any money either, but according to Moody Mike, it's not as simple as that. The school is supposed to be more or less self-financing. It's my problem, apparently, not the LEA's. If I can't find the money for bloody pencils, how am I supposed to get a roof fixed?'

'Do you know anyone? I'm trying to think if I know a roofer. Sammy Small does all sorts of building work. I'm sure I've got his card somewhere.' Kate started to root around amongst the order pads and receipt books by the side of the till.

'I can't see Small Sam being able to do it,' Ruth said. 'He needs a ladder to get up the steps.'

'I'll get his number anyway and text it to you,' Kate said. 'He can have a look at least.'

'Thanks, Kate. But my real worry is what someone's going to find. Nobody's looked at that roof as long as I've been here, so God knows what state it's in. Now I've told Mike about it, it'll have to be done properly, too, not a patch-up job. I can see someone who knows what they're talking about taking a look and condemning the whole roof.'

'It can't be that bad, surely?'

'Who knows? But we all know how these things go. You think it's a small job, but it grows. If it does, we can't afford it. End of.'

'So what then?'

'Worst-case scenario – and I have to look at that – is that

the school has to close. Like any other business, if you can't pay your bills, you go bust. The kids will all have to jump on a bus and go up the road to Llandewi, and I come and ask you if you need any staff.'

'You know I'd love to have you,' Kate said, 'and God knows I could use an extra pair of hands so I can have the occasional day off if nothing else, but unless you can do it for nothing, I'm afraid I wouldn't be able to help.'

'That might be an issue,' Ruth replied with a sad smile. 'Anyway, thanks for listening, Kate. I'd better get off and go and stare at spreadsheets for a bit. Then I'll drink too much wine and messy-cry over Skype with Phil.'

'Good luck with that!'

'He'll make me laugh. He always does, and I might be able to forget about it for the weekend.' Ruth gathered her files together. 'Same time next week,' she said.

'I'll be here,' Kate said. 'Where else am I going to be?'

Kate watched Ruth climb the steps up to the road, with her head down like she had the weight of the world on her shoulders. She had made light of it, but Kate knew how serious the situation was. The school was the heart of the village, and Ruth was the heart of the school. If the school went, it could very well be the beginning of the death of the village. To think, some days she worried because she sold a few sandwiches less than usual. She didn't know how lucky she was.

8

Frank got off the train at Holyhead and stood on the platform while people bustled around him. He took the ticket out of his inside pocket and noted the time on it, even though he knew it perfectly well. He had a good hour and a half before he even had to think about checking into the Ferry terminal. Another couple of hours and he would be on his way to Dublin and a new life. He looked around and spotted a snack bar on the other side of the station and decided that a coffee would fill some time in, maybe even something to eat if anything took his fancy. He hefted his holdall onto his shoulder and crossed the footbridge to the other platform.

The steamed-up windows of the snack bar successfully disguised how basic it was. In these days of coffee shop chains, it was rare to come across a place like it, even though there was a time when such places were all there was. It served a purpose, Frank supposed, a place where you could get a drink and grab something to eat on your way between here and there. At least, he was gratified to note, it had a decent coffee machine. He had half expected an urn and a jar of instant served in glass cups or enamel mugs. He ordered a latte and was pleased to see that the middle-aged woman behind the counter knew what she was doing. He looked at the meagre cake display in the glass cabinet and selected a Danish pastry. It looked slightly dry and not particularly appetising. Still, it was preferable to the alternative, a sad-looking custard slice in which the filling suggested it belonged more in a baby's nappy than in an item of confectionery. He paid (rather more than he had expected) and took his plate and cup to an empty table.

Once he had sat down, he looked around at his surroundings and his fellow travellers. At a table near the counter, a young couple held hands across the debris. They weren't saying anything, but the looks they were giving each other spoke volumes. It had been a long time since Frank had given or received a look like that. Next to the window, a woman wearing a niqab was trying to comfort a fractious baby, with limited success. Various other people sat concentrating on their drinks, and all carried an impatient air, which betrayed the fact that they were not where they wanted to be but merely on their way somewhere else. There was one person Frank recognised, though. The young Goth girl he had spotted on the train from Liverpool was sitting at a corner table. She still had her ear pods in and her book in front of her, but the book was unopened. Frank was alarmed to see that her heavy mascara was smudged around her eyes and grubby lines were sketched down her face. She had been crying, but worse, didn't care who saw. Frank felt sorry for her but turned his attention back to his coffee. This was no time to get involved.

The coffee was okay, not great, but acceptable, but he couldn't concentrate on it. The sadness on the girl's face had disturbed him too much. She was, he guessed no more than seventeen or eighteen, and it bothered him that she was sitting in a café full of strangers and crying. He sighed, picked up his coffee and the uneaten Danish, and crossed the café to her table.

'Mind if I sit here?' he asked.

The girl barely registered his presence.

'I don't want to intrude, but the thing is, I've got a pastry going spare. I thought I wanted it, but I don't. I wondered if you might like it.'

The girl looked at him properly for the first time, and Frank was dismayed to see apprehension in her red-rimmed eyes. He had played it all wrong, and now she probably thought he was some kind of pervert. He rapidly changed tack.

'I'm waiting for my husband,' he said. 'He's been held up.' At the mention of the word 'husband', the girl visibly relaxed. 'Look,' Frank said, 'are you okay?'

'I'm fine,' the girl said in a small voice.

'Are you sure? Only I've not seen makeup in that style before, but then I'm pretty old. Is it a new thing?'

The girl self-consciously wiped a hand across her eyes, which only served to make matters worse.

'Are you sure you don't want the pastry?' She shook her head. 'I can't think why.' He picked the pastry up and tapped it on the plate, then frowned and tossed it down again. 'It can only be a couple of days old. You could build a wall out of these.'

This time the girl rewarded him with the shadow of a smile.

'I'm Frank,' he said. 'And you are...?'

'Beth,' the girl said.

'Pleased to meet you, Beth. Now that we know each other, maybe you'd like to tell me why you're sitting in this bloody awful place and ruining your makeup which, let's face it, must have taken hours to do.'

The girl didn't reply, but two fat tears spilled out of her eyes and followed the tracks down her cheeks.

'Hey,' Frank said, 'come on. Whatever it is can't be that bad, can it? Tell me. I might be able to help.'

'You can't,' she said. 'No one can.'

'Try me. You might be surprised.'

'I'm going to Dublin,' she said and then said no more.

'I don't know if that's a very good reason. Dublin's not a bad place, from all accounts. I've heard the Guinness is bloody expensive, but you don't look like a Guinness girl to me, unless you're looking for a drink to match your clothes.'

'My boyfriend's there,' she said. 'He's working.'

'You're going to see your boyfriend,' Frank started to count on his fingers, 'and he's got a job...No, sorry. They sound like good things. Can't see anything to cry about there.'

'I'm pregnant,' the girl said, and her face crumpled again.

'Ah. That makes it more complicated. Does he know?'

'That's why I'm going. We're going to get married.'

'Right. So far, so good. Then why...?'

'I've lost my ticket,' the girl said, then covered her face and broke down in uncontrollable sobs.

Frank moved his chair around the table so it was next to hers and laid a hand on her shoulder.

'And I'm guessing you haven't got the money for another ticket.'

The girl shook her head and snorted wetly.

'That's easily solved,' Frank said and took out his wallet. 'I'll lend you the money for a ticket.'

Beth looked up and frowned.

'You'd do that? Why?'

'Because you need it and because I can.' Frank opened his wallet and looked inside. There was a solitary ten-pound note. He took the note out and looked at it, as if willing it to breed. Then he remembered MOT woman on the train. His last Good Samaritan act was going to stop this one in its tracks. He had a bank card, but until the money cleared through his account, which probably wouldn't be until tomorrow, ten pounds and change was all he had. 'Except that I can't. Shit.' He tucked the tenner in his trouser pocket in case he needed it quickly and put his wallet back in his jacket.

'Never mind,' Beth said. 'It was kind of you, but I'll be okay. I'll find a way.'

'How? No, sorry, Beth, but you can't stay here hoping something will turn up.'

'What about your husband?'

'My...? Oh. Him. No, he never carries any money either.' Frank thought for a moment, even though there was nothing to think about. He had a simple choice; he could leave this girl here and walk away, and nobody could blame him for that. She wasn't his problem, or... In the end, it wasn't a choice. He reached into his pocket again and took out his ferry ticket. He put it on the table, kept his hand on it briefly, and then pushed it across the table to Beth.

'Here,' he said.

'But that's yours! You can't do that.'

'I'm sort of doing it.'

'No. No, I can't take that. What will you do?'

'I just remembered that—er—Seamus is bringing his credit card with him. We'll get another ticket with that.'

'Seamus?' Beth asked, and a smile crept across her face. 'Really?'

'He can't help his name. Now, are you going to take my bloody ticket or not?'

Beth hesitated and then picked the ticket up.

'Thank you,' she said. 'I don't know what else to say.'

'You don't need to,' he said. 'Now go and get your ferry. If it goes without you, that ticket won't be any good to either of us.'

She stood up, stuffed the ticket into her coat pocket and then threw her arms around him.

'Thank you,' she said again. 'I'll never forget this.'

'You'd better not,' he replied, pulling away from her embrace. 'Tell you what, if the baby's a boy, you can call it Frank.'

'Not Seamus?'

'Go and get your ferry, Beth.'

She gave him one more radiant smile, then hurried out of the café. Frank looked down at his cooling coffee and the stale Danish. *Shit*, he thought. *What the hell do I do now?*

9

It was early afternoon before Gemma went for her first forage of the day. She normally liked to be out and about before starting work, but the postman had brought a couple of bills that needed sorting out and there were one or two emails to answer, including, miracle of miracles, a small order from her online store. She had spent a little too long chatting with the postman, and it had set her back by a good half hour. She didn't mind because Rhodri, the postman, was quite good company, always cheerful and pleasant. He was in his early forties, at a guess, and Gemma had a strong suspicion that he fancied her. Much as she liked his chat, she didn't fancy him at all; there was no way she could go for a man of that age who still thought wearing his hair in a man-bun was a sensible fashion choice. She secretly enjoyed the attention, though, in much the same way one would enjoy a glass of water in a drought, but at the same time, wished he would bring her something other than bills and junk.

The order was a nice surprise, too. She had begun to wonder if her online store was an expensive waste of time, but getting an order from it, even if it was only for two items, now made her think that perhaps she should be doing a bit more to promote it. She added it to her mental list of things to ponder and possibly even do something about. She printed the order out to deal with when she got back from her forage. She knew she had all the materials in stock to sort it out and should be able to get it done and ready in time to catch the afternoon collection at the post office. But foraging came first. It was the part of her day that she lived for.

It didn't matter which of the local beaches she went to, there was always something new to find. Every tide brought in fresh flotsam and uncovered the buried treasures the sand had concealed. Often the most surprising things washed up on the shore and were proof, if any were needed, that the sea retained far too much human debris, tossing it back onto the shore as if returning an unwanted present. The seaweed, which marked the reach of the last high tide, was always tangled with bits of netting, enough rubbish to fill several large bins and the inevitable selection of used condoms. She could never forget the first time she had found an example of that particular item on the beach. She had been out beach combing with her father and had wandered off on her own a little way. She had come across this strange, waterlogged thing and come running back to her father, dangling it from her little hand.

'Daddy!' she had exclaimed. 'I found a jellyfish.'

The look on her father's face, a mixture of horror and amusement, was something she would never forget. He had carefully taken it off her and held it at arm's length with clearly no idea what to do with it next. In the end, he had thrown it back onto the sand.

'It's not a jellyfish,' he said. 'It's...something else.'

'What is it then?' she asked, in the insistent way only small children who are asking unanswerable questions can.

'You don't need to worry about that,' her crimson-faced father replied. 'Just never pick them up. Promise?'

'Okay, Daddy.'

'Also, never pick up jellyfish. You know they can sting you, don't you?'

'I forgot.'

'Well, don't,' her father said, on safer ground now. 'There are things that have more of a right to live here than we do and some of them can defend themselves. Crabs nip, jellyfish sting...always remember we are only visiting their home.'

Gemma never forgot that advice, just as she never forgot the shame she felt when she finally found out the truth about the thing that wasn't a jellyfish and pictured herself running across the sand holding it. There were things that stayed in your memory forever.

Today, fortunately, there were no 'not-jellyfish' around.. There was one actual jellyfish, but only a small one and it was so close to the water's edge that Gemma was content to leave it where it was, secure in the knowledge that the tide, which was on its way back in, would soon lift it back to safety. She found a good size razor clam, which was virtually complete apart from a tiny nick out of one edge, which could be sanded smooth, and a handful of delicately coloured periwinkles. She tucked these away in the satchel she always carried and continued on her hunt. About two-thirds of the way along the beach, something glinted in the sunlight and caught her eye. It was a piece of glass, which was by no means unusual, but what really attracted her attention was the colour. She had come across green glass fragments on many an occasion, and sometimes blue glass too, but she did not recall ever seeing glass this shade of turquoise before. She picked it up for a closer inspection, wary of jagged edges. Not all glass was worn smooth by the sea, and it wouldn't be the first time she cut herself on a razor-sharp edge. She always kept a packet of plasters in her satchel for such an accident. She studied the piece of glass, trying to make sense of it. The colour didn't belong to any bottle she had come across, not even the very old ones that occasionally appeared from somewhere, and the shape was all wrong. The glass had a gentle curve to it as if it had come from something spherical. Gemma was so fascinated that she looked for more. Once she started to scour that part of the beach, they were everywhere. Some were lying on the sand, some half-concealed, one was buried under an old crisp packet (Smiths Crisps, Gemma noted, and how long had it been since they were in the shops?), and one piece of glass almost eluded her altogether until she picked up and shook a clump of bladder wrack and a shard of turquoise glass dropped out onto the sand. Gemma gathered all the pieces up, maybe a dozen in all and laid them out on the sand. They definitely formed a hollow sphere, and as far as she could see, she had found all the pieces. She gathered them all up and put them in her satchel, with a vague idea that when she had a quiet moment, she might try to glue them all back together to see what she got. Then she was distracted by a piece of white bone she spotted nearby. She scraped away the sand around it and was delighted to find the complete skull of a rodent, a mouse, or maybe a shrew. That went in the satchel too. A good soak in bleach and a quick look in one of the books she kept for such purposes to identify it, and somebody with macabre tastes would be happy to wear that on a thong around their neck. Satisfied with her foraging, Gemma fastened her satchel and headed back to the workshop.

She unloaded her haul on her workbench and immediately filled a jam jar with diluted bleach. She dropped the skull and the shells she had picked up into the liquid and set the glass fragments to one side to look at properly later. By the time she had done that, her internal body clock informed her that it was time for lunch, so she locked up the workshop again and went to see Kate and find out what was on the Specials Board today. If she had looked back, she might have seen the faint, turquoise glow coming from the corner of her workbench that flickered briefly, then faded.

10

It probably hadn't been the best idea for Kate to pick up a couple of bottles of wine on the way home. She had called into the village shop, which was known to everyone as Parry's, even though Mr. Parry had retired years ago and the shop was now run by Tomasz and Ewa, a lovely couple who had moved from Poland a number of years ago and set up home in the village with their two children. Tomasz was a plasterer by trade, but when Mr. Parry decided that at seventy-two, he was getting a bit too old for the long hours the shop entailed, they had invested their savings and bought the shop. They worked hard and were always friendly and welcoming and although some of the older residents of the village still complained that the shop wasn't like it used to be when Mr. Parry had it, most people were glad of the fact that the stock had more variety now and you would be greeted with a smile and chat.

Kate had called in to pick up something to throw in the microwave for her evening meal, but when she took her tagliatelle to the counter, she spotted the sign on the fridge that told her that one of her favourite Pinots was on offer at two bottles for £10.00. She wavered for a moment, but Ewa caught her looking.

'Come on, Kate,' she said, with a smile, 'you know you want to.'

'That's the trouble,' Kate replied, 'I do want to. And that's probably the worst time to buy wine. Oh, go on. You've tempted me.'

'That's the idea,' Ewa said, putting the wine and the meal in a carrier bag and ringing the sale through. 'And how was your day?'

'It was okay,' Kate said, putting her debit card in the machine and hoping for the best.

'Only okay?'

'I'll settle for that. Okay is about the best I'm going to get at the moment.'

'Things will pick up soon. They always do.'

'Thanks, Ewa. Let's hope so.'

Kate made her farewells and walked up the lane to her cottage. She put the wine in the fridge, her meal in the microwave and a pouch of brown slop in The Cat's bowl and hung her coat up. As she did so, she noticed that there were a couple of envelopes on the mat. They were both junk, but what drew her up short was that one was addressed to Al. Six months later and the message still hadn't got through to everyone.

'Not known at this address,' Kate said grimly and put the envelopes in the bin.

When the microwave dinged, she took her meal out and ate it at the kitchen table. She didn't bother with a plate because there was no point in creating washing up if you didn't have to. Anyway, who was going to know? In the same way, nobody was going to know that she ate her meal using a plastic fork she found at the bottom of the drawer and when she had finished, threw everything in the bin on top of the discarded envelopes. There was a tiny amount of satisfaction in how the remains of the carbonara sauce stained the envelope bearing Al's name. It made it permanent. There would be no taking the envelope out again and keeping it just in case. Just in case of what? The impossible? Al wasn't coming back.

After she had eaten, Kate opened the fridge door and looked at the two bottles of Pinot in the door. She quickly shut the fridge again, deciding it was way too early and switched the kettle on instead. She opened a cupboard and looked at the array of herbal teas she had bought for those occasions when she was wired from drinking too much coffee during the day, but after some consideration realised that she didn't fancy any of them and went into the living room, letting the kettle click itself off.

She turned the television on and sat down, flicking

through the channels with the remote, trying to find something, anything, that she might like to watch. She never thought she would miss the days when she and Al would debate what they wanted to see. She would usually make suggestions, and Al, while never expressing a preference, would make non-committal noises at every suggestion until Kate would hand over the remote and say, 'You decide then.' She could watch what she liked now, but somewhere along the line had lost sight of what that was. She didn't want to watch the news or a programme about how people with more money than sense paid for a gardening celebrity to come along and ruin a perfectly good garden. Al liked the cooking shows, but Kate had enough of preparing food during the day and anyway, the idea of smearing sauce on a plate with a paintbrush and then serving a portion of food that wouldn't satisfy a vole was alien to her. She opened a café because she wanted to feed people and make them happy; if she wanted to overcharge credulous punters for a canapé as a main course and make them want to call in at the chippy for some proper food on the way home, she would have trained as a chef. In desperation, she switched to the iPlayer to see if there was a box set of any comedies she and Al liked. She found one and started to watch one of their favourite episodes, but after ten minutes realised that there was little pleasure in laughing at something if there was nobody beside you laughing along. She turned the television off and opened the wine. Because she knew Al would have disapproved, she poured a healthy measure into a mug. It was one of those ideas that are simultaneously a good one and a bad one.

By the time she had finished the first one and refilled her mug, she was beginning to feel maudlin. What a sad bloody life it was to sit on your own apart from a cat that didn't want to know, drinking wine and not even being able to find something decent to watch on the telly. It was all Al's fault. Kate should never have let her go, but by the end, couldn't bear for her to stay. That's the trouble when you realise that a person you have known and loved for so long is no longer someone you know, or even like that much.

Kate and Alison had been friends forever. Their mothers had been school gate, and coffee afterwards friends and the two girls had gravitated to each other. Once they had found each other, they had become inseparable all through primary and secondary school and had made their university choices together. They got a flat together and started the next phase of their lives, Kate studying English Literature and Al studying History, neither of them giving a thought to what they might do afterwards. Neither of them really expected that they would become lovers, either, but when it happened, suddenly everything made sense. It was as though they had found the one thing absent from their relationship, a piece of the jigsaw that they hadn't noticed was missing. They had been in love for years but never given it that name.

After three years of study, parties and the occasional march, they graduated and tried to find their place in the world. The trouble was that they both had degrees that were useful for jobs requiring a graduate rather than a non-graduate, but, unless you were very lucky, were of no use in themselves. Neither of them wanted to teach, and while Kate thought she might quite like to get a job in a library, and Al thought museum work might suit her, no opportunities in either field presented themselves. Kate went to work for an insurance company and Al went into the Civil Service. They didn't particularly like their jobs, but they paid the rent and the bills and enabled them to go out sometimes. They had each other, though, and that, as they often said, was enough.

And for ten years, it was enough. They were happy with each other's company and that of a small circle of friends. They might have stayed that way if the Recession hadn't come along. They read about it in the papers and saw the news reports, and thought it was sad but wouldn't affect them. They had been in their jobs long enough to be safe. Reality hit them like a hammer when first Al, then Kate, was made redundant. They used a bit of their redundancy money to take a holiday to recharge their batteries and decided what to do next. The Anglesey air and the peace and quiet made them forget their situation for a while and maybe that was why, when they went for a walk around their surroundings and saw the seafront café which had a To Let sign on it, they both thought at more or less the same time, *Well, why not?* Once they had calmed down and talked the whole thing through at length, the answer was still the same. There was no reason why not.

Almost before they knew where they were, they had invested a substantial amount of their redundancy money in deposits for the café and a lovely cottage up the lane from it. They debated what to call it for ages, throwing names backwards and forwards. In the end, they settled on *Kate's* as the best they could come up with. The fact that Al didn't want her name on it should have been a sign, but somehow wasn't. They spent their evenings working out costings. They put in many long days cleaning and painting. Kate was so caught up in learning how to make the different coffees, coming up with menus and decorating the café, that she believed they were both enjoying themselves equally. Maybe if Al had complained sometimes, Kate would have noticed that she wasn't happy, but there was so much to do getting the café ready to open that she couldn't see that her partner wasn't sharing her enthusiasm. Even when *Kate's* opened, Kate put Al's moods down to tiredness or the stress of opening a new business. She was under no illusions that it would take a little while for the café to establish itself, and their business advisor at the bank had told them so in no uncertain terms. But all Al could see was money draining from their bank account far quicker than it was being replaced. Any attempts to discuss it inevitably finished in an argument. Kate accused Al of premature negativity, and Al countered by calling Kate a Pollyanna, blinded by hope and unable to see that they had invested their money in a white elephant. Kate put it down to teething problems, but the more she threw herself into the business, the more Al drew back. This went on for most of the first eighteen months or so that they were in business. Even then, Kate never saw the end coming. She had never considered that there might be any such thing as an end with Al, so when it came, it floored her.

It came, ironically, after what had been quite a busy day in the café. Kate had certainly been busy, especially after Al had announced she was going home after lunchtime, claiming to have a headache. Kate finished the day, cleaned down and came home to find Al sitting in the living room without the lights on as darkness gathered around her.

'Sorry I'm a bit late,' Kate said. 'Couple of late customers. You okay? How's your head?'

'It's not working,' Al said.

'What, your head?' Kate asked, trying to joke so she wouldn't feel sick.

'All of it. The café. Us. I'm sorry, Kate. We can't go on like this. I want out.'

Kate stood and stared, willing herself not to cry even though she knew she already was.

'Why?' she asked. 'I thought we were happy.'

'No,' Al replied. 'You're happy. I'm not.'

'Then we'll stop,' Kate said, coming over and kneeling at Al's feet. 'We'll do something else. What would you like to do?'

'You can't stop,' Al said. 'It's a three-year lease. You can't afford to give it up.'

'Then I'll run the café. You do...whatever you want to.'

'Around here? There's nothing here, Kate. It's a place you come for a holiday for a week because two weeks would get boring. It's not somewhere you come to live.'

'Well, I like it,' Kate said and cursed herself for sounding like a petulant child.

'Then you stay,' Al said. Her voice sounded gentle, and for a second, Kate felt some hope. 'But I can't.'

The words, *please don't leave, please don't leave,* were on Kate's tongue, so she closed her mouth in case they came out. She swallowed those words and picked some more.

'Don't you love me?' she asked.

'Oh, Kate,' Al said, tears now shimmering in her eyes, 'I loved you so much.' It was the *loved* that sealed it.

Kate didn't open the café for a day after Al left. She couldn't bear to be in there on her own. She had intended to keep it closed for longer, but on the second day, there was a knock at the cottage door. Kate was reluctant to answer it because she was still in her dressing gown and knew that her face was so puffy from crying that it looked like she had been in a fight. But the knocking continued, and whoever it was clearly wasn't going away. She opened the door, and there was Tomasz from the village shop standing on her step with a carrier bag in his hand.

'Are you okay, Kate?' he asked. 'Are you sick? I brought some things for you. Ewa thought you might need them.' Kate mutely took the carrier bag. 'Maybe rest,' Tomasz said. 'Come back soon. We need you.'

Kate croaked a thank you, and Tomasz walked away backwards down the path, a look of concern in his deep brown eyes. Kate closed the door and looked in the bag. There was a loaf, a bar of chocolate, a packet of paracetamol and a Tupperware container with what looked very much like homemade soup. She heated the soup up and ate it, ravenously finishing every delicious morsel, then showered, got dressed and went to open *Kate's. We need you.*

Nobody asked where Al was. Ruth Prior told Kate later that someone had seen her getting on the bus with her suitcases, so everyone knew anyway. Kate threw herself into the café. It was hard work, especially since she had been used to talking all the decisions through with Al but now had to do it on her own. She never heard Al's voice again; their only communication was by text and email as they worked out an amicable arrangement whereby Al could get back the money she had invested without sinking the business, but it was all cold and formal. Once that was sorted out, even the texts stopped.

Kate was never lonely during the day. Even when there were no customers in the café, there were always things to do. It was in the evenings that she still felt Al's absence, and much as she knew that wine was a poor substitute for love, at least it made the hurt a bit less. Some nights she needed it more than others and she did wonder on occasions if she was developing what her mother would doubtless call 'a drink problem', but then her mother thought that anyone who drank even a glass every night had a problem. Kate dreaded to think what she would make of her own daughter's recycling box. It was a rare week when it wasn't full, and more often than not, it was so packed that a few bottles had to be slotted in upside down. There were nights when Kate felt disgusted with the amount she had drunk, but those nights were rare. Most nights, she would have a glass or two at the most (large glasses, but glasses all the same), but there were times, like tonight, when the loneliness and boredom got to her and she would finish one bottle off and open another if she had it. She was always up on time to open the café, though. Since that one day, she had never been late. Tomasz's words, *we need you*, stuck with her and she tried not to wonder whether it was Kate they needed, or *Kate's* the café.

Kate sat and drank her wine and looked out of her window. Sometimes she struggled to remember Al's face, Al's body. All that existed of Al now was a lack—a lack in Kate's arms, in her heart and in her bed. Night was drawing in and the sky, while not yet black, was a deep blue, studded with stars. One star. in particular, was very bright and Kate remembered being told that the brightest star in the sky was usually Venus. She raised her mug to the star.

'Thanks a lot, Venus,' she said. 'Thanks for nothing.'

11

Frank had been walking for an hour and several things were dawning on him. The main thing, the thing from which the other things all sprouted, was that he hadn't thought this through. He had made the decision a couple of weeks earlier that he needed to get away and that Ireland might be a good place to go. He had ordered his ferry ticket online, and as soon as the envelope had dropped through his letterbox, he had emailed his notice to his landlord and started to pile things he wasn't going to need any more into bin bags. There wasn't that much. He had never been one to accumulate possessions; material things didn't mean that much to him. He had sorted through his clothes and thrown the ones he wanted to keep into his holdall. The day he left, he had locked the flat, passed the keys onto a neighbour, got on a train and left. He had enough cash to pay for anything he needed on the way and a cheap B&B when he got to Dublin, and the plan, such as it was, was to play things by ear from there. Little by little, that vague plan had now come totally unravelled. He was stuck on Anglesey until the cheque cleared in his account the next day (hopefully) without enough money to pay for anywhere to stay, no credit card (he'd never had one) and now no plan.

The second thing was that he really should, at some point, have invested in a better pair of shoes. He had gone out in the first pair he had found that morning, his reliable Nike trainers, the ones he'd had for years. They were comfortable, didn't smell too bad and had given him reliable service. He should have checked that they were still going to be reliable and hadn't picked today to retire from service. He could feel a slight draft on his left foot, and it seemed very likely that the body of his shoe was starting to part company with the sole. There had been occasions in the past when he was skint and had repaired such damage to previous trainers with gaffer tape, but strangely, a roll of gaffer tape, like a change of shoes, was something he hadn't thought to bring with him. It looked like one of the first things he would have to find tomorrow would be a shoe shop and that certainly wasn't in the plan, such as it was.

It was also starting to sink in that if you're going to call anyone in a crisis, Mick Rogers probably wasn't the best person. Frank had known Mick for years. The Leisure Decree had toured a few times with Mick; they had done a tour of the clubs of the North with Mick's first outfit, Nevermore, and then, once they had started to make it a bit, with his more successful band, The Riflemen. When Decree had split, Frank and Mick kept in touch to an extent, but where Frank was content to live off the royalties and whatever work he could pick up, Mick hadn't been able to give up the rock'n'roll lifestyle and had been gigging with the Riflemen ever since. There was nobody left from the original line-up apart from Mick, but he still kept going and kept himself in the public eye by popping up every time there was a 90s nostalgia celebrity edition of any popular TV game show. When Frank thought of Mick, he thought of late nights spent drinking (and other things) and those memories were made hazy by the sheer amount they consumed. They were all kids, making music and having a good time. None of them ever thought there might be any kind of real world afterwards, and Mick still hadn't got there. He had calmed down a bit, by all accounts, but still liked a good time. How he had managed to stay married to the lovely Nina for all these years was a complete mystery, but it had somehow happened.

When Frank realised that he was stranded on Anglesey for the night, his thoughts turned to Mick Rogers. He hoped that Mick was still living on the island and wasn't off on tour somewhere. The Riflemen were still very popular in Germany for some reason, and rumour had it that Mick kept a place near Hamburg because he spent so much time there. But Mick had answered the phone when Frank rang and readily offered him a bed for the night.

'The only problem is I can't come and get you,' he said. 'Nina's away at her ma's, and I'm still on my ban. I'd say get a taxi, but it'll cost you.'

'I haven't got much cash 'til tomorrow,' Frank said.

'I'd pay this end,' Mick said, 'but Nina hasn't left me any money. She knows what I'd do with it. It's not that far to walk. It'll be good to see you, man. We'll have a few, and it'll be like the old days.'

'I don't really drink much these days, Mick.'

'Don't blame you. I reckon my liver's pretty fucked too. I've got some decent blow in, though.'

'I don't do that either. I've gone boring these days.'

'Jesus, you have. I'm sure I can find you some Ovaltine or something, Granddad. Okay, so you're on Holy Island now, so you need to get to Four Mile Bridge and cross over to the main island...'

'Four Mile?'

The bridge isn't four miles. I don't know why they call it that—some Welsh thing. No, actually, scrub that. Get on the A5 and head for Valley. That'll take, I don't know, an hour maybe...'

'An *hour*?'

'You could probably get a bus, but if you're skint...'

'I could manage a bus, Mick.'

'Okay, get a bus...'

'To Valley?'

'No, you need a bus to Llanfaethlu, then give us another ring. I'll give you directions from there. I'm probably about half an hour from there.'

'That's better. I'll talk to you in a bit.'

Frank found the nearest bus station and tried to work out which bus he needed to catch. As he stared at the bewildering array of place names, all of which had too many 'l's and not enough consonants, he had the sinking feeling that maybe he should have asked Mick to spell it out for him. All the same, he found a name that looked like it might have been what Mick had said and saw that the bus was due in ten minutes or so. It was only when the bus pulled up and Frank had managed to make his destination apparent to the bus driver, who was obviously used to English idiots and their pronunciation, that he reached into his trouser pocket for the ten-pound note he distinctly remembered putting it in there back in the café and found that all that was in there was a few coins, copper ones at that. Somewhere between the café and the bus station, he had lost the only note he had.

'I'm sorry,' he said to the bus driver, 'I haven't got any money. I don't suppose....'

'You'd better start walking then, hadn't you?' the driver suggested helpfully and rang the bell. Frank got off the bus and took his phone out to ring Mick and say he might be a bit longer than he thought. Inevitably, the indicator on the screen showed him he had probably about enough charge left on the phone to make one call and decided it would be better to save that until he got to whatever that place was that Mick had said and call him from there. It couldn't be that far, could it? Anglesey was only a small island, after all, or at least that was how it looked on the maps he remembered seeing. He selected a direction he hoped was the right one and started to walk.

Now he was on a road he could only hope was the right one, walking to a place he couldn't pronounce or spell, with no money and one of his trainers dying on its arse. He was regretting the time he had wasted at Llandudno Junction and the kindness he had felt compelled to show to two total strangers who could have been lying about their situations for all he knew. It felt like someone had weighed his bag down with bricks, and he was very much aware of how unfit he was. Of course, it was going to start to rain. It was only a spot at first, and he was able to convince himself for a minute or two that he hadn't felt it at all. But then it started to pour down and Frank knew there was only one thing to do. He stuck out his thumb and hoped to God that some kind person would stop for a miserable-looking drenched Scouser. The prospect didn't seem very promising, and indeed the first few cars that passed ignored him completely. He was surprised, then, when a white transit van pulled up ahead of him. He jogged a few yards to reach it and the driver wound the passenger window down. Frank could see that the driver was a man in his fifties with a very incongruous looking mullet, badly dyed blonde.

'Where you going?' he asked.

'Llan-faithly, is it?' Frank attempted.

'You're going the wrong way then,' the driver said. 'I'm going up past Llandewi. I could drop you off round there. Looks like you could do with finding some shelter. It's a hell of a walk back to Llanfaethlu from here.'

'Okay,' Frank said, 'thank you.'

'No problem,' the driver said. 'Better still, I'll drop you in Chapel Bay as we go past. They don't mind strangers there.'

12

Gemma sat and looked at the mess on her workbench and was utterly perplexed. It was one of those words you read in books and pictured ladies in crinoline dresses, but you never think will happen to you. But there was no better word for it. She was perplexed and didn't much like it.

It had started when she got back from lunch and sat down to start work on the order she had received. It was a simple job and should have taken half an hour maximum. The customer wanted a jasper pebble mounted on a chain and there was nothing easier than attaching a silver cap to the narrowest part of the stone. She had the perfect stone already polished and lacquered. It was simply a matter of threading the chain through the mount and putting the whole thing in a gift box that would then be wrapped in a bubble-wrap pouch, placed in a jiffy bag and posted. Simple. But where she would normally be completely focussed on the job in hand, she found it difficult to concentrate. It was as if she had forgotten something important and couldn't quite put her finger on what it was. She was all fingers and thumbs when it came to putting the cap on the stone. She ruined one cap altogether by opening it too far - a very basic mistake - and snapping one of the wings. She put it back in the cellophane bag in which it had come and tossed it into the cardboard box she kept for items she intended to return one day as faulty and tried another. This time, she very nearly squirted too much adhesive into the cap, so much that had she tried to attach it, it would have run down the stone, ruining that, too. Luckily, she caught that in time and was able to rescue it before any irreversible damage was done.

By the time she had finished faffing about, a half-hour job had taken nearly twice as long, and she still had no idea what it was that was nagging at the back of her mind. She was normally very organised. She kept her paperwork in ring binders and her accounts up to date. She knew at any one time exactly what she had in her inventory and what was running low. It was rare that she forgot anything. In fact, all through school, it was her memory rather than any particular academic prowess that got her good marks. She was very good at exams, because anything she didn't quite understand, she was able to learn parrot-fashion and trot out in the exam. In subjects like maths or physics, she gained enough marks for her working out to get by, even if she was never sure if she got the final answer right. Nothing annoyed her more than forgetting something or losing something. On the rare occasions, for example, when she put her keys anywhere other than the hook she had screwed into the wall by the door of her flat for that purpose, she had been known to fly into such a rage with herself that she virtually dismantled her flat trying to find the keys, rather than calmly thinking about where they might be. They were, in fact, usually by the kettle, since putting the kettle on for a cuppa was one of the first things she did when she got home. She was too hard on herself at times and had been told that before but was probably a bit too long in the tooth to change now.

She finally finished the customer's order and addressed the envelope, setting it aside to post later. She debated whether or not her finances or her caffeine levels could stand nipping next door for another coffee and was on her feet ready to go when something caught her attention, something out of the corner of her eye, a glint of the purest turquoise. The sun had clearly caught the pieces of broken glass she had left in the corner, which was odd because the afternoon sun was coming through the open door of the workshop and making a triangle of light on the other side of the room. No light was shining on the corner where the glass was.

'Is it you?' Gemma asked aloud. 'Is it you that I've forgotten? I hadn't really, you know.' She stopped herself and frowned. 'Jesus,' she said, 'I'm talking to broken glass.'

All the same, for want of anything better to do, and deciding that her problem might be that she had drunk too much coffee anyway, she gathered up the glass fragments and took them to the small sink in what the estate agent had hilariously described as 'the kitchen area' of the workshop. Her kitchen was a sink with only one tap (the cold one) set into a worktop covered in grey Formica that would never convince as marble even in poor light. The bijou kitchen area had the extra luxury of an electric socket, ideal for the kettle with which one could cook one's gourmet Pot Noodle. She ran some water into the sink, as ever, filling it fuller than she needed so that the ill-fitting plug would not cause all the water to run out before she had finished. She laid the pieces of glass on the work surface and, using a sponge, gently cleaned each one. In truth, they didn't need all that much cleaning; despite some of them having been semi-buried, they didn't seem to have much sand clinging to them. She gave them a good wash anyway, paying particular attention to the edges. If she had any hope of gluing them back together, the edges had to be completely clean and free of any sand or grit. Once she had finished washing every piece, she laid them on a tea towel to dry. She always preferred to let things dry in the air, rather than trying to dry them herself, especially glass – she had sliced a finger more than once on a sharp edge which had been concealed by a tea towel or piece of kitchen roll. While they dried, she organised herself with everything she would need for the job, the felt mat she used for such jobs, a sheet of finest grade sandpaper, the adhesive, the cotton buds to apply it and the masking tape to hold the pieces together while it set. Then she carried the pieces of her glass jigsaw puzzle over to her workbench, laid them on the mat and tried to decide where to begin.

She was lucky, she supposed, that whatever this glass thing was, hadn't broken into too many pieces, and a cursory glance told her they all looked to be present. It would be awful and very frustrating to go to all the trouble of trying to repair it, only to find that a small piece she might never be able to find could make it incomplete. She picked up two of the larger pieces that obviously went side by side and put them together, holding them up to the light. They fitted together perfectly, making a seamless join that allowed no light to get through. So far, so good. She cut off a couple of thin strips of masking tape and stuck them lightly to the end of the bench. To try and do that when she had stuck some of the pieces together would have taken a third, and possibly even a fourth hand she often regretted not possessing. She gave the edges a delicate rub with the sandpaper, buffed them with a cloth and then applied the thinnest layer of adhesive to the edge of the larger of the two pieces. She pressed the edges of the two pieces together and, holding them with one hand, picked up a piece of masking tape to keep them in place. She added a second piece of tape to be sure and carefully rested the joined sections on the mat to dry, a process that should have taken seconds. That was where things began to get perplexing.

She was sorting through some of the other pieces when she heard a quiet 'tink'. Despite the glue and the masking tape, the two pieces she had stuck together had fallen apart. That really shouldn't happen. The adhesive she used wasn't cheap Poundland three-for-a-quid stuff. It was the real thing, the kind used by all proper jewellers. It should bond anything to anything else in seconds and frequently did, especially when you didn't want it to. Before now, it had bonded stones to workbenches, jewellery fittings to tools and fingers to any number of things. Two pieces of the same glass should be no problem at all. Her first thought was that something was wrong with the glue, but she had only bought it the other week, and she had done a couple of other jobs with that same tube. Maybe she hadn't applied it properly. She had, after all, proved herself to be rather distracted that afternoon already, but deep down, she knew she had. She could picture herself doing it. She picked the pieces up to look at them, and it was then that she noticed the sticky patch on the mat below them. She didn't need to touch it to know it was glue; there was no mistaking it. Somehow, inexplicably, the adhesive had run off the glass. She examined the edge where she had applied the glue. At the very least, it should be slightly tacky, but there was nothing there. Her next thought was that perhaps she hadn't let the glass dry sufficiently. She was sure it hadn't still been damp when she applied the glue, but in case she did it again, this time making absolutely certain that there wasn't the tiniest part of the surface that she didn't coat with glue. She pressed the pieces together again, reapplied the masking tape and waited. Within seconds, the pieces, which shouldn't have been able to move at all, fell apart. Now she could definitely describe herself as perplexed. This went against all her experience and made no sense at all.

'What's your game?' she asked the glass. 'What *are* you?' And then she felt ridiculous, not for talking to the glass again, but for asking the question. It was glass. It was a broken glass *something* that someone had left on the beach. It was a pretty colour, but nothing special. She collected the pieces together and put them back in the corner of the workshop. If it was truly a mystery, it was one that would have to wait for another day, possibly with the assistance of the Internet. It would be another couple of weeks before she would give the glass another thought. By that time, something would have happened, which would be enough to perplex anyone.

13

When she woke up next morning, Kate immediately regretted the previous night. Her head regretted the wine, and her heart regretted the thoughts and memories it had awoken. She sat up in bed for a few minutes, furious with herself for being so weak, then made a decision. No more. She was leaning on the wine too heavily and she was doing it to try not to think about Al, and none of it was working. So that was it. Al was gone and wasn't coming back, and a river of wine and all the hangovers in the world weren't going to change that. There was only one direction in which to go now and that was forwards. She had as cold a shower as she could stand, made a coffee and got herself dressed and ready for the day. The Cat wandered into the kitchen and eyed her suspiciously but didn't turn down the food she put in its bowl. She even stooped down and gave it a quick tickle behind the ears while it ate, which made it stop eating and look at her with the cat equivalent of raising an eyebrow.

'You need to lighten up,' she told it and, picking up her keys that had miraculously ended up in the right place the night before, left the cottage.

The spring sunshine helped her mood, and she stood outside the cottage breathing in the air, with its tang of salt from the sea and the delicate fragrance of the early hyacinths, which reliably sprung up every year in the flowerbeds by the front door, and the honeysuckle that framed the door itself. She felt frivolous enough to pluck one of the young blooms from the honeysuckle and suck the end as her father had shown her, filling her mouth with the incomparable sweetness. Her heart felt lighter than it had done for quite some time as she walked down the lane to the café. Behind one of the hedges that lined the lane, she could hear old Huw calling and cursing Gwyl and even that made her smile.

She arrived at the café a good ten minutes before Dour Dairy Dave turned up and even he couldn't put a damper on her mood.

'I think I've put my back out,' he said, dumping the milk down. 'I was cutting back the bush out the front for the wife, and I think I overdid it.'

'Tell your wife to trim her own bush in future,' Kate couldn't stop herself from replying.

'Talk like that'll get you a reputation,' Dave said.

'No thanks. I've already got one. Have a nice day, Dave. Don't work too hard.'

'I can't,' Dave said over his shoulder. 'I think I've strained my coccyx.'

'That would be a first,' Kate said, but by then, he was well on his way back to the van.

When Kate carried the milk to the fridge, it occurred to her for the first time that day that her own back wasn't hurting, or at least no more than a dull ache with which she could more than cope. She decided that the best thing to do was thank the Universe for small mercies and try not to think about it too much. She switched the radio on and before long was singing along. She was giving her best version of Mr. Blue Sky, including the instrumental bits, when she realised she was no longer alone. Briony had arrived with the bread and was watching her with amusement from the shop doorway.

'You haven't got a bad voice,' Briony said. 'It's kind of sexy.'

Kate smiled and finished the song, her eye on Briony all the time.

'Someone's in a good mood today,' Briony said. 'Did you get some last night, then?'

'You know I'm saving myself for you,' Kate replied, realising as soon as she said it how daring it sounded. She backtracked rapidly. 'It's a lovely day.'

'Your smile would brighten any day, my lovely. You should do it more.'

'Time for a cuppa?' Kate asked, turning away so Briony wouldn't see her blush.

'Go on. I've got myself a bit ahead.'

Kate made two coffees while Briony loaded the bread onto the counter.

'So what has put you in such a good mood? Not that I'm complaining.'

'Nothing in particular,' Kate replied. 'I've decided to let go of some of the stuff that was holding me down, you know? It's time to go forwards.'

'That's my girl,' Briony said, sipping her coffee. 'Mmm. You make the best coffee around, you know that?'

'Thanks, Bri. I try.'

'You do very well.'

They drank their coffee in silence for a while. Kate looked up once to steal a glance at Briony but had to look away because she was acutely aware that she was also being watched. She was also aware that Briony had the prettiest sky-blue eyes and wasn't sure she wanted to think about that.

'So I was wondering,' Briony said eventually. 'You doing anything a week Saturday night? The 14th, I think.'

'I doubt it. The usual pizza and crap telly. Why?'

'I've got a couple of tickets to see a band in Caernarfon. I was going with a mate, but she cried off because of some childcare bullshit. It's Space. You remember them?'

'Did they do that one about Tom Jones, with whatshername?'

The lovely Cerys,' Briony said, putting on a heavier Welsh accent than usual. 'I thought that now I've caught you in a good mood for once, you might like to come.'

'What do you mean 'for once'? Am I that bad?'

'No, of course not. I'm joking—a bit. You can be a bit serious, though. Happy suits you better. You've got dimples. Who knew?'

Kate laughed.

'Hey, I don't show my dimples to everyone, you know.'

'I'm flattered then. So what do you think?'

'I don't know, Bri. I'm usually pretty knackered by the end of the week.'

'Aren't we all? Doesn't mean you can't have a bit of fun. I

promise I won't keep you out late.'

'Go on then. Why not?'

'Really? That's brilliant. I'll see you before then and sort out times.' Briony looked at her watch. 'Jesus is that the time? I'd better shoot. Thanks for the coffee, Katie.'

'You're always welcome. Thanks for the invitation.'

'No problem.'

Briony picked up her empty crate and started towards the door.

'It's just mates, you know. The gig. No pressure.'

'Mates is good,' Kate said and waved Briony off. As she watched the van pull away, she had to smile as Briony did her best to wake the whole village up with Barry White on full volume. She had something else to smile about, too. Not since her childhood had anyone called her Katie. Even Al stuck to 'Kate'. But Briony had called her Katie, and she liked the way it sounded.

She washed the cups she and Briony had used, trying not to pay any attention to the smudge of pink lipstick Bri had left on the cup, and began to get herself ready for the day. As she did so, she glanced through the café window and noticed that a man was sitting on the low wall that separated the beach from the path. She didn't recognise him, was certain she had never seen him before and wondered for a second if she should be worried. But he looked harmless enough, someone passing through, judging by the holdall on the wall beside him. Maybe when he stopped staring out to sea, he might be her first customer of the day. Any day, which started that early, was bound to be a good one. She had no idea that this stranger was about to change things forever, or of the trouble he was going to bring with him.

14

Frank sat on the low wall, watching the gulls wheel in the sky and plunge into the sea. Their squawks, as they yelled instructions or insults to one another and the gentle hiss of waves retreating over the pebbles at the edge of the sand, were the only sounds he could hear. Everything else was quiet. It wasn't like the city, where there was a constant background noise of traffic, shouting and dogs barking. Here you could hear your own thoughts without distraction. Unfortunately, the main thought Frank could hear was how much his body ached. His feet throbbed, and the tendons in the back of his calves felt tight as guitar strings. If he moved his head the wrong way, a sharp bolt of pain ran up his neck. He was getting way too old to have spent the night outside. None of this was going to plan. By now, he should have been waking up in a Dublin bed and breakfast, looking forward to fortifying himself with a large fry-up before starting to discover what a new life in a new place would hold for him. Instead, he was sitting on a hard stone wall in a place he didn't know. Something was damp, and he wasn't sure if it was the wall or his trousers. There was an odd, slightly earthy smell coming from somewhere, too, and he was rather afraid it was him. He needed to change his clothes, but this wasn't the right place to do it, not in full view of the café behind him. There was someone in there and he didn't want to strip off in front of them. The sooner he could get to a bank, withdraw some money and get back on his way, the better.

Spending the night in a barn had not figured in his plans at all. He hadn't thought about what he would do next when the mullet-haired driver had dropped him off. The rain had stopped by the time the driver, who had said his name was Ian (or possibly Owen, it was hard to tell with his accent), had pulled up at the side of the main road, pointed to a side road and told him that Chapel Bay was 'just down there.' He had thanked Owen (or Ian), watched the van drive off and started to walk down the road. It was dusk by now and the air above was filled with small birds with forked tails flying backwards and forwards at speed, making high pitched shrieks. He thought they might be swallows, but it was as likely they were swifts. Mick Rogers would probably have known, seeing as he was a country boy now. He wondered if Mick would be worried about where he had got to, but knowing Mick, he would have quite possibly started on that weed he said he had, in which case he had probably forgotten about Frank by now. All the same, once he'd got some charge back in his phone, he'd give Mick a quick ring out of courtesy, if nothing else. The road was one of those country roads with high hedges on either side and where you normally got stuck behind a very slow-moving tractor, with no room to pass. Other things were darting in and out of the hedges, small, black, flappy things and Frank was concerned they might be bats. He wasn't sure why he was concerned; he was pretty sure that there were no vampire bats in Britain, not even in the wilds of Wales. All the same, they were flying disconcertingly close to him, and he didn't want to get one in the face. He hurried on down the road until he spotted a sign, half in and half out of the hedge. It announced that he had now arrived at Chapel Bay and something else in Welsh that he couldn't begin to read. The sign also suggested that he might like to drive slowly through the village, as if there was a chance of doing anything else. Despite the fact that he was now officially in Chapel Bay, he had to walk for another ten minutes before he saw any sign of civilisation, other than one farm.

Civilisation, when it arrived, consisted of the smallest village Frank had ever seen. If you talked about one-horse towns, this place would struggle to house a small Shetland pony. There were several cottages, all of which might have been very picturesque, but it was difficult to tell in the diminishing light. Down from the cottages was a sandstone building that could possibly have been a school, though it was so small that it could equally have been a village hall and next to that was an older building with a wooden cross erected outside, obviously the Chapel which gave the bay its name. Over the road from the chapel was another row of cottages and what looked like a general store. It had a post box outside, but, as far as Frank could see, no cashpoint. It was, of course, closed, as was the tiny chip shop next door. Another narrow road ran off to the left, but as far as he could see, only contained houses. After that, the lane seemed to go on further, but it didn't look like there were any more buildings. The warm welcome for strangers, which Ian the Mullet had predicted, was nowhere to be seen. There wasn't even a pub, as far as he could see, unless it was down the side road, but even if there was, it would almost certainly be closed by now. There was no sign of life at all. There were lights on in most of the cottages, and some had smoke coming out of their chimneys, but Frank didn't think any of them would appreciate a bedraggled Scouser knocking on their doors requesting free lodging for the night. All the same, he had to find somewhere to sleep and maybe dry off a bit. The rain might have gone off for now, but that was no guarantee it wouldn't return.

He remembered the farm he had passed on the road into the village and went back for another look. A padlocked gate marked its entrance, but, peering into the gloom, Frank could see several outbuildings and a barn. There was enough distance between the barn and the farmhouse to make it a promising prospect, so, looking around to make sure he wasn't observed (he was more than aware that farmers might possess shotguns and an aversion to trespassers), climbed the gate, which wobbled uncomfortably, but at least didn't fall over under his weight. He landed on the other side with a squelch. Something seeped in through the split in his trainer, and he hoped it was only mud because something around there smelled a bit ripe. As cautiously as he could with one very soggy foot, he crossed the farmyard and made his way to the barn, hoping that whatever had made the smell wasn't also lodging there. The barn was a large one and fortunately filled with bales of hay rather than incontinent cattle. The bails at the front of the stack were damp from the rain, but he climbed up a bit and discovered that the bails behind were not only dry but pleasantly warm. He did his best to make himself comfortable and took off his damaged shoe, placing it on the bail next to him in the vain hope that it would dry out a bit before he needed it again. He closed his eyes and did his best not to think about how unpleasant his damp clothes felt against his skin or to wonder about how long trench foot took to develop. He was soggy, alone and miserable and beginning to think he might have been better off staying in Liverpool and facing the music.

He was hungry too. Having abandoned the stale Danish pastry at Holyhead, the last thing he had eaten was the sandwich many hours earlier, but now there was no chance of anything to eat before morning. His usual policy was only to eat when he was hungry, which often led to a lack of forward planning. If he had known how the day was going to pan out, he might have picked something up to keep him going, but now he would have to wait. Frank had always had a love/hate relationship with food. As a child, he had tended towards fat. His mother was a feeder, showing her love through providing food, and this love did him no favours, not with his father, or the other kids at school who bullied him for the way he looked, and it was only his love of, and his aptitude for music that saved him. Later, when he was on the road, the exercise and adrenaline of performing stopped him piling on the pounds that a diet of junk food and beer would otherwise have made inevitable. Once the touring days finished, his weight began to fluctuate again through inertia and comfort eating. But since the one horrible morning when he had taken a good long look at his flab in the mirror, he more or less had it under control, through diet, common sense, and sometimes practices that would not necessarily be recommended by any dietician. Mostly now, he only saw his old friend, the inside of the toilet bowl, when he had been drinking. But he still hated to be watched while eating. One of his biggest dreads was the buffet at parties, and he tried to avoid them whenever possible. Even though everyone else was piling their plates sky-high, he generally only took enough to be polite, in case anyone was watching and thinking *look at all that – no wonder he's so fat*. He had no real idea if anyone did think that or if they were all too busy stuffing their own faces to notice, but it was enough that he thought it. Now he was sitting on straw and wondering whether it tasted as much like Shredded Wheat as it looked.

If the hunger wasn't enough to keep him awake, he was getting a bit concerned about the small scuffling noises he could hear coming from somewhere behind him. This was undoubtedly the wrong time to remember the television programme he had once seen in which a farmer unleashed a couple of Jack Russell terriers on his barn, causing a furry, squealing tsunami of rats to come flooding out. Who would have thought there were so many in there, lurking unseen amongst the hay? They were probably here now, sneaking about between the bails, waiting for him to go to sleep. Between the hunger and the fear that he would wake up covered in rodents, Frank fully expected that he would get no sleep at all.

***

Frank woke with a jolt, dazzled by the low sun that was streaming into the barn. Somehow, he had managed to sleep for hours without dying of starvation or being nibbled to death. According to his watch, it was just gone seven, which hardly seemed possible. The realisation that the new day could lead to his discovery made him get up, despite the protests from most of his muscles. He just about remembered to put his trainer back on, pleased to find that it was more or less dry, and cautiously left the barn. He fully expected to be confronted by a shotgun-wielding farmer, but luckily the farmyard was empty. Somewhere nearby, he could hear a gruff voice calling someone (presumably a dog, or at least that's what he hoped) a 'hairy wanker' and decided that this was the ideal opportunity to climb back over the gate and into the lane. This left him with the decision as to what to do next. He checked the change in his pocket and was pleased to discover that he had at least enough money to buy a cup of coffee if there was anywhere to buy one and if they didn't charge city prices, so wandered back down the lane to the village to see what it looked like in the daylight and if there was anywhere he had missed.

The village looked, to all intents and purposes, exactly the same as it had the previous night. Clearly, the villagers liked a lie-in. He walked through the village and followed the lane a short way. Up ahead, he could hear the sea and had a strong urge to go and see it. It was a sudden tug and reminded him of being a child again, on holiday by the seaside and unable to wait to go to the beach. He hurried down the lane as quickly as his stiff legs would carry him and there it was. The lane opened up onto a road, which ran along the cliffs, and there below was an expanse of sand and rocks and the sea itself, the sun sparkling on the waves like the memory of every best holiday he'd had. There was a van with the logo of a bakery parked on the road, and as he passed it, he could see steps leading down to the beach. There were a couple of buildings down below, and he jingled the change in his pocket, hoping that one of them might be a beachfront café. The steps appeared to have been carved out of the cliff a long time ago, back when health and safety standards were not nearly as rigorous, and he almost stumbled a few times in his haste to get down them. He forced himself to slow down, because after all, he wanted a look at the sea and a coffee, not A&E and a drip, even holding onto the handrail once or twice, which didn't feel a great deal safer. Before too long, he was on the safer ground at the bottom of the steps. One of the two buildings certainly was a café called *Kate's,* and it was quite a nice-looking one at that, but it didn't look like it was open yet. An attractive blonde woman was coming out carrying a plastic crate, and Frank watched her navigate the steps back up to the bread van. He wondered what had happened to put such a smile on her face and a spring in her step. She positively bounded up the steps, climbed into the van and drove off with Barry White growling about someone being his first and last and everything. There was obviously something in the bread. It was only a shame Frank didn't have the money for a sandwich as well.

A wall separated the beach from the forecourt of the café, although Frank had his doubts that it was big enough to offer much protection if there was a particularly high tide. Not wanting to hassle the café owner too early, he went and sat on the wall and looked out across the beach to the sea. After coffee, he might well be tempted to have a wander on the beach, but for now, he was content to keep his eyes on the horizon, breathe in the clean, fresh air and feel at peace. There would be plenty of time later to make any decisions that needed to be made.

15

It was exactly the sort of day Gemma liked best, bright, but with a gentle breeze to stop it getting too warm. Much as she loved the feel of the sun on her skin, the workshop had no windows and, even with the door wide open, it could become an oven when the weather was hot, and that kind of heat made her grouchy and gave her a dull headache. Today was perfect, though, and she put on one of her favourite summer dresses, the cream one decorated with tiny cornflowers, and felt like she was floating as she negotiated the fire escape down from her flat to the workshop. For once, there was nothing of any concern thrown away in the passage and the door to the workshop opened easily. The Universe had obviously decided that today would be a good day, and most of the time, she trusted the Universe to know what it was doing. Every morning on waking and every night before going to sleep, she sent a wish list to the Universe and thanked it for the small blessings of the day. It was her way of praying and had always served her well.

Years ago, she had given up believing in the God her parents prayed to, and with good reason, but had always believed there was something guiding her, even if wasn't some bloke with a beard who made capricious decisions about who lived and who died, who had robbed her of both her parents within two years, her father of a heart attack and her mother of a cancer she didn't have the heart to fight without her soul-mate by her side. Gemma had been left to fend for herself at the age of twenty-four and had decided at her mum's funeral, while everyone prayed and sang to God, that either they were praying to someone who had a sick sense of humour, or who was cruel and uncaring. She walked away from the church that day and had never set foot in one since. She only had herself to rely on now, and she would put all her faith in that instead. At least she knew where she was. If she made mistakes, they would be because of her decisions, not because of some entity that didn't give a damn about her.

A few years earlier, a friend of hers (back when she had a few friends before leaving them all behind) had given her a book about the Law of Attraction. Esme had been very much into such things and had become quite the evangelist about them, telling everyone the book had changed her life. Gemma had read the book and had, at first, dismissed it as quite possibly the biggest pile of bollocks she had ever read. Apparently, if you wished hard enough, you could make anything you wanted happen. A good job and loads of money? No problem. The ideal man? All you had to do was want it enough. If you didn't get what you wanted, you didn't want it enough and had to try harder. The whole thing made Gemma feel distinctly uncomfortable. Obviously, the people, who had loads of money and wonderful lifestyles and didn't give a shit about anyone else, had wanted it more than the people who were living below the breadline, desperate to survive. She couldn't get her head around how *that* bit of logic worked. She had finished the book out of politeness and because Esme kept asking her if she had read it, and then put it in a bag with the other books she no longer wanted and really would take to the charity shop next time she had a chance.

She didn't think about it anymore until the car crash, the accident that put beautiful, cheery, positive Esme in a coma in the intensive care unit. Gemma and her other friends took turns relieving Esme's parents at the bedside while Esme, unrecognisable beneath bandages and drips and a respirator, fought for her life. It was during one such vigil that Gemma remembered the book. As the machine breathed for her lovely friend, she wondered how on earth Esme could possibly have wished for this, and she got angrier than she had been for a very long time.

'How could you do this?' she hissed quietly, even though there was nobody who could hear. 'How could you fucking do this? Go on. Show me. If it's as easy as that, do something.

There is nothing I want more than this, so save her.'

The monitors bleeped. The respirator breathed. Nothing happened. But something had changed in Gemma. For the whole of this four-hour vigil, she fiercely challenged the Universe to save her friend. She held Esme's hand and thought over and over again, *prove it, save her.* She wished so hard that it felt as though she was pushing the wish out through her forehead and into the air. She shut every other thought out of her mind and concentrated furiously on that one thing. By the time Esme's parents, who looked as though they had both shrunk over the past few days, arrived to start their shift, Gemma had a headache, but there were no visible results. Gemma went home raging.

The first thing she did when she got back to her flat was grab the stupid bloody book out of the carrier bag.

'You are no fucking help,' she said and took it to the bin, ready to throw it in and bury it amongst the food scrapings. She was never sure what stopped her. She could never be sure why she felt compelled to sit down and read the book again. Maybe it was sheer desperation, or maybe some higher force intervened, but read it, she did. She skipped through the passages about wealth and ideal men because neither seemed appropriate or relevant, instead concentrating on the practical applications it described. One passage leapt out at her. It instructed the reader that if they really wanted a thing, they should act like it had already been granted. If you wanted that fantastic new job, start dressing like you deserve it. If you want that man, start planning where the first date is going to be. It was a matter of eliminating doubt. Something about this resonated strongly with Gemma, and she understood she had been going about it the wrong way. She had been approaching it from a point of view of cynicism and doubt. She found the best picture she had of Esme on her phone and placed the phone face up on a table so that she could see the image of her friend at all times and went and found a notepad and pen. She spent the next hour writing Esme a letter. It had been a long time since she had written a letter to anyone, but the words poured out of her, and they were good words, full of love and hope. She wrote it, imagining that Esme had woken from her coma and was on the road to recovery and filled it with gratitude and optimism, plans for what they were going to do when Esme got out of hospital. By the time she had finished, tears were pouring down her face and onto the paper, but they were not tears of grief, they were tears of joy and relief. Gemma picked her phone up and smiled at the picture of her friend and *knew*. She knew how she would feel when she got the call she was waiting for. She knew how wonderful the good news would feel. When the phone started to ring, ten minutes later, Gemma didn't need to look at the caller display. She knew who it was. She cried again when Esme's mother told her through her own tears that Gemma's beautiful friend had woken up briefly, squeezed her mum's hand and smiled. Three days later, Gemma was able to give Esme the letter she had written in person and had not needed to change a word of it. The book went on Gemma's bookshelf and had stayed with her ever since.

From that day on, Gemma never went to sleep at night without listing the small blessings she had received during the day and giving thanks and then sending out her wishes to the Universe. They were mostly wishes for other people, but there were a few long-term things she wished for herself. The things she wished for others were usually granted in one way or another. She was still waiting for her own wishes to be granted but clung to the belief that this was only because it was not the right time for her yet. One day.

Esme was married now. The accident had the bonus effect of galvanising her on/off boyfriend Jacob into realising what he had nearly lost, and he had stunned everyone (though no one more than Esme) by proposing as soon as Esme left hospital. They were happy, and it made it that little bit easier for Gemma to leave Esme behind when she walked away and escaped to this beach retreat. It wasn't as though she had much choice, but it still hurt not to have any contact with those she had left. One of her wishes was that her friends had not forgotten her and she would see them again. One day, but not yet.

The Universe still delivered good days and bad days to Gemma. The good days were a blessing, and the bad days were a lesson. Today, the sun was a blessing, and it made her wonder what else the day had in store. She spent the first hour tidying and cleaning the workshop. It was a job she usually put off as long as she could, but then enjoyed it when she finally got around to it and wondered why she had put it off for so long. It had gone ten o'clock when she wiped the last traces of dust from her workbench, and definitely time for a coffee. As she came out of the workshop, she noticed a stranger sitting on the wall outside Kate's, a takeaway cup in his hand. He didn't look that threatening or suspicious, just a bit scruffy. He looked to be in his forties or thereabouts, with untidy dark hair that was threaded with grey in places. His leather jacket had obviously seen better days, and so had he, and although he seemed fascinated by the sea and was taking no notice of Gemma whatsoever, she still made sure that the workshop door was locked before she went into the café.

Kate was busy when Gemma came in, not with customers, takeaway man was the only one, but with organising and cleaning one of her fridges.

'Be right with you, Gem,' she called.

'No hurry,' Gemma replied, but then there was a shriek and a thump. Kate was doubled over at the fridge, clutching the small of her back, the milk bottle she had dropped on the floor with its contents pooling around her feet.

'Shit,' she said. 'My back's gone.'

16

Gemma rushed over to Kate and nearly skidded on the spilt milk. She grabbed the top of the fridge in time to stop her dragging them both over. She took hold of Kate's arm.

'Come and sit down,' she said. 'Do you need an ambulance?'

'No,' Kate said firmly. 'It's only a spasm. I'll be okay.'

'Let's get you sat down anyway.'

She put her arm around Kate's back and hooked a hand under her armpit.

'Lean on me, Kate. Come on.'

'I'm too heavy. I'll pull you over.'

'I'm stronger than I look.'

'Do you need a hand?' Gemma looked up and saw that the scruffy stranger who had been sitting outside was now standing at the counter. 'I heard a scream.'

'We're fine,' Gemma snapped. 'Come on, Kate. Easy does it.'

Gingerly, Kate tried to move, but another shriek escaped through her gritted teeth. 'I can't!'

The man was suddenly on the other side of Kate, and Gemma caught a strong odour of something very unpleasant, like manure and old hay.

'Jesus,' she said, 'have you been sleeping in a barn?'

'Well, he *was* born in one,' the man replied. Then he spoke to Kate and his voice was gentle this time. Gemma could detect a Liverpudlian accent.

'Put your arm around my shoulders,' he said. 'Sorry about the smell. You can wash your hands in a minute.'

Kate looked at him uncertainly but did as she had been instructed.

'Good,' he said. 'Now let me and this young lady take the

weight. This might hurt a bit, but we could do with getting you sat down, okay?'

Kate nodded.

'Okay. Here we go.' The stranger looked at Gemma and, with him taking most of the load, they managed to get Kate to the nearest chair and sat her down.

'There you go,' the man said. 'That wasn't so bad, was it?'

'It was bad enough,' Kate replied, and Gemma could see how ashen her face was. 'But thanks.'

'No problem. You got any painkillers?'

'I haven't,' Kate said. 'They're at home.'

'No good there, are they?' he turned to Gemma. 'What about you?'

'I think I've got some aspirin in my flat.'

'It'd probably do in a pinch, but she could do with something stronger. Anti-inflammatory.'

At that moment, the café door opened, and two men in yellow high visibility jackets came in.

'Can we get two lattes to go?' one asked.

'One skinny. Extra hot with a vanilla shot,' the other one added.

'Just a minute,' Kate called.

'We're in a bit of a hurry,' the first man said. 'We're due on site in five minutes.'

'You'll have to hang on,' Gemma interrupted.

'It's okay,' Kate said and tried to get up. Her eyes screwed up in pain.

'Stay there,' the scruffy, smelly stranger said. 'I'll do it.'

'No, you can't...' Kate began, but he put a hand on her shoulder and held her down.

'I know my way round a coffee machine,' he said. 'I've had plenty of experience. Milk in here?'

Without waiting for an answer, he washed his hands at the sink, then pulled a bottle of full-fat milk and a bottle of skimmed milk out of the fridge, went over to the coffee machine and looked at it. He smiled and got to work. As he did so, he called to Gemma over his shoulder.

'Is that shop open yet?'

'Should be. Why?'

'You want to go and see if they've got any ibuprofen?'

'I can't just leave!' Gemma protested.

'I've got this,' the stranger said. 'Go on.'

Gemma hesitated, but frustratingly, it made sense. She went out of the café, almost slamming the door as she went. The arrogance of the man, walking in there and taking over! Who the hell did he think he was, ordering her about like that? She stomped up the lane to Parry's, her earlier good mood now forgotten. She would get the tablets for Kate, and then that bloody tramp could get back under whatever hedge he had crawled out from. She arrived at Parry's, only to see a sign on the door saying, 'Back in five minutes'. That often happened. If Ewa or Tomasz were on their own in the shop, they often had to lock the front door while they took a delivery round the back. Gemma leaned against the doorframe and waited. Five minutes stretched to ten, then fifteen. Gemma kept checking her watch, willing the time to pass faster, aware all the time that Kate was in pain and stuck in the café with some rancid, cocky stranger. Finally, she heard a click, and through the glass in the door, she could see Ewa going back to the counter. The bell over the door tinkled and Gemma even found that irritating. Ewa gave a cheery, 'Good morning!' which Gemma forced herself to return.

'You got any ibuprofen, Ewa?' she asked.

'Yes, of course,' Ewa replied, taking a box from the shelf behind her. 'Are you okay, Gemma? Are you ill?'

'Not me. Kate's done her back in.'

'That is a pity. She works too hard, that one.'

Gemma went to get her purse out, but Ewa stopped her.

'It's okay,' she said. 'Take them. Kate is always bringing us leftover cake. She is very kind.'

'Well, if you're sure...Thanks, Ewa.'

'No problem. Oh, and Gemma, be careful. Make sure you keep your door locked. Huw was in earlier and he thinks he had a trespasser on the farm last night. He said he saw someone climbing over the gate. Took him a long time to calm that dog down.'

'Thanks, Ewa, I will.'

Gemma headed back down the lane as quickly as she could. She knew there was something about that guy. She'd lived in Chapel Bay long enough to know that nobody showed up here without a reason. He was probably going around the island, sleeping rough and looking for places to burgle. That's what happens when you let bloody Scousers out of Liverpool, she thought. Well, Kate could close the café today and go home. She'd go with her and look after her if needs be, but that thieving tosser would be gone. He'd be lucky if she didn't call the police on him, or worse, get Huw down here with his shotgun.

She was very surprised, then when she opened the door of the café and saw Kate on her feet and behind the counter. If that surprised her, then she was absolutely gobsmacked to see the robbing Scouser behind the counter with her and that the two of them were laughing together like old mates.

'Oh Gemma, thanks!' Kate said when she finally looked up. 'I did have some in my bag after all, but thanks for going. I can always use them.'

'You should be resting,' Gemma replied, scowling at Kate's new friend.

'They're kicking in now. Anyway, I've got an extra pair of hands.'

'What, *him*? Kate, are you sure that's a good...?'

'It's fine, Gem. He passed his audition with flying colours. Two perfect lattes, and he even sussed the till out. I'd better introduce you, hadn't I? You're going to be seeing a lot of each other. Frank, this is Gemma, who has the lovely workshop next door. Gemma, this is Frank. Once I've got him sorted out with somewhere to stay and a shower – definitely a shower – he's going to be helping me out here for a bit.

17

Kate arrived at the café early on Wednesday morning. Her back still felt tender after the spasm the day before, but at least she could move. She had soaked in a hot bath the night before, despite worrying a little about how she would get out if her back went into spasm again and there was no one around to help. The bubbles and the hot water had helped considerably, and she had gone to bed without a drink and slept right through until 4 o'clock when her brain woke her up by choosing that moment to wonder what the hell she thought she was doing when she offered Frank Davies a job.

Yes, he seemed like a nice guy, and yes, he had been very helpful when she needed it. She also couldn't deny that he made a great cup of coffee, but you could say much the same about a lot of people, but you didn't necessarily offer them a job. They got talking when Gemma went off to the shop, and Kate had found Frank very easy to talk to, although he seemed quite reluctant to give much away about himself. He was on Anglesey by chance, he said, on his way somewhere else, travelling around for a bit. Kate hadn't had to ask where he had come from because his accent gave him away. He had admitted he was from Liverpool but said no more about that. He had independent means but needed to get to a bank to access the money, which he proposed to do that day. He planned to move on as soon as he had. It was then that Kate, through a pain and painkiller fog, blurted it out.

'I don't suppose you fancy giving me a hand for a bit?'

Frank looked at her with a frown that could have meant any number of things, then grinned.

'I might do,' he said.

'I can't pay you much,' Kate added, 'I mean, this place barely pays me, but I'll feed you and pour enough coffee down you to turn you into an owl.'

Frank grinned again, then turned away to serve another customer who had come in. He took the order, and while Kate limped off to serve the customer's cake, Frank made a cappuccino on which the foam was so soft and white that it looked like meringue. He finished it off with a sprinkle of chocolate and handed it to the customer.

'Tell you what,' he said, 'I need today to sort myself out. I need to find the nearest bank and sort out somewhere to stay, ideally somewhere with a shower, because, well, these clothes aren't too fresh. What if I come back tomorrow and give it a try? I'll do it for nothing for a week or two and then we'll see. How about that?'

'Really? Are you serious?'

'Why not? It's as good a place as any.'

And that was that. Once the painkillers had fully kicked in, and Gemma was back to keep an eye on her, Frank disappeared, a piece of paper in his pocket with the name of the next town written down in capital letters and the address of a B&B that Kate knew to be fairly cheap but nice. She spent an uncomfortable half-hour fending off Gemma's objections to what she had done before packing her neighbour off to her workshop. She hadn't thought too deeply about Frank again until the nagging voice of her brain woke her up at 4am demanding to know what the hell she was thinking of. She had invited a man about whom she knew nothing to come and work in her café. All Gemma's objections came back to her.

He could be anyone! Look at the state of him. I think he slept rough in Huw's barn last night. He smells like he slept in a pigsty!

Gemma was right, of course. Frank had given very little away about his background or his reasons for being there. As the sun began to rise outside her window, the horrible thought struck Kate that maybe Frank was on the run. Maybe he was a criminal, a murderer even, and she had invited him into her business because he made a decent latte. She didn't get back to sleep after that.

It was for that reason that she arrived early at the café.

She had to be sure that now he had seen the layout, this Frank, if indeed that was his real name, hadn't broken in during the night and ransacked the place. She half expected to find her business in ruins and police tape everywhere. It came as some relief, then, when she arrived and found that everything was exactly as she had left it the night before. All the same, she unlocked the door as stealthily as she could and crept inside, ready for someone reeking of the farmyard to jump out on her. There was no one there. She turned the lights on and started to wonder how she was going to break it to Frank that it had all been a huge mistake and that she didn't need him at all—assuming, of course, that he turned up. She had told him to come at nine o'clock, so she could get the café ready before he started, and it was still only half past seven. She turned the coffee machine on to heat up, made herself a cup of green tea using the kettle, and went to sit outside in the fresh morning air, enjoying the peace before what had the potential to be a difficult day.

Dreary Dave had delivered the milk and Kate was about to put it away in the fridge when she heard the door go. Standing in the doorway, looking slightly nervous, was Frank. It was, however, a rather different Frank from the previous day. He had washed, shaved and brushed his hair. He was still wearing the same leather jacket but had obviously made an effort to clean it up a bit. Underneath, he was wearing a neat, pale blue shirt and clean jeans. He looked very presentable indeed.

'I'm a bit early,' he said. 'Sorry. The bus service is a bit... er...'

'Crap?'

'I was going to say unpredictable, but yes. I didn't want to be late. So I'm early.'

He noticed the cartons of milk on the counter and said, 'Here. Let me get them. You need to watch that back of yours.'

He picked the milk up, two four-pint cartons in each hand and put them away.

'Now what?' he asked, with a grin that made Kate forget

all her doubts.

'Now you make yourself a cup of coffee, and I'll take you through the rest of the day as it happens. How did you get on with Dorothy Evans?'

'She's a bit of a character,' Frank replied, sorting himself out with a black americano. 'She wanted references, so I mentioned you. I hope that's all right. She didn't mind the cash, though. The room's okay and the shower worked, which is the main thing.'

'You found the bank okay then?'

'Yes. I found money in it, too, which was nice. And an excellent charity shop next door. You must have thought you were taking on a right scruffy bastard.'

'The thought occurred.'

'I'm not usually like that. It's been a strange couple of days.'

'Listen, Frank -'

Before Kate could ask any more, the strains of *Disco Inferno* broke the peace of the morning, heralding the arrival of Briony. She bounded into the café but stopped so suddenly when she saw Frank that Kate nearly burst out laughing.

'Well,' Briony said, 'who's this?'

'Briony, this is Frank. He's going to be helping me out here. Frank, Bri has the best bread delivery service on the island.'

'Oh,' Briony pulled an exaggerated sad face, 'is that all I am?'

'She's also my friend and a cheeky cow,' Kate laughed.

'I suppose that'll do,' Briony said. 'As long as you haven't forgotten the Space gig and he's not competition.'

'No, I haven't forgotten, Bri. I'm looking forward to it.'

'Good. Now are you going to stop flirting with me and give me your bread order?'

After Briony had left, Frank helped put the bread order away, and Kate was pleased that he was discrete enough not to ask any questions about Briony. She would have had trouble answering them because she had far more questions than answers herself. In truth, she had tucked the prospect of the concert away in the back of her mind, filed under 'things I'd rather not think about right now', but time was running out. She would quickly have to decide whether to come up with a sudden reason why she couldn't go and risk upsetting Briony. It would also mean missing the first night out she'd had for a long time. It wasn't as if she and Alison went out all that much; they were usually too tired or too broke. Thinking about Al raised the other doubt Kate had about going to the gig. She simply wasn't sure if she had the courage or the will to see someone else right now. The hurt was still raw, and she absolutely refused to risk going through that again. She wasn't even sure if Bri thought of her that way or if she was only being a friend. A friend was something she would very much welcome, but more than that, she didn't know. It had been a very long time since Kate had been out in the world of dating. She hadn't liked it very much then and now had no idea what the rules were. She also had nothing to wear. These days, all her clothes were work clothes or things that could be thrown on while she pottered about on Sundays. She didn't have much time to go clothes shopping or any particular inclination to do so, even if she had. There never seemed much point. Now, suddenly, she was faced with the prospect of something she wasn't even certain was a date, and it was all a bit too big and scary. She filed it away again and got on with her day.

For the first time, she had a member of staff to train, which was an entirely new experience. All the health and hygiene regulations had become habit these days, so she would have to refresh her memory. She had a file, which she kept rigorously up to date because even in the wilds of Anglesey, she still had periodic inspections and was proud of her five-star rating. At least Frank seemed mature and quite intelligent, and so many of her routines were simply common sense. She hoped he possessed that, too, as she knew only too well that intelligence and common sense were not always the same thing.

She snapped herself out of her daydream and looked around for her new employee. She found him on his hands and knees, his head in the under-counter milk fridge. When he emerged, he had a bottle of cleaning spray and a cloth in his hand.

'I noticed a few bits on the bottom of the fridge, so I thought I'd give it a quick wipe down while it's quiet,' he said. 'Hope that's okay.'

Oh, you'll do, Kate thought. *You'll do very well indeed.*

18

Even if an international super-criminal had strapped him to a table and aimed a laser beam at his genitals, Frank would have been unable to explain why he said yes to Kate. He hadn't meant to, really he hadn't, but once the words 'I might do' had slipped unbidden from his mouth, he had realised that he meant them, even if he didn't fully understand why.

He felt sorry for Kate, yes, and didn't want to see someone who seemed very pleasant stuck and in such pain. Surely that would have been enough to stick around until the pain eased, at which point Frank could have gone on his merry way, collecting his money from the nearest cashpoint and going back to Holyhead to catch the next available ferry without passing 'GO' or looking back. Something in his head or his heart (he never knew which one was in charge of his decision-making process) suggested to him that if he was running with no definite plan as to where he was running *to*, then there were surely worse places than this. It was quite remote, quiet and beautiful, and that was what he had wanted. There was always the option of going on to Ireland at a later date if it didn't work out.

He had bluffed his way through his audition, if the truth were told. He had never used an espresso machine in his life. He was, however, a great observer of people, a habit easily acquired when you spend so much time on your own. With only instant coffee at home (when he remembered to buy any), Frank frequented coffee shops for his caffeine fix, always preferring small independent ones to the big chains who thought writing your name on a cup was a nice, personal touch. One of his favourites, which was around the corner from his flat, had an almost identical coffee machine to *Kate's*, and he had watched in fascination as the shop's owner, a young man improbably called Alf, who had an equally improbable beard, made all the different kinds of coffee. Frank knew which ones had a single shot of espresso and which ones required a double shot, and the apparently scientific process of frothing the milk fascinated him. He watched in admiration as Alf created elaborate patterns on the tops of the drinks, even though there were occasions when he would have preferred his own coffee a bit less patterned and a bit hotter. Until he made the drinks for the two workmen in *Kate's* café, Frank wasn't sure if he would be able to pull it off and had a horrible moment of doubt about how many shots went into a latte, but he pictured Alf doing it in his mind and instinct took over. He didn't attempt any artwork on the top, though; even if he was able to pull it off, he didn't think the Hi-Viz lads would appreciate it all that much, especially since they were in a hurry. He had been a bit apprehensive about using Kate's till as well, but either it was very straightforward, or he had been very lucky. Either way, he got it right first time.

Maybe if he'd cocked the drinks up, he might have thought differently about Kate's offer, if she had made an offer at all to someone who couldn't make a cup of coffee. But something about successfully completing the order and sending the customers away happy (he assumed—they didn't complain) felt right and felt good in a way the rest of his life had failed to do for a while. When Kate asked him to stay, instead of wondering how far and how quickly he could run, he immediately started to think about the logistics of it, and almost before he knew where he was, he had asked if he could have a bit of a wash at the café's sink before going off to sort out money and somewhere to stay.

His only doubt was that he wasn't sure how he would get on with the neighbours. The fierce girl with the long, dark hair seemed to have taken an instant dislike to him. He didn't blame her. He must have looked a sight, and certainly not particularly trustworthy, but luckily Kate had ignored her objections, and she had gone back wherever she came from in a bit of a huff. He hoped she wasn't too much of a regular. She had a lovely face but a hell of a tongue on her. It was something he would worry about later, he thought, as the bus trundled along narrow roads towards the town with the impossible name, where Kate had assured him he would find such technological marvels as a functioning cashpoint.

The town was actually only a village, but compared to Chapel Bay, it was a metropolis. There was a newsagent and general store, a butcher's, a charity shop of some kind and, quite bizarrely, a shop that advertised gun repairs. He found the cashpoint sign outside the smallest post office he had ever seen. It hardly looked any bigger than the telephone box outside it, but inside seemed to sell pretty much anything you could wish for and a few things you might never have thought of. The cash machine was in one corner, and Frank had to wait until an elderly lady had finished collecting her pension before he could get anywhere near it. He assumed that she was collecting her pension as she was speaking to the lady behind the counter in Welsh. She could equally have been reciting the first three books of the Old Testament, for all Frank knew. She certainly took long enough. Eventually, Frank got to the machine, inserted his card and reluctantly agreed to the exorbitant charge it proposed to impose on him for the privilege of withdrawing his own cash. He checked his balance first and was considerably relieved to see that his royalty cheque had cleared and there were enough funds in his account to keep him going for the next few months at least. He withdrew the maximum amount of cash the machine would allow, then consulted the piece of paper on which Kate had written the address of the B&B she had suggested. He thought about asking the lady at the counter for directions but then thought again. She was Welsh and he very much wasn't. The address had Welsh words, and Frank didn't trust his non-existent grasp of the inexplicable way some of the letters were supposed to be pronounced. Not wanting to offend, he approached the counter, said 'Good morning' and pushed the piece of paper through the gap in the window. The woman behind the counter shot backwards in alarm on her wheeled chair as if Frank had passed her a note demanding all the money in the safe. He realised that the arrival of a stranger who looked like a scarecrow and smelled like a cow might be a bit suspicious, so did his best to reassure.

'Sorry!' he said. 'I'm not from round here.'

'I see that,' the woman said, her words loaded with meaning.

'I'm after directions. Could you tell me where that address is, please?'

'I *could*...' the woman began and eyed him slowly again. 'But I'm not sure what Mrs. Evans would make of the likes of you.'

'I understand,' Frank replied, forcing the most charming smile he could manage. 'But I don't always look like this, I promise. I clean up quite well.'

'I'll let Mrs. Evans be the judge of that. Go past the phone box and turn left. It's the third house along.'

'Thank you. Thank you very much.'

'Don't mention it. But don't be surprised if she sends you on your way. She has *standards* has Mrs. Evans. She never misses chapel.'

'I'll bear that in mind. Thanks again.'

Frank got out of the Post Office as quickly as he could and followed the directions he had been given. He passed the phone box and turned left into a cul-de-sac. There were only about half a dozen houses, and it wasn't hard to spot the one that had a weather-beaten Bed and Breakfast sign outside. In common with the other houses in the road, it was quite a modern house compared to the rest of the village, possibly built as recently as the 1960s. It had a very well tended garden at the front, and the net curtains were so white they were almost dazzling. Frank pressed the doorbell and waited.

After a few minutes, the door opened, and Frank found himself looking down at one of the smallest women he had ever seen. She came up to no higher than his chest, and if her eyebrows were on a mission to take over the whole of her face, they had half succeeded. Her hair was black but threaded with silver and scraped back in a severe bun, and she was, in Frank's estimation, anywhere between fifty and seventy. She looked at him with sharp, dark eyes and raised one of her voluminous eyebrows in query.

'Good morning,' Frank said, suddenly feeling like a small child trying to explain to his teacher how he had come to wee himself, 'I was wondering if you have a room.'

'That depends,' the tiny woman said, 'on whether you always smell like that.'

'No. No, I don't. Honestly. I'd rather not smell like this at all. Kate sent me. Kate who has the café in Chapel Bay. It *is* Mrs. Evans, isn't it?'

'Hmm. Always thought she had more sense.'

Mrs. Evans scrutinised Frank once again, and he felt an irresistible urge to confess to something, anything.

'References?' she asked.

'References?' Frank repeated, incredulous. 'Do you ask for references from everyone who stays here?'

'Only when they look like you.'

'It's not the sort of thing I carry round with me.'

'I didn't really think it would be.'

'I'm sure Kate would vouch for me. I'm going to be helping her out at the café, and I could do with somewhere to stay.'

'Kate's a nice enough girl, but she has some funny ideas. They say she's one of those lesbians, and I don't hold with that at all. Don't get me wrong; it's none of my business what people get up to in their bedroom, but all I'm saying is if she met a decent man, she might have better taste in shoes. You'd better come in. But wipe your feet—*properly*—or you'll be going straight back out again.'

Frank did as he was told and followed Mrs. Evans into the house. It was clean and very tidy, even if the décor didn't look like it had been updated much since the house was built. Mrs. Evans also had a predilection for the type of religious painting that would give you nightmares rather than comfort. There was also a lingering aroma of lavender polish and cabbage in the air. She led him upstairs and opened a door on the landing. The room she showed him was small but functional in that it had a bed and a wardrobe, and the view through the window across the fields was a pleasant relief from the migraine-inducing carpet.

'It's thirty pound a night, with breakfast,' Mrs. Evans announced. 'I don't negotiate—no pets, visitors, smoking or alcohol. Front door is locked at eleven prompt, so if you're going to be out later, I need to know in advance so I can lend you a spare key, otherwise, you'll have to find somewhere else to sleep. Not in the shed, though. That's where I keep my lounger.'

'That all sounds fine,' Frank said, taking a wad of cash out of his pocket. 'What if I pay you a week in advance now and see how we go?'

'A week? You're sticking around then?'

'For now.'

'Hmm. Bathroom's next door and there are clean towels out. I think you'd better wipe the bath down when you've finished. Probably twice.'

'Thanks, Mrs. Evans. And thank you for trusting me. You'll hardly know I'm here.'

The landlady gave him one more look, which clearly said *We'll see about that* and left him to it. By the time he had showered, scouring his body until the water ran clean, wiped the bath down (Mrs. Evans was right, it really did need it) and changed into the one spare set of clothes he had brought with him, he began to feel more human. He plugged his mobile in to charge, and while it did so, he opened the window in his room and looked out, breathing in the fresh air. Two fields away, there were a couple of cows, and somewhere nearby, he could hear sheep. It was peaceful and he could feel some of the tension leaving his muscles. Nobody would come looking for him here.

As soon as the phone had enough charge, he rang Mick Rogers to apologise for not showing up the previous night, but Mick was vague and probably stoned and left Frank wondering if he remembered anything about it at all. He wasn't sure whether to feel hurt or relieved. His duty done; he went off to explore his surroundings. He bought a pie and some sandwiches at the general store and found that the charity shop was quite well stocked. He bought a pair of jeans which looked hardly worn and a couple of shirts and had a look at what shoes they had, but the only ones in his size were one pair which had ridiculous tassels on them and were not him at all and a pair of trainers which were rather more luminous than he would normally have worn, but he didn't have the luxury of choice. He picked up a couple of chunky paperbacks he didn't think he had read and still had enough money left to see him through the next couple of days.

Back at the B&B, he settled down to read. Mrs. Evans didn't have to worry about her curfew that night; he was in bed and sleeping soundly by nine o'clock.

***

The next morning, after a remarkably good breakfast, he caught the earliest bus he could, hoping it would take him straight to Chapel Bay, but giving himself plenty of time if it didn't. As a result, he was at the café far earlier than Kate had said, but then he had always been the type of person who preferred to arrive anywhere early rather than late. Kate seemed half surprised and half pleased to see him and they chatted easily while he helped her get the café ready for the day, although he remained on his guard when the questions got a bit too personal.

'Not got a girlfriend, then?' Kate asked at one point.

'No,' Frank replied simply.

'I'm surprised, a good looking guy like you.'

'As if! No, I've never met the right person, I guess. I'd rather be free, really. Do what I want, when I want.'

'There's not a huge amount of talent round here, I'm afraid. Most people are either in couples or on their own for a reason.'

'Like Mrs. Evans, you mean?'

Kate laughed.

'Not exactly a prize catch, is she?'

'What happened to Mr. Evans?'

'No one knows, and believe me, plenty of people have tried

to find out. Theories range from him having run off on her, to her having murdered him and buried him under the shed. The most likely answer is that there never was a Mr. Evans, and she uses the 'Mrs' for the sake of respectability.'

'And to stop her lodgers chatting her up?' Frank suggested.

'I think her face is enough to do that,' Kate replied. 'Anyway, speaking of eligible young people....'

Frank looked around as the door opened. The dark-haired girl who had tried to talk Kate out of taking him on had come in and, judging by her face, was not in a much better mood today.

19

There was a microwave in the passage at the bottom of Gemma's fire escape that morning. A microwave! Who the hell would dump a microwave there? It was a white, cheap one, but half of the white shell was obscured by black scorch marks. The door hung open, and it wasn't hard to see why its former owner had no use for it. The meal that had killed it was still inside. Gemma recognised that it was what was left of a Tesco budget lasagne and momentarily felt angry with herself for even being able to identify it. It wasn't the lasagne that had proved the microwave's undoing; however, it was the metal fork that was sticking out of it like King Arthur's sword. Gemma kicked it. It was bad enough that somebody had dumped the bloody thing outside her home, but what thoroughly infuriated her was that this somebody was obviously too stupid to know how to use it properly, even though microwaves had been on the market forever and everybody (well, nearly everybody) knew you didn't put metal in them. She would have to figure out how to get rid of it later. She didn't have a car, and the nearest tip was miles away. She certainly wasn't going to take the damn thing there on the bus. She also couldn't imagine who in the village would do such a thing. She knew most of the residents reasonably well now and they knew her. It was almost certainly not someone from Chapel Bay who had left it there. Somebody had made the effort to drive to the bay and fly-tip it there. Somebody existing in the world whose brain worked it in such a way that they would blow up a microwave and decide to put it in their car, drive to Chapel Bay in the middle of the night and leave it there. Gemma often despaired at the human race. This was more proof. And now she had kicked a microwave oven wearing espadrilles and had a sore toe. As starts to the day went, this was not very promising.

Of course, the key stuck in the lock of the workshop; there were some days when it was inevitable. It took her a considerable amount of manipulation and cursing, and when the door finally opened, it did it so suddenly that she was nearly propelled into the workshop headfirst. She turned the lights and her laptop on and stood next to the workbench. *Now what?* she thought. She had no orders to fulfil and there were no gaps on the displays where stock needed to be replenished because she hadn't sold anything. She had a whole day in front of her and nothing to do. Even her accounts, such as they were, were up to date, which was unusual in itself. Normally Gemma loved days like this. She would have a latte and maybe a chat with Kate, then put the 'Back Soon' sign on the workshop door on the off chance that someone called by, and then take a walk on the beach to see what she could find. Today, though, she felt thoroughly unsettled and not particularly inclined to bother with anything. Out of habit, she checked her emails to see if there had been a miracle and an order had dropped in during the night. She was not at all surprised that her inbox consisted entirely of spam, which she deleted and closed the programme down. Determined to shake herself out of this mood, she decided that a coffee and then a long stroll on the beach would sort her out. Caffeine and fresh air, that was what she needed. She locked the workshop, telling the lock to fuck off when it stuck again, and went to Kate's. That was when her morning instantly got worse.

She didn't see him at first. Kate was behind the counter when she came in and greeted her with a smile.

'Morning! Lovely day.'

'Would be if some wanker hadn't dumped a microwave outside the workshop. Can you believe it?'

'A microwave? Why?'

'Don't know. Maybe they don't know how barbecues work. I'll have to get whatshisname with the van to take it away and he'll probably want paying for it. Anyway, enough about me. How's your back today?'

'It's better, thanks.'

'Really? Or are you only saying that as usual?'

'No, really. It is.'

'Good. You had me worried for a bit. Well, since you're here, I need a coffee.'

'I'll do that,' said the milk fridge. Only it wasn't the fridge speaking, it was someone crouching down behind the open door. They stood up, and Gemma was dismayed to see that it was *him*, or at least a cleaned-up version of him, maybe his cleaner, tidier twin brother.

'What's he doing here?' Gemma asked Kate.

'I told you yesterday. He's helping me out for a bit. Scrubs up well, doesn't he?'

'Are you out of your mind? Have you any idea...?'

'I *am* still here,' Kate's new friend said, coming over to the counter. 'What can I get you?'

'Hazelnut latte,' Gemma said, not feeling like saying 'please'. 'Double shot. That's...'

'I'd guess it's a latte with a double shot of espresso and hazelnut syrup, am I right?' He gestured towards the row of syrup bottles. 'And I'll take a stab in the dark and say the hazelnut syrup is the one with a picture of hazelnuts on it. Is it to drink in or to go?'

'To go,' Gemma said. 'Definitely to go.'

'No problem.' He started to make the coffee and Gemma was aware that Kate had stepped back to let him. She watched intently as he made the drink, scrutinising every move and waiting for a mistake. Frustratingly, he did everything exactly as Kate would do, slapped the lid on the takeaway cup with what looked annoyingly like a flourish and quoted her the correct price without consulting the menu. She fumbled in her purse for some coins and slapped them on the counter. She had no desire to put them in his hand; she still didn't trust where those hands might have been. She grabbed the coffee and when she looked up, she was aware that Kate was trying hard not to laugh.

'The day can only get better, Gem,' she said. Then she turned to the smug Scouser. 'Sorry, Frank, we didn't get time for introductions yesterday. Gemma has a workshop next door and makes lovely gifts.'

'Really?' Frank said. 'I must have a look sometime.'

'I doubt there'd be anything there to interest you,' Gemma replied.

'I might surprise you there.'

'I doubt it. Got to go, Kate. Loads to do.'

She hurried out of the door and stamped back to her workshop, flinging herself down in her deckchair. She was tempted to throw the coffee in the bin, but the need for a caffeine hit took over, and she lifted the lid instead and sniffed at the contents. It smelled okay, so she took a tentative sip. The velvety liquid had slipped down so easily and tasted so good that she sighed before she could stop herself. She sat and finished the whole cup and thought *whoever this Frank character is, I'm going to have to keep an eye on him.* His name bothered her more than she cared to admit, too. *Probably wasn't even his real name.* She went into her workshop, dropped the empty cup in the bin and tried to put him out of her mind.

20

Gemma managed to keep the Liverpudlian invader out of her head for several hours while she went for a slightly unsatisfying forage on the beach and then called Vince, the local Man with a Van, to come and take the microwave away, which he kindly agreed to do free of charge, seeing as it wouldn't take up much space. He was doing a tip run that morning anyway. She told him that there would be a bacon butty and a coffee with his name on in the café any time he wanted it, but as she hung up, her promise reminded her (as did her stomach) that it was about lunchtime and that meant she had to make the decision she had been putting off; whether to go to Kate's and find out if the Scouser could make food as well as he made coffee (she secretly hoped not), or to take a wander up the lane and pick up a pre-packaged sandwich from Parry's. In the end, homemade won over made by God knows who and God knows when, so she locked up the workshop and went next door, hoping that maybe *he* got a lunch break and was on it now.

The minute she walked in through the café door, it was apparent that her timing was wrong. Not only was he there, but he was hurling himself into the preparation of food and drinks for Ruth Prior from the school and two rather severe-looking men in suits who were sitting with her. Not only that, but he was doing it at speed and with good humour. She wasn't sure why that set her teeth on edge, but it did. She waited while he sorted out lunch for Ruth and her dour associates, trying to catch Kate's eye, but her friend was staring fiercely at some paperwork in the corner of the kitchen area and had apparently not noticed her come in. Food and drinks delivered, the new boy turned his attention to Gemma and seemed genuinely pleased to see her.

'Good afternoon,' he said with a smile. 'What can I get for

you? Hazelnut double shot latte?'

Gemma was taken aback that he had remembered. 'Yes, please,' she stammered. 'And can you do a tuna and cheese panini?'

'I think I can probably manage that,' he replied, not unpleasantly. 'If not, I'm sure I can find a YouTube video. Take a seat, and I'll bring it over.'

Gemma nodded and sat down at a table by the window. Normally, she sat near the counter so she could chat with Kate while she had her lunch, but that wasn't an option today. She stared out of the window so she wouldn't have to watch him work. Two herring gulls were stalking about on the outside tables, and as she watched, one jetted a white stream of guano onto the tabletop. Gemma couldn't help but think that this somehow summed up her day so far. The unpleasant sight outside forced her to turn her attention back to the interior of the café. Much as she hated to admit it, the Scouser was moving from panini grill to coffee machine to salad with ease, fluidity and efficiency. He was good and she would have liked to think he knew it, but she didn't think he did. The fact that Kate was letting him get on with it showed she trusted him, and Gemma didn't like that thought much either.

Gemma didn't trust Scousers at all and had good reason. It wasn't the natural, inbred antipathy that came with living in Manchester for so long, but from experience. It was one person from Liverpool in particular who was directly responsible for her being where she was now. While she wasn't the sort of person to tar the entire population of a city with the dirty brush of a couple of its citizens, it had left her with a very bad taste in her mouth and a deep mistrust of anyone with that horrible accent. Not that Latte Man's accent was especially pronounced, but it was there and that was enough. If you added the fact that he seemed to have arrived out of nowhere and had wasted absolutely no time in getting his feet under the table, it was hardly a surprise that she viewed him with suspicion. And yet here he was, at her table with a delicious looking sandwich, a perfect latte and a smile.

'I don't think it's turned out too badly,' he said.

'We'll see,' Gemma replied, although she was dying to tuck in. He gave her another smile (she wished he'd stop doing that) and retreated back to the counter to clear up. Once she started eating, any resentment was forgotten for the time being because it was one of the best paninis she had ever tasted and she didn't stop eating until she had cleaned the plate. She drained her coffee and sat back, replete. Latte Man noticed and was there in an instant to collect her dishes. He looked at the empty plate and did the smile she was beginning to want to slap.

'Do I have to ask if everything was okay?'

'It was okay,' she replied, and a smile twitched unbidden at the corner of her mouth.

'I don't think we got off to the best of starts,' he said. 'I noticed the Manchester accent. Is it only me you don't like, or all Scousers?'

'I don't know you well enough to say.'

'Would it help if I told you I'm not really a Scouser? I was born and bred on the Wirral.'

'Which is what?'

'It's a peninsular. That's -'

'I know what a peninsular is. I did first year geography at school.'

'Peninsulars and oxbow lakes. All crucial stuff. The Wirral's over the water from Liverpool. Different postcode and everything.'

'I do know where the Wirral is. I was winding you up. I even went there once. It rained.'

'It does that. Mind you, I lived about half my life in Liverpool. Does being half a Scouser get me any points?'

'We'll see,' Gemma said and was aware that was becoming a bit of a catchphrase. 'Can I pay now, please?'

'Of course. I'd say it's on the house, but I know for a fact that Kate is only pretending to work and is actually listening to everything.'

'No shit,' Kate said without looking up.

Gemma paid and left without saying goodbye. She felt a

bit rude not speaking to Kate, but she couldn't very well say goodbye to one and not the other; that would have been far too obvious. Instead, she slipped out of the café and hurried back to her workshop. Now she was trying not to think about Latte Man's smile.

We'll see indeed, she thought.

Part Two

21

Derek Cooke pulled his car into a parking space but kept the engine running. Further up the road, two traffic wardens were slapping a penalty notice onto the windscreen of a silver Audi and taking photographs of their handiwork. Cooke could see that the whole of the road was a residents' only zone, and while he didn't want to risk a ticket, especially when it wasn't his car, he also didn't know Sheffield at all well and didn't want to have to go looking for somewhere he could park in peace. He had a job to do and had to be in and out quickly; the last thing he needed was to go hunting for the car after he had finished. To be on the safe side, he eased out of the space he had found and drove around the block. When he came back to the street, the traffic wardens were getting into a white van. He went around the block once more and by the time he got back to the street, the white van had gone. He stopped the car once more and, this time, turned the engine off. Even if the wardens had plans to come back, he would be well gone by the time they did.

Cooke glanced at his reflection in the rear-view mirror and straightened his tie. He hated ties; it always felt like he was being strangled. The only other time he had worn one in the years since he left school was at his cousin's wedding a few years earlier. Even then, he couldn't wait to take it off as soon as the ceremony was over. Mind you, he found a use for it later when he got off with one of the bridesmaids and went back to her room. He didn't think she minded being gagged with the tie, but it was hard to tell with all the incoherent noises she was making. It was certainly a bit too damp to use again afterwards, so it had gone in a bin outside the hotel as he left. He'd had to borrow the tie he was wearing and didn't like the colour, but sometimes you had to do things you didn't like when there was a job to do.

He picked up the clipboard from the passenger seat and checked the address he had been given. No.16 was across the road, and there was a light on in the living room, not that it was easy to tell; the house had a privet hedge at the front which badly needed cutting back. Some people, he reflected sadly, have no pride. He opened the front cover of the clipboard and folded it back, then opened the clip to remove the ID card that had been pinned there. He fastened it to the breast pocket of his suit jacket and got out of the car. The gate of No.16 squeaked as he opened it, and he noticed that the windows, and indeed the front door, badly needed a clean. He hated to think what the inside of the house looked like, but he wasn't going to be there long. There was no bell, so he knocked on the door, checking his knuckles after he had done so and wiping the muck they had picked up on his trouser leg. There was a long pause before the door opened to reveal the lady of the house, resplendent in a grubby pink onesie. *Jesus*, Cooke thought, *it's two o'clock*, but he kept the thought to himself and put on a cheesy grin instead.

'Good afternoon,' he said. 'Mrs. Ashcroft?'

'Who's asking?'

'Nothing to worry about. I'm from Vox Pop Surveys, and I wanted a quick word with Mr. Ashcroft.'

'He's not in. And I'm not Mrs. Ashcroft. I'm Ms. May' She tried to close the door, but Cooke put his foot in the way.

'That's a pity,' he said. 'It looks like the money he has won will have to go back into the pot then. I really need his signature today. I know three grand isn't much, but...'

Ms. May peered at him around the door, and he could read the thought process in her face. You always could.

'Three grand?' she said.

'Shame he's not in.'

'Can't I sign?'

'I'm afraid not. It was Mr. -' he made a show of checking the clipboard, '- *Mr. Dean Ashcroft* who took our survey, so it's him who's won the prize. I'm sorry. I don't make the rules.'

Ms. May thought again for a moment and then yelled

'Dean!' into the house in a voice that almost made Cooke feel sorry for Dean Ashcroft. Almost. The woman disappeared into the house and was replaced at the door by a weasly-looking man dressed in a Motorhead T-shirt and jogging trousers, even though it was quite apparent he had never jogged anywhere in his life. He took one look at Cooke, gasped, '*Shit!*' and tried to shut the door. Again, Cooke's foot stopped the door from closing, but this time he used his shoulder to force it open. Ashcroft took a step back and nearly stumbled over the step into the porch.

'Deano,' Cooke said. 'It's been a while.'

'Jackie!' Ashcroft shouted. 'Call the police!'

'You don't want to do that,' Cooke said, advancing on him. 'You don't want them coming round here and maybe having a little look at what's on the hard drive of your laptop.'

'What do you want, Degs?' Ashcroft demanded. 'I haven't done nothin'. It wasn't me.'

Cooke took a step forward and grabbed Ashcroft by the front of his manky T-shirt.

'Now that isn't exactly true, is it, Deano? It mightn't have been you, but Mr. James is of the opinion that you know something.'

'I don't know anything!' Ashcroft protested, struggling to break free of Cooke's grip. There was a rip as one of the sleeves of the T-shirt parted company with the rest of it. 'What does he think I know? I don't know anything!'

Cooke leaned in and head-butted Ashcroft sharply in the face. Ashcroft reeled back, clutching his nose, rivulets of blood seeping through his finger.

'Fuck!' he said. 'My nose, Degs! You've broken my -'

'It's a start,' Cooke said, reaching into his inside jacket pocket and taking out a kitchen knife. 'Mr. James believes you know a name, Deano. If I were you, I'd think fast.'

22

Derek Cooke had got carried away again. He'd promised he wouldn't, and it was on that condition that Mr. James had sent him to do this job, but there were times when you couldn't help yourself. He'd always been that way. He couldn't count the number of times he was suspended from school for fighting, but if someone looked at you the wrong way, you had to do something about it, didn't you? It had started on his first day at school, when he was a small, lost and lonely child, bewildered by all the other bigger kids, not understanding their games or the teachers' rules. He had been in the playground, standing on his own, not knowing what he was supposed to do, when two older boys came over to him. They looked like they wanted to be nice to him at first, but then one started to laugh, so Derek hit him. He was too small for it to do any damage, and the older boy laughed it off and walked away, but Derek never forgot that day, never forgot how small it had made him feel, and vowed there and then never to feel like that again.

After a number of suspensions, he was finally expelled from school when he was fifteen. It was the day he put Stephen Robinson in hospital. He had been aware of Robinson for a while, a broad, fat lad who pushed his way around, muscled into football games even though he was crap, the sort of kid who would be picked on himself, so made it his business to pick on weaker kids first. He wanted everyone to think he was cock of the school, but Derek knew that wasn't how you did it. Derek had no interest in being known as a hard man; he knew the other kids were afraid of him because they had seen what his temper could do if he lost it, but he didn't go looking for trouble. He didn't need to; trouble had a way of finding him. That was exactly what happened that day, which is why Derek was so resentful of the fact that he was the one who got blamed for it and ended up being kicked out. It was all because of a doughnut. Derek was sitting enjoying his lunch when Stephen Robinson arrived late at the dining hall. A kid from a couple of years below, whose name Derek never knew, had selected his lunch, including, for dessert, the last doughnut. Derek had started his own dessert (apple crumble, as it happened) when he heard Robinson say, 'Hey, shitface, I wanted that.'

'Sorry,' the kid stammered. 'It's the last one.'

'I know,' Robinson said. 'So give it to me.'

'But it's mine,' the kid protested.

'I don't give a shit. Give it to me.'

Derek watched the scene unfolding, clocked the fact that there were no teachers around and that the catering staff were taking no notice and put his spoon down. Robinson was standing over the other kid, at least a foot taller than him and far wider. The poor kid must have thought the sun had gone out, but still, he clung to the plate with the offending doughnut.

'Fuck's sake, Robinson,' Derek said. 'Let him have it. It's not like you need it.'

Robinson turned to look at where the voice had come from and when he saw it was Derek, he stopped for a moment. Then bravado took over and all common sense went out of the window. It made what happened next sadly inevitable.

'Stay out of this, Degsy,' he said. 'This is between me and Shitface.'

'Let him have the doughnut,' Derek said. Robinson then made a classic mistake.

'Or what?' he said.

Derek felt the old red mist rising and before he knew what he had done, he had slammed his dessert bowl into Robinson's face, shattering it into small pieces, and had his hands in the other lad's hair, forcing his face down into what remained of a vat of school custard. He remembered watching in fascination as veins of blood threaded through the custard, looking for a moment like raspberry ripple ice cream. Then Mr. Cooper, the woodwork teacher, escorted him out of the dining hall and his school career was over. Stephen Robinson had needed stitches for the cuts on his face and a skin graft for the scald on his forehead caused by the custard. It was probably the custard that saved Derek from Borstal. Robinson's parents had wanted at first to press charges but had suddenly changed their minds. Presumably, their darling son had persuaded them that he didn't want to be known as Custard Boy forever and made them let it go. Derek was out of school with no future. He never knew if the other kid enjoyed his doughnut.

No provision was made for what Derek might do with no school to go to. He wasn't the school's problem anymore and he was a bit too old for Social Services to bother about. His father had run off years ago and his mother didn't have a clue what to do with him. She had a new man and a new daughter to worry about, so she didn't care that he was rarely in the house. In fact, it suited her not to see his miserable face around the place. He got in first with one gang and then another when the first one only did things for kicks and had no real ambition. The second gang, run by a man called Skid (Derek never found out his real name), was better organised, and there was a chance of making real money for a bright, keen teenager who didn't mind using his fists. After a year or so of running with Skid's gang, Derek learned that it was the junior branch of a much bigger organisation, and for the right person, the prospects of advancement were good. He worked hard to be the right person. He began to do small jobs for the organisation, a bit of dealing, a bit of delivery and collection, a bit of paying calls on people who needed a chat. Derek did everything that was asked of him and started to attract the attention of the right people, the people higher up, the ones who could offer him a future.

Derek learned to drive; his lessons paid for and were taught by a guy who was guaranteed to get him through his test with no questions asked. He now found he had a valuable skill. He was given a nice car and a phone and was on call day and night to drive anyone who needed it to anywhere they needed to go. He also learned an important lesson; that once people are in the back seat of a car, the driver becomes invisible. By keeping his mouth shut and his ears open, he discovered that things could be changing within the organisation and soon. The feeling was that the ones at the top of the organisation were becoming old, tired and stale, and the time was right for someone younger and more energetic, more imaginative to make a bid to take over. There were a couple of people vying for the role, but Derek gathered that the smart money was on Derry James, a good-looking, highly intelligent Irishman. He allied himself to Mr. James and it proved to be the right decision.

Was it Derek Cooke driving the car containing Derry James away from the canal the night John Carlin, the now former head of the organisation, went for a bullet-assisted swim? Derek, of course, was too discrete to say, but if anyone wanted to think that, he wasn't going to argue. For the last ten years, he had worked hard and become one of Mr. James's trusted officers. Yes, he had to be careful, and yes, he still lost his temper every now and then, but these little indiscretions were quickly forgotten and covered up. Derek Cooke was too good to let go, just because a minor dealer had ended up in A&E, or a nameless (and now faceless) prostitute had been pulled out of the Mersey.

As he drove away from Dean Ashcroft's house, he knew he would have a bit of explaining to do. He wasn't even sure why he had lost his temper this time. Deano had given the name up quite quickly, but there was something pathetic about the way he did it that really pissed Derek off. Deano's ugly bird wouldn't talk. Derek had left her with more than enough money to compensate for the french window her husband had accidentally fallen through. She was also left in no doubt about what might happen if she told the paramedics when they arrived that her partner's untimely death was anything other than an unfortunate, drunken accident. If necessary, she was a loose end that could be tidied up later.

Derek gradually calmed down the more miles he put between himself and Deano's house. By the time he had joined the motorway that led back to Liverpool, he was feeling relaxed enough to take out his phone and make a call to Derry James's personal number. The road ahead was clear when he started the call. The line was engaged, so Derek texted the name to Mr. James instead, feeling slightly smug at his ability to text and drive at the same time. Unfortunately, he was feeling so pleased with himself as he replaced his phone and turned the car radio up for a bit of loud rock music to accompany his journey, that he failed to notice the lorry that had turned onto the motorway from a slip road. He never stood a chance. He was doing nearly eighty when he hit the side of the lorry and was catapulted through the windscreen like a crash test dummy. Considering that he had spent most of his career as a driver, making two fundamental errors, like not wearing a seatbelt and using his phone while driving, was a ridiculous way for Derek Cooke to die.

23

'What do you mean he's dead?'

Jonathan Liddell didn't like the look on Mr. James's face. He had seen that look many times before, and an explosion always followed it. Liddell didn't want to be caught in the blast (he had experienced it once before and it was only Mr. James's bad aim that stopped him from having his head knocked off by a flying coffee pot), so he edged backwards to be a bit closer to the door. Mr. James's face was often quite red (everyone knew he was on blood pressure medication), but right now, it was heading towards purple and that was not a good sign at all.

'I'm sorry, Mr. James.'

'Why? Was it your fault? Did you kill him?'

'No, Mr. James.'

'Then don't talk shite about being sorry. What happened?'

'Apparently, he drove into a lorry, Mr. James.'

'A lorry. A fucking lorry!'

Mr. James brought his fists down on his desk and Liddell took another step backwards.

'You know what the problem is with this organisation, Jonny? Do you know why I haven't made enough money yet to retire to somewhere sunny and have a yacht the size of the Titanic? Have you any idea why I have to come in here every day and work like everyone else?' Mr. James came around the front of his desk and Liddell shrank back a bit further. 'Shall I tell you why I have to pop pills like a kid eating Smarties? Shall I?'

'Yes, Mr. James.' Liddell's mouth was now getting so dry that he could barely speak. *Here it comes...*

'I'll tell you. The problem with this organisation is that people don't seem to have read their fucking job descriptions!' Mr. James's face was now completely purple, right past the hairline (which everyone knew was a weave, but nobody dared say), and he was beginning to shake. 'I've got an army of accountants who don't notice that a chunk of my yacht money is missing for nearly a year, so now I've got to have the accountants sorted out and find some more, but now it turns out that I've got drivers who *CAN'T FUCKING DRIVE!*'

Mr. James turned away from Liddell and leaned on his desk, his shoulders hunched. There was a long, dangerous pause and Liddell wondered if he should use the time to run out of the door. But then Mr. James turned to him, and this time, he spoke quietly. The quiet was often worse than the storm.

'The one good thing about Derek Fucking Cooke topping himself is that it means I don't have to do it. Give me some good news, Jonny. Tell me the mess Cooke left behind has been cleared up.'

'It has, Mr. James,' Liddell replied, feeling a little safer. 'Dean Ashcroft has been disposed of and his woman was more than happy with the fee she got for forgetting all about him. I think she was glad to see the back of him, to be honest.'

'She isn't the only one. The one good thing Cooke did, apart from saving me the trouble of killing him, was that he sent me the name.' Mr. James picked up his gold iPhone and consulted it. 'Frankie Davies,' he said. 'So Frankie Davies is the person to whom, for some reason, that Ashcroft wanker passed my money, instead of giving it to me. What do we know about Frankie Davies, Jonny? Anything? Nothing?'

'Nothing at the moment, Mr. James. We're on it, though. We'll find him.'

'You'd better, Jonny. It's as simple as that. You will find Frankie Davies, or they'll never find you again. Is that clear?'

'Yes, Mr. James.'

'Good. Two more things. When you find where Frankie Davies is, I want the best people we have to go and get him. Is that clear? No amateurs. No idiots. I want the best.'

'Totally clear, Mr. James.'

There was another pause.

'You...er...said there were two things, Mr. James?'

'Yes. Fuck off and tell Elise I don't want to be disturbed for any reason for at least an hour. I am very upset, Jonny and feel the need to watch cat videos.'

'Yes, Mr. James.'

With a considerable feeling of relief, Liddell made his exit from the room and closed the door behind him. Elise, Mr. James's immaculate personal assistant, looked up from her computer and gave him a warm smile. He liked Elise. She was beautiful and unflappable and always friendly, though not quite friendly enough for him to think he had the remotest chance with her. He had no idea what someone like that was doing working for a man like Derry James.

'How was it?'

'Grim. He wants to watch cat videos for an hour.'

'Shit. I'll hold all calls.'

He flopped down in a comfortable armchair near Elise's desk.

'I'm getting too old for this,' he said.

'Too old? You're what? Forty?'

'Thanks, Elise. You're very kind. I'm forty-six and spending my life working for a man who threatens to kill me every time anything goes wrong. Most places, you'd get a verbal warning, but I get, 'They'll never find your body'. That wasn't in my contract.'

'You've got a contract?'

'No, of course, I haven't. But if I did, I don't think I'd have signed up to capital punishment being part of the disciplinary section.'

'He won't have you killed,' Elise said. 'He needs you.'

'Was that supposed to be reassuring? It means I've got to keep flogging myself to make sure he keeps needing me. Nobody gets the sack from this organisation. Nobody gets, 'I'm sorry, we don't require your services anymore'. You don't walk out of here with a nice clock and a reference. I wish I'd followed my mum's advice and gone into teaching. At least I'd only be dealing with small lunatics.'

'I just can't see you as a teacher, Jonny.'

'No, neither could I. That's why I ended up here.'

'So what then? What's he want you to do about this guy who's got him all worked up?'

'I've got to put a couple of our best people on it, he said. God knows who I'm going to get. Malik is out of the country at the moment, and I think Mr. James has forgotten that Knox is inside. I'm thinking it might have to be Sutcliffe and probably Dawson.'

'Sutcliffe? But he's...'

'A psychopath. Yes. I know. I'm almost starting to feel sorry for this Frankie Davies.'

24

Jonathan Liddell found Sutcliffe in a pub. He hadn't expected to find him anywhere else; it was merely a question of which one. He could have saved himself a lot of time if he had come to the King's Head first but had hoped that Sutcliffe hadn't reached that stage yet. Sutcliffe's alcohol consumption was legendary, and so was his routine. If anyone wanted to find him, they would have known that he started in the Slug and Lettuce for a couple of pints, then moved on to the Midland when it was time to hit the shorts. He only progressed to the King's Head when he was in the mood for a fight. Nobody used this well-known routine to find Sutcliffe, however, because Sutcliffe wasn't somebody you wanted to find; he was someone you hoped wouldn't find *you,* especially not at this time of the night. The landlord of the King's Head, an ex-docker named Larry, had tried to bar Sutcliffe once, but only once. Rumour had it that Sutcliffe had only had to give Larry a look, and the barring had never been mentioned again. The roll of money Sutcliffe left on the bar that night might have helped too; it would have at least paid for the repairs without Larry having to bother his insurance company.

Larry didn't have to worry that Sutcliffe, and others like him, were bad for business. The King's Head, or as it was universally known, The King's Arse, wasn't the sort of place you happened to come across and think it might be a nice venue for a quiet pint. It was tucked away down a side street on the outskirts of the city and was the sort of establishment where a certain breed of man came with drinking and fighting in mind. The clientele was almost exclusively male, apart from the occasional prostitute who didn't know better. Larry had never had to worry too much about providing an extensive cocktail menu. The King's Arse was the kind of pub where you went when you were angry or depressed and came out feeling worse. It was a place where nobody knew your name.

Liddell had only been in the King's Arse once before. He had been sent there as a joke by a man named Arthur. He didn't know whether this was his first name or surname and never found out because Arthur was shot on an industrial estate a couple of months later. He was still relatively new to Derry James's organisation and wet behind the ears, so was at the stage where he did what he was told to do without asking questions. His instructions were to go in, go to the bar and ask for a Harvey Wallbanger and wait. It seemed ironic to him now that the only thing he had worried about at the time was that he didn't drink that much and, although he knew what a Harvey Wallbanger was, he wasn't sure how strong it was and hoped that Arthur wasn't trying to get him drunk to make him do something that would make a fool of him. He had walked into the pub, trying to appear confident and ignore the fact that the place was dead quiet. The only customers in there were sitting silently at their tables, apart from one giant of a man who was sitting on a stool at the bar staring at a large whisky, the stool straining under his enormous buttocks. Liddell didn't want to contemplate the builders' cleavage that was very apparent over the top of the man's jeans. He took a deep breath, went to the bar and caught the eye of the barman, who raised an eyebrow, which was clearly his version of *yes, sir, and how may I help you?*

'Harvey Wallbanger, please,' Liddell said. The barman looked at him as if he had asked for a weasel on a bun, then looked at the giant at the bar and gave a flicker of a smile. The giant hauled himself off the stool and turned, causing a waft of sweat and booze to hit Liddell in the face. Before Liddell could protest, the giant had seized the lapels of his jacket, lifted him off his feet and slammed him into the wall so hard that it knocked the wind out of him completely. Liddell slumped to the floor and tried desperately to catch his breath, wondering if he would ever breathe again and if this was how he was going to die, lying on the unpleasantly sticky carpet of the worst pub he had ever been in. As the breath returned to his lungs, he became aware that the giant was standing over him, inexplicably grinning and revealing the fact that he was not acquainted with a dentist. More surprisingly, he was extending a hand. Liddell tried to shrink back against the wall, but there was nowhere to go.

'Come 'head, lad,' the giant said. 'Don't sit there on your arse all night.'

Knowing he had no choice, Liddell reached up, took the man's greasy hand and was dragged to his feet. He didn't know whether to run, cry, or wet himself.

'Jesus, lad,' the man said. 'Don't look so scared. I'm not going to do it again—the name's Harvey. I've got a message from Arthur. He says you need to start going to the gym. Now fuck off.'

Harvey the Giant sat on his stool and turned his attention back to his drink. Liddell left the King's Arse as quickly as he could. He had never returned to that particular pub, but he hadn't missed a morning session at the gym since.

It was with considerable reluctance that Liddell pushed open the door of the King's Arse to seek out Sutcliffe. Part of this reluctance stemmed from the humiliation he still felt after the last time he was here, but there was also the fact that this was Sutcliffe he was looking for and he was not known as the most tolerant of men. Although Liddell was considerably stronger and fitter than he was the last time he had crossed this threshold, he didn't fancy his chances if Sutcliffe happened to be in the wrong mood.

As soon as he entered the pub, he could tell that he would probably be all right. It looked very much like Sutcliffe had already got his frustrations out of his system. He was sitting at the bar, much as Harvey the Giant once had, and all was calm. The only evidence that anything had happened was the man lying in the corner of the bar amidst the wreckage of a barstool. He was just about alive and moaning slightly, but none of the occupants of the pub were taking much notice. With a certain amount of trepidation, Liddell approached the bar.

'Sutcliffe,' he said. Sutcliffe turned to look and, considering the empty shot glasses lined up in front of him in a neat row on the bar, seemed totally sober.

'Jonny Liddell,' he said. 'Fancy a drink, Jonny Liddell?'

'No, I'm all right, thanks.'

'Larry,' Sutcliffe said to the landlord, ignoring Liddell, 'get my mate Jonny Liddell a large Jack. I'll have another one too.' He turned his attention back to Liddell. 'So, how are you, Jonny? Long time.'

'I'm good,' Liddell said. 'You?'

'Been worse, Jonny, been worse. Although, if that knobhead in the corner doesn't stop moaning, I'll wrap another stool round him.'

'Not another one!' Larry protested, putting the drinks on the bar. 'I'm running out.'

'You could do with some new ones, Larry,' Sutcliffe said. 'These are getting a bit tatty.' He picked his drink up and raised it to Liddell. 'Cheers.' He knocked the drink back in one. Liddell raised his glass, said, 'Cheers,' but only sipped his.

'So, Jonny Liddell, what brings you to this fine hostelry? Is it the fine menu of gourmet food on offer? Is it perhaps the splendid variety of craft ales? Or is it the general ambience of the place?'

'I was looking for you.'

'I thought you might be. There's no other reason to come to this shit hole. Go on then, what's it all about?'

'Mr. James needs someone found.'

'Found and presumably dealt with?'

'Terminally if necessary.'

'That's how I like it.'

'Good. It's probably a two-man job, so you'll need to round up Dawson.'

Sutcliffe waved at Larry for another drink. He waited until the drink had arrived before he replied.

'Dawson,' he said, 'is a dick.'

'We're a bit short on options,' Liddell replied.

'Do you happen to recall the last job Dawson did with me?

The burger fiasco? It made me look very bad.'

Liddell did indeed recall the incident. Sutcliffe and Dawson had been sent with a very simple instruction, to torch The Burger Palace, a fast-food joint owned by Derry James's rival Elijah West, as a warning to the Jamaicans not to encroach on the James territories. Dawson had the instructions, and he and Sutcliffe had sneaked out in the dead of night, broken into the kitchen and, with the assistance of a can of petrol, set fire to the store of cooking oil. Dense plumes of black smoke had been visible from several streets away, and the Fire Brigade took a couple of hours to get the flames under control. The takeaway had been gutted, along with the shop next door. The only problem was that the takeaway they had torched was not Elijah West's Burger Palace, but a different takeaway altogether, on the opposite side of the road, called The Burger Place, which was, as bad luck would have it, owned by Derry James. The shop next door was, equally unfortunately, a vintage clothing shop owned by one of Derry James's girlfriends. The incident had not gone down well. Sutcliffe had blamed Dawson, who, in turn, blamed a badly placed crease in the piece of paper on which he had written down the name of the place they were to torch, which had rendered the second 'a' in Palace illegible. It was only the fact that both Sutcliffe and Dawson had good records up to that point that saved them from suffering a similar fate to The Burger Place. But since then, it had been noticeable that the better jobs went to other people, and Sutcliffe had vowed never to work with Dawson again.

'I think lessons were learned that night,' Liddell said carefully. 'It was quite an easy mistake to make.'

'It was a fucking stupid mistake to make,' Sutcliffe replied. 'And the lesson it taught me was never, ever to work with a dickhead like Dawson again. I mean, look at me, Jonny. I used to be feared. I used to be the first person Mr. James turned to when he needed something doing because he knew I'd get it done. Now I get scraps if I'm lucky. I have to come to places like this, hoping someone will spill my drink so I can get a decent fight. Look at that sad sack of shit on the floor over there, Jonny. I had to bump into him twice before he spilled my drink. So, no. Not Dawson. Never again.'

'It's a chance for you to redeem yourself. Look, Sutcliffe, I have the greatest of respect for you and what you do. I want to see you back up there. This could be your chance. It's not a difficult job, and with you in charge, not even Dawson could screw it up.'

Sutcliffe finished his drink and thought for a moment.

'I'm in charge?'

'Totally. Dawson is there for back-up.'

'And there's definitely no chance of him fucking it up?'

'None.'

'Okay, Jonny. I'll do it. Only this once, and only because you asked me nicely. I'll tell you one thing, though. If Dawson puts one foot out of line, there will only be one of us coming back. You know that, don't you?'

'Understood. I'll be in touch.'

Liddell went to leave but only got halfway to the door before Sutcliffe called after him.

'Hey, Jonny! There is one other thing. I'm trusting you on this. If it goes wrong and Dawson fucks up again, I'll be coming for you when I get back.'

Liddell let the door to the King's Arse shut behind him and stood in the cold night air, breathing hard. He tried to tell himself that everything would be all right and as long as he got the details and sorted it out properly, nothing could go wrong. He didn't get much sleep that night.

25

It hadn't taken Jonathan Liddell very long. The Internet made it almost impossible for anyone to move through life without leaving a breadcrumb trail behind them. The more social media platforms that were created, the more people liked to display all the stupid little details of their lives for the whole world to see. It had become very much a 'look at me' society. Without looking very far, you could find out whereabouts someone lived, where they worked, their marital status, what teams and political parties they supported, even what they liked for breakfast. Far too many people thought that everyone else would be fascinated by all the stuff that you once kept private. It made tracing people much easier. But if conventional methods failed, there were darker places on the Internet, if you knew where to look, where you could find out so much more. Liddell didn't often have to resort to such places but knew where they were if he needed them.

He hadn't needed them this time, or at least he thought he hadn't. Merseyside had more than its fair share of people called Frank or Frankie Davies. It wasn't exactly an unusual name. All he had to do was eliminate the unlikely ones and look at what was left. He found three that had connections of one kind or another to the Liverpool club scene, but on closer examination, he learned that one had retired years ago, and his Facebook page hadn't been updated for over a year, not that he used it much anyway. In all likelihood, he was probably dead by now. The second was definitely dead, according to the Liverpool Echo. He had been a doorman at one of the shadier clubs, but had been stabbed to death eighteen months ago, well before Derry James's money had gone missing. The third one, though, ticked enough boxes to raise Liddell's interest.

This Frank Davies had been in a band Liddell had never

heard of but, here was the most interesting thing, the surname of the drummer in this band was Ashcroft. Jonny Liddell didn't believe in many things. He didn't believe in ghosts, the Loch Ness monster, or that the moon landings had been faked by Stanley Kubrick. He definitely didn't believe that there was any such thing as coincidence. He thought he'd probably know if Deano Ashcroft had a brother in a band, but if you're looking for a name, and you find it in connection with another name you recognise, it bears further investigation, which is exactly what Liddell did. Another article in the Liverpool Echo provided a reason for why Frank Davies was keeping a low profile these days. It also provided a motive for someone to need to do a runner with a load of cash. It was enough to convince Liddell that he had found the right person. He picked up his phone and called Elise.

'Elise,' he said, 'have you still got that mate in those people who send the polling cards out? ...Great. Do us a favour. Tell them I've got a couple of tickets for the Anfield derby if he's interested...Yeah, they're good ones too. I need him to find me an address.'

26

Elise's contact certainly earned his Derby tickets, even though he'd never been able to use them because the authorities at Anfield don't tend to approve of forged tickets. He would not discover that yet, though and three days later came back with an address. Liddell had passed the address on to Sutcliffe, who had paused only to collect Dawson and headed straight there.

Sutcliffe stopped his car in a disabled bay, fished the blue badge out of the glove compartment and put it on the dashboard. Neither he, nor Dawson, who was in the passenger seat next to him looking at something on his phone, was disabled, but it was handy to be able to park anywhere you liked. Mr. James wasn't keen on getting parking tickets on cars he owned. He could afford to pay for them, of course, but generally preferred not to if he could avoid it. The disabled bay was in the street next to the one they wanted, but near enough. There were parking meters right down the street they were visiting, including one directly outside the building they were going to, but this was near enough.

'You finished there?' he asked Dawson.

Dawson looked up from his phone, ratty little eyes in a ratty little face, and prodded the screen with a nicotine-stained finger. Sutcliffe tried not to frown but wished, and not for the first time, that if he had to do a job with someone, it would be someone who washed a bit more.

'Yeah,' Dawson replied. 'There's this dog that got frightened by a firework and came looking for its mum, only she was sitting in the bath at the time, and the dog came and sat in the bath with her.'

'Really? A dog?'

'Yeah. Would you believe it? It's sitting there in the bath, getting its arse all wet and this dead sad look on its face.'

'I think maybe you need to get a life. Come on. Let's go and do this.'

'Just a quick in-and-out?'

'Should be. Get the money if he's got it, or kick him until he tells us where it is. Piece of piss.'

'Good. Because there's a programme on the History Channel I want to catch later.'

Sutcliffe looked at Dawson and frowned.

'Mr. James is paying us to do a job, not to watch the fucking History Channel. What's the programme about? Dogs?'

'Not on the History Channel. They don't show programmes about dogs. They show programmes about history. That's why it's called —'

'—The History Channel. Yes, I got that.'

'It's about the Ottoman Empire.'

'Get out of the car, Dawson.'

Once Dawson had disentangled himself from the seatbelt and got out of the car, Sutcliffe pressed the lock button on the key fob and checked the address again on a piece of paper that he pulled out of his pocket.

'He'd better be in,' he said.

'What if he's not?' Dawson asked.

'Then we wait. The Ottermen will have to do without you.'

'No, it's —'

'I know what it is, Dawson. Come on.'

They walked in silence around the corner into the next street, a street of tall, grey houses which Sutcliffe thought were probably Victorian or something, but all of which were converted into flats. They found no.17 about halfway along, and Sutcliffe looked at the block of doorbells for the individual flats, noting with some relief that there was no video camera at the top. Most of the bell pushes had names written on the space next to them, but the one for flat 3 was blank, and he wondered if maybe that was deliberate. He pushed the button for flat 3 and waited. After a second or two, the intercom crackled.

'Yeah?'

'Got a delivery for flat 3,' Sutcliffe said. These days, when people ordered everything online, that usually worked. The occupant of the flat didn't reply, but there was a buzz and a click as the lock on the main door was released. Sutcliffe nodded to Dawson, and they went in.

Inside was a dark, dingy hallway with a staircase and a bank of pigeonholes for post. There were two doors off it, which Sutcliffe presumed were flats 1 and 2, so he motioned to Dawson that they were going upstairs. At the top of the first flight of stairs was a door with a crooked brass number 3 on it. Sutcliffe knocked on the door, shouted, 'Delivery!' and braced his shoulder against the door. As soon as he heard the chain being removed and the latch opening, he shoved hard with his shoulder and slammed the door into the person behind it. He and Dawson stepped into the flat to be confronted by an indignant middle-aged man in his dressing gown and underwear, who was now sitting sprawled on the floor.

'Who are you?' he demanded. 'You're not Amazon.'

'Tax dodging bastards,' Sutcliffe replied. 'Get up.'

'Get out of my flat!' the man shouted, making no attempt to rise.

'Get up,' Sutcliffe repeated calmly, advancing on the man, making him scuttle backwards like a frightened crab. 'I'll give you a count of three and if you're not up, you'll be staying down there for good. I haven't got time to piss about. My associate here has a programme to watch. One—'

The man didn't wait for 'two' but struggled to his feet, getting one foot tangled in the cord of his dressing-gown, which was hanging loose.

'I'm up! I'm up!' he said. 'Now will you leave?'

'We've only just started, Frankie,' Sutcliffe said.

'Started? Started what?' There was panic in the man's eyes now, and Sutcliffe caught a foul smell as the man involuntarily passed wind. 'Who are you? What do you want? And who the hell is Frankie?'

'It's probably best if I ask the questions,' Sutcliffe said.

'Let's start with an easy one. Where's the money?'

'What money? I don't know what you're —'

Before he could finish, Sutcliffe glanced at Dawson, who stepped forward and punched the man hard in the stomach, doubling him over. Sutcliffe grabbed the man's hair and pulled his head back up.

'The money, Frankie,' he said. 'Where is the money?'

'I don't know what you're talking about,' the man managed to gasp. Sutcliffe pushed the man's head back down and brought his own knee up sharply. There was a muffled crunch, and the man slumped to the floor clutching his nose. Sutcliffe crouched next to him.

'Stop fucking me about, Frankie. The next one will be harder and we're not going to stop until you tell us. Is that quite clear?'

'My name's not Frankie,' the man said and spat what looked like a blood-covered tooth onto the carpet. 'It's Brian.'

'Brian what?'

'Brian Sharkey.'

'Then where's Frankie?' Sutcliffe looked at Dawson, and Dawson moved away and started looking around the flat.

'I don't know any Frankie,' Sharkey said. Sutcliffe considered this for a second and then backhanded Sharkey hard across the nose, causing the other man to scream in pain.

'This is Frankie's flat. Where is he?'

'It's *my* flat. I moved in three weeks ago.' Sutcliffe raised his hand, but Sharkey shrank back, trying to cover his face. 'I don't know any Frankie. Honestly! Please, I've not long moved in.'

'He is Brian Sharkey,' Dawson called over. 'Got his wallet here. Photo on the driver's licence looks like him. Well, it *did*.'

'So where's Frankie?' Sutcliffe asked again. 'Didn't he leave a forwarding address, Brian?'

'Not with me. Maybe with the landlord.'

Sutcliffe sighed and stood up.

'Shame,' he said. He nodded to Dawson, said, 'Follow me down,' and walked out of the flat, closing the door behind him. He went down the stairs at a leisurely pace and walked over to the pigeonholes. There were several envelopes protruding from the pigeonhole, which was marked with a 3 in very old, red Dymo labelling tape, and when he pulled them out, he saw that they were all addressed to F.Davies. Two looked like junk, but one was a bank statement. As he opened it, Sutcliffe looked up at the sound of a dull thump coming from upstairs. He heard a door open and close and then turned his attention to the statement as Dawson came down the stairs.

Nasty accident with his dressing gown belt,' Dawson said. 'Poor bastard. What have you got?'

'Bank statement. Recent one too. Last thing on it is a ferry ticket. Looks like Frankie's gone to Ireland.'

'As opposed to Hollywood?'

Sutcliffe ignored Dawson's bad joke and stared at the statement.

'How the fuck are we supposed to find him there?'

Part Three

27

K ate surveyed her wardrobe and quietly despaired. Then she surveyed it again and despaired rather more noisily to The Cat who had chosen the occasion to sit for a while on her bed and keep her company. She suspected it was there to enjoy her misery.

'You can take that look off your face, as well,' she told it. 'You don't have to wear clothes. You come ready equipped.'

She sat down on the bed, next to The Cat.

'I don't know what to do,' she said. The Cat regarded her briefly and then decided it would be more interesting to give its genitals a thorough wash. She didn't know why she should imagine The Cat would be interested in what she planned to wear when it wasn't ever something to which she gave much thought herself, not since Al left and probably not for some time before that. She had practical clothes which she wore for work, several pairs of trousers and a selection of tops, which at any one time were either on, in the wash, or washed and ready to put on. The same outfits were rotated regularly because there was enough to think about most days without thinking about what to wear. When she wasn't in the café, she wore jogging trousers, T-shirts and pullovers, what she always used to call her 'sloping about' clothes, back in the days when there was anyone there to speak to about them. The problem was that it was Saturday, and she had less than an hour before Briony was due to pick her up, and she had allowed the time to sneak up on her without giving it any thought. Now she was sitting on her bed, staring at her wardrobe, and The Cat was being no bloody help at all.

It wasn't as if Briony hadn't given her enough notice. Ten days should have been plenty. It also wasn't as if Bri hadn't reminded her, either. She said something pretty much every other day, whether it was confirming the time she was going to pick Kate up, commenting on how much she was looking forward to it, or the time Kate hated most, the ones where Bri tried to tease her about what she would be wearing. 'Some sexy little number,' was one such suggestion. Bri always laughed after she said such things but treating it as a joke only served to make Kate even more confused about what was expected of her. Bri hadn't called it a date; in fact, she had specifically said it *wasn't* a date, simply a mates' night out. But Kate was acutely aware that in these circumstances, what you said and what you hoped to convey were two different things. It had been a long time since Kate had been in the position of reading between the lines of what someone said and didn't think she could trust herself to get it right anymore. She pulled out a denim dress that had remained on a hanger at the back of the wardrobe since Al left. Kate had always liked it because it was comfortable and disguised her figure, but Al wasn't so keen, possibly for exactly the same reasons. She held the dress against her body and looked in the mirror. The length looked okay, and at least it didn't need ironing, so she laid it out on the bed and continued her inspection of the wardrobe. After another fruitless five minutes, she decided that nothing else was going to leap out at her, so the denim it was.

She put the dress on, brushed her hair, which was not used to being out of the confines of its usual scrunchie and put on enough makeup to hide the dark rings under her eyes and to look like she had at least made an effort. She finished the outfit off with the only pair of shoes she possessed that had any kind of a heel at all and elected not to look in the mirror again. Briony would have to take her as she found her because right now, this was the best she felt like doing. She poured herself a small glass of wine to steady her nerves while she waited for her friend – not her date, definitely not that – to arrive.

She wasn't sure quite why she had expected Bri to turn up in the Disco Bread Van, but it was still a surprise when a neat silver Fiat pulled up outside the cottage and Briony got out. Kate was a bit taken aback when she saw her because Bri looked frankly stunning. She was wearing a short black dress and a black leather biker jacket, and as she came up the path, her blonde hair looked almost luminous. Kate felt a catch in her throat and an undeniable attraction. Even in her bread delivery casuals, Briony was pretty, but dressed up, she was gorgeous. Kate suddenly felt frumpy and wanted to run upstairs and get changed, or simply stay there. But it was too late; Bri had spotted her through the window and waved. Kate swallowed hard and went to answer the door. It came as some surprise when Briony looked her up and down, smiled and let out a whistle.

'Hey you,' she said. 'Looking good, lady.'

'Hardly,' Kate replied, blushing. 'I just threw this on. Not like you. You're, well —'

'Hot, yes, I know. Bet you never expected Bread Girl to scrub up like this. Come on, stop staring and let's go. We need to have time for a drink before the gig.'

Kate followed her friend to the car and climbed in. As Briony fastened her seatbelt, Kate stole another look. *Definitely hot*, she thought and then tried to push the idea out of her head. This was friends and nothing more. Once they had got underway, and Briony started to chat about her day (who'd have thought that delivering bread could produce so many funny stories?), Kate slowly began to relax and enjoy herself. Hot or not, Bri was great company. Despite not having much of an accent herself, she was a terrific mimic and brought her tales of the eccentric customers she encountered to life. By the time they finally arrived at Caernarfon and pulled into the pub car park, Kate's sides were hurting from laughter. Come what may, it was going to be a good night.

The pub was already getting packed when they arrived, and a support band, a Welsh punk group with a name Kate struggled to pronounce, despite the length of time she had lived on Anglesey, and the beginners' Welsh course she and Al had decided they really ought to take. It was noisy, very warm and the sort of venue in which she had not set foot for far too long. They found a space near the bar–sitting down was totally out of the question–and Briony insisted on going to the bar.

'But you've paid for the tickets!' Kate protested.

'You get the next one. Beer okay?'

'Yes, great. Thank you.'

Briony blew her a kiss and went to fight her way to the bar, leaving Kate more confused than ever. What was that all about? Was Bri like this with all her friends, or was there more to it than that. Kate tried to convince herself that she was going to enjoy the night and stop looking for subtext in everything, but her eyes were drawn to Briony, who was leaning against the bar shouting her order to the barman, who looked about twelve, and again she felt that tug of attraction. *For God's sake, grow up,* she told herself. *You're not a bloody teenager anymore.*

Bri brought the beers back and handed one to Kate. She clinked the bottom of her own bottle against Kate's and said, 'Iechyd da,' but pronouncing it, 'Yacky Da,' like most non-Welsh speakers did, which made Kate smile. She noticed, too, that Bri's beer was non-alcoholic. As they sipped their beer, Briony surveyed the crowd.

'Not much talent here tonight,' she said. Kate hesitated, not sure of how to reply, but then Briony caught her eye, smiled and said, 'Just as well I don't need any.' If Kate intended to answer, it would have been lost because at that moment, the support band launched into their set, and for a while, conversation was impossible. The band were, as far as Kate could tell, of the opinion that what they lacked in talent, they could make up for in sheer volume. They sang, or more accurately shouted, most of their songs in Welsh, which didn't help, but even when they attempted the occasional cover version in English, it was so hard to tell that they needn't have bothered. After about six numbers, Briony leaned in close and shouted into Kate's ear.

'Jesus, they're bloody terrible. Mind if I nip outside for a quick smoke?'

'They're awful,' Kate shouted back. 'No, you go ahead.'

'Don't worry. I don't smoke much anymore. A couple a

day, for old time's sake. Do you want to get some more beers in before we get some proper music?'

'Of course. Same again?'

Briony gave her the thumbs up and picked her way through the throng to the door. Kate watched her go and headed for the bar.

The queue at the bar was two-deep and the bar staff were rushing back and forth trying to keep up. Kate jostled for a space and then kept her eyes fixed on the bar waiting for her turn. As she did so, she became aware that two lads were observing her from further down the bar, nudging each other and grinning. They didn't look old enough to be out drinking, let alone to have the slightest idea who Space were. She tried to ignore them and concentrated on not losing her place at the bar. If she didn't pay attention and be at least a little assertive, she had a tendency to be one of those people who become invisible at a bar and have to watch everyone around getting served, whether it is their turn or not. When she was finally served, by which time the support band had finished their set, she didn't have to shout quite so loudly. She ordered two bottles each, partly to repay Briony for her generosity and partly so that neither of them would have to brave the crush once the main event began. She paid and pushed her way back through the mass of bodies to somewhere near where they were standing, keeping an eye on the door so that she could see Bri, even if Bri couldn't see her. She was so intent on the door that she didn't realise that she had company until a voice said, 'Saw you at the bar.' She turned and saw that the two lads had followed her from the bar. They were drenched in sweat and clearly very drunk.

'You here on your own?' asked a gangly redhead whose face, punctuated with spots, betrayed his age. Kate wasn't sure whether she should be flattered or dismayed that she was probably old enough to be his mother.

'I'm here with my friend,' she said.

'She's got a friend,' the redhead's mate, a dark-haired Goth wannabe, said and laughed in a way Kate didn't much care for. 'We could all hang out together.'

'Isn't it past your bedtime?' Briony asked, appearing at Kate's side. 'She's with me, kids, so fuck off.'

The two lads shot Briony a resentful glance, but they backed off. All the same, the redhead couldn't resist saying 'They're fucking dykes,' to his mate as they went.

'Well, I don't know about that,' Bri said, accepting the beers that Kate was holding out. 'The night is still young. You okay?'

'I'm fine,' Kate replied. 'They were only kids.'

'You can tell you're getting old when the dickheads start looking younger.'

'Men are dickheads any age.'

'Very true. That's mainly why I don't bother with them. Your man at the café seems all right, though.'

'Frank? Yes, he's a godsend. I was lucky to find him.'

'You know, I'm sure I recognise his face. Can't put my finger on it, though.'

'Maybe got one of those faces.'

'Maybe. So what's the deal there? Are you—?'

'No!' Kate nearly choked on her beer. 'He works for me and he looks like being a good friend, but that's all.' Made bolder by the beer, she looked Briony directly in the eye. 'He's not my type.'

'And what *is* your type?' Briony asked, holding her gaze.

'Right now?'

Kate was interrupted by a voice booming over the PA systems, imploring the crowd to give a warm welcome to the main act of the evening. A roar went up and the moment was lost. The band took to the stage, and Briony grabbed Kate's hand.

'Let's see if we can get nearer!' she shouted and tugged Kate through the crowd and closer to the stage. With a roll on the drums and a crashing chord from the guitars, the band launched into their first number.

The rest of the evening passed in a euphoric blur. Kate and Briony danced, jumped, sang along to all the familiar songs and never stopped grinning once. Kate felt alive in a way that she realised she hadn't done for years and hadn't fully understood how much she missed it. Alison would have come along to a gig like this one but stood coolly on the sidelines, watching the younger people throw themselves about. Kate would have loved to join in but felt the disapproval and resisted. Briony had no such inhibitions, and for once, Kate felt like she was back in her student days—young, carefree and with no worries about the future.

All too soon, the band was performing the encore, and Kate reached out for Briony's hand again. Briony gave her hand a squeeze but then let go and snaked her arm around Kate's waist instead. Kate allowed herself to be drawn in closer and rested her head on Bri's shoulder. Something brushed her hair, and she wasn't sure, but it felt like Bri had kissed the top of her head. Then the lights came up and Briony let go. Kate felt a sudden loss and knew then that she wanted that closeness to go on.

'I must look a right bloody state,' Bri said. 'Jesus, I'm soaked.' It was true; her blonde hair was plastered to her head and darkened with sweat, but her smile was radiant.

'You look fine to me,' Kate said. 'I'm sure I don't look any better.'

'You're a mess,' Briony said and reached out to brush away a tendril of hair that was clinging to Kate's face. 'A gorgeous mess, but a mess all the same. Come on. We'd better make a move.'

'Thanks, Bri. It's been an amazing night.'

'They definitely don't make music like that anymore.' Briony laughed. 'Jesus, I sound like my dad.'

'You're right, though. It took me right back. I think I'd forgotten how to have fun.'

'Stick with me then. Fun is my middle name. But we're also grown-ups with jobs that need early starts. We could do this again, though.'

'Yes, I'd like that. I'd like it a lot.'

'Good. We will then. Mind if I have a quick ciggie before we go?'

'No, of course not. I'll come out with you. I could do with some air.'

While Briony smoked, keeping a respectful distance, Kate closed her eyes and enjoyed the cool air on her face. Her ears were still ringing from the noise, and her head was full of the band's last song. She could also still feel the warmth of Briony's arm around her. She opened her eyes and saw that her friend was watching her. Briony slowly breathed out a cloud of blue smoke and winked. Then she ground her cigarette out in the bin on the pub wall, put her cigarettes away in her bag and produced her car keys. She flicked her head to gesture *come on,* and Kate followed her to the car. Bri started the car, but before she drove off, she excused herself and leaned across to fumble for something in the glove compartment.

'I know it's here somewhere,' she said, pulling out a wad of CDs. She shuffled through them until she found the one she wanted and slid it into the CD player. 'Here we go,' she said, and as the car moved off, the Best of Space began. They sang along all the way back to Chapel Bay. Kate wished it were further, but all too soon, Briony pulled up outside the cottage.

'Thanks again, Bri,' she said. 'What a night.'

'Yes. Like I said, we'll do it again soon.'

There was an awkward pause. Kate took a deep breath and, before she gave herself a chance to change her mind, said, 'Listen, do you fancy coming in for a coffee or something?'

'I'm not sure,' Briony replied. 'Early start and everything.'

'Start from here,' Kate said, and then leaned in and kissed her.

28

Frank had found the perfect place to spend his lunch breaks. Tempting as it would be to stay in the café, he chose not to. Kate had always said that he was more than welcome to make himself a sandwich or something. After all, it wasn't as if she was paying him all that much, but he politely declined, making some vague remark about watching his weight and how everything was far too tempting. That was partly true; the food he served to customers did look very tempting, which meant he preferred to get a break from it. The café was far too public, anyway. He didn't want customers who came in regularly to have to witness him shovelling food down. It was also true, in a sense, that he was watching his weight, but that was a permanent state of affairs. He ate enough to live but was always conscious of how the waistband on his trousers felt. Although he had come to terms with his weight many years previously, he still experienced that pang of dread every time he tried a new pair of trousers on for the first time, the fear that this time he might not be able to fasten them properly and that he might have gone up a size. He had given up weighing himself when he was in his twenties and had developed the makings of an obsession. The day he seriously contemplated buying a notebook to record his daily weight was the day he threw the scales on the nearest skip, and the only way he observed any fluctuations in his weight now was by how his trousers felt. At the moment, they felt about right, and he wanted it to stay that way, so when he wasn't working, he took himself off, out of temptation's way.

The first few days, he had wandered about a bit, exploring Chapel Bay and the lanes around it. Once he realised that he was walking for the sake of it, and that all the lanes looked pretty much the same, he began to hunt for somewhere he could sit and think. He found it on the cliffs that rose up either side of the bay. He had followed the wall that bordered the beach until he got to the end of it, and there he discovered a stile. It was an old, wooden thing that looked like it would snap in two if you put too much weight on it, but it was stronger than it looked, and he was able to climb over it onto a rough path which bisected two hedges of brambles. The first time he had followed the path, he had expected it to become overgrown and impassable but had been surprised when he encountered a second stile and saw that beyond it was an open field. He was even more surprised when he jumped down from the stile, and his feet landed on soft, springy turf, which practically made him bounce when he walked. The grass was peppered with pink, blue and yellow wildflowers, all of which attracted bees and butterflies by the dozen. He wished he could put a name to all the flowers, but apart from dandelions and what he thought might be clover, he drew a blank. They were nice to look at, though, and he walked on, trying not to step on them. He walked over a rise and was greeted by a view that made him stop short. To his right, he could see the whole of the bay, stretching out in a crescent to the cliff face on the other side. To his left was nothing but the sea. A small outcrop of lichen-covered rock jutted out from the turf and was big enough for him to sit on. He made himself comfortable and gazed out at the view. This was exactly the place he had been looking for, and from then on, he came on every lunch break, whatever the weather. It was on his third visit that he spotted Gemma.

Since he had started working at *Kate's*, Gemma had come in nearly every day, usually for a takeaway latte, but once or twice she had stayed for an early lunch. Frank served her politely, but on the days when she stayed, she chatted to Kate, and he left her to it. He wasn't quite sure what he had done to offend her but hoped that if he kept himself to himself and didn't say anything to make things worse, she might thaw in time. When she talked to Kate, she sounded like a nice person, with a good, dry sense of humour, but at the moment, her laugh was reserved for Kate. He was the guy who made the coffee. He watched her walking slowly across the beach, head down, concentrating on the sand beneath her feet. Her dark hair was untied and because of the light breeze off the sea, she frequently had to brush it away from her face. When she spotted something, she would crouch down, examine whatever she had found, rinsing it in the seawater. Sometimes she would drop it in the canvas satchel that was slung over her shoulder, and other times she would place it carefully back on the sand. Even from his high vantage point, he could tell that she was putting whatever she had found back exactly where she had found it as if offering it back to the sea. Then she would stand, brush her hair back and carry on scouring the tide-strewn debris for more treasure. He watched her, fascinated by the way she moved backwards and forwards across the beach and wondered what she was collecting. He thought that perhaps he might drop by her workshop at some point and find out what she did. It could be a way of breaking the ice. He waited until she had disappeared out of sight under the cliff beneath him and decided that this was an opportune moment to go back to the café. There was something about Gemma that made him reluctant to bump into her by accident. He would rather be ready.

When he got back to the café, he mentioned to Kate that he had seen Gemma and casually asked what it was that she did. She made things, he learned. She made jewellery and gifts out of items she foraged on the beach. She polished and lacquered shells and mounted them on leather thongs. She decorated boxes and mugs with shell mosaics and turned driftwood into exquisite ornaments. If only, Frank thought, he had someone to buy a gift for. That would give him the excuse to visit. He could make someone up, of course, or find some other pretext to go.

An opportunity unexpectedly presented itself the next day. Kate was in the middle of sorting out an order, which had recently arrived, and there were no customers in the café.

'You couldn't do us a favour, could you, Frank?' Kate asked.

'Sure. What can I do?'

Kate picked up an envelope from the top of the fridge and held it out.

'Postman delivered this before, but it's for Gemma next door. Do you mind running it round to her? It mightn't be important, but you never know.'

'No problem.'

Frank took the envelope and crossed the small alleyway to Gemma's workshop. He stood outside the door for a moment or two, undecided about whether he should knock, but in the end, pushed the door open and went in. The workshop was only small, but Gemma had made the most of the space, turning the front section into a display area to sell her wares, while the rear was dominated by a large table, where she sat, surrounded by the tools of her trade. Frank watched her as she sprayed lacquer over a razor clam, which she had polished, transforming the dull browns of the shell into an extraordinary array of patterns. Her face was hidden behind a pair of oversized industrial goggles and it wasn't until she had finished spraying, taken the goggles off and blown some straggling hair away from her face that she noticed Frank was there at all. She smiled when she saw him, and as soon as he saw it, he knew he wanted to make her smile more.

'Sorry,' she said. 'Miles away. I didn't hear you come in.'

'Don't worry. I didn't want to disturb you.'

'No, please. Disturb away. Especially if you want to buy something. That would be a bit of a novelty today. Hey, it's Latte Man, isn't it?'

'That's me.'

'You do make the best lattes. But I can't keep calling you that. Kate did tell me your name, but I've got a terrible memory.'

'Oh yes. Sorry. It's—ah—Frank,' he said.

'Pleased to meet you, R. Frank. I'm Gemma.' She held out her hand, and he shook it rather formally.

'Postman delivered this next door by mistake,' he said, holding out the letter.

'Oh, thanks. Probably junk.' She took the letter and tossed

it onto the workbench.

'You make beautiful things,' he said, turning his attention to a display of shell necklaces.

'Oh, I don't make the beautiful things. Nature does that. All I do is show them off. You know how you see a lovely coloured pebble underwater, but it goes dull when it dries off?'

'I used to hate that when I was a kid. It was always disappointing when you saw them dry. I kept pebbles in a bucket of water so they'd stay like that.'

'Hey,' she said, spreading her arms out, 'I'm the bucket. The lacquer keeps the shells and pebbles looking like they do when they're wet, but that's all. The beauty is already there.'

Yes, Frank thought, stealing a glance at her. *It is.*

29

Kate woke with a start and, for a moment, felt completely disorientated. She thought at first that it was because her alarm hadn't gone off until she remembered that it was Sunday, the one day her alarm didn't wake her. It wasn't that, though; there was something else...something about the bed didn't feel right. Then it all began to sink in. The bed felt wrong because she was on the right and usually slept either on the left or more usually in the middle, and the reason she was on the wrong side was Briony. Briony, who had been there when she went to sleep and now wasn't. *Typical*, she thought. *Stupid, stupid Kate.*

She might have known it was all too good to be true. Briony had accepted the offer of a cup of coffee, and while they drank, they talked, first about the gig and then about other things.

'This is a beautiful cottage,' Briony had said. 'You've got it so nice. Must be nice to have all this space to yourself.'

It is, usually. Do you share, or...?'

'With my parents, yes. I know. How sad is that? Still living with the parents at my age. It's a convenience thing, really. They're both getting on a bit. I keep an eye on them; they keep a roof over my head. Delivering bread doesn't pay that well, and I keep trying to save up for a place of my own, but, you know, stuff happens.' Briony shrugged and glanced around again. 'Don't you get a bit lonely on your own?'

'I suppose. Sometimes. I have a cat that visits, but I don't think it likes me very much. It comes in for food.'

'Doesn't count then. I know you weren't on your own when you moved in... Sorry. People talk. Tell me to mind my own business.'

'No, it's okay. It's old news. Alison's been gone a while. It tore me to bits for a while, but I'm used to my own company now. I like it, in fact. I see enough people during the day.'

Briony had moved a little closer on the settee, so close that their thighs were touching. Kate felt a warmth she had forgotten.

'So you wouldn't want any company then?'

'It depends on the company,' Kate said and kissed her. This time the kiss went on for a long time. By the time she broke away, they were both slightly breathless.

'There are other rooms in the cottage,' she said, taking Bri's hand and pulling her to her feet. 'Do you want to see?'

Now, on the morning after, Kate drew her dressing gown around herself and blushed at the memory. She had given more than she thought she could and received more than she had expected and still woken up on her own. It probably served her right for being so bold. Maybe that wasn't how it was done these days. She had been out of the game so long now, and maybe there were different rules. It had been nice, very nice, but now she felt stupid. Surely they were grown-ups. If there was something wrong, then they should have been able to talk about it. There was no need for Briony to walk off without a word. Perhaps there might even be a need to find a new bread supplier. *Shit.*

Kate went into the kitchen and filled the kettle. The Cat had appeared from somewhere and was sitting by its bowl, giving her the slightly disappointed look of a parent whose teenager had come home late from a party and not phoned.

'Who are you looking at?' Kate asked. The Cat looked at its bowl and then back at Kate. If it could have cleared its throat, it probably would have done.

'Oh, all right.' She reached into the cupboard and took out a pouch of cat food, ripped it open and emptied it into The Cat's bowl. The intended recipient sniffed it and then looked at her again.

'It's tuna, for God's sake. Just eat it, you ungrateful little shit. I'm sure it tastes better than it smells.'

The Cat sniffed again, then put its head down and tucked in.

'You only love me for food, don't you?' Kate said. 'You

don't give much back. Never mind. That's you and everyone else. You want me for what I can give to you. One of these days, someone's going to wonder what *I* want.'

The kettle clicked off. She took a mug out of the cupboard and made her coffee. It wasn't even her favourite mug; that one was in the living room on the table with her second favourite, which probably had traces of Bri's lipstick on it, and she didn't want to see that right now, let alone have to wash it off. She took her coffee to the back door of the cottage to get some fresh air. One of the cottage's attractions was the two-section stable style back door. She could open the top half, look out across the fields at the back of the house and lean on the bottom half while she drank her coffee. There was a low shroud of mist sitting on the fields at the moment, but the day promised to be a fine one. Kate felt the need to get dressed and go for a very long walk, but at the moment, she couldn't be bothered. She would probably drink her coffee, then waste the day sitting in her dressing gown and watching crap on the television. Except...Sunday was her shopping day, and her cupboards were getting to the point where even someone as resourceful who hated shopping as much as she did would struggle to rustle together anything worth eating.

She finished her coffee with a sigh, which sounded overly dramatic even to her, and closed the door. She was going to have to shake herself out of this funk and do something. She put her mug in the sink and then talked herself out of leaving it there for later. One of Alison's more irritating habits was to let mugs accumulate in the sink rather than wash them. They only got washed when there were no more in the cupboard, and even then, it was usually Kate who ended up washing them. She washed her mug, dried it and put it away and then decided that while she was at it, she might as well wash the mugs she and Briony had used the previous night. She thought she could probably do it now without thinking about what the use of those mugs had led to. But of course, trying not to think about it inevitably made her think about it, and the feeling of sadness and shame came rushing back. Best to get the bloody mugs sorted and then she could try and forget about it. She went into the living room and snatched the mugs off the table, not thinking, definitely *not* thinking about the red smear on the second favourite. As she did so, a flashing blue light caught her eye. She had left her phone on the table last night, and its notification light was winking insistently at her. It was almost certainly junk, but in case, she checked anyway. She had two texts and they were both from Briony. Expecting the inevitable 'Can we forget that ever happened?' message, she opened the first one and had to read it twice before she took it in properly.

```
Sorry to run out on you, but the
bread doesn't stop for Sunday. You
looked so comfy that I didn't want to
disturb you.
B xxx
```

She allowed herself a smile after the second reading. That was nice, anyway. At least there were no hard feelings. Her smile grew broader when she read the second text.

```
Last night was beautiful. You're beautiful.
Can we do it again, please?
Xxx
```

Yes, Kate thought as she read the text again and again. *Yes, we bloody well can.*

30

Gemma knew that Frank had started to spend most of his lunch breaks sitting on the cliff top, watching the beach below. At first, she resented his presence, feeling self-conscious about being observed while she combed the beach for new treasures to take back to her workshop. It was *her* place and *her* time, and she wasn't used to company, even from a distance. But since he had visited her in the workshop, something had changed. He had made a point of spending money with her that day, paying £15.00 for an auger shell mounted on a brown leather thong. She had asked if he wanted it gift-wrapped as a present for someone, but he had said, 'No, it's for me,' and slipped it straight round his neck. She had liked that, the straightforwardness, the honesty of it. He was obviously a man who liked what he liked and wasn't bothered about what anyone else thought. Not that there seemed to be an anyone else. She had spoken to him in *Kate's* a couple of times after that (and yes, he was still wearing the shell pendant) and tried to tease information out of him. While not explicitly saying so, he made it pretty clear that he was here on his own and made no mention of anyone waiting for him anywhere else. It was probably because of this that she told him about the beach party. It was Ruth Prior who had mentioned it to her. Some of the younger folk from the neighbouring villages had been talking about it in Parry's and invited her along and told her to spread the word. Impromptu parties on this, and the other beaches on this stretch of coast, happened quite often during the summer, apparently. Gemma had never fancied them, too many kids getting drunk and stupid she reckoned, and not the sort of thing it was much fun to go to on your own. It was while she was having her morning latte and Frank made some casual joke about the lack of nightlife in these parts that she spoke without thinking about it.

'There's a party on the beach on Thursday night,' she said. 'You know, a bonfire and stuff. Don't know if you fancy it. Probably not your sort of thing.'

'Why? Do you reckon I'm a bit old for it?'

'No! I didn't mean that. I meant—'

'It's okay,' Frank replied with a grin. 'I'm only kidding you. Sound like it could be fun. You going?'

'Might do.'

'What about you, Kate?'

'I don't know,' Kate said, pausing in buttering some bread. 'I'm usually well in my pit before parties like that even get going.'

'Bring Briony. I bet she'd be up for it,' suggested Gemma.

'Briony?' Frank raised an eyebrow. 'Briony the bread?'

'Didn't you know?' Gemma laughed. 'Kate and Briony are dating.'

'We're not!' Kate protested, flushing crimson. 'We went out once. As mates, that's all.'

'You never told me,' Frank said. 'That's great. I like Briony.'

'I never said because it's none of your business. Or yours, Gemma. Haven't either of you got anything better to do than gossip about me?'

'Ask her,' Gemma said. 'Go on. Let your hair down. As for you, Latte Man, give me a knock about nine if you're going.'

'I'll think about it.'

'Do that.'

Gemma gave them both a little wave and left the café, but not before she heard Kate say, 'She's a force of nature, that one.' She was still smiling when she got back to her workshop.

***

Frank hesitated outside the door of Gemma's workshop. He raised his hand to knock twice and stopped. It was five to nine on Thursday night, and he wasn't entirely sure what he was doing there. The party had already started on the beach. The bonfire had been lit, and judging by the voices and the choice of music, the party seemed to be attended mainly by young surfer dudes, who were not Frank's usual choice for company. He felt old and redundant and had managed to convince himself over the past couple of days that Gemma had invited him out of something like pity. He hadn't yet decided what he wanted from her, but pity was a long way down the list. He was about to turn and go, when the door opened.

'Oh, sorry,' Gemma said, giving him a smile that instantly changed his mind about going anywhere. 'I didn't hear you knock.'

'I hadn't yet.'

'Well then, I've saved you wear and tear on your knuckles. Are we set?'

'I've got beer,' Frank said, raising the carrier bag he had been clutching.

'I've gone one better,' Gemma replied, indicating her beach-combing satchel. 'Hope you like Coke with your Jack Daniels.'

'I haven't had any for a while,' he replied, now wondering if he was still going to be able to use the darkness to conceal the fact that the lager he had brought for himself was non-alcoholic.

'Shall we go then? It's a long walk, and we don't want to miss anything.'

Gemma started off down the beach. Frank watched her for a moment, admiring the easy way she crossed the sand as though she owned it. She was wearing a lilac dress that swished around her legs as she walked, and she waved at some of the other partygoers as she went. Frank hurried to catch up with her. By the time he reached her, she had found Kate, who had obviously persuaded Briony to come along, and the teacher from the school, Ruth Somebody. Kate and Briony were hand in hand, but Ruth was paying more attention to the bottle of wine she had brought with her.

'Glad you two could make it,' Kate said. 'I think we're the

oldest here.'

'It feels like the parents have arrived to break the party up,' Frank remarked.

'Well, I intend to have a good time,' Ruth said, and Frank could tell by the slight slur in her voice that this probably wasn't the first bottle of wine of the evening. 'Might as well enjoy myself now, while I can.'

'Are you okay, Ruth?' Kate asked. 'You're going for it a bit.'

'I'll tell you another time. Don't want to be a downer tonight.'

'No, it's okay. Might as well tell us now.'

'Well,' Ruth took another gulp of wine, 'it looks like I might be moving on.'

'You're leaving the school?'

'It's worse than that, Kate. Unless someone can come up with a big pile of cash pretty soon, there isn't going to be a school. The roof has been condemned, and unless I can find the cash from somewhere by Christmas, the school will have to close. And I'll be out of a job.'

'Oh no. That's awful, Ruth. Surely something can be done. Would any businesses be prepared to sponsor it? They sometimes like being seen to do good works like that.'

'Not so far, and don't think I haven't tried. There's a feeling that it's throwing good money after bad. You know, if the roof's falling to bits, what else is wrong with the place? One place I spoke to, a horrible guy said he reckoned that if he sponsored us once, we'd always be coming back with our hand out. But I know we wouldn't. The roof is the cause of all the problems. Anything else is cosmetic. There you go. Told you it'd be a downer.'

'There must be something we can do,' Kate said. 'A fundraiser, maybe. Look, let's enjoy ourselves tonight and have a chat in a day or two. See what we can come up with.'

'Thanks, Kate. I don't think it'll do any good, but I'll try anything. In the meantime, the enjoying ourselves bit sounds good to me.'

'Anyone fancy anything to eat?' Gemma asked, neatly changing the subject. 'I think they're doing hotdogs over there. I haven't eaten since lunch.'

Kate, Briony and Ruth all declined, so Frank said he'd go with her, even though a hotdog, cooked God only knew how, was the last thing he felt like. He didn't want to let Gemma out of his sight yet. There were plenty of young, fit, good-looking men around, and he was more than aware that she had been attracting glances.

'Sorry about that,' Gemma said as they went. 'Typical village. You can't come for a night out without some crisis.'

'Poor Ruth, though. She must be stressed out of her mind.'

'Kate will sort her out. I get the impression she likes a bit of a cause. Here we are. You having a hot dog?'

'Not for me, thanks,' Frank said, as Gemma put her order in with the enterprising young couple who had set up a trestle table and were selling hot dogs and burgers.

'You sure? They look great. Onions, mustard and ketchup for me, please.'

'Mustard *and* ketchup?' Frank asked.

'It's the only way. You sure you can't be tempted?'

'Honestly, I'm fine, thank you.'

'Your loss.'

Gemma took a huge bite out of her hot dog, sending pieces of onion tumbling to the sand. She used a napkin to wipe away a ketchup smear that had found its way onto her chin.

'Did I get it all?' she asked. 'This is great. Nothing like a hotdog in the open air. Are you sure—?'

'Yes, I'm sure,' Frank snapped. 'Sorry. Yes, I'm sure, thanks.'

'You don't eat a lot, do you? I'm not sure I've ever seen you eat.'

Frank looked away, unsure how to answer. It was too soon, the wrong kind of night for that sort of honesty. But Gemma pressed on.

'It's not a criticism. Just an observation.' She paused. 'Oh dear. I've said the wrong thing, haven't I? I do that. Ignore me, Frank. I'll eat my hot dog and shut up.'

'No, it's okay. It's a bit of a sensitive subject. I used to be...well, I didn't always look like this. Let's leave it at that.'

'Oh, you're dieting! Fair enough. I don't know that there's much in a hot dog, though.'

'It's not a diet. Not really. I'm very careful about what I eat. I used to be fat, Gemma. I mean properly fat. It's not somewhere I ever want to go back to. Now can we leave it?'

'Yes, sorry. Can I say that you look pretty good to me?'

'Yes,' Frank smiled. 'Yes, you can say that.'

'Good. Because you do.'

'Thank you. You look pretty good to me, too. Even with ketchup on your chin.'

'What? Really?' Gemma frantically wiped her chin with the napkin again, and when it came away clean, she slapped Frank on the arm. 'Bastard! Come on. Let's get back to the others in case they think we've run away together.'

Frank thought that didn't sound like a bad idea at all. He was starting to feel uncomfortable and was already regretting having said anything about his weight and his eating habits. He liked Gemma and wanted her to like him, too, but didn't want to feel as though she was watching him for all the wrong reasons. She chatted away as they picked their way through the party-goers, who were standing or sitting in groups, some talking, some dancing to the music from the sound systems which had been set up on the beach wall. She didn't seem to be treating him any differently, but he was now wary about what he said to her. He'd crossed a line by being too honest, and even though he hadn't told her the whole truth, he still wished he could take it back. They found Kate, Briony and Ruth, who seemed even tipsier now, and sat down with them on the sand. As Gemma laughed and joked with the other women, Frank listened and joined in at what he hoped were appropriate moments, drinking his beer with his hand firmly around the label on the bottle. At one point, Gemma leaned back against his arm. He held his breath and tried not to move, in case she realised her mistake and pulled away, but she didn't. She seemed quite comfortable and relaxed, and Frank was tempted to put his arm around her. He restrained himself, though. That might be one step too far.

As the sky began to darken, Kate announced that it was probably time for her to call it a night. Briony had an early start, and Ruth needed escorting home; she could barely stand on her own, and when she tried to walk, her feet seemed reluctant to obey her. Kate gave Frank a mock-stern instruction not to stay out too late, and she and Briony led the inebriated teacher back up the beach.

'Do you want to stay?' Gemma asked.

'If you do.'

'For a bit. I haven't been out in company for quite some time.'

This remark raised plenty of obvious questions, but Frank asked none of them. One of the lads in the group next to them had produced a guitar and was singing Beatles songs passably well. Gemma sang along in a pleasant soprano, amusing him by getting some of the words wrong. After a few songs, the guitarist held the guitar up.

'Anyone else play?' he asked. Frank kept his mouth shut. The young man had no takers and laid the guitar down on the sand next to him while he concentrated on his beer and his girlfriend. Frank kept looking at the instrument, trying to resist, and on one occasion, Gemma caught him looking.

'You do play, don't you?'

'A bit. I used to. I haven't for ages.'

'Go on, Latte Man. Give us a tune.'

'No. I'd better not. I'm very rusty.'

'Go on. You know you're dying to. I won't listen.'

Frank deliberated and almost resisted, but the lure of the guitar was too strong. He picked it up and started to pick out a few chords. The guitar was slightly out of tune, so he tuned it and started again. Before long, the old, comfortable feeling of having a guitar in his hand came back, and he began to sing the first song that came into his head, one of the lesser-known tracks from The Leisure Decree's second album, a ballad called The Reason of You. He figured that if he was going to sing anything, it was better if it was a song nobody here was likely to have heard. As he sang, he became aware that Gemma was watching him and smiling.

'You're not bad,' she said. 'You've done this before. I don't know that song. It's lovely.'

Frank smiled back and carried on singing. He reached the end of the song and was about to pass the guitar back when he realised that there was applause coming from the group of kids sitting next to him. He made what he hoped were the appropriate modest gestures.

'Give us another one!' one of the kids called out, and one of his mates wolf-whistled. Against his better judgement, Frank did as he was asked and this time upped the tempo with a song he had always quite liked called You'll Be Mine, which was the nearest The Decree had to a hit. He still thought he was safe enough, though. Most of these kids probably hadn't been born when the song had failed to trouble the top 10. He finished the song with a flourish, and this time he did hand the guitar back. He knew that if he didn't, he would be hooked and sing all night. As he did so, he saw that one of the kids in the group was looking at him curiously.

'You're him, aren't you?' the kid asked.

'No,' Frank replied. 'I'm not anyone.'

'You are,' the young man persisted. 'You're Frankie from The Leisure Decree. Man, I *love* your stuff. My dad used to play it all the time.'

'Thanks, but you're mistaken. I'm the guy from the café.'

He got to his feet and brushed sand from his trousers.

'I need a bit of a walk,' he said to Gemma. 'My leg's going to sleep.'

'Do you want company?'

'Up to you. I'm not going far.'

'I could do with stretching my legs too.'

She linked her arm through his, and together they wandered down the beach towards the waterline.

'So,' Gemma said. 'Who is Frankie from the, what was it, the Leisure something? Truth, please. Why Frankie?'

'Frankie is who I used to be. A long time ago. I'm Frank now.'

'Don't talk in riddles. If we're going to be friends, we need to be honest. That is if you *want* us to be friends.'

'Okay, okay. There isn't much to tell. I was in a band once. The Leisure Decree.'

'Wanky name, but go on.'

'They all had wanky names in those days. That was the rule. We nearly made it, too. One of our songs—that second one I did—almost bothered the top 40, but, well, didn't. You can find it sometimes on those one-hit-wonder compilations. Then we got fed up with not making it and split. That's the story. It's not very exciting, not exactly rock'n'roll, but it was the same for so many other bands. Nearly getting there but then going off and getting proper jobs.'

'I must have a listen to some more.'

'If you must, but prepare for crushing disappointment. Do us a favour, though? Listen to the music but don't look at the videos. If you think the name was wanky, you definitely don't want to look at the hairstyles.'

Gemma laughed.

'You realise that I'm definitely going to look now, don't you?'

'Oh God, please don't. I shouldn't have said anything.'

Gemma didn't reply. Instead, she gasped, 'Look at *that!*' Frank looked up, following the line of her pointing finger and saw what had made her react in that way. Arcing across the night sky was probably the most beautiful, perfect shooting star he had ever seen. It was a bright silver-white and so clear that for a second, he could see nothing else and couldn't tear his eyes away.

'It looks so low!' he whispered.

'Optical illusion,' Gemma replied, her voice also hushed. 'You should see the moon some nights. You'd swear you could touch it. Quick, close your eyes and make a wish!'

Frank did as he was told and closed his eyes, but the brightness of the shooting star was burned across his vision, and he could still see its trace. He could feel Gemma's nearness and the smell of her perfume and couldn't think of a thing to wish for, other than this moment. When he opened his eyes, the shooting star was disappearing over the headland.

'Did you make a wish?' Gemma asked and then laid her finger on his lips to silence any reply. 'Don't tell me, or it won't come true. Come on, let's go back. I think that's probably the perfect way to end tonight.'

31

Gemma climbed the fire escape to her flat on aching legs. It had been a long time since she had been out so late and was normally either sitting on the battered old sofa in her flat watching something on the television, or more usually, in bed, trying to sleep and watching the hours tick by on her alarm clock. Sometimes she got three or four hours sleep before waking up right before the alarm was due to go off. Her brain had an unerring knack for dragging her from sleep at exactly the same time pretty much every day; it was a rare night when she was tired enough to hear the alarm go off. It had been a good night, though. She felt that she had finally made an effort to integrate herself into the local community, something she had been reluctant to do before. There had never seemed much point in making yourself at home somewhere if you're not sure how long you were staying. She was now more settled than she had been for a long time. She hoped that people like Kate and Ruth and even Briony had been given a chance to see that Gemma was a real person, not some hermit who wandered around on the beach like a lunatic and then hid away in her workshop playing with shells. All the same, there was the old nagging doubt at the back of her mind that warned her not to get too settled. There was always the strong possibility that something (and she was all too aware what that might be) could come along and ruin everything and force her to leave. She didn't want to become too attached because she knew only too well how much that would hurt.

And then there was Frank. Once they had both decided that the beach party had reached the time when there was more fun to be had by the younger partygoers than by the slightly older ones, they had made their way back up the beach, more or less in silence. The shared sight of the shooting star had changed things somehow, and it was a moment neither of them wanted to break. Frank had escorted her to the foot of the fire escape and said goodnight. There had been an awkward pause, during which neither of them had made a move to do anything at all. He then said he'd better get his bus, gave her a wave and vanished into the night, leaving her to make her ascent to her flat on her own. She was glad that nothing more had happened. She was still getting used to the idea that she might have been wrong about him, and anything more would have been too confusing right now.

He had, she admitted to herself, been much better company than she had been expecting and she was now not sure why she had taken to him so violently in the first place. It was almost certainly a territory thing. It had taken her a while to start feeling that this place could be anything like a home to her, but he had, it seemed, walked straight in and got his feet firmly under the table. That made her feel far more resentment than the situation warranted, and she had to confess (but only to herself for now) that he was all right. He had been very guarded at first, but once he had started to open up, she had been flattered by his trust. She definitely got the impression that it was something he didn't make a habit of, and that, in turn, made her wonder why. So he'd had a problem with his weight at some time. So what? Didn't everyone have days when they looked in the mirror and thought they could lose a pound or two? He certainly didn't look like he was overweight. If Gemma had to describe his figure as anything—and it wasn't something she wanted to think about too much at this early stage—she would probably describe him as *solid*, and there wasn't anything wrong with that. He had seemed almost more reluctant to talk about his band, if anything, and that made Gemma go straight on YouTube on her phone and look to see if, amongst the videos of cats doing silly things, there was any trace of The Leisure Decree.

It didn't take much hunting. Entering the band name into the search bar threw up a good selection of results. It seemed that, contrary to what Frank might have thought, there was still a bit of a following for his band, even if, closer inspection revealed, that there were only a few actual clips of the band in action. Gemma selected one; apparently, the official video for You'll Be Mine, and hit play. She waited until she was allowed to skip the adverts and settled back to watch the video. It started with a close up on the drummer, who looked to be about twelve, beating out an introductory riff, and then, as the rest of the band kicked in, the camera pulled out to show that the band were performing in a field, complete with a rather nonplussed-looking cow. Gemma was a bit confused at first. The guy singing the song had bleached blond hair and an unconvincing beard, but it definitely wasn't Frank. Then she spotted him. He wasn't, as she had imagined, the frontman of the band at all. He stood towards the back, nearer the drummer than the singer, his head down, concentrating on his guitar (his *bass* guitar, which was a bit of a surprise) rather than the camera. His fringe was considerably longer than it was now, and with his head bowed, hung over his face like a curtain, but it was unmistakably him. There was something about the set of his jaw and the overly serious line of his mouth that Gemma would recognise anywhere. It was also apparent from the way he hid at the back and wouldn't look at the camera that he would rather have been anywhere but there. In return, the camera paid him considerably less attention than the other members of the band, especially the lead singer, who was at least attempting to give some kind of a performance. It was no real surprise that Frank had decided that the life of a rock star wasn't for him. Instead of watching the visuals, Gemma restarted the video, turned up the volume and listened to the song. It was catchy, the lyrics managed to avoid too many obvious clichés, and she knew that she would probably wake up with the tune lodged in her head the next morning and would have difficulty shaking it off. She listened carefully, trying to pick out the bass line, all too aware that it was the bit nobody noticed in a song, and was pleasantly surprised to find that it was actually very good. Frank was obviously a skilled musician, and his bass line, rather than simply providing a rhythm, had a melody all of its own. She made a mental note to listen to any other tracks she could find, but tomorrow. Right now, her bed was calling her. She took one last look out of the window at the night sky and its patchwork of stars. You could wish on stars all you like, she thought, but stars are gone by the morning, and very often, so are your wishes.

32

When Kate's alarm went off the next morning, she did something she very rarely did; she reached out and slapped the snooze button. Normally, she turned the alarm off and got straight up, no matter how tired she was or how little sleep she'd had, because if she didn't, she knew she would sleep in and incur the wrath of Dour Dairy Dave. This morning, however, there were two reasons why she hit snooze. The first was the nagging headache she always got from drinking red wine, which she could usually deal with by downing a couple of paracetamol with a pint of water and then getting on with her day. She didn't often drink red wine on a weeknight, but that seemed to be all that was floating around at the party last night, and it was better that than nothing. In any case, when she had decanted Ruth Prior through the front door of her house, she had been left holding more than half a bottle of a very drinkable Cabernet Sauvignon, and what was she supposed to do with it? Since Frank had started helping her, she was used to waking up with so much less pain from her back, that a headache was a real annoyance and needed dealing with.

The second, and much more compelling reason to put the alarm clock on snooze was lying next to her in the bed, propped up on one elbow, watching her and smiling.

'You stayed,' Kate said.

'Well, of course I did,' Briony replied. 'Couldn't run out on my beautiful girl, could I?'

'Is that what I am?'

'My girl? I know we haven't talked about it, but I hope so, yes.'

'No, I meant beautiful.'

'Have you even looked at yourself? Come on, babe. You've

got mirrors, haven't you?'

'Yes, but I don't bother with them much. I don't always like what I see.'

Bri frowned briefly, then smiled again and reached out a hand and stroked Kate's cheek.

'Then let me be your mirror. If you could see what I see, then you'd know you're beautiful.'

'You're bloody soppy, you are,' Kate said and rested her face against Bri's palm.

'Don't you dare ever tell anyone. It would ruin my reputation.'

Briony pulled back the duvet and slid out of the bed.

'And before you fish for any more compliments, I need to use your shower and get moving. 'There are going to be people gagging for my buns.'

'I can see why.'

Briony struck a pose, laughed and then headed into the bathroom. Kate watched her go and pulled the duvet up to her neck. Bri seemed so at ease with herself, and Kate wondered if she could be that self-confident. Alison had been very self-critical but did it in a way that always felt like it was being extended to Kate too. She never said she wanted to cut back or diet. It was always, 'We need to lose a few pounds,' and Kate could never work out whether it was because she wanted company or if it was a criticism. Kate knew there wasn't anything badly wrong with her body, but when she saw some of the young girls parading around on the beach, she knew she would never look like that again. The years were starting to tell on her waistline, and she felt frumpy and middle-aged in comparison. She wasn't exactly sure when middle age officially began these days, but she was pretty sure she wasn't there yet. Maybe the mirror of Briony's eyes could help her turn back a few years. *My beautiful girl*, Bri had said, and Kate knew a line had been crossed, a line between the past and what could be a very nice present indeed, and maybe even a future. She was beginning to daydream when the alarm clock went off again. This time, she switched it off altogether. As she did so, she was aware that the water had stopped running in the bathroom and that Briony was calling to her.

'You okay, Bri?' she called back.

'Yeah, fine, I just said, any towels?'

'Any one that's dryish. I don't have a guest towel as such. I don't really have guests.'

'You do now,' Bri replied, coming back into the bedroom with one towel wrapped around her and rubbing her hair with another. 'And you need to do a wash. I don't demand Egyptian cotton, but not damp would be good.'

'I'll buy some new ones. Just for you.'

'Do that. I don't mind what colour.' Briony discarded the towel with which she had been rubbing her hair. 'That'll have to do,' she said and started to gather up her clothes from the floor where they had been strewn the night before. 'So, have you had any ideas yet?'

'Ideas?' Kate raised an eyebrow.

'Get your mind out of the gutter. Not that sort of idea. Don't you remember? That long conversation you had with Ruth Thingy about the school roof?'

Kate buried her head in her hands. 'Oh, God. Yes, I had forgotten that. I was distracted by other things. I suggested a fundraiser, didn't I?'

'Nope. You offered to organise a fundraiser. Have you seen my bra?'

'It's on the dressing table.'

'How did it get there? Oh, I remember. You were pretty definite about it. 'No problem, Ruth,' you said. 'I'll sort it for you. I *love* things like that'. You made it sound like you couldn't wait to get cracking.'

'Oh God. I did. What am I going to do?'

'Well, there are two possibilities. One is that Ruth was so pissed that she won't remember, but seeing as the school roof was all she could talk about, I don't see that happening.'

'What's the other?'

'That you start thinking about what kind of fundraiser you're going to organise. It's not a bad idea, actually. Makes you come over as public-spirited, and that can only be good publicity. How do I look? Do you think people will be able to tell that the bread lady has spent the night in a den of sin with her new girlfriend?'

***

Kate managed to put off thinking about Ruth Prior and her roof for several hours. By the time Briony had left and she had got herself ready, she was already running late. She practically ran down the lane, nearly colliding with Huw, who was standing in the middle of the lane. Huw was calling impotently for Gwyl, who, wherever he was and whatever he was doing, was taking no notice whatsoever. She got to the café in time to intercept Dave in the two-minute window between his getting out of his van and giving up and getting back into it again. She made sure he was definitely unloading the milk before hurrying down the steps to the café, where Frank was already waiting. He looked remarkably fresh, considering that he and Gemma had still been at the beach when she and Briony had helped Ruth lurch home. It crossed her mind to wonder if Frank had perhaps stayed at Gemma's, seeing as they did seem to be getting on rather better than they had been, but she was fairly sure Frank was wearing a different shirt yesterday.

'Sorry I'm a bit late,' she said as she unlocked the door.

'It's no problem,' Frank replied. 'I have to get that bus. I think the one after that is a week next Sunday or something. But listen, if you ever want a lie-in, I could open up for you. I'm pretty sure I know what you do. You could always leave me a list.'

'Thanks, Frank. I'll get you a key cut.' As the words left Kate's mouth, she felt surprised and pleased with herself at the same time. If you'd asked her even twenty-four hours earlier if she would consider someone else opening the café, you'd have been met with a flat refusal, but the memory of how hard it was to drag herself out of the Briony-warmed bed that morning had made her accept straight away. This week was turning out to be full of plot twists and it was still only Friday. She left Frank to deal with Dave and the milk and made some coffees, which had now become their morning habit. It was funny how you fell into routines. Kate had run the café by herself for so long but now rather liked having Frank about the place. She hoped that she could continue making enough money to ask him to stay on at the end of the summer. It would be awful now to let him go.

She had just handed Frank his coffee when she spotted Gemma through the window. She had obviously been out beachcombing early, and Kate marvelled at how someone could look so windswept and so good at the same time. But then she checked herself and remembered that Briony thought *she* was beautiful and hoped she didn't blush. Instead of going to her workshop, Gemma hurried straight into the café, which was unusual.

'Morning, Gemma,' Kate said. 'Usual?'

'No, I'll have it later if that's okay. Sorry. Morning. It's actually Frank I wanted.'

'Won't be minute!' came Frank's voice from somewhere behind the open fridge door.

'Enjoy yourself last night?' Kate asked.

'Yes, I did,' Gemma replied, and a look crossed her face that Kate found hard to identify. Not quite a smile, but... *something*. 'Did I hear you offer to organise a fundraiser for the school? That's so good of you.'

'Oh God, it really happened, didn't it? Shit.'

'I'm sure you'll come up with something brilliant. Let me know if I can help. Hey, maybe you should have a word with Frank. He's a genuine rock star.'

'A rock star? Frank, you never said.'

'Look up the Leisure Decree. He's not bad. He played for us on the beach last night.'

'He's also a retired rock star,' Frank said, emerging from the fridge. 'And wasn't much of one to begin with. So do *not* look up the Leisure Decree. It was a very long time ago, and no one knew about us then. Now, what can I do for you, Gemma? Though I'm not sure I should do anything after that.'

'Can you come to the workshop at lunchtime? There's something I want to show you.'

Well well well, thought Kate. *She wants to show him something. Looks like there's something in the air.*

33

Like Kate, Frank had also wondered what Gemma's motives were for summoning him to the workshop. The previous night had felt like unfinished business somehow, and he had hoped he might run into her today and perhaps talk more. He had been waiting for the bus for a good half hour. He had started to wonder if the night bus actually existed, whatever the ancient timetable on the bus stop said, so he had that time and the time the bus took to navigate its way through pitch-dark lanes to think about the events of the evening. By the time he got off the bus, he had concluded that he had no idea what to think about it. He liked Gemma. That was a fact and one he couldn't deny. He found her attractive, too. But then who wouldn't? Where he was conflicted was over whether he had enjoyed the evening or not. The conversation had been relaxed and easy, almost too easy, and that was where he had the problem. Because Gemma had been so easy to talk to, he had let his tongue run away with him and said too much. He knew from bitter experience that as soon as you start giving too much away, you become vulnerable, and the more you tell people, the more ammunition you give them to hurt you. He had vowed not to let anyone in anymore because once you let them in, they see all the reasons to want to get out again. He thought he and Gemma might be becoming friends, possibly (hopefully?) even good friends and wasn't quite ready to put her off. And yet there he was, telling her things he should have kept to himself, even playing the guitar and singing in front of her for Christ's sake. Now she wanted to see him, and in the privacy of her workshop, rather than in public in the café, and that probably meant that there would be a conversation that sounded like 'It's not you, it's me', but really meaning 'It's you'.

When it came close to his lunchtime, he tried to find things to do, essential stuff like rearranging the condiments and tidying up the pot of wooden coffee stirrers, but it didn't fool Kate.

'Go on your break, Frank,' she said with what could only be described as a smirk. 'Don't you want to see what Gemma's got to show you?'

He couldn't think of a reason that would be convincing enough, so hung up his apron and left the café. Once outside, he was torn between seeing Gemma and getting it over with or running away up to his usual haunt on the cliffs and hoping nobody noticed. In the end, he decided to be a grown-up and go to the workshop. If it were quick enough, he would have time to retreat to the cliffs for a bit afterwards before he was due back. It came as something of a surprise, then, that Gemma really did want to show him something, and it was something that had her looking even more flustered now than she had been earlier.

'What do you make of this?' she said by way of a greeting, indicating the object that sat on her workbench. Frank was slightly lost for words. He wasn't sure whether it was a trick question or not.

'It's a paperweight, isn't it?' he replied.

A paperweight was certainly what it appeared to be. It was a sphere, at a guess around six inches in diameter, made of glass that could have been blue, green or turquoise, depending on how the light hit it. It was quite attractive, if you liked that kind of thing, but, as far as he could make out, no real cause for such urgency.

'I don't know what it is,' Gemma replied. 'I thought it was a paperweight too, but now I don't quite know what to make of it. Seriously, you're not going to believe this.'

'Go on,' Frank said. 'Tell me.'

So she did. She told him how she had got up early, despite the late night and gone out for a walk to clear her head before starting the day. She had, as usual, taken her satchel with her, on the off-chance, but hadn't been looking for anything in particular. The tide had been a long way out, so she had ventured around the headland to the next bay and had nearly reached the other end of the beach when she saw it. It was half buried in the sand, but when she pulled it out, she was surprised to find that it was intact. She had a sudden weird feeling that reminded her so much of her father telling her to leave things as she had found them, but put it in her satchel anyway and came back to the workshop to have a proper look at it. That was when she started to notice peculiar things.

'I should have known,' she said, interrupting herself. 'Because of the way I found it.'

'How do you mean?' Frank asked. 'Someone must have dropped it or something.'

'Do you take a paperweight to the beach, Frank? I know it's not something I usually do.'

'Well, no, but...'

'I took a photo of it before I picked it up. Look at this.'

She scrolled through the gallery on her phone until she found the one she wanted and held it up for Frank to see. He couldn't quite get what she was talking about; it was a picture of a glass thing stuck in the sand, as she said it had been, but then he saw where she was pointing and understood. The sphere was at the end of a furrow in the sand. It was hard to judge from the angle of the picture, but the furrow could have been several feet long.

'Looks like it rolled,' Frank said. 'It *is* round.'

'It didn't roll,' Gemma said. 'If you rolled that along the sand like a big marble or something, it might leave a line, but not as deep as that.'

'Then what?'

'I don't know. But that's not the strangest thing. This is where it gets totally bloody weird. What colour would you say it is?'

'I don't know. Blue? Turquoise? Depends on how the sun catches it.'

'That's the point. Look properly. There is no sun on my bench. I don't get it 'til much later.'

Frank looked at the bench and then the floor and saw that she was absolutely correct. The morning sun was only just coming through the window and illuminating a patch of floor near the door.

'It shouldn't change colour like that. There's no reason. It doesn't make sense. Now pick it up.'

'Why? I don't...'

'Just do it, Frank.'

Frank picked the sphere up, expecting it to be heavy, but it wasn't. It was light as a feather, which didn't seem possible, and there was something else.

'It's warm,' he said, putting it rapidly back down again.

'I know. It shouldn't be.'

'Well, I guess if it was buried in sand...'

'The sand wasn't warm at that time of the morning. If anything, it was damp. But anyway, it's been in here since then, so it should have cooled down. And if that wasn't enough to freak me out, there's another thing.'

'Another? Don't tell me it speaks as well,' Frank laughed.

'Do you think I'd still be in here if it did? No, the thing is, this isn't the first one of these I've found.'

Gemma went over to the corner of the workshop by the sink and picked up something that was covered in a tea towel. She brought the towel to the workbench and opened it up. Inside was another similar sphere, or rather what was left of one. One half was relatively intact, but the rest was in bits.

'This is what I wanted you to see. I found it ages ago, in roughly the same place. I tried to repair it but couldn't, so I stuck it in the corner and forgot about it until today.'

'Pity it's broken. You could have sold them as bookends or something.'

'That's the thing, though, Frank. Yes, it's broken, but it was a lot worse than this last time I saw it. All of it was in pieces, not just half.'

Frank stared at the glass, then at Gemma.

'No, sorry,' he said. 'My brain can't take that in. What are you saying? That it's repaired itself? That can't happen. It's impossible.'

'Yes, impossible, like the colour thing it does, or like how it's warm when it shouldn't be. There isn't much about this thing that makes sense.'

'Then what do you suggest? What do you think it is?'

'There's only one thing I *can* suggest, and it's one of those thoughts you get and then wish you hadn't. Remember that shooting star last night? What if...what if, well, something came down?'

'Woah! Wait. So this is a paperweight from *space*? Come on, Gemma. I know it's a bit odd, but seriously? Is that why there are two of them? Is it a tiny little invasion?'

'I don't know!' Gemma waved a hand to gesture at the spheres. 'Shit!' As she waved, her hand caught the intact sphere and it rolled to the edge of the bench. She made a grab for it, but it rolled off the bench towards the floor where it.... slowed, then landed gently on the ground.

'What the bloody hell did I just see?' Frank gasped. 'Did you see that?'

'Yes,' Gemma replied, and Frank couldn't help but notice that the colour had drained from her face. 'I saw.'

'Okay,' Frank said. 'Paperweights from space. *Now* what?'

34

Kate was still smiling at Frank's apparent reluctance to go on his lunch and see Gemma, when customers started to trickle in. She was half tempted to text Gemma and ask her to put Frank down and send him back but stopped herself. She'd managed before Frank turned up, and so far, there was only a couple of tourists wanting coffee and cake, and Geraint, who was in his usual seat by the window sipping his first flat white. Kate served the couple with their lattes and lemon drizzles while Geraint's teacake was toasting. Nothing she couldn't handle. If it got much busier, she might consider giving Frank a call, but for now, she'd leave them to it. Let them have their fun.

She was buttering the teacake when the door flung open and Ruth Prior came in, looking like death. Kate gave Geraint his teacake and his second flat white and immediately started making a strong coffee for Ruth.

'How are you feeling, Ruth?' she asked.

'Can't you tell?' Ruth replied, flinging herself down on a chair. 'Oh, God. I'm never drinking again.'

'Yes, you are.'

'Probably. But not *that* much. Jesus, how much did I have?'

'Hard to tell, babe. You were half gone when you got there.'

'I was, wasn't I? I think I had most of a bottle before I left the house. Bloody Moody Mike Tremaine. It's all his fault. I only wanted a nice night out, but he had to phone yesterday afternoon, didn't he? Do us a lemon drizzle, will you, Kate? I don't really feel like it, but I've got to get something down me. Did you have a good night?'

'It was a very nice night,' Kate said.

'Ooh! Very coy. You seemed very cosy with the nice Bread

Lady, I have to say.'

'My *girlfriend*, the Bread Lady, you mean?'

Ruth squealed, then grimaced and held her head.

'Remind me not to do that. Seriously though, Kate, I'm made up for you. She's lovely, and you can tell she thinks the world of you.'

'Really? Can you?'

'Of course you can. She never took her eyes off you, you lucky thing. It suits you, as well. Phil's away so often, I'm thinking of giving it a try myself.'

'Sorry, I'm spoken for.'

'I didn't mean you, you muppet. Not that you're not gorgeous...I'm going to stop now and eat my cake before I dig any deeper.'

Kate smiled and watched Ruth ravenously attack her cake. Behind the smile, her mind was racing. *Don't ask about the fundraiser. Don't ask about the fundraiser...*

'So, about the fundraiser,' Ruth said. 'That was very kind of you, offering to organise it like that. Have you had any ideas yet?'

'Not as yet,' Kate replied, trying hard not to admit that the only ideas she was interested in were for good ways of getting out of it. 'Nothing concrete. We only thought of it last night, Ruth, and I've slept since then.'

'Or not.'

'Stop it.'

'Sorry. And I'm sorry to be pushy. I'm only panicking. I'm supposed to get it sorted before Christmas or the school won't be opening in January. I'm worried that if I don't get it sorted sooner rather than later, the weather might turn and then I'll never get roofers out. I need to know I'm going to be able to do it as soon as possible, or I might as well give up.'

'I know, Ruth. Honestly, I'll get cracking and do what I can. Maybe we could do, I don't know, a concert or something. See if we can get some musicians to play. I don't know. Only an idea.'

As she said that, Frank walked in through the café door.

'Speaking of which...' Kate said.

'Sorry,' Frank said. 'Am I late?'

'No. You're early, if anything.'

'Oh, okay.'

Frank went to the back of the café, put his apron on, which he seemed to have some difficulty tying, and started wiping surfaces down that didn't actually need wiping.

'What's up with him?' Ruth whispered.

'Come outside a second,' Kate said, her voice slightly louder than necessary. 'I'll show you that thing we were talking about. Frank,' she called, 'I'm going outside with Ruth for a second.'

Frank waved vaguely, and Kate ushered Ruth outside.

'What's all that about?' Ruth demanded.

'I didn't want him to hear in case he thought I was gossiping about him.'

'Aren't you?'

'Well, yes. But not only about him.' She glanced next door to the workshop, but there didn't seem to be any sign of life. Ruth followed her line of sight and her jaw dropped visibly.

'What? You mean Frank and...?'

'I'm saying nothing.'

'Are you sure?'

'Well, put it this way, he was here before me this morning and Gemma asked him to come to her workshop, 'to look at something'. And you've seen the state he's come back in. He looks stunned.'

'Bloody hell, Kate. What are you putting in that coffee?'

'I know! Maybe it's because the sun's shining. Always puts people in a good mood. Anyway, I'd better get back in. He's so distracted, he could burn the place down.'

'I'll grab my things. I need to get back and sit in the school while it crumbles around me.'

'We'll get it sorted,' Kate said, opening the door and holding it for Ruth. 'Leave it with me. I'll have a think while Love's Young Dream does all the work. Although he might be able to help. Something Gemma said.... Frank?'

Frank, who was holding a metal milk jug that Kate was sure she had only just washed, looked around, startled. His mind was definitely elsewhere.

'Frank, you know how Gemma was saying before about you being a musician? We're organising a fundraiser for the school roof, and we were thinking of putting on a concert of some kind. Do you fancy playing a few songs? It would be a real draw to have a name there.'

'What?' Frank asked. 'Sure. Whatever.' He went back to polishing the chrome off the jug.

'There you go, Ruth. We're up and running. Check Frank's band out. Gemma said they were called The Leisure Decree. Hey, maybe he could get the band back together.'

There was a resounding *clang* as Frank dropped the jug. It bounced off the counter and onto the floor.

'Wait!' he said. 'Hang on. *What* did you just say?'

35

Later, Frank would look back on that day as when his life started to get strange and run out of control. Control was, and always had been, a huge part of his life. He controlled his weight by being completely conscious of how much food he ingested. He controlled his feelings by strictly monitoring how close he allowed people to get to him and what he allowed them to see of him. He had resisted the excesses in which his fellow musicians indulged because he knew that if he lost control, whether it was through drink or drugs, then anything could happen. If things went really bad, he could end up like his father.

Jack Davies wasn't really a bad man. He was, Frank supposed, very much a product of his time and his upbringing. He was what would probably be called 'A Man's Man', very much of the opinion that he worked long hours on the Docks to put food on the table and clothes on Frank's back. In return, he thought it only reasonable to expect a clean house, a hot meal when he came home, and the right to go to the pub whenever he fancied, to stay as long as he wanted, and to drink as much as wanted to. He didn't expect to be bothered in his own home by his wife and child or to be questioned about where he had been. When that happened, he had to take control of the situation, which he did by silence. He never raised a hand to Frank, or Kathleen, his mother; he rarely even raised his voice but went silent and ignored them. The silence was, Frank always thought, worse than any shouting. The silence of bitter disappointment always left Frank feeling like he had done something wrong, something bad, but didn't always know quite what.

Frank had, unfortunately, inherited neither his father's temperament nor his build. Where Jack was lean and muscular, Frank had a tendency to chubbiness. Where Jack was loud and everyone's mate (when he was in a good mood), Frank was quiet and introverted, preferring to read a book or listen to music rather than watch the football, or worse, play it. In Jack's monochrome view, everything was connected and, as a result, meant that his son was often a let down. If Frank got off his arse, got his head out of that book and moved a bit more, he wouldn't be so fat, the other kids wouldn't laugh at him and he could play footie with them. Frank, on the other hand, knew that the truth was rather different. He was fat because his mother liked to provide food. But because he was fat, he was never invited to play football with the other kids, whether he wanted to or not. He had tried sometimes, but he was last to be picked so often he began to think his name was You Can Have Frank. After that, he stopped bothering. He would rather read anyway, but music was his real love, and he inherited that from his mother, who liked to have music on while she cleaned or cooked. Despite the bizarre fashions and haircuts that populated the music scene of the 1980s, Frank preferred the music his mum played, most of which was from the 60s, or if she was in a good mood, glam rock anthems from the 70s. Where the other kids at school wanted to play for Liverpool or Everton, Frank wanted to be in the Beatles, or possibly T-Rex.

When he was fourteen, his mum bought him a second-hand guitar with money she had somehow saved from her housekeeping allowance. She also found in a charity shop a battered copy of the Beatles' Complete songbook that showed all the chord shapes you needed to play the songs. In a stroke, she changed Frank's life. As soon as he got home from school and had eaten his tea, he went to his room and practised. He fumbled with the chords at first but gradually got better. He practised until it felt like his fingers would start bleeding or until his father got home. On one occasion, he had made the mistake of being too absorbed in the song he was working on at the time (Get Back, as it happened) to hear Jack come home. His father had explained patiently that no son of his was going to be a musician because he'd either end up taking drugs or gay (Jack wasn't clear which was worse) and that if he ever heard that fucking awful noise in the house again, he'd take the guitar out the back and burn it. Then he had lapsed into one of his disappointed silences, which lasted days. Frank continued to practice, but his father never heard him play again. Once he finally left school, got a job and started playing a few gigs in a local bar, Jack's silence became permanent. He spent more time at the pub (though not ones with any live music) and less time at home. When he *was* at home, he was usually so drunk that he could barely stand. It was that sight that made Frank determined never to have so little control of himself. After Jack's death, when Frank was nineteen (a heart attack on his way from work to the pub) and once he had extricated himself from his mum's cooking, he became much more conscious of his own health and made a concerted effort to get the weight off and keep it off.

Since then, even during the Leisure Decree years and after, Frank had kept that control, and there were times when he was proud of himself for doing so, though more usually, he hated it. He'd had relationships, but they tended not to last very long. Melissa was probably the longest, and she only stuck around for about eighteen months before she became frustrated with how little Frank let her in. 'All this time,' she said to him once, not long before she left, 'and I've still got no idea who you are.' By and large, it suited him better to be on his own because that way, at least, he'd only get on his own nerves. He had only seriously lost control once, but that was bad enough to make him want to forget the life he'd led, flee to Ireland and begin again. Unfortunately, whatever was guiding his life had a very warped sense of humour, and he was now stuck on Anglesey, getting dangerously close to another person, and things were getting out of hand. By the time he got back to the B&B the previous night, the beer he had drunk, even though it was non-alcoholic and he'd only had two bottles, was weighing heavily on his stomach. After the less than smooth bus ride, he knew he would be able to feel it creeping up his throat when he lay down. It was better to get rid of it. Luckily, he was well practised in doing these things quietly and did what he had to do without disturbing Mrs. Evans. He doubted very much that she would understand.

If things hadn't been confusing enough last night, things had got much worse today. He had apparently agreed to perform again for the first time in years and all because those bloody spheres of Gemma's distracted him. Shortly after one of the damn things had failed to smash itself on the floor, Frank had used the excuse of being needed back at *Kate's* to get away. If the spheres really *had* fallen from the sky, he wanted nothing to do with it. There was only a certain amount of weirdness he could cope with, and that amount was very small. Extraterrestrial table ornaments, and he was not yet convinced that's what they were at all, was a much larger amount of weird than he ever wanted in his life. He felt bad about leaving Gemma there with them but had promised to come back later. If thinking about them had landed him with a very unwanted gig, then he might be inclined to come back with a sledgehammer. *Repair yourself now, you little glass shit.* For the time being, he was stuck in the café. Ruth had gone back to school, and Kate was going on and on about the fundraiser.

'It's a pity about the band,' she said for what felt like the forty-seventh time. 'Mind you, Lennon and McCartney fell out, too, didn't they? And Simon Garfunkel and Whatsisname.'

'Me and Sean were hardly Lennon and McCartney,' Frank replied, not correcting her. 'We only wrote two albums together and you've probably sold more coffees than we sold copies of them. If you want someone to sell tickets, it was never us.'

'I don't suppose...this is going to sound cheeky. I don't suppose you know anyone else.'

'Kate, I'd love to be able to tell you I've got Elton John and Tom Jones on speed dial, but I didn't back then, and I certainly haven't now. Those days are a long way behind me. I'm only a guy who makes coffee.'

Frank was so startled by his mobile ringing, right on cue, that he didn't check the caller display when he answered. He might not have bothered if he had, and things could have turned out quite differently.

'Hello?'

'I'm calling about your internet speed,' a voice said.

'I haven't got the internet....' Frank began, his thumb poised to hang up.

'How do you watch porn then?' the voice said. 'It's me, you daft bastard.'

'Mick?'

'Where the hell are you, Frank? I was expecting you.'

'That was weeks ago! And I rang you?'

'Did you? Yeah, well, you know what it's like. Nina came back and, well, you know. So where are you? On the ol' Emerald Isle?' Mick's attempt at an Irish accent was woeful.

'No, I'm still on Anglesey. Chapel Bay?'

'Jesus, that's only up the road. What are you doing there?'

'Long story,' Frank said, and then a thought occurred to him. 'Listen, Mick, long shot, I know, but I don't suppose the Riflemen fancy a gig?'

'Where and when, mate? You know me. I'd play at the opening of an envelope these days. Any cash in it?'

'No, it's a charity thing. School needs a new roof.'

'Charity's good. Great publicity. Sure. Tell us the date, and I'll round the boys up. Have you got a PA?'

'I doubt it.'

'We can sort that. What about you? You playing?'

'I was going to. But I won't need to now.'

'No, mate. You don't get out of it like that. I'll play if you do.'

'Okay, okay. I'll do a short set.'

'Good lad. Listen, got to go. Nina's calling me. Glad you're alive, mate. Let us know the date.'

'Will do, Mick. And thanks.' He hung up and turned to Kate. 'There you go. That's your headliner. Mick Rogers and the Riflemen.'

He was about to put his phone back in his pocket, thinking *shit, I haven't even got a guitar* when he spotted the icon for a new text. Gemma. With a strange sense of unease, he opened the message.

```
Can you come round after your shift,
please? They're singing to each other
            and it's beautiful
                    x
```

36

The time could not pass quickly enough for Gemma. It had been over an hour since she had texted Frank, and while she had hoped that he would drop everything, make an excuse to Kate and come round, it was looking increasingly likely that she was going to have to wait until the end of his shift. It meant that although she didn't want to stay inside the workshop with that sound, she also couldn't go up to her flat or down to the beach in case Frank did come around, found she wasn't there and left again. She wanted someone to see what she had seen, hear what she had heard, and she wanted that someone to be Frank. As a compromise, she took her deckchair outside and closed the workshop door behind her. Then she sat and waited. She needed to think, and there was no way she was going to be able to do it inside.

At the point when Frank had fled back to *Kate's* (*as if his arse was on fire,* she thought wryly), things had been bizarre enough. She could maybe accept the fact that these two strange glass spheres might have fallen out of the sky. Things did, she knew that; she'd been to museums. When she was growing up, there was a large boulder in one of the local parks and for many years, she had believed the stories that it was a small meteorite that had come crashing to Earth at some point in history (though it was never clear exactly when). She was in her twenties when she learned the disappointing fact that it wasn't extraterrestrial in origin at all but was, in fact, a big lump of rock, probably granite that had been deposited in the park for no apparent reason. She had loved the story and in all her years of scouring beaches for unusual things, she had longed to unearth something truly unique. But most of the things that fell from space were lumps of rock, and only an expert would know where they had really come from. They certainly weren't perfectly formed spheres of glass that behaved like nothing else she had ever seen.

The way the complete sphere had slowed itself down to lessen the impact when it rolled off the bench had been weird but could have been a fluke or an optical illusion, but after Frank had left, Gemma tried it again three times, each with the same result. The sphere defied the rules of gravity as Gemma understood them and landed gently as a feather. At first, it baffled her that, if they could preserve themselves like this, the first one she had found had been broken. But she reasoned that perhaps the velocity with which it fell from the sky was too great, and these weird powers were enough to stop it being pulverised as it should have been, but not enough to stop it breaking if it hit a rock. The second one had landed in the sand, creating the trench she had seen but not causing any damage. Then there was the self-repairing thing. The damaged sphere had resisted any attempts Gemma had made to fix it, but once its mate had arrived, it had started to repair itself. She had left the broken sphere and all its pieces on the workbench next to the whole one to see what would happen. This presented another mystery. She could see that the sphere was becoming complete and that the pile of fragments was diminishing, but she couldn't see it happening. It seemed likely that the proximity of the complete sphere was helping somehow, but she could not work out how. Then she gave herself a talking to for trying to explain something that was working to rules and patterns that might not have been devised on Earth and would have probably bewildered the best scientists in this field. They were alien and had alien ways.

Gemma was quite surprised by how calmly she was taking the whole situation. She didn't have a problem believing in the existence of life on other worlds; in fact, it was the idea that humans were alone in the Universe that made no sense to her. Out here in the countryside, with less light and air pollution, she was often treated to clear nights and skies blanketed with stars. If only some of those stars had planets orbiting them, that was still millions of planets, and the thought that humans existed through some massive cosmic coincidence seemed statistically daft. Her own pet theory was that if aliens had the technological capability to travel this far, then in all likelihood, what they would see was a species so primitive it was hardly worth their notice. All the same, she had seen enough science fiction films to be aware that celluloid aliens only came to Earth for one of several reasons; to study mankind, to improve mankind, or to conquer mankind. She had also heard all the rumours about exactly how aliens were alleged to study humans, and she had no particular desire to have a probe up *there,* thank you very much. She had absolutely no idea if these spheres were sentient or even alive in any real sense, but the thought that they were so far from home made her feel sad in a way she could understand only too well. She had also left her home and friends and ended up somewhere nobody knew her, with no way of ever going back.

With her thoughts, a wave of loneliness washed over her, and a tear escaped and rolled down her cheek. She didn't try to stop it, and it landed on the workbench. As it did so, there was a barely perceptible *tink,* and the sphere that had been broken was suddenly complete. That was when the singing began. She wasn't sure what it was or where it was coming from at first; it was just there, in the air and in her head. But when she saw that the spheres were pulsing with a faint blue light, she realised that the sound was coming from them. It was a sound unlike anything she had heard before, an eerie, gentle sound, not exactly music, but music was about the only thing she could equate it to, in much the same way as whales' songs weren't exactly songs, but that was a word that described them best. One sphere would make a pattern of sounds, not a melody as Gemma would normally understand it, but something like that. There would then be a tiny pause, and the other would repeat the same pattern, each pulsing in turn in time to the sounds. There seemed little doubt that they were communicating with each other somehow, though what they were saying was purely their business. All Gemma knew was that it was probably the most heartbreakingly beautiful thing she had ever heard, and she didn't want to be hearing it on her own. She wanted Frank there with her to hear it and wanted to weep because he wasn't. That was when she sent him the text. She sat staring at her phone for ten minutes or so, all the time unable to escape that sound, which was ringing in her ears and filling her head, but he didn't text back, and she hated him for it. She spent the next fifteen minutes pacing backwards and forwards across the workshop, rehearsing all the things she was going to say to him when he finally showed up, veering wildly between wanting to slap him for leaving her alone and simply wanting him to be there, to hear what she was hearing and feeling what she was feeling. Most of all, she wanted the spheres to shut up for a minute so that she could think. She hunted around and found an empty cardboard box, which she turned upside down and placed over the spheres. It dulled the sound for a moment and allowed her to gather her thoughts. She wasn't sure what had happened, but she did know it was most unlike her.

Gemma had never been one to wear her heart on her sleeve. She felt things, felt them deeply, but rarely allowed anyone to see them. It was a lesson she had learned at an early age from her mother. Where her father was a quiet, calm man, her mother tended to express exactly what she was feeling pretty much the moment she felt it. If she was angry or upset, you knew it straight away. She was very capable of saying hurtful things in anger and then apologising profusely when she had calmed down. She didn't seem to realise that some things, once said, can't be unsaid and 'I didn't mean it' didn't always carry any weight. 'If you didn't mean it,' Gemma said to her on more than one occasion, once she had reached an age to stand up for herself, 'why did you say it?' Gemma had her father's temperament, outwardly calm, preferring to give things some thought before she spoke, and most of the time not speaking at all. It made some of the other girls at school think she was stuck up and certainly made the boys think she was cold. Anyone she allowed to get close would have found that she could be every bit as warm and loving as anyone else, but most people didn't bother to try. She'd had boyfriends (she didn't know what the average number of partners you were supposed to have had by her age was but suspected she was there or thereabouts). One or two had lasted long enough for her to believe that she was in love, but she had carried her broken heart stoically and privately when it ended, and they would never know. The only time she had felt that her emotions were running away from her was the last time, with that scumbag boyfriend. That had led to her doing the most impulsive things she had ever done, the things she had run from in the middle of the night and still had her looking over her shoulder even now. But even then, when she was hastily packing a bag and preparing to flee, she had known what she was doing. She had never felt like she felt right now and didn't like it. The only thing that made any sense was that it was something to do with that noise the spheres were making even through the cardboard and she had to get out. That was why she had grabbed her phone and was now sitting on a deckchair outside her workshop, wishing that the sun would hurry up and come around this way, so she wouldn't have to risk going back in for her coat. She sat and stared out to sea and tried to work out what was going on.

She felt calmer now. The sound of the waves whispering onto the shore always calmed her down, but she also had the distinct impression that it was being away from that strange sound that was coming from her peculiar houseguests. The most bizarre and probably scariest thing about it was that she had started the day rather conflicted about her feelings towards Frank. There was something there that much was certain. She had felt more at ease with him at the party last night than she had with anyone else for a long time. He was good company, seemed to be kind, was certainly attractive, but at the same time, it was obvious that he was keeping something hidden. There were hints—odd stuff he said about his weight and how reluctant he was to show what a good musician he was—but Gemma knew only too well that you didn't reach their age and not have some secrets. That he had revealed anything at all felt special and left her convinced that he had told her things he wouldn't tell anyone else, like Kate, for example. But at the same time, the way he kept clamming up every time it looked like they were getting somewhere worried her. It was very similar to how she behaved herself and knew only too well where that could lead. And now he was probably hiding in the café, thinking she was all kinds of lunatic. She had been watching *Kate's*, and it was obvious that they weren't very busy. If he wanted to, he could certainly have got away. Her text must have put him off. *Yeah,* she thought, *singing bloody paperweights from another planet. How do you think that sounds?*

But then there he was, emerging from the café, looking, what? Embarrassed? Hesitant? He paused outside the door, then saw her sitting there and walked across the pathway towards her.

'I got away,' he said.

'I see that,' she replied.

'I told Kate I needed to come and see you. She didn't seem to mind. Practically shoved me out of the door for some reason. So. Singing.'

'Yes, singing.'

'Show me.'

She led him to the workshop door, but with her hand on the handle, turned to him.

'Be careful,' she said. 'I don't know what the sound does. I think it had a weird effect on me.'

'Weird? In what way?'

'Best showing you. Be careful, that's all.'

She opened the door and went in. It was all exactly as she had left it, quiet and still apart from that sound coming from the cardboard box.

'Are they under there?' Frank asked. He was behind her but close.

'I don't think it helps much.'

'What *is* that? I've never heard anything like it.'

'I don't know. I'm not sure if they're talking to each other or trying to talk to us.'

Before she knew what was happening, Frank's hands were on her shoulders, and she was leaning back against him.

'No,' she said. 'Don't trust it. It's them.'

'Is it?' he asked and turned her round to face him. 'Maybe it's us.' Before she could reply, he kissed her.

It was some time before either of them noticed that the spheres weren't singing anymore.

37

Kate was busy making phone calls. She had spent most of the day on the phone and her ear was getting sore.

'Ruth? IIi. Good news. I think we're in business. Frank's got one of his old mates lined up, and he's going to do a set too.... They're called The Riflemen, apparently.... No, I hadn't either. We might be a bit young. I looked them up, and they had a few hits. I think I recognised one. Might have been on an advert or something. All we need is a date and a venue. Do you think the school field would be big enough?.... No, good point. We want to get as many people there as we can. What about the field next to the school? That's Huw's, isn't it? I'll ask him. I was thinking maybe the 17th...of next month, yes. That gives us a few weeks to plan it. I'll get on to the Chronicle. I'm sure they'll do something. It's local interest and a good cause.... Okay, I'll tell Frank and get him to book his mate. Speak to you later.'

'Hello? Is that Huw?.... It's Kate, here.... Kate Wilde from the café.... Kate's Café by the beach.... That's the one. Listen, Huw, I wonder if I could ask you a massive favour?... Sorry, I can't hear you very well...yes, I'll wait while you let him out.... So, what it is, is this. The school roof's in a really bad way and needs replacing, but they can't afford it.... No, I'm not asking for money. We want to put on a concert to raise funds for it, and we were wondering if we could borrow your field, you know, the one next to the school.... It's only for a day.... Well, could your cows go somewhere else, just for a day? ... Yes, both of them.... No, there wouldn't be any money in it for you. It's a charity event. You'd be doing a wonderful thing. We'd tell everyone how nice you are.... Okay, a free breakfast every week for a month, how's that? ... Fine, two months. Thank you, Huw, you're a star.... What? No, I'm very sorry Huw, but I'm seeing someone. Thank you anyway.'

'Oh, good afternoon. Could I speak to the News Desk? Oh, that's you, is it? Great. My name's Kate Wilde, and I own the café by the beach in Chapel Bay. I've got a story I hope you'll be interested in....'

***

Less than a week after Kate's phone calls, another phone call was taking place over a hundred miles away. Jonathan Liddell had not expected anything much from the alerts he had set on his phone for any news reports containing a particular name, but when one came through, he read it, read it again, and then made his call.

'Mr.Sutcliffe? Jonathan Liddell. I've got some good news for you. I need you to round up Mr. Dawson and get ready to move. We've found him.'

Part Four

38

Frank and Gemma agreed it had been a bad idea. It was a mistake. They had both got a bit carried away with the strangeness of the moment, with the weird noise the spheres had been making—with everything. They weren't looking for a relationship, they said. They were better off on their own right now, for various reasons, but they both agreed that they could do with a friend. Friends were good. Relationships were complicated and messy, and neither of them wanted that. Frank helped Gemma pack the cardboard box with bubble wrap, tuck the spheres in tight and seal it firmly with parcel tape. She stowed it away in a cupboard under the sink unit, shoving it right to the back behind a box of cleaning materials. Then Frank excused himself and went back to finish his shift at *Kate's*. Before he made it out of the door, though, Gemma touched him lightly on the arm.

'A thought,' she said, 'but do you fancy coming down to the beach with me one day to do a bit of beachcombing and see what I do? I know you like to have a bit of time to yourself at lunchtime, so it's okay if you don't. I thought...'

'That would be nice, yes. I'd like that.'

'Just as friends.'

'Yes, Gemma. Just as friends. Text me.'

'I will.'

Frank backed out of the workshop, doing one of those awkward half-waves people do when they're not sure if they're supposed to be waving or not. Once outside on the path, he looked up to the sky and sighed. *Friends,* he thought. *Text me. Bloody hell, how old* are *we?* He hurried back to the café, hoping to God that the embarrassment of it all wasn't showing in his face. The good news was that Kate was on the phone when he got back. The bad news was that she appeared to be confirming arrangements for the damn concert he had forgotten all about. Tempting as it might be to run from a situation that was starting to feel like it was closing in on him, getting away was going to be even harder now. He owed Kate and couldn't very well let her down. At the end of the shift, he went straight past the bus stop and walked back to the B&B, hoping it would clear his head. It took over an hour and didn't work.

The next couple of days were overcast, threatening, but never quite delivering rain. Gemma called in for her coffee, and they made polite small talk, but the idea of going down to the beach to help her root in the sand was not mentioned again, and he half hoped she had forgotten about it. The other half of him was slightly put out that she obviously either hadn't meant it or had changed her mind. He was not quite sure how to feel when one morning he woke up to bright sunshine streaming into his room at the B&B and a text on his phone from Gemma.

```
It's a lovely day for beachcombing.
    What time's your lunch? Xxx
```

Frank, trying not to question if there was any significance to the three x's (first time for that, it was usually only one), replied simply that he'd let her know, then sat indecisively on the edge of his bed for somewhat longer than absolutely necessary wondering what the protocol for how many x's he should add to his reply. Politeness dictated that he matched her number, but then he didn't know why she'd done it, and therefore what message he would be sending by matching it. He decided that Gemma was probably the sort of person who put x's on texts to everyone and that it didn't really mean anything, like the people who call everyone 'babe' and 'darling' but don't attach any meaning to them at all. He settled on two as a compromise, but before he pressed 'send,' he added a third in case and sent the message. Then he wondered why, for the first time since he was a teenager, he was overthinking the contents of a simple message and told himself not to be a fucking idiot.

Yes, that was a clean shirt he was wearing when he called at the workshop on his lunch break, but only because he'd splashed coffee on the one he was wearing yesterday. Yes, he had shaved that morning, but only because it was about time he did. But yes, he was pleased that Gemma's smile when she saw him proved that he was right to make a bit of an effort.

'Any word from...you know?' he asked, nodding towards the sink unit.

'Not a peep,' she replied. 'They're probably miffed that we've stuck them away and are planning the invasion even as we speak.'

'This is going to sound a stupid question, but we didn't... we didn't imagine it, did we?'

'Both of us? At the same time?'

'Told you it was a stupid question.'

'No, Frank. We didn't imagine it. Any of it.'

Frank had a fair idea that she wasn't referring to their pair of glass mysteries but let it go in case he was wrong.

'So what the hell are we going to do?' he asked instead.

'We're going to try and forget about it and go for a lovely wander on the beach in the sun.'

Which is exactly what they did, and it *was* lovely. Gemma's enthusiasm and joy were infectious, and Frank delighted in her company and was also very impressed by her knowledge. The things that he usually crunched under his feet on the beach and dismissed as 'shells' had names, and the names had a magic of their own. There were augers and razor clams, periwinkles and whelks, and each one was as individual as a snowflake. She showed him the delicate colours and patterns on the outside and the iridescent layers of nacre inside. She pointed out the white clusters of whelk egg cases and the black skate egg sacs, which truly earned their nickname of mermaid's purses. She knew the different kinds of seaweed, the difference between bladder wrack and knotted wrack, sea lettuce and gutweed, and she found beauty and fascination in all of them. When they reached the furthest edge of the bay, where the rocks rose from the beach and joined with the cliffs, she found a large rock pool and showed him limpets and sea anemones and pointed out where a crab was lurking under a rock shelf, its claws and antennae barely visible. As they walked back across the beach, she took his arm and then started to point out seabirds to him.

'Woah! Hang on!' he protested. 'Information overload!'

'Sorry,' she said, but the sparkle in her eyes said she wasn't sorry at all. 'I do go on a bit. I get that from my dad. He taught me everything I know.'

'Is he...?'

'Dead? Yes. Mum too. I'm like Little Orphan Annie without the hair.'

'I'm sorry.'

'Don't be. It was a while ago. I'll tell you all about the birds next time. If you want there to be a next time.'

'Yes. Yes, I do.'

'Good. Come on, race you back to the café.'

'I don't run.'

'Then you'll lose!'

With that, she took off across the beach, her satchel bouncing at her side as she ran. Frank muttered 'Shit' under his breath and ran after her. By the time they reached the other end of the beach, Frank was red in the face and out of breath, but Gemma looked no different, apart from the fact that she was laughing. She was doing *a lot* of laughing.

'The state of you!'

'Jesus, I'm out of condition,' Frank gasped. Gemma took his arm again and leaned in close.

'Don't be dying on me,' she said. 'Couldn't have that on my conscience.'

Then, suddenly aware that they were staring a little too intently into each other's eyes, she let go of his arm and took a step back.

'Sorry,' she said. 'I know. Friends.'

But as they parted company outside the café, Frank made the same mistake as they had the day the spheres sang and kissed her. She compounded the mistake by kissing him back.

Two days later, they made what they later said was the worst mistake of all and slept together. They were wrong, though. The worst mistake had been made a while ago, and preparations were already in hand for that mistake to follow them to Anglesey.

39

June gave way to July, and on an unseasonably rainy day, a bus made its way onto the island, its occupants sitting rather less than comfortable in their seats. Dawson thought that if the bus hit one more bump in the road, he'd probably puke all over the mum and toddler in the seat in front of him. He knew Wales was a different country and everything, but he'd always assumed they had proper roads.

'Fuck,' he said as the bus hit another bump, making him grip the back of the woman's seat.

Sutcliffe, slouching in the seat next to him, his head buried in a book, looked up.

'There's no need for that,' he said. 'There are children present.'

'Yeah, I know,' Dawson replied. 'But Jesus, these roads.'

'They're not so bad. You ever been to India? Some of the roads there are like ploughed fields.'

'But this is supposed to be a civilised country. I mean civilised for a load of sheep shaggers who can't speak without spitting on you.'

'That's a bit prejudiced, isn't it? Welsh is an older language than English. They've got a right to speak it.'

'It's not even a real language! It's a bunch of letters. It's like someone dropped a Scrabble set. I mean, look at that!' He pointed as an ambulance sped past them. 'What the fuck's that? 'Ambiwlans'? What the fuck's that all about? That isn't a real language. It's English spelled wrong.'

'Keep the language down,' Sutcliffe warned again, nodding towards the toddler, who wasn't that bothered about Dawson swearing. He (or she, it was hard to tell) was much more concerned about making sure that there were no bits on their face that weren't covered liberally with jam from the sandwich they weren't so much eating as trying to absorb through their skin.

'*Fnuk!*' the toddler exclaimed with a giggle, nearly making its mother look up from her Snapchat page.

'You see?' Sutcliffe said. 'They're impressionable at that age.

'*Fnuk!*' the toddler opined once again, in case everyone had missed it the first time.

'I don't even get why we've got to go by bus,' Dawson said. 'They have trains in Wales. I saw it on that show. The one with that Tory ponce who wears yellow trousers and shit.'

'He's a twat. You watch that show, and you'll turn into a Tory.'

'Language,' Dawson said and laughed.

'*Trat!*' the toddler shrieked.

'Jesus, it's like a fucking parrot,' Dawson said. 'So why *are* we going by bus?'

'You heard what Mr. James said. We've got to look like tourists. Why else would we dress like this?'

Sutcliffe indicated his own attire, a T-Shirt with the Guinness logo emblazoned on the front and camouflage shorts. And sandals with socks. Dawson was more conservatively dressed in a short-sleeved shirt and jeans. Anything he needed for the job was stashed in a holdall at his feet.

'Anyway,' Sutcliffe went on, 'there aren't any stations on this side of the island. It's either the bus or walk. Do you fancy walking?'

'We could have driven.'

'No, we're tourists. There's a vehicle waiting for us at the other end, Mr. James said. We wander in looking like tourists, pick up the motor and find this Frankie Davies. We sort him out, get the goods and get out. It's simple. It's a nice couple of days out in the countryside.'

'I hate the countryside,' Dawson said. 'It's full of fucking sheep.'

'*Fnukken sheet!*' the toddler yelled. Dawson sank down in

his seat and waited for the journey to be over.

Three miles from their destination, the bus broke down. It had stopped in a village Dawson couldn't begin to pronounce and simply refused to start again. It happened, the bus driver said with a shrug. A replacement would be along in maybe an hour. Dawson and Sutcliffe got off the bus and sat on a dry stone wall, trying to decide what to do.

'I knew it,' Dawson said. 'I knew the bus was a bad idea.'

'We might have to walk,' Sutcliffe replied. 'It's only a couple a miles.'

'Walk? Jesus. I'm not walking that far. How long did he say the replacement bus would be?'

'An hour. That probably means three round here. He didn't look particularly arsed about it. We could walk it in that time.'

'You expect me to walk miles with that bag? You know what's in it. What if someone stops us?'

'Do you see any bizzies? I haven't seen a police car on the island. They probably only have one.'

'I'm not walking three fucking miles with a gun in my bag.'

'But you'd sit on a bus with one.'

'I didn't want to do that, either. Jesus. This is a disaster. I don't even know what we're doing here. Who is this Davies anyway? Why's Mr. James so pissed off at him?'

'That's not for us to know.'

'So we've got to find him, get the money he took back off him and then do him in, and we don't know why? Do we even know what the poor bastard looks like?'

'No. I showed you the text.'

'So we've got to ask around for this Davies guy. You do know Davies is a Welsh name, don't you? Probably every fucker on the island is called Davies. They're interbred.'

'Not everyone. Some are called Hughes.'

'You know what, Sutcliffe? You're a big fucking help.'

'So are we going to start walking, or what?,

40

Three weeks into what seemed to be turning into a very nice relationship, and Briony had already said the words Kate had dreaded.

'We can't go on like this.'

Well, that didn't take long, she thought.

It had come out of nowhere, or so it seemed. Briony had stayed over again, as she did most nights now. She came around after work, and they had a meal together, then spent the evening watching television or a film together and then bed. Their tastes in terms of what they ate and watched were broadly similar, though Briony refused to eat asparagus. Kate had served it once as a treat, or so she thought, but Bri had pushed it to the edge of the plate and apologised, saying that one time she had eaten it by accident, and it had turned her wee green. She assumed it was the asparagus but didn't want to risk trying again. She also didn't like anchovies on pizza (or indeed anywhere else), but Kate didn't either, so that wasn't a problem. So there were no issues in terms of compatibility in taste. There were certainly no issues over compatibility in the bedroom either. Briony was much more giving and entirely more enthusiastic than Alison had ever been. This, in turn, encouraged Kate to be less inhibited than she had been used to being, an adjustment she found surprisingly easy to get used to. They got on very well, and Kate had even caught the 'l' word forming on her lips before she stopped herself because it was far too soon, wasn't it? Bri had used the word once, but it was in the context of, 'That's one of the things I love about you,' and seeing as Kate couldn't even remember what that specific thing was, it didn't count. Even The Cat liked Bri and often sat on the arm of the settee next to her, allowing her to tickle it behind the ears. It purred for Bri, and that wasn't a sound Kate had heard before.

Now she had said it, though. 'We can't go on like this.' She had said it first thing in the morning while she was rushing around getting dressed, which she did a good hour or more before Kate even had to think about getting ready. Kate tended to stay in bed and out of the way while Bri quickly sorted herself out before dashing back to her parents' house to do a quick change and pick up the van and the bread and start her rounds. She'd had her top half over her head at the time, but Kate was sure she had heard right. Bri had definitely said, 'We can't go on like this.' Kate hadn't been sure how to reply, so she had said, 'Oh, okay,' and sunk back into her pillow.

'Shit. Look at the time. We'll talk later, my lovely,' Briony said, giving her a quick kiss, and as far as Kate could see, couldn't get out of the door quick enough. At least she's coming back later, Kate reasoned, trying to talk herself out of the deep, black mood that was descending on her. And she called me 'my lovely'. But then Briony even called The Cat 'my lovely', and that didn't exactly prove anything.

The dark clouds followed Kate around all day. She was quiet at work, barely giving Frank the time of day because it was all right for Frank, wasn't it? He and Gemma were all bloody loved up. They hadn't said it wasn't working out, had they? When she felt like this, she wished she'd never taken Frank on. It was bad enough having to be cheery with customers, but having someone around all day that you had to be nice to and gave you concerned looks if you wanted to be quiet, was too much to cope with. The only relief she got was at lunchtime when Frank went off to see his girlfriend, but even that relief was short-lived because Kate had forgotten that Ruth was coming in for another planning meeting for the damn fundraiser. And unlike Frank, who knew when to keep his distance and didn't ask too many questions, Ruth wouldn't shut up. Eventually, when Ruth had asked her what was wrong for what felt like the thirty-seventh time, Kate snapped.

'Briony wants to finish with me, all right?' she said. 'Can we get on now?'

'What? Oh no, Kate. I thought you two were great. She always looks nuts about you. What happened?'

'I don't know. She said it out of the blue this morning.'

'What, that she's dumping you?'

'She said we can't go on like this. Just like that. Exact words.'

'Did you ask what she meant?'

'There wasn't time. She was out the door like her life depended on it.'

'Can't you ring her?'

'I don't like to call her when she's on her rounds. She says she's fine hands-free, but I don't like to. I wouldn't want to hear her crash. She's coming round later.'

'Well, that's a good sign. You need to find out what she meant. It mightn't be what you think at all.'

'It is. I know it is.'

'How?'

'Because that's what Alison said. Exactly that. She said we couldn't go on like that, and we didn't.'

'Oh, Kate. That might be one of the daftest things I've ever heard. I've seen you and Briony together. I've seen the way she looks at you. I didn't know Alison well, but I did meet her a few times, and I have to say I wasn't that keen. One thing I can say for sure is that Bri isn't Alison.'

'But she said...'

'It's an expression. Phil and I use it probably once a month. You want to try being married to a picture on a screen.'

'I'm sorry, Ruth. I didn't think...'

'I don't need an apology, Kate. I'm not complaining. Yes, when I'm stressed out of my head about the school roof, I'd really like a cuddle, rather than a whinge to you—no offence— but that's how it is, and we get on with it. All I'm saying is don't prejudge what Briony meant. See her tonight and find out what she has to say. But I'd bet that when I see you next, you'll have a smile on your face and probably a bit of a funny walk, if you know what I mean.'

Kate couldn't help but laugh then, but the mood still followed her around the rest of the day. She could picture herself as a cartoon, trudging along with a grey cloud following her. By the time she got home, she was nearly ready to text Bri and put her off coming for fear that she would get in with a pre-emptive strike and be the one who finished it first. But something stopped her. She wasn't sure if it was Ruth's words or the way The Cat walked past her in the hall when she got home and sat looking at the door waiting for the other one, the nice one. Whatever it was, it made her leave her phone in her pocket, pour a glass of wine, curl up in an armchair and wait.

She didn't have to wait that long. About half an hour after she got in, there was a knock at the door, and it was a knock that normally made her heart leap, but today made it sink. She decided to be a grown-up and went to answer the door.

Briony breezed in as she always did, heading straight into the hall and hanging her coat up, leaving a trail of perfume behind her.

'Is something up with your phone?' she asked. 'I've been texting you. Sorry, I'm a bit late. Dad had a bit of a funny turn. Nothing to worry about, he's fine now, but at his age....'

She stopped and looked at Kate, who had not moved away from the door.

'Are you okay, babe? What is it? Has something happened?'

'What did you mean?'

'What did I mean by what?'

'This morning. You said we can't go on like this. What did you mean?'

'Oh no, Katie. You haven't been brooding about that all day, have you? Why didn't you call me?'

'Because...well...you're busy. And I didn't want to make you tell me.'

'Tell you? Tell you what?'

'That it's over.'

'Right. Come and sit down.' Briony strode into the living room, plonked herself on the settee and patted the seat next to her. 'Right now, Kate, please.'

Feeling more like a six-year-old than her true age, Kate mutely obeyed.

'Kate, you have to not do this. We're adults, you and me. We're a long way past playing games. If we have something to say, let's say it, sort it and move on. What I meant was that as much as I love staying over with you, it's a bit of a pain in the arse dashing out an hour earlier in the morning so I can run home and get changed. I was going to suggest leaving some stuff here, that's all.'

'Oh.'

'Oh? Is that all?'

Briony paused for a moment, looking stern. Then she cracked up.

'Your face!' she cried between gales of laughter. 'Stop being so serious! Listen, Kate, there's no need. We have fun, don't we?'

Kate nodded.

'We're good together, you must feel like that. You need to know, though, that if I've got something to say, I'll say it. I won't ever mess you around, Katie. That's not something you do to someone you love. But you need to be honest with me, too.'

'Wait, hold on. Say that again.'

'You need to be honest with me.'

'No, not that bit. The bit before. The bit about it not being something you do…'

'To someone you love. Well, it isn't.'

'Do you?'

'Do I what? Love you? Of course I bloody do. Did you not know?'

'You never said.'

Briony gently put her arm around Kate and drew her close.

'Well, I'm saying it now. So there's no doubt. I love you, Kate Wilde. I was half in love with you for months before I even asked you out. Do you mean to tell me that you never noticed? All my best flirting, and it was for nothing! You know how to make a girl feel appreciated, don't you?'

'I thought it was a bit too good to be true.'

'Thanks. I'm good, but I'm not all that. I'm just me.'

'You are all that. You're all that and more, and I love you too.'

'Yes, I know. Now let's stop being bloody daft. You can afford to trust me more. You can be a bit more secure than you are.'

'I'm sorry. It's not you. It's just that Alison said the same thing to me and then left.'

'Well, obviously, I didn't know that. I get it, Kate. You've been hurt. We've all been hurt. You don't get to our age without getting kicked by life a few times. I've never told you what happened when I came out, have I?'

'No,' Kate said, talking Bri's hand and stroking her knuckles with one finger. 'Tell me.'

'I didn't actually come out, not really. I always knew I liked girls but hadn't done anything about it. My parents are total Chapel goers. They live there every Sunday and most of the week, too, so there was no way I could sit them down and tell them. There was a girl at school called Rhian, and I liked her so much. I was obsessed, you know, in the way only teenagers can be, but I didn't tell anyone. Not Rhian, not my parents, nobody. I poured it all out into a diary. I'd sit in my room all evening, listening to crap music and writing all this *stuff* in a load of exercise books. I even wrote some seriously shit poetry. And then I came home from school one day, and my parents were waiting in the living room with a pile of exercise books on the coffee table.'

'Oh no.'

'That's one way of looking at it. I've never seen them so angry. It was like they'd been all the way through angry back to calm again, and it was horrible. I genuinely thought my dad was going to take his belt to me. He never did that, never would. He's a lovely man, my dad, really. But in that moment, I thought he might. There was a long conversation about how disappointed they were and how they would never, ever be able to hold their heads up in Chapel again. They wanted to drag me to see the Minister there and then and seek forgiveness.'

'Did they?'

'Did they shite. I refused to go. I told them if they tried to make me, I'd run away and go and live on the streets. My mum didn't speak to me for three weeks, but they never told the Minister. So, yes, I know a bit about hurt. The looks my mum gave me in those weeks, that was the hardest thing I've ever had to take because I couldn't do anything about it. I couldn't change who I was.'

'How are they now?'

'Oh, they're great now. My dad loves the fact that I'm doing the bread deliveries now. It's like I'm his heir.'

'And your mum?'

'I don't think she'll ever understand it properly. I think she's still waiting for me to grow out of it, but the fact that the Minister's son is now living with a lovely accountant called Simon kind of helps. Turns out I wasn't the only one in the village.'

Kate laughed and held Briony's hand tighter.

'The thing is, Kate, you get over it. Hurt fades if you let it. If you carry it around with you, you never get over it. All you have to do is find something that makes you happy instead. I have. So, are you going to give me a bit of wardrobe or not?'

Kate thought for a second. This was a serious conversation, but she wanted to sing and dance. If it were a movie, there would be a big musical number around about now.

'I've got a better idea. Why don't you move in?'

'Wow! That escalated fast! Kate, are you sure that's what you want? This is your place. You've got it the way you want it. Are you sure you want my dirty washing on the floor and my hair clogging up your plughole?'

'Yes. I really do,' Kate said and knew beyond a shadow of a doubt that she meant every word.

'Okay. I need to have a word with Mum and Dad. They've kind of got used to me being around, and I might need to organise a bit more care for Dad, but that's fine. I'm a bit too old to be living with my parents. I think I'd much rather live with my girlfriend instead.'

'The Cat will be pleased.'

'Sod The Cat. What about you?'

'Me?' Kate said, taking her now live-in lover by the hand and leading her from the settee to the stairs. 'Can I show you how happy I am rather than telling you?'

41

'My feet are fucking killing me. How much further is it?'

'Bloody hell, Dawson, we've only been walking for fifteen minutes.'

Sutcliffe had spent years among the hardest, most dangerous people Merseyside had to offer. He had been shot at six times (they all missed) and stabbed twice. The second stabbing had left him on life support in hospital for weeks and relieved him of a small part of his intestines, though luckily a non-essential part. Another few inches, the doctor had told him, and he would have been cruising the mean streets of Liverpool with a colostomy bag for company. Despite the obvious risks, he would still rather be there than traipsing down a country lane with a dejected whinger like Dawson trailing behind him. This wasn't the life he had signed up for.

'It's these roads. Why haven't they got pavements?'

'We're in the countryside,' Sutcliffe replied. 'They have pavements in towns.'

'That's why I stay in towns.'

'Well, once we've got the job done, you can go back to Liverpool and walk on all the pavements you like.'

They trudged on a bit further along the lane. Sutcliffe could smell something strong and unpleasant coming from behind the hedge that bordered the lane. Dawson had obviously noticed it too.

'Jesus, is that shit?'

'They have cows here. They shit a lot.'

'How the fuck could anyone live here?'

Up ahead, the lane split into two and Sutcliffe could make out a signpost, partly concealed by the hedge.

'That way,' he pointed.

'Oh, for fuck's sake,' Dawson protested. 'It says two and a half miles.'

'You'd walk further than that for a pint on a Saturday night.'

'I'm not going for a pint, though, am I? I'm two miles off civilisation of any kind. It's getting darker too. You know there aren't any streetlights here, don't you?'

'We'd better start walking a bit quicker then.'

Dawson was quiet for a minute, apart from the laboured breathing of the chronically unfit, but Sutcliffe knew it was too good to last.

'So what's this Davies character doing out here? You'd have thought with all that money he'd be in Spain or Portugal or somewhere.'

'He probably reckons it's safe. He probably thinks that people like us wouldn't come here looking for him.'

'He's got a point. I wouldn't come here out of choice. Is that shit getting stronger?'

'Keep walking, Dawson. You're doing my head in. If you don't shut up, I might think about shooting you first.'

It was pretty inevitable that they would get lost. They had been walking down the lane for maybe twenty minutes when, rounding a bend, they found that the lane abruptly ended. A T-junction sent the lane off left and right, but of course, there was no signpost to give them any idea which way to go. Sutcliffe pulled out his mobile phone to try and get some assistance from his map app, but he couldn't get a good enough signal. He did notice, however, that there was a text message from Jonathan Liddell saying that Mr. James was enquiring about their whereabouts and how close they were to completing the job. For now, he decided that he would ignore it and blame the signal.

'Give us your phone a minute,' he said.

'What for?' Dawson asked.

'I want to play a game. What do you think I want it for? I need to find out where we are. Can you get a signal?'

Dawson took his phone out and looked at it.

'I've run out of charge,' he said.

'Didn't you charge it before you left?'

'I thought we might be going somewhere that had electricity.'

They stood at the junction, looking first one way, then the other trying to get some clue as to which direction they should choose. The hedges on either side of the lane were too high to get their bearings, and the lanes on both sides looked pretty much the same.

'Do you want to toss a coin?' Dawson asked.

'No, I don't want to toss a fucking coin. We need to work it out.'

Sutcliffe looked at the alternatives again. He pointed to the lane on the left.

'Does that look like it goes down a bit? I think it does.'

'Can't tell. It might. Why?'

'I reckon the coast is down. Water always runs down, doesn't it? If we go down, we'll get to the coast. I think we should go this way.'

He was wrong.

They first suspected that he might have been wrong when the lane began to narrow. Their suspicions grew when they noticed that grass was growing in a strip down the middle of the lane and grew still more when the strip of grass became noticeably wider. The theory that they should have gone right instead of left was confirmed when the lane ended at a padlocked gate leading to a field of placidly chewing cows. Dawson looked like he was about to make either a helpful suggestion or a smart remark, but Sutcliffe glared at him, snapped, 'Fuck it', and stomped off up the lane in the direction in which they had come with Dawson in hot pursuit. As he walked, small brown birds darted into the hedges, as they might when there was a storm coming. Right now, Sutcliffe felt like the storm and couldn't wait to get out of this alien environment and back to more familiar surroundings. The sooner this Davies was dealt with, the better. It would be another hour and a half before they finally found the village they were looking for and another day before they could even think about moving on and searching for their quarry.

42

Three days after Gemma and Frank made the mistake of spending the night together, and one day after the second time they did it, which was starting to feel a bit more deliberate, Gemma came to *Kate's* for her morning coffee. She also hoped to see Frank as she hadn't seen him for a couple of hours. When she entered, she found Kate serving on the counter but Frank nowhere to be seen.

'I don't know,' Kate said, in response to the query Gemma hadn't even made yet. 'His phone went, and he went outside to take the call. He'll be around somewhere. So,' she leaned on the counter, ready for all the gossip, 'how are you getting on?'

'It's a bit of fun, Kate. Nothing to get excited about.'

'There's not much excitement round here. You have to take what you can get.'

'I would have thought you'd be getting quite enough. Has Briony moved in yet?'

'Sort of. She's doing it a bit at a time, a box a day, type of thing. She says she hasn't got a lot of stuff, but let's put it this way, my box room is starting to live up to its name. Has Frank moved out of Mrs. Evans's place yet?'

'No, and he's not going to. He's paid a couple of weeks in advance and doesn't dare ask for a refund. Anyway, like I said, it's not serious. We're taking it as it comes.'

'Two weeks takes us up to the Fundraiser. Make sure you keep him happy 'til then if you would. Don't want him buggering off before then.'

'He's his own man, Kate. He can do what he wants. He won't let you down, though. I'm sure of it.'

As she spoke, Kate nudged her to warn her that Frank was coming back into the café. He looked troubled but still smiled when he saw Gemma.

'Hey,' he said. 'You all right?'

'I'm fine,' she replied. 'You're not, though. What's up?'

'Nothing. I've had Mick Rogers on the phone. Wants to have a chat about the arrangements for the gig.'

'Well, that's good, isn't it? At least he's still on board.'

'He wants to meet in a pub tonight. In Ross somewhere?'

'Rhosneigr?' Kate asked.

'If you say so,' Frank said. 'Sounds about right? Where's that?'

'It's about half an hour from here. Give yourself an hour if you're getting the bus.'

'I'd probably be quicker walking than getting the bus. It's a pity he's not a little bit closer, but that's apparently the nearest decent pub.'

'There are good pubs nearer than that,' Kate observed.

'What Mick thinks is decent and what you call good probably aren't the same thing. I'll risk the bus.'

'Tell you what,' Kate said, 'I'll give Bri a ring, see if she can give you a lift.'

'No, there's no need for that. Honestly.'

'I've got you landed with this gig, Frank. Let me see what I can do.'

Kate retreated to the rear of the café, presumably, Gemma thought, because there would be parts of the conversation she didn't want anyone to overhear. Frank, however, still looked concerned.

'What is it?' she asked. 'It's not only the distance. And don't say 'nothing' again.'

'You haven't met Mick,' Frank said. 'He's a real throwback. Thinks he's still twenty and drinks and smokes weed as if he is. There's no way I can keep up these days. Never could, really.'

'Then don't. Tell him you don't want to drink much.'

'You've not been around many rockers, have you? Mick isn't going to listen, not unless his wife's with him, which is not very likely. He'll keep on going and expect me to join him. I'm dreading it.'

'I'm sure it wouldn't hurt you to let go this once. Where's

the harm? We've all done it.'

'Gemma, you don't understand, do you? Look, I have to get back to work. I'll go back to the B&B tonight. I'll call you tomorrow.'

Gemma was about to protest, but Frank turned his back to her and started to clean the gleaming chrome of the coffee machine. She had been dismissed but wasn't sure why. One thing she did know, though, was that Frank was totally bloody out of order. So she turned on her heel and stormed out of the café and down to the beach, where she spent a furious half-hour hurling pebbles into the sea. Despite the fact that it was a clear, dry day, there was nobody on the beach, so nobody heard her shout *bastard, bastard, bastard!* With every pebble she threw. It nearly, but not quite, made her feel better.

***

By ten o'clock that evening, the anger had subsided and was replaced by worry. She hadn't seen Frank like that, certainly not since they had become...friends? Lovers? Whatever they were. He had smiled more and talked more. He had even started to open up a bit. But the prospect of going out for a few beers with an old friend had closed him down again, and he had completely shut her out, and she was unable to read his mind or figure out what was going on. She had texted him an hour or so earlier to ask if he was okay, but there had been no reply. She initially hoped that meant he was enjoying himself and hadn't looked at his phone. But as time went by, she began to worry that it had more significance than that. He was either still cross with her for her lack of psychic abilities, or something was wrong. Unsure exactly what to do, she rang Kate.

'Kate, sorry to disturb you. Did Briony give Frank a lift in the end? I want to make sure he got there all right. He's not answering my texts.'

'Yes, she dropped him off in Rhosneigr about seven, I think. Is something wrong, Gem? Have you fallen out?'

'Not exactly. I don't know. There's something...'

'You're telling me. I hardly got a word out of him all afternoon. Bri said he hardly spoke when she was giving him a lift. He wasn't horrible or anything, just quiet. What was that, Bri?...' Gemma could hear muffled talking in the background. 'Bri says he seemed anxious.'

'Shit. I hope he's okay.'

There was more muted conversation at the other end.

'Bri's on her way, Gem. She'll run you over there.'

'No, Kate. I won't disturb your evening. He's a big boy. I'm sure he can look after himself. He'll probably have a bad head in the morning, and I'll take the piss out of him.'

'Too late. She's left. Get your coat on, Gem. She'll be there in a minute.'

'Thanks, Kate. I appreciate this.'

Gemma had barely had a chance to grab her keys and a jacket before she heard a car crunch to a halt down below. She locked up and raced down the fire escape. Briony's car still had its engine running.

'Come on,' Briony said as Gemma climbed into the passenger seat. 'Let's go and find out what's going on with your man.'

'He's not...' Gemma began but then stopped herself. 'Thanks, Bri.'

They drove most of the way in silence or at least conversational silence. Briony apologised initially for the music, explaining that she was quite unable to concentrate on driving if she had to do it without some sounds on. Gemma didn't mind. She would much rather listen to the Goombay Dance Band than her own thoughts right now. In all likelihood, Frank was having a nice time with his old mate, or at least that was what she hoped. Her plan was to stick her head through the doorway of the pub as discretely as possible and, if all was well, withdraw again without being noticed. After that, she would never mention it again unless Frank brought it up. Even then, she hoped she would never have to mention that she had even been there.

Briony pulled up on the far side of the car park from the

pub. Gemma suggested that Bri should leave her there to get a taxi back, but it only took one look to tell her that this wasn't going to happen. She gave Bri a smile that was far sunnier than she felt and got out of the car. Considering what Frank had implied about the tastes of this Mick character, the pub was far nicer than she had expected, more Toby Carvery than Den of Iniquity, and Gemma wondered at first if she had the right place. It looked out over Rhosneigr beach, which, even at this time of the day, was busy with surfer dudes. Another reason why it didn't look like the sort of place geriatric rock stars would hang out, but then she spotted a lone figure leaning against a rail that bordered the car park. From her position, it was hard to tell if he was looking out to sea or down at the ground, but Frank was on his own and didn't look very steady. Gemma crossed the car park and put a hand on his shoulder.

'Hey,' she said softly. 'Fancy seeing you here.'

Frank looked up, and it was obvious he was drunk even before she saw the drool glistening on his chin and the splatter of vomit at his feet. The smell hit her nostrils, and it was plain that it was fresh. There was a guitar case propped up on the fence next to him, and fortunately, he had missed it.

'Why are you here?' he slurred. 'Go 'way.'

'I've come to take you home, Frank.'

A look of confusion passed over his face. He raised a finger, apparently to prod her in the shoulder, but missed and nearly lost his balance.

'You don't drive,' he said.

'I do, actually. But I haven't got a car. Briony gave me a lift.'

'I'll get the bus.'

He did his best to stand up straight and lurched a few steps towards the car park exit. Then he stopped and looked around.

'You don't even know where the bus stop is, do you?'

'I do. It's over...there.' He waved his hand in a vague direction that could have indicated anywhere.

'No, you don't. State you're in, you could end up in Bangor or Caernarfon. And you've got that guitar to carry.'

'It's Mick's. He's lent it to me. Some musician I am. Haven't even got my own guitar.'

'That was good of him.'

'He's got loads.'

Frank picked up the guitar case and nearly got his legs tangled in it.

'Give that here,' Gemma said, taking it from him. 'Come on. Let us take you home, Frank.'

'It's all your fault,' he said. 'I didn't want to stay here on fucking Anglesey. Should be in Ireland now. Fucking Dublin.'

'I didn't make you stay.'

'Yes, you did. With all your...your hair and your face and your bloody weird bloody alien things.'

'I think you might be a bit pissed, Frank.'

'Nah. I got rid,' he pointed towards the general vicinity of the puke-spattered grass. 'Be fine.'

'Okay. If you say so.'

She turned to go, thinking how easy it would be to go to the car and ask Briony to drive. She didn't need this kind of complication in her life. A couple of days ago, she had thought that she and Frank were going to have a pleasant little friendship, fling, whatever it was. But instead, she was standing in a car park while he admitted to making himself sick and wouldn't let her in to understand the reason why. After the last time, she had vowed that she would never again get involved with secrets or bloody stupid men who kept them. She had vowed not to have anything to do with men at all or even other human beings if she could help it. But that's the trouble with staying in one place too long; you get sucked into other people's lives, into their problems. She had meant it when she said never again, but here she was.

'I thought you liked me,' she said, and it came out more petulant than she had intended. She waited for his response, but when it didn't come, she started to move towards the car.

'I do,' came a rather pathetic voice from behind her. She stopped and turned around.

'Then why the hell are you doing this? We're supposed to be friends, Frank, whatever else we are. Stop pushing me away. *Talk* to me.'

'I can't.

'Fuck you, then. Stay here if you want, but whatever you do, stay away from me.'

'It's not you. I wish...bloody Mick. I knew this would happen. I *told* you.'

'You wish what?'

He took a couple of wobbly paces towards her. She stood where she was, torn between wanting to hold him and wanting to punch him hard in the face.

'We like each other too much,' he said. 'I wish we didn't, in a way. This wasn't supposed to happen.'

'Why not?'

'If I tell you, you won't like me.'

'Let me make my own mind up. Tell me.'

'Not here.'

They walked back to the car in silence, Frank lingering a pace or so behind, but at least going in something like a straight line. She opened the rear door and let him pour himself into the back seat, put the guitar in after him, then got into the passenger seat between Briony.

'Sorry, Bri,' she said.

Briony smiled and mouthed *Is he okay*? Gemma shrugged.

'Buckle up, Frank,' Briony said out loud. 'And do me a favour. Let me know if you're going to puke, so I can pull over. I don't want your second-hand beer on my upholstery.'

***

The drive back to Chapel Bay seemed to go on for hours. Gemma made small talk with Briony, who, bless her, really didn't seem to mind having been dragged out and then made to wait. She even gave Gemma a kiss on the cheek before leaving them outside the workshop and driving off.

'Here we are,' Gemma said. 'Are you going to be able to get up the fire escape?'

'Can we sit outside?' Frank asked. 'I could do with the fresh air.'

'Tell you what, I'll make us some coffee and bring it out. You get your air.'

'Should be me making the coffee. It's my job.'

'It's your night off, Latte Man,' Gemma said and steered him to one of the tables outside the café. She left the guitar propped up against the wall at the bottom of the fire escape. It wasn't as if anyone was going to come past and steal it. Once Frank was safely seated, she took her keys out and opened the workshop door, hoping that there was still some coffee in the jar she kept in the cupboard under the sink for special occasions. In her haste, she had the door open before she remembered it wasn't only the coffee that she kept under the sink. She was reminded quickly, though, because when she opened the door, she saw that the cupboard was filled with a gentle turquoise light. The cardboard box had two perfectly round holes in it, and the alien glass spheres were sitting side by side on the shelf, throbbing softly in time with each other. Gemma tentatively reached into the cupboard to get the coffee, and as she did so, the sphere nearest to her rolled across the shelf a few inches and nudged her hand.

'Not now,' Gemma said. 'I'll deal with you later.'

The sphere rolled back to its original position.

'Okay.... Do you know what? I totally haven't got the time to worry about whether you actually understood me.'

She filled the kettle and tried to put her visitors out of her head while it boiled. She made the coffee and, once again, was in too much of a hurry to think about what she was doing. She was halfway over to Frank before she realised she hadn't closed the cupboard door, but it was too late to go back now.

'Here you go,' she said, setting the coffee in front of Frank and sitting opposite him. 'Get that down you and tell me everything. And I mean everything.'

He did, but it wasn't what Gemma had been expecting at all. He gave her an abbreviated version of the story of his upbringing and glossed over a great deal of what went on in the Leisure Decree years. Then he told her what happened after. He told her how, after he left the band, he had become disillusioned with the whole music business. Even though he could play guitar pretty well, those people who knew him at all knew him mainly as a bassist, and there wasn't much work there. Once the session work began to dry up, he made the decision. He put his guitars away and tried to find work in the real world. While he was trying to make a living, his mother had started slowly dying, or at least that was how Frank described it. Kathleen Davies had stopped cooking and trying to feed her son and had begun an inexorable descent into dementia. At first, it was a case of forgetting the odd word or being completely unable to recall the name of someone she had only been talking about a few minutes earlier. Frank put it down to the general malaise called Getting On A Bit. He did, however, start to call around a bit more often, just to keep an eye, and also made sure that the neighbours had his phone number in the event of any problems. In the meantime, Frank worked in a call centre, advising customers on their banking requirements. While his mother's mind was destroying itself, so was his soul. The job lasted until the day he received a phone call from one of Kathleen's neighbours who said she was wandering up and down the road and didn't seem to know where she was and would he come. He asked his supervisor if he could leave early, and when the supervisor, who was apparently not long out of school, refused, Frank walked out and didn't come back.

Eventually, he got another job, this time as a taxi driver. It meant he could keep tabs on his mother during the day and pay a carer to sit with her at night while he worked. This arrangement worked quite well for nearly two years. Kathleen was reasonably safe, although Frank was exhausted most of the time. It was physically and mentally draining to work what hours he could while all the time was worrying about someone who didn't always know who he was. Sometimes she thought he was Jack. Sometimes she knew he was Frank, and sometimes she had no idea who he was at all. It was always pot luck which Kathleen he would find. He was starting to consider whether she would be better off in residential care (he hated the term 'in a home'; it wouldn't be her home) when the slight cold that had been nagging her for a week or so turned into a chest infection and then to pneumonia. He stayed with her at the hospital for two days while she slipped away and then made the fatal error of going straight back to work to give himself something else to think about. Unfortunately, it wasn't him for whom the error was fatal.

Tim Barnes. That was the name that was destined to haunt him, to follow him around, and eventually send him heading for the hills, or the hills of Ireland anyway. Sometimes it's a name we have never heard before that ends up having a huge impact on our lives. Sometimes crossing a path that five minutes earlier or later we would have missed can change our lives forever. That was the case with Frank and Tim Barnes. The problem was that Tim Barnes crossed Frank's path on a bicycle, at night and in the pouring rain. He had no lights on, came flying out of a side street, across a lane of traffic, and Frank had no chance. He didn't even hit Tim; Tim hit him. Frank would wrack his brains for months afterwards about his state of mind that night. Was he concentrating on the road ahead, or was he thinking about the funeral? Could he have seen Tim coming, or was he busy picturing his mother looking blankly at him and asking the carer if he was a doctor? These were questions he would never be able to answer no matter how many times or in how many different ways he asked them. All he knew was that one minute he was slowing down (not speeding up, definitely not speeding up) in case the traffic lights changed, and the next minute there was a sickening thump on the passenger side of his car. He stopped the car straight away and hit the hazard lights, but what he saw was the sight he would see every time he closed his eyes for a long time after. There was a buckled bike on the pavement and lying under it was a man. Because this man was wearing no helmet, even in the dark, Frank could see the blood running down his face quicker than the rain could wash it away. He called an ambulance and the police, then pulled the bike off the prone figure and started to try CPR. He was still desperately doing compressions when the paramedics dragged him away so they could take over. Tim Barnes's life ended before he reached the hospital. Frank's life effectively ended in the rain on the pavement.

Two wonders of modern technology saved Frank. There was CCTV at the traffic lights, and even through the rain, it was clear that Frank was slowing down, and the cyclist shot out of the side road without stopping. Tim Barnes wore no helmet but did wear a body cam that survived the crash, which showed that it was Tim who hit Frank, not the other way around. No charges were pressed, but Frank still had countless conversations with the police, juggling this with organising his mother's funeral and facing the accusing eyes of Tim Barnes's family at the inquest. One of Tim's brothers walked past him on the way into the court, but as he did so, he looked at Frank, kept eye contact for what felt like hours but was actually only seconds, and then carefully spat on the ground at Frank's feet and walked on. His barrister told him to ignore it and steered him inside, but Frank felt he had got off lightly.

Once in the court, Frank tried to give his evidence calmly and clearly, but his throat felt like it was closing over every time he tried to speak. He sat through evidence and testimonies that painted Tim Barnes as a saint, a devoted family man and loved by everyone he met. The worst anyone could say was that he had a 'cheeky sense of humour'. Nobody mentioned the fact, which Frank's barrister had imparted to him, that Tim Barnes, and indeed other members of the family, including the brother who had spat at Frank's feet, were all well known to the police. Fortunately, the court thought that, while it was very sad, it was not Frank's fault in any way. It was one of those tragic accidents. The inquest exonerated Frank, but his own conscience did not. Nor did the taxi company, who regretfully let him go. He spent the next few weeks clearing out his mother's rented house and made the decision that he could no longer stay in his hometown. He was tired of looking over his shoulder in case any of Tim Barnes's family wanted to exert their own cheeky sense of humour on him and tired of wondering if any of the faces he passed in the street had seen his own face in the local papers and were judging him. He packed a bag and booked his one-way ticket for Ireland.

'So now you know,' Frank said. By now, he had talked himself more or less sober. 'That's me. That's all there is to know. I killed a man and ran away.'

'It wasn't your fault,' Gemma said. She couldn't think of anything else to say.

'Doesn't matter. It was my car he hit. Nobody else's.'

'But that was—I don't know—bad luck.'

'It was very bad luck for him, that's for sure. If you want to walk away, it's probably best to do it now.'

'I'm going to walk away as far as the workshop, and only to make another cup of coffee. Don't you go anywhere.'

Gemma picked up their mugs and went back inside. Her mind was reeling from the story she had been told, and she didn't quite know how she was supposed to feel. On the one hand, she was very sorry for Frank and the burden he was carrying on his shoulders. On the other hand, a small, selfish part of her told her that she had unresolved weight on her own shoulders and wasn't sure she was ready to help anyone else carry theirs. Maybe another cup of coffee would wake her up and help her think more clearly. She wasn't quite prepared for the sight that greeted her when she walked into the workshop.

She was sure the light hadn't been on when she left earlier. She didn't think she had switched it on at all. In any case, the light in the workshop was a rather harsh and occasionally flickering fluorescent strip light. It certainly wasn't blue and not a shade of blue that seeped into your heart and soul and made you want to weep with its beauty. But that was what she saw. The cause of it was immediately apparent. Two glass spheres were floating in mid-air in the middle of the workshop and glowing cobalt blue.

'Oh,' Gemma said and felt ridiculous for doing so, 'you're out, are you? You might have put the kettle on.'

As she said it, she realised that the kettle *had* been on, was boiling away merrily to itself and was reaching the point of clicking off.

'I don't know how you did that,' she said, 'but don't do it again. You're freaking me out.'

The spheres hovered briefly, then shot out of the open door.

'Shit,' Gemma said. She put the mugs down and went after them. There was usually nobody around at this time of the night, but all the same, there was no way she could risk anyone seeing them. She'd seen those sorts of movies, and it never ended well. She followed the spheres outside and found them harassing Frank, who had clearly been trying to leave. *Well, of course he had*, she thought.

'They won't let me go,' he said.

'I've been training them,' Gemma replied.

'What? Seriously?'

'No, Frank. If I had my way, I'd let you go. Be a dickhead if you want. Do what you like.'

'I thought that would be what you wanted.'

'Did I say that? Did you even ask me? Look, Frank, I get it. You feel guilty. You've been through some shit. But hey, guess what? We all have. I've done things too, things I'm not happy about. One way or another, we all have things we want to run away from. If you want to run away from me, that's fine. I'd rather you didn't, but it's up to you. I'm too old and too tired to run after you, though.'

'All right, all right!' Frank said, raising his hands in surrender. 'If you want me to stay, I'll stay. Now could you call them off before they zap me with a death ray or something?'

Before Gemma could say anything, the spheres flew past her and back into the workshop. She watched them go, open-mouthed.

' 'Zap with a death ray'?' she said. 'Did you really say that?'

'I think I'm still pissed,' Frank said. 'Tell you what, though, if your mates are going to keep doing things like that, maybe you should give them names.'

43

Sutcliffe was in the middle of a patch of wasteland in the arse end of nowhere. It was one of those patches of land where tourists park up to look at the view and drink tea out of thermos flasks. He and Dawson were the only tourists here at the moment, though. Them and the guy Sutcliffe currently had by the throat. He wasn't in the best of moods.

His mood had been getting steadily worse over the last twenty-four hours. He'd had to put up with Dawson complaining about every single step he took along a selection of country lanes. By the time they had reached what passed for a town, the contact they were due to meet had sent them a text saying he'd given up waiting and would come back the following morning. They had found a pub that advertised rooms and had checked in. The guy who took their money had a thick Welsh accent and, Sutcliffe thought, a face that even a sheep would struggle to fancy. From what he could make out, he seemed to think they were a couple and kept apologising that he only had one twin room left. Before they had even climbed the narrow flight of stairs to the room, Sutcliffe had pictured himself killing the landlord and burning the pub to the ground. He would, he vowed, remember and come back one day. Not today, though. They needed something to eat, a drink or two and a bed for the night and at least the rates were cheap.

The food in the bar was reasonably priced, too, but when it arrived, it became fairly obvious why. The steak, which Sutcliffe had requested rare, was virtually cremated, and the chips were at the opposite end of the badly cooked spectrum — anaemic, limp and strangely damp. Sutcliffe held one up by its end and watched it droop sadly.

'Look at that,' he said. 'This explains everything. This is why pubs like this are closing all over the country.'

'Because of a chip?' Dawson asked.

'It's not merely a chip. It's a symbol. It's a symbol of everything that's wrong these days. All these pubs have got fifty-seven different craft ales that nobody wants to drink because they're all piss. They've got a load of different flavour gins. I mean, flavoured gin? What the fuck's that all about? Gin is gin. It's fucking *gin* flavour. You want a drink that tastes like lemon or, I don't know, rhubarb, you don't buy gin. Gin's horrible stuff anyway. It's a drink for middle-aged women who think colouring books are cool. But what people want is to come to the pub, get a decent pint and a fucking chip that's cooked properly. That's why they're all going out of business. They've lost touch with the common man.'

'So, are you going to send your symbol back or let it go cold?'

'No, I'm going to eat it,' Sutcliffe demonstrated the point by shoving the flaccid fry in his mouth and chewing aggressively. 'I'm going to eat all of this shit meal, and if it makes me sick, I'm going to puke on the floor and leave it there for them to clean up. That'll teach them a thing or two about customer service.'

True to his word, Sutcliffe cleaned his plate, and luckily for Dawson, managed to keep it down. That did not mean that he passed a peaceful night, though. The bed was uncomfortable for a start. He didn't expect the height of luxury, certainly not for that price, but he didn't expect the mattress to have one raised spring dead centre, which dug into one part of him or another no matter how he tried to position himself. The almost inedible steak, while not exactly making him sick, had given him such bad acid indigestion that at one point, he nearly had Dawson call him an ambulance because he was convinced he was having a heart attack. Not that Dawson would have been much help; he was sleeping like a baby. Admittedly, it was a baby that snored, occasionally talked in its sleep and from time to time passed explosive wind, but a baby, nonetheless. The fact that Dawson could sleep, and he could not, was yet another reason why Sutcliffe got up the next morning in a very bad mood. The breakfast they were served, which, if anything, made the previous night's meal look like haute cuisine, only served to add to his temper. When they came to check out, the landlord presented them with the bill. Sutcliffe took one look at it and laughed. There was no humour in the laugh.

'This,' he said, 'is a joke. The food here is so bad that I wouldn't serve it to my wife, and I really hate her. I've had better nights' sleep on the pavement. And there was a pubic hair on the soap in the bathroom. I know it wasn't mine because I'm not ginger. So I'll tell you what we're going to do. You are going to take this bill and tear it up and forget we were ever here.'

'Or what?' the landlord asked, clearly not getting the message.

'No, there was no 'or' about that. It was a statement because that is what is going to happen. If you want an 'or', I can give you one, but you don't want to hear it. That will mean we have crossed a line that you seriously do not want to cross.'

'I'll call the police,' the landlord said and reached out for the phone. Sutcliffe looked at Dawson, who had the landlord's arm up behind his back and his face pressed down on the counter before he could even lift the receiver.

'No,' Sutcliffe said. 'You won't.' There was an audible *crack* as the landlord's shoulder gave way. He screamed and dropped to his knees. 'You might need to call an ambulance, though. But if you so much as breathe a word about us being here, I'll know. And then I'll be back.' He punctuated this last threat by kicking the landlord in the face, then he and Dawson picked their bags up and left the pub.

Sutcliffe was feeling considerably better by the time they got outside. It was a bright day and already starting to warm up. His phone had pinged—finally, they seemed to be somewhere with a signal—and there was a text from Jonny Liddell telling him that their contact would meet them in an hour with transport. A map showed the location, which only seemed to be a short walk from where they were towards another no-horse town with too many consonants in its name. The contact would be waiting in a lay-by, it seemed, which Sutcliffe found quite reassuring. He didn't know there were any roads on this bloody island big enough for a lay-by. Dawson seemed less impressed.

'Walking?' he asked. 'Again?'

'Stop moaning,' Sutcliffe replied. 'Only for a bit, and then we'll have wheels. Sounds like we're nearly done here.'

'Tell you what,' Dawson suggested, 'why don't you go and get the wheels and come back and pick me up? I've still got a blister from yesterday.'

'I'll tell you what,' Sutcliffe said. 'No. Now let's get moving.'

***

The brief lifting of Sutcliffe's mood hadn't lasted long because he was now standing in the tattiest lay-by he had ever seen and had their contact by the throat. The walk had been longer than the map had implied and took them along another boring country road. At the end, a T-junction revealed a road that was practically a motorway by the standards they were used to; it actually had white lines down the middle and traffic on it. A short way along this road, they spotted a man in a leather jacket, jeans and sunglasses standing next to a very smart, black Jaguar.

'Sutcliffe?' he asked as they approached.

'Who else is it going to be out here?' Sutcliffe asked.

'This is more like it!' Dawson said, appraising the Jag. 'Very nice.'

'Thanks,' the man said. 'But it's mine. *That's* yours.'

He indicated the other vehicle in the lay-by. That was the moment Sutcliffe grabbed him by the throat and said, 'You have got to be fucking kidding me!'

'Look, mate,' the man gasped. 'Not my problem. I'm only delivering. Take it up with Liddell.'

'Oh, I will,' Sutcliffe said. 'Now give me your keys.'

'No chance. That's not in the deal.'

'I don't give a shit about the deal. Right now, the only shit that matters is the one Dawson is going to kick out of you if you don't give us the keys.'

Sutcliffe could never be quite sure where the guy got the strength from, or what the fuck Dawson was doing at the time, but one minute he was squeezing the delivery guy's windpipe, and the next he was on his knees on the rough ground with an excruciating pain shooting through his groin. The pain was compounded by the shower of grit that hit him when the Jaguar screamed out of the lay-by. Suddenly Dawson was there, helping him to his feet. Sutcliffe had to hit someone, so he cuffed Dawson hard across the back of his head.

'Where the fuck were you?' he demanded.

'Didn't expect him to have any fight in him. Soz.'

Sutcliffe started to push Dawson across the lay-by, giving him a shove to emphasise every word.

'Never—*ever*—use—the word—*soz*—again!'

Dawson sat down hard on the grass at the edge of the lay-by, narrowly avoiding what looked very much like a discarded and extremely used nappy.

'What are we going to do?' Dawson asked miserably.

'Well, first of all, I'm going to call Jonathan Fucking Liddell and give him ten seconds to explain exactly what the hell he thinks he's playing at. And if his explanation isn't adequate—and I doubt it will be—I'm going to suggest that he makes plans to emigrate before we can get back to Liverpool, because when I get my hands on him, I'm going to take a blunt butter knife and carve him a new arsehole.'

'I'm not being funny or anything, but he'll have time to emigrate and start a whole new life before we get back to Liverpool in *that*,' Dawson observed, pointing out the vehicle that had been supplied for their use.

He was probably right. The vehicle did not look particularly capable of going at high speed. It didn't look capable of going at moderate speed. But then speed isn't usually of the essence when you are driving a pastel pink coloured van with a giant plastic ice cream cornet on the top and has, emblazoned on the side in yellow letters in a friendly, cartoony font, the words 'Mr. Creamy'.

44

It was, Frank thought, uncanny how quickly chords came back to him. Apart from the night on the beach, he hadn't picked up a guitar for a few years now. Mick had hardly been able to comprehend this when he had told him on the phone. Mick had called to suggest meeting up, and it occurred to Frank for the first time since agreeing to play in public that he didn't have anything to play *on*. He wasn't sure why, but he hadn't even considered it. Perhaps he had been hoping that if he said 'Oops, I forgot I haven't got a guitar', they might let him off. There didn't seem to be much hope of that. So he had asked Mick if there was a music shop anywhere in reach. There was one in Bangor apparently and one in Conwy, but getting to either of them would involve taking time off from work and relying on public transport or trying to get a lift. Luckily (or not, depending on how you looked at it), Mick had offered to lend him a guitar straight away. He had fired off a few makers' names as if they would impress Frank, but he had never been that interested in names. The guitar and the bass he had used for years had been ones he had picked up, tried and liked the sound. The guitar Mick had brought had stayed in its case all through the previous, weird night, and it was only the following morning, when Frank woke up feeling surprisingly good, that he opened the case for a look.

He perched on the end of Gemma's bed and flipped the catches. Despite not knowing a great deal about guitars, he knew a Yamaha when he saw one, and this was a very nice electro acoustic, with a sunburst design body and a tortoiseshell pickguard. He ran his fingers gently across the strings, and even at that volume, it was obvious that the instrument had a beautiful tone. He glanced over his shoulder to make sure he hadn't woken Gemma because there was probably a conversation coming, and he wasn't sure it was one he was ready to have yet. It had been a little after one o'clock before they had gone to bed the previous night, and Gemma had surprised him by going straight to sleep. He had remained awake, picking over every word he had said to her and every word and nuance of what she had said, trying to work out if maybe this time he had gone too far. That was enough to think about, without even getting onto the subject of the (still nameless) spheres, which had followed Gemma back into the workshop like obedient puppies and stayed there. The fact that it had been way too late to think about going back to the B&B prevented any discussion about whether he should or not. But all the same, he was in no hurry for her to wake up so he could see how quickly she threw him out. He glanced at the clock Gemma kept by the side of her bed and saw that it was a little after five. He'd had, by his reckoning, two- and a-bit hours' sleep and hoped that Gemma would at least let him have a quick shower before sending him on his way. The prospect of a full day's work in the café was like standing at the foot of a mountain looking up. He pulled his clothes on, picked the guitar up, went outside, sat on the wall where he had sat when he first arrived and tried a few tunes out.

A bit of Nick Drake suited his mood, and the muscle memory in his fingers found the chords more easily than he had expected. He vaguely remembered his early days, teaching himself to play with the battered Beatles Complete, a book that almost certainly had more simplified versions of the chords than John, Paul and George played. His first guitar had what he later learned, a high action. He had to press down hard on the strings for the notes to sound at all clear rather than muddy and indistinct. That hurt. He would finish a session with deep depressions in his fingertips and the firm belief that he was never, ever going to be able to play the guitar. He heard somewhere that soaking your fingertips in white spirit would toughen the skin, and he followed this advice so regularly that he was probably not safe to be around a naked flame. Something helped, though. Whether it was the white spirit or the practice, he started to get better. He started to expand his repertoire by having a go at songs he heard on the Chart Show on the radio, and while he wasn't always sure he was exactly right, he was close enough.

Nick Drake had inevitably not lifted his mood very much, so he turned his attention to Dylan, someone he had always regarded as a great songwriter, but one whose songs always sounded better sung by someone else. He was strumming his way through 'Lay Lady Lay' when he was aware that someone was standing behind him. Instinctively, he stopped playing.

'No, don't stop,' Gemma said. 'You play well.'

'It's been a while,' he said. 'We used to do that one for an encore. Sean sang it better than I can.'

'You've got a nice voice.'

'Thank you. There are worse, I suppose.'

He put the guitar down and turned to look at her. She gave him a half-smile and sat down on the wall next to him. She was wearing the T-shirt she wore to bed and leggings, and because it was still quite cool, hugged herself for warmth.

'So how come you played bass then?' she asked. 'Yes, I looked. You'll have to tell me what that cow was about sometime.'

'Well, it wasn't our manager. He was into a different kind of grass. No, I sort of fell into the bass thing. Sean was a mate of a mate, and I'd heard they were looking for someone. Everyone wanted to be in a band in those days. They already had a guitarist but needed a bass, so I said I'd have a go. Luckily nobody else knew what they were doing, so by the time we were anywhere near ready to do anything, I'd got it sussed out enough that no one noticed.'

'You're too modest, you know. You were good. The band, I mean. You should have been bigger.'

'There were a lot of bands around in those days who should have been bigger. That's the business, though. A few make it. Loads don't.'

They both stared out across the beach for a while. Several black and white birds with bright red beaks that Frank thought Gemma had called oystercatchers were wading in the shallows, looking for breakfast. Frank had been amused by the name. As far as he knew, oysters didn't move fast enough for catching them to be worth boasting about. A gull of some kind (that was something else he had learned, that there were different kinds; he had thought they were all called seagulls) hovered over the water, then plunged in with barely a ripple. Frank waited to watch it emerge with its catch before he spoke.

'Is there going to be a difficult conversation?' he asked.

'Difficult? No. Except...'

'Except what?'

'Except thank you.'

'For what?'

'For trusting me.'

They watched the gull and the oystercatchers a bit more.

'I have to say,' Frank said eventually, 'that wasn't what I was expecting.' Gemma looked at him and raised an eyebrow. He loved the way she could raise one at a time. He'd never been able to do it without gurning.

'What were you expecting?' she asked.

'Something along the lines of 'Get lost, Frank, you murderer'. That sort of thing.'

'Why would I say that? You're not.'

'Might as well be.'

'No. Stop that, Frank, please. It was an accident. If it was murder, you'd have had to plan it, and I believe you're too kind to plan to hurt anyone. I need to know, though. Are you planning on hurting me?'

'What? No! I wouldn't do that!'

'You're restless, though, aren't you? I bet you don't stay in one place for long. How come you've never married? Or have you?'

'No. The opportunity has never presented itself.'

'Restless. I thought so.'

'Yes, okay, smartarse. What about you? I'm not exactly the only single one round here, am I? What's your story, Gemma?'

'I haven't got a story,' Gemma said, looking away.

'Everyone's got a story. Come on, I've told you mine. It

can't be any worse than that.'

'All right. I'll tell you. But not now.'

'Why not?'

'Because,' she said, standing up, grabbing him by the hand and pulling him to his feet, 'you need a shower, my friend. I don't think Kate would thank me for sending you into work stinking of ale.'

She let go of his hand and started to walk back to the fire escape. He put the guitar back in the case and snapped the catches closed. He watched her climb the fire escape. When she was halfway up, she turned to make sure he was following. It was then that something she said the previous night came back to him. *One way or another, we all have things we want to run away from*, she'd said. He hoped that whatever she was running from would not make her want to run again. Not now that there was every possibility he was falling in love with her.

45

Kate tapped on the tabletop with the end of her biro. The meeting had been due to start fifteen minutes earlier, but Ruth had been running late, and now she and Briony were having a lovely catch-up session, while Kate wanted to get the business of the meeting done and go home. She had been on her feet for a busy ten-hour day, and those same feet were letting her know about it. Ruth and Briony carried on gossiping, so Kate tapped harder. Her biro broke.

'Can we start, please?' she asked, getting up and going over to the cash register to find another biro. She scribbled on an order pad with the first two she found but to no avail. The third one worked, but it was red. It would have to do.

'Sorry, Kate,' Ruth said. 'Bri was telling me your plans. Sounds exciting.'

Kate scowled. The plans she and Briony had been discussing—only discussing, mind, nothing concrete— involved installing a couple of bread ovens at the back of the café, for which one of them would almost certainly have to take out a loan and they hadn't even got on to looking at which of them had the better credit score. Assuming they could get the ovens, the idea was for Briony to make her own artisan bread and sell it in the café initially and then spread further afield. There were far too many ifs and buts for the plans to be anything like solid yet. There was the matter of the family business, for which Briony's father relied on her and which also provided a steady wage, and there were plenty of conversations to be had about that. They had only started talking about the whole thing a couple of days earlier, and Kate thought it was a bit premature to be discussing it with anyone else yet, even a friend like Ruth. Besides, there were more urgent things to talk about, which was why they were there, rather than sitting at home with a glass of something, watching the television.

'It's early days, Ruth,' she said. 'But in the meantime...'

'Sorry, Katie,' Briony said, but the mischievous twinkle in her eye said that she was anything but sorry and also made it difficult for Kate to stay cross.

'Yes, well, the sooner we get through this, the sooner we can all go home. So, here's where we're up to. Frank assures me that his mate Mick has everything in hand as far as the music is concerned. His band is all booked, and he's got the PA organised. He knows someone who's going to bring the staging over the day before and get it set up—all free of charge, which is good of them. Frank is going to remind Mick about it all. Apparently, they got very pissed when they met to talk about it.'

'Do we need to worry about this Mick?' Ruth asked. 'He *is* going to turn up, isn't he?'

'Frank says so. He's going to talk to Mick's partner about it, though, just in case. It sounds like she's more of a carer than a partner. Mick enjoyed the 90s quite a lot from all accounts.'

'As long as he does. It would be awful if people turn up to an empty stage.'

'It won't happen. Honestly. Speaking of which,' Kate consulted her notes, 'we've sold sixty-two tickets so far. That's over the counter and online. Ruth, could you send a reminder out to the parents, please? I know there aren't that many of them these days, but they need to be spreading the word.'

'Will do. They're bloody slow to respond to anything, that lot, especially if it means spending money. I'll lay it on thick again that the school will close if we can't get the roof sorted out. You'd think they'd be desperate to help, but no. It's always somebody else's problem.'

'How did we get on with the chairs?'

'Great. The high school in Beaumaris will let us have as many as we want and bring them here in the school minibus. As long as they can get them back before the Monday, they're happy.'

'Ace.' Kate ran her finger down the list. 'Bri's got the

crowdfunding page set up, and donations are already coming in, but we need to push that a bit more. Oh, go on, Bri. Tell Ruth what you found.'

Briony laughed and scrolled down her phone until she found what she was looking for.

'Check that out,' she said and passed her phone to Ruth.

'Is that...? Oh bloody hell, a *fan* page?'

'Hey, don't knock it,' Briony said. 'The Leisure Decree nearly had a hit, you know! Of course, they've got a fan page. I've made contact, and they're going to shout about it. The lady who ran the page nearly fainted when she heard that Frank was appearing in public. She made it sound like the Second Coming. I think we could pick a lot of sales up from that.'

'If only they knew they could come here and get a cup of coffee made by him too,' Kate said. 'We could all be rich. I think Frank would run a mile as well. On the subject of coffee, I've sorted the coffee van for the day, so that's okay. We could do with something for the kids as well, but I'm still on the lookout for that. Oh, and did I tell you about Huw?'

'No, what's he done now?' Ruth asked.

'Actually, it's pretty good for him. He's given over one of his fields for camping for that weekend. Reckons he's nearly filled it too. He says he'll give us a percentage of what he takes, but equally possible he'll tell us that bloody soft dog of his ate it or something.'

'If it works, he might keep doing it, though,' Briony suggested. 'Can't do any harm to have a few more tourists around here, especially if you, say, run a café or something. God knows what toilet facilities he's providing, though. A bucket in the barn, probably.'

'And on that note,' Ruth said, pulling a face, 'I think maybe we'd better call it a day. Unless there's anything else...?'

'Can't think of anything right now,' Kate said. 'I'll text you if I do.'

'No problem. Any time. And thanks, girls. I do appreciate all you're doing.'

'You don't have to keep saying that,' Kate said. 'It's okay,

Ruth. We know.'

'Well, my mother always brought me up to be polite,' she looked at her watch, 'which is more than Phil will be if I'm not home in time for his call. Speak to you tomorrow.'

Ruth dashed out of the café and off up the steps. In the silence that followed her explosive exit, Briony got up from her seat and went over and put her arms around Kate.

'I'm sorry for blabbing about the bread idea,' she said. 'I could see you weren't impressed.'

'It's okay. But it's early days yet. I don't want to jinx it.'

'You won't. We'll make it work, Katie. All of it. I think that's why I got a bit carried away. I'm not used to talking about a future like that.'

'Is that what I am?'

'The future? No, babe. That's what *we* are. Come on. Let's go home and talk about it some more.'

Kate had already cleaned the café, so all she needed to do was grab her bag, turn the lights off and lock up. As she walked up the steps, hand in hand with Bri, she noticed an ice cream van parked up along the road. It was hard to tell from where she was, but there didn't seem to be anyone around. The windows of the van were closed and dark.

'Hey, look at that,' she said. 'I said I wanted something for the kids. I'll see if he's around tomorrow and have a word.'

'I'm not so sure about that,' Briony said with a grin. 'I'm not sure I want any girlfriend of mine having anything to do with a guy who calls himself Mr. Creamy.'

46

Sutcliffe and Dawson had spent the night in the ice cream van, and it had not been comfortable for either of them. Sutcliffe had pulled rank and insisted on taking the driver's seat, leaving Dawson to doss down in the back, occupying the narrow expanse of floor between the serving hatch and the freezers. The temperature outside was comparatively mild, but by its nature, the interior of an ice cream van was never going to be very warm, and they were both dressed for summer. There was something that looked like it could have been heating in the van's cab, but no matter how he tried or how loudly he swore, Sutcliffe could not persuade it to work. It was just one more thing on the list of things for which he owed Jonathan Liddell a slap.

After the deliveryman had raced out of the lay-by, presumably heading back to Liverpool and a nice warm bed, Sutcliffe had rung Liddell to have a little chat about the situation, but the conversation had not gone the way he hoped.

'Liddell, you melt,' he had begun, 'explain the transport situation to me.'

'Did he get it to you?' Liddell asked from a very safe distance. 'Great.'

'No, I'm sorry,' Sutcliffe said, doing his best to keep calm. 'You've lost me there. What, exactly, would you consider to be great about stranding us on this godforsaken island with only a clapped out ice cream van for transport? How could that possibly be great?'

'It's the perfect cover,' Liddell said. 'Who's going to suspect an ice cream van?'

'Let me put it another way. Get us a proper fucking car, right now, or the job's off. But seeing as we're all set to kill someone, it might as well be you.'

'It's only for a couple of days. Find Davies, get the money, and that's it. No more ice cream van.'

'No. We're not doing it.'

'I think you're being a bit ungrateful. I've gone to a lot of trouble and expense to get that van. I had to find one first, then get hold of the owner and get him to leave it there. Of course, he wanted compensating for loss of trade, especially with it being summer.'

'Have you got any idea how much of a shit I don't give about that?'

'On the positive side, the van should be stocked. If you sell anything, you get to keep the money.'

'You want me to sell ice cream?'

'If you want, yes.'

'You want me to sell ice fucking cream?'

'Up to you. It was just a thought.'

'Here's another thought. No. You need to sort this, Liddell.'

'Well, I'd have to speak to Mr. James about it. It was his idea.'

'Then speak to him. *Now*. Tell him what I told you. Proper transport or we're heading back.'

'I'll call you back.'

Liddell hung up before he heard what Sutcliffe called him next. Sutcliffe was about to start complaining to Dawson, but when he looked around, Dawson was nowhere to be seen.

'Hey, look at this!'

Dawson was inside the ice cream van, grinning like an idiot as he poured ice cream into a cone.

'I think I'm getting the hang of this,' he added as he continued to pour the white foam over his hand and then the floor. 'Shit,' he said, trying desperately to find out how to turn it off. Once he had, he stood there licking ice cream off his hand.

'Do you want crushed nuts?' Sutcliffe asked.

'I don't think there are any,' Dawson replied, glancing around. 'There are hundreds and thousands.'

'I didn't mean on the ice cream. I meant in general.'

'Very funny. Hey, did you hear about the ice cream seller

who was found dead in his van covered in hundreds and thousands and strawberry sauce? They reckon he topped himself!' Dawson roared with laughter until he saw the look on Sutcliffe's face.

'Wait there,' Sutcliffe said and strode over to the van, nearly pulling the door off as he wrenched it open. He grabbed Dawson by the lapels, making him skid on the white and sticky puddle that wasn't quite ice cream anymore. He hauled Dawson towards him so that they were virtually nose-to-nose.

'That wasn't funny,' he said. 'There is nothing about this clusterfuck that is remotely funny. Now get this mess cleaned up before it starts to attract wasps or something.'

'Sorry,' Dawson said. 'Just trying to lighten things up.'

'The only thing that's going to lighten things up is Jonathan Liddell's head on a plate. And once we get back to Liverpool, that is definitely going to happen.'

A tapping on the window of the serving hatch interrupted him. While he had been busy, he had not noticed a car pull up in the lay-by and its occupants get out, a man, a woman and two small children, a girl and what was probably a boy, but its hair was so long that it was hard to tell.

'Excuse me,' the man said.

'We're closed,' Sutcliffe replied.

'Your window's open.'

'We're still closed.'

'We wanted a couple of ice creams. It's for the kids.'

'And what was it you wanted?'

'Just a couple of cones, please?'

'And did you want flakes in those?'

'Only in one,' the woman said. 'Alfie can't have chocolate. He's intolerant.'

'I wondered if he might be,' Sutcliffe said. 'And what about sprinkles? Or are they a choking hazard?'

'Oh, they could be,' the woman said, apparently in all seriousness. 'And a bottle of water.'

'The water isn't organic, I'm afraid,' Sutcliffe said. 'It's just water.'

'How much?' the man asked, reaching into his pocket.

'Here's the thing,' Sutcliffe said, 'we're closed. Like I said.'

'But you took our order!' the man protested.

'No, I didn't. I asked what you wanted. I didn't say you were going to get it. We're closed.'

'Look, this is ridiculous. You can't talk to us like that. Your sign says, 'Stop Me and Buy One'.'

'Did you stop us?'

'Well, no, but...'

'Or were you, in fact, the ones who stopped?'

'I suppose we were.'

'Good,' Sutcliffe said. 'Glad we got that sorted out. Now fuck off.' With that, he closed the window. The man slapped on the window for a bit, but Sutcliffe ignored him. He was too busy answering the phone to Jonathan Liddell.

'Give me good news, Liddell,' he said.

'It's sort of good news,' Liddell replied. 'Mr. James says he'll send a car for you...'

'Good.'

'...to drive back in once you've done the job.'

'Not good.'

'Best I can do, I'm afraid. Mr. James is convinced that the ice cream van is the best cover for you to get in and out, and you know what he's like when he's got an idea. You can't move him.'

'I can see the getting in bit, Jonny. That isn't the bit I've got a problem with. It's not ideal, but I can see where he's coming from. The problem I've got is with the getting out bit. Let me set the scene for you. We find Davies and relieve him of Mr. James's money. That is assuming, of course, that he co-operates. If he doesn't, and we have to persuade him, that could get messy, up to, and including, shooting the bastard. All good so far. But the bit that bothers me, and it's the bit that I don't think Mr. James has thought through, is that afterwards, we then have to make our escape in an ice cream van. Now, I would imagine that the authorities round here aren't so backward that they don't have cars and go round on bikes or horses or something. That being the case, I don't fancy our chances of getting away in a vehicle that only goes at about ten miles an hour and plays fucking Greensleeves as we go. Now, do you see the problem?'

'Yes, I do. Which is exactly why you let us know when you're going to do it, and we'll have a car there in two hours tops. Oh, and Sutcliffe...'

'What?'

'Mr. James says can you save him a Strawberry Mivvi?'

Sutcliffe hung up.

'Right,' he said. 'Let's find this Chapel Bay place, deal with Davies and get the hell out of here.'

Finding Chapel Bay had turned out to be a bit easier than they thought. Even in this Day-Glo death trap, it was easier and quicker than on foot. It only took them the rest of the day, and that was because they took a wrong turn somewhere and found themselves back at the Menai Bridge twice. Once they understood the correct way they were supposed to go around the island, it looked straightforward. By the time they saw the first signs for Chapel Bay, they were both feeling a bit hungry, so they stopped at the next pub they came to, which served a very acceptable fish and chips. It also served a beer which wasn't completely gnat's piss, and several pints of that went down quite easily. It made the few miles' drive up the coast in the gathering dusk rather more hazardous, so they parked where they could at Chapel Bay and tried to get the best night's sleep, resolving to get down to business the following day.

They were woken from their fitful slumber by the sound of a van driving past. It wasn't the van that disturbed them, so much as the fact that it was blasting out *Daddy Cool* at a volume that wasn't fitting for that time of the morning. They were settling down again when there was a knock on the side of the van.

'Who the fuck...?' Sutcliffe asked, trying to straighten himself up from the capital L shape he was starting to fear he might be stuck in for the rest of his life. He opened the van door and was greeted by the sight of two attractive women, one blonde and extremely shapely and the other smaller and darker.

'Good morning,' the dark-haired one said. 'I'm really sorry to bother you. My name's Kate, and I have the café down there. Look, I know it's probably short notice, and you're probably very busy, but we're running a charity concert on Saturday, and we could do with an ice cream concession. I don't suppose you'd be interested?'

Sutcliffe was about to make an obscene suggestion when a thought occurred to him.

'This wouldn't be the concert Frankie Davies is playing at, would it?'

'Yes, it is,' the woman called Kate said. 'Have you heard of him?'

'Oh, we certainly have. We've been dying to see him. So yes, I think we can definitely arrange to be there. You can call me Mr. Creamy, by the way. And my associate in the back there goes by the name of Mr....er...Sprinkles.'

'That's great!' Kate said. 'I can't thank you enough. Listen, why don't you come down to the café when you're ready and have breakfast on us?'

'Thank you,' Sutcliffe said. 'We'd like that, Kate. We'd like that very much.'

47

Gemma didn't mind that Frank was spending most of their evenings together practising. When he confessed that he was a bit shaky on some of the songs he used to perform with the Leisure Decree, she had looked on eBay and located copies of the band's only two albums. The first self-titled album was quite easy to find, but she had to pay over the odds for an American import copy for the second, which had the unlikely title 'Exit Pursued By A Bear'. When she asked why they had called it that, Frank replied, 'We thought we were clever. It's probably why it didn't sell.' Gemma had played both CDs and preferred the second. The songs weren't as commercial or as immediately catchy, but they had more depth and, where the lyrics on the first album were at times extremely pretentious, the songs on 'Bear' seemed more like the work of serious musicians rather than art-school kids. Frank laughed when she told him this and observed that none of them had been to art school. Sean was a welder by day, and Darren, having failed tryouts with both Liverpool and Everton, worked for Littlewoods Pools. They were all self-taught and had little idea what they were doing. They were lucky that Britpop was in such high demand at the time, and smaller record labels were springing up everywhere. They were, however, unlucky that the real demand was for slightly edgier bands from Manchester and London. Liverpool, once the capital city of pop music, hardly got a look in.

The CDs had brought the memories flooding back, and Frank had worked up a set list that would last an hour or so of the Leisure Decree songs he thought the audience might like and some cover versions of songs he liked himself. He even asked Gemma if she had any requests. She thought for a moment.

'What about Have I Told You Lately That I Love You?' she

suggested. She caught a look on his face and started back-pedalling. 'No, sorry. Too much, I know.' But Frank had smiled, played the song through, or at least as much of it as he could remember, and promised to look the lyrics up and include it in the set. He sang it so well, not too schmaltzy, with the right amount of grit, that Gemma allowed herself to wonder if he was singing from the heart.

Over the next couple of days, they had developed a routine. Gemma would work in her workshop as there were more tourists around. She was actually selling things and had to restock frequently, and Frank was Latte Man. In the evenings, Frank practised while Gemma read. They ate together, and Gemma was pleased that Frank seemed more relaxed about doing so in her presence. They then watched television or a film. She couldn't pinpoint the exact day that Frank had moved out of the B&B and into her flat but presumed that Mrs. Evans wouldn't mind. It was the time of year when there were plenty of people looking for somewhere to stay. It was comfortable and relaxed, and they didn't talk about anything important. For those days, the past stayed exactly where it belonged.

The mystery of the spheres remained unsolved. Gemma had not put them back in the box after that night Frank had got drunk with Mick. She left them on the side of her workbench, where they seemed quite content to glow quietly to themselves. Twice, customers had spotted them and asked if they were for sale. But Gemma had said they were for display and had no intention of selling them at any price. She was almost able to forget they were there at all, most of the time. Then two things happened in fairly quick succession that made her question once again exactly what she was sharing her workshop with.

The first thing happened one evening when Frank had finished at the café, and Gemma was working late trying to get a couple of orders finished. She could hear the guitar playing upstairs, though not distinctly enough to pick a tune out, and then heard the clang of footsteps on the fire escape as Frank descended.

'Have you got a minute?' he asked.

'If I can carry on doing this,' she said. 'If I don't glue it now, it'll be wrecked.'

'No, you crack on. I wanted to see what you thought about this. I quite like the idea of doing a Neil Diamond song.'

'Jesus, not Sweet Caroline. It's not bloody karaoke, Frank.'

'No, not that. I thought maybe Solitary Man. Have a listen.'

Frank perched on the edge of the workbench and started to pick the song out. He was about halfway through when it happened. One of the spheres began to glow deep blue, then shot off the bench and cracked Frank on the knuckles. He stopped playing, grimaced and shook his hand.

'Shit! What did you do that for?'

The sphere gave a peculiar hum and dropped back into its place on the bench as if nothing had happened.

'What the hell?' Frank said. 'It wasn't that bad!'

'Are you okay?' Gemma asked.

'Ow. Yes. I haven't had a rap on the knuckles like that since school. Everyone's a critic, though. I won't tell Neil. He'll be devastated.'

'I wonder...' Gemma said. 'Play something else. Play Have I Told You Lately.'

'You're joking, aren't you? I need this hand.'

'I think it'll be okay. Just try it. Please?'

'Okay, but if your little mate breaks my hand, you can explain it to Kate.'

Frank started playing. A bit apprehensively at first, but once it became apparent that nothing was going to happen, he grew in confidence. The spheres stayed where they were, pulsing a gentle green in time to the music. Gemma couldn't take her eyes off them. By the time Frank finished, those eyes had tears glistening in them.

'Oh, Frank,' she said. 'I think they know.'

'Know? Know what? That they prefer Van to Neil? Come on, Gemma. That's ridiculous.'

'No, I think they know what the songs are about.'

Frank put his guitar down and stared at her. Then he laughed.

'That's even more ridiculous. I think you've been overdoing it, Gem. I've never heard anything so...'

'You explain it then.'

'Obviously, I can't. We don't know what these things are, or where they came from or anything.'

'Yes, we do. They came from the stars.'

'We *assume*. We don't know, though. It's more likely they come from Japan. But in any case, it's a bit of a leap to think that they understand English and an even bigger one to think that they have taste in song lyrics. No, sorry, Gem. This is a bit too much for me.'

'Think about it. They stopped you playing the one about being solitary but liked the soppier one. They must have been picking up on something. I don't know that it's the words, exactly. Maybe it's the feeling.'

'No, this is getting too weird for me. They're made of glass! They don't feel things.'

As he spoke, there was a noise from the workbench, and the two spheres rolled towards him. They were both glowing the same dark blue as before.

'I think you'd probably better apologise, Frank. That doesn't look too friendly if you ask me.'

'Okay, okay! I apologise. Clearly, you do have feelings, and if I have hurt them, I'm sorry. You've got to appreciate that this is hard for us to understand. We're only human.' Frank watched as the glow died down to a lighter shade, and the spheres rolled backwards to their original position and muttered, 'I can't believe I said that.'

'I have a theory,' Gemma said. 'I think they want us to be together. Remember when you were drunk and walking away? They made you come back. And just now, the difference between the two songs. They're happier when we're together.'

'What, seriously? I can just kind of accept that they're alien. I'm getting my head round the idea that they could have some kind of sentience. But alien matchmakers? No. Sorry. Why would they do that?'

'Frank, it's obvious. We brought them back together. One

was broken, and it was only when we found the other one that it repaired itself.'

'They're a *couple*?'

'Of some kind, yes.'

The spheres, in perfect unison, rose from the workbench.

'So what the hell are they doing now?'

Slowly, the spheres, glowing a soft turquoise, rose into the air and began to move, circling around the space Gemma and Frank occupied. They made two wide circuits and then began to get nearer with each pass until they brushed against Frank's shoulder as they flew by, forcing him to take a step forward, a step nearer to Gemma. As they hovered, they started making their singing sound again. They nudged Frank once more, and Gemma laughed.

'Give them what they want, Frank.'

'Oh, I don't know,' Frank replied, but he was laughing now too. 'I think I'm being manipulated here.'

He moved forwards again, and Gemma was in his arms.

'They've got a point,' he said and kissed her. The spheres abruptly stopped singing and innocently settled back down on the workbench.

'I've got a name for them,' Gemma said when they came up for air. 'Seeing as they like Mr. Morrison so much, how about Moondancers?'

'I think that sounds perfect,' Frank said, his face buried in Gemma's hair. 'You know what else sounds perfect? You packing it in for the night and coming upstairs. On your own, though. Our friends have done their job for the day.'

***

The second thing the Moondancers did was rather more troubling and happened two days later. There were only a couple of days to go to the concert, and Gemma and Frank had woken early. Gemma knew that Frank had slept badly. It wasn't hard to tell in a bed that size. He had got up at least twice, whispering an apology and telling her to go back to sleep. The first time, he came back to bed an hour or so later.

The second time, at around five, he didn't come back to bed at all. Gemma got up and found him drinking coffee in the flat's small kitchen.

'Come back,' she said. 'You haven't had much sleep.'

Frank shook his head. 'I'll only disturb you. I'd be getting up in a bit anyway.'

'It's the gig, isn't it? Are you worried?'

'I'm shitting myself if I'm honest. I haven't been on a stage this century. Even then, I hated it. I didn't mind playing, but I've never liked being watched. At least in the band, everyone was looking at Sean, not me.'

'You're good, though. Really good.'

'Am I? I don't know anymore. I'm not sure I did then.'

'What's the worst that can happen?'

'The worst? Only that a load of people who remember the Leisure Decree being better than we were, all turning up, seeing me and saying I'm crap. At least I'm only the support act, and Mick's band will blow them away. Otherwise, they'll all be asking for their money back. That won't help Ruth much.'

'They won't want their money back. You'll go down a storm. I can understand you being anxious, though. I couldn't go anywhere near a stage, let alone perform on one. Anyway, another couple of days and it'll all be over, and you'll never have to do it again. You can go back to being Latte Man.'

'If I can ever show my face in public again.'

'Stop it now. You'll be fine.'

'I might have a quick practice before work, if that's okay.'

'It's fine. I'll grab a shower first.'

Gemma had her shower, dressed and went down to the workshop to give Frank some space. She only hoped he could calm down before the concert. Otherwise, he ran the risk of letting his nerves make his prediction come true. She had meant what she said; he *was* good, and if he could control his anxiety, everyone else would see that too.

When she reached the bottom of the fire escape, she could see that Kate already had customers at the café. She and Briony were sitting at one of the tables outside with two middle-aged men who were tucking into cooked breakfasts. It was quite unusual for Kate to have customers that early; it was only just gone seven, and the café didn't open until eight. Briony would normally have left by now, too, so there was obviously something going on. As she wrestled with the lock on the workshop door, one of the men looked over, a large chunk of sausage on his fork and his mouth open, ready to take a bite. There was something about his face that seemed vaguely familiar, one of those faces that you think you've seen somewhere before but can't place where. He turned back to Kate, and they all started laughing at something someone had said. Whoever he was, there was something about him that Gemma didn't trust and definitely didn't like. Her instincts about people didn't usually let her down, not since that one time they had let her down totally, of course, but that was why she was so much warier now. The lock finally turned and allowed her to open the door and go inside. As she opened the door, it banged against something on the floor behind it. She nearly jumped out of her skin when she went in, and one of the Moondancers rolled over her foot.

She bent down to look, and both the spheres were on the workshop floor near the doorway, as if they had been trying to get out. They were glowing that disquieting deep blue and rolling backwards and forwards restlessly. If an alien glass sphere could look agitated, she thought, this is what it would look like. She scooped them up, one in each hand and carried them over to the bench. She sat down and brought her hands together so she was cradling them both in the cup her palms made.

'Shh,' she whispered. 'It's okay. I'm here. What's got you guys all worked up then?'

As she cooed and whispered to the Moondancers, their colour changed, from the angry dark blue to a deep green and then a more gentle emerald. Their restless movements began to calm.

'That's better,' she said. 'It's okay. You're safe with me.'

The Moondancers were now glowing a pale peridot colour and felt still in Gemma's hands.

'There you go,' she said. 'Don't worry. Nothing's going to harm you.'

But as she said that, another burst of raucous male laughter came from outside, and the Moondancers turned dark blue again. Gemma could feel their tense vibration in her palms.

'It's them, isn't it?' she said. 'There's something about them. We won't let them harm you. Me and Frank, we'll look after you.'

For the first time since she had arrived on Anglesey, Gemma felt suddenly and inexplicably afraid.

48

The day before the concert had to be a hot one, didn't it? Kate was glad in one way that the weather was good and was forecast to be sunny all weekend. There would, at this point, be nothing worse than rain. People might not mind paddling through a swamp at Glastonbury, but here it would be more likely to put them off coming at all. She could, however, do with it being a bit cooler today when there was so much setting up to do. She wiped the perspiration from her forehead with the back of her hand and started the next row of folding chairs. It had been slow going at first, but now she had got into a rhythm, it was picking up pace nicely. Her back would probably have something to say about it later, but hopefully, a hot bath and painkillers would sort it out. On the other side of the field, Briony, who had raced through her bread round to come and help, was matching her chair for chair and didn't seem bothered by the heat at all.

At least, she thought, she wasn't Mick. The first she had seen of Frank's old friend was when a large removal van had managed to get itself stuck in the lane near the field. Kate had gone to see what the fuss was about and had seen a man with hair longer than was appropriate for someone of his age, leaning out of the passenger window of the van and producing a very colourful litany of swear words, some of which Kate had never heard before. Luckily, Huw was on hand (supervising, rather than helping). He was able to assist the van driver in negotiating a very awkward reversing manoeuvre, which finally got him back down the lane and through the gate onto the field. Once the van had parked, the sweary, long-haired man jumped down from the cab.

'Fuck me,' he said. 'Thought we'd never get here.'

Kate introduced herself and shook his hand, which was rough and calloused. She caught a whiff of something fragrant and smoky that she was sure owed nothing to any cigarettes John Player produced. But fair play to him, once she had explained that Frank was running the café today and would be down later, he and his mate (whose name seemed to be Rags) got straight down to it, unloading the stage blocks from the van and setting them up where Kate directed. They seemed to be making good progress despite the heat and the urgent need for frequent water and smoke breaks. Kate was happy to let them get on with it while she and Bri started the chairs. Ruth had said she'd be along when she could, and Ewa and Tomasz from the shop had offered to help too as and when they were free. Kate had decided not to wait for anyone else but to get on with it. There would be plenty to do later; the coffee van was due to be delivered at some point in the afternoon (no, they couldn't give an exact time), and she hadn't seen the two strange ice cream sellers. She could only hope they would turn up and was kicking herself for not taking their contact details. Just as she was beginning to curse people who promised to help and then didn't, she saw the familiar figure of Ruth coming through the gate. A tall, very well-built man with close-cropped hair and an impressive beard followed her onto the field.

'Sorry, Kate,' she said. 'I was on my way, but then look who turned up on my doorstep out of the blue! He's only taken time off without telling me.'

'Phil!' Kate said, giving him a hug. 'How lovely!'

'Hey, Kate. Good to see you. This is a great thing you're doing. I had to come and support if I could. I was due some leave anyway. What can I do?'

'You could give us a hand with the chairs, if you wouldn't mind.'

'No problem,' Phil said and got down to it straight away, assembling and arranging chairs at probably twice the speed Kate had been managing.

'He's good,' Kate said to Ruth. 'Bloody hell, look at him go!'

'I could watch those muscles for hours,' Ruth replied. 'You're lucky to have him, you know. This isn't how we normally spend the first couple of hours after he comes home.'

'That's probably a little too much information.' Kate surveyed the field. 'I can't believe we've got here. If we fill these seats, you should get your roof.'

'To say nothing of it being one in the eye for Moody Mike Tremaine. Really, Kate, I'm never going to be able to thank you and Briony enough. And Frank, of course. How's he feeling about it all?'

'He isn't talking much about it, but I think he's quite stressed. I feel sorry for him. I don't think he expected all this when he turned up here. But on the positive side, he's got the lovely Gemma looking after him, so that must be a bit of a bonus.'

'Is it serious between those two, do you think?'

'I'm not sure. They seem to be enjoying each other's company at the moment, but seeing as they both showed up in Chapel Bay out of nowhere, I'm not sure either of them is the settling down type, if you know what I mean.'

'Not like you and Briony.'

'Not like us, no. Speaking of which, I don't think it's fair for us to stand here gossiping like fishwives while our spouses do all the work. Go on, you go and give Phil a hand, and I'll help Bri. Bet we get our side done first.'

'You're on.'

Ruth went off to join her husband, and Kate crossed the field to where Briony was working. Bri looked up when she saw her coming and smiled.

'It's about time,' she said. 'Thought you were going to leave me to it.'

'That's Ruth's husband,' Kate replied. 'He's come back from the rigs to support her. That's sweet, isn't it?'

'That's love. You support the people you love. It's why I'm here rather than driving round dropping bread off.'

Kate picked up a chair, and for a while, they worked in companionable silence.

'We work well together,' Briony said once she had finished a row and paused for a breather.

'We do,' Kate agreed.

'So, have you thought any more about my offer?'

'What, for the café? Yes, I've thought about it. I don't know, Bri. Are you sure it's what you really want?'

'Don't you?'

'Of course I do. Only it's a massive step for you. What does your dad think about the idea?'

'He's all for it. He's wanted to sell the bread round for ages and retire properly. He thought he'd be selling it to me, not to some stranger and all, so I can go off and bake bread with my girlfriend.'

'Could we do it, do you think? Work together, I mean. Could we spend all that time together and not get fed up?'

'Yes, Katie. We can. I don't know about you, but I feel like any time I don't spend with you is time wasted. I've waited a long time for you, and now I want to make the most of every minute. Does that sound selfish?'

'No,' Kate said. 'It sounds just perfect.'

'So it's a yes then?'

'Yes. It is. There is one snag, though.'

'What's that?'

'Frank. How am I going to tell him I won't need him anymore?'

'You've got a bit of time. It's not like it's going to happen overnight.'

'I know. And he probably knows that this is only for the summer. He's not stupid by any means. I hope he doesn't pack up and go. I've got used to seeing his face around the place, and I think it would probably break Gemma's heart.'

49

There was, Sutcliffe thought, something faintly disturbing about how much Dawson seemed to be enjoying selling ice cream. Part of the deal the woman from the café had offered was that in exchange for the pitch at the gig, they wouldn't give her any competition by selling around the village until the day of the gig. Sutcliffe had agreed readily. The gig would give them the best possible cover, with plenty of people around, to take Davies, but he certainly didn't intend to be an ice cream salesman in the intervening days. That wasn't part of the plan. In any case, being a salesman meant being a people person, an expression he hated and one that could never be applied to him. A people-hating person, perhaps, but not a people person. All Sutcliffe wanted to do was find a bed and breakfast somewhere for a few days, hole up there and wait for Saturday, when they would deal with Davies, take the vehicle Liddell had promised and get the hell off this island.

The first part had been relatively easy to solve. They had pulled up in the next village, gone for a wander and spotted a bed and breakfast sign quite quickly. The tiny Welsh woman with enormous eyebrows who had answered the door was very happy to rent them two rooms, especially when Sutcliffe turned on the charm. He explained that they were salesmen and allowed her a glimpse of the large roll of cash he had concealed about his person. They were very lucky, she said. Someone had moved out just the day before at very short notice, and she could do them bed and breakfast at forty pounds a night. Sutcliffe paid a week in advance, even though they weren't going to be staying that long. It was worth it just to spend the next few nights in a bed rather than on the floor of an ice cream van.

Dawson's career as an ice cream salesman began later that day when they went back to make sure that nobody had stolen the van. It was unlikely in this backwater because, as Sutcliffe had said, 'You won't get many hardened criminals hanging round here.'

'We are,' Dawson replied, and there wasn't any arguing with that, so they had gone to check anyway. As they approached the van, they could see that two small children, a boy and a girl, were hanging around outside.

'Oi!' Sutcliffe shouted, stomping towards the van with his fists raised. 'Get away from that, you little bastards.'

He had thought they would run, but they didn't. The little girl started to cry, and the boy looked up at Sutcliffe with the saddest eyes he had ever seen.

'Sorry, Mister,' he said. 'She just wanted a Mini Milk.'

Sutcliffe was about to reply, but Dawson interrupted.

'I think we might have one of those,' he said. 'Shall we see, Mr. Creamy?'

Without waiting for an answer, he had jumped into the van and opened the window. He had two of the appropriate ice creams in his hand.

'Here you go,' he said, handing them to the boy and taking some sticky coins in return. 'They're buy one get one free, but only to you. Don't tell anyone.'

The boy thanked him, and, after getting a dig from her brother to prompt her, so did the girl, and they scampered off with their spoils.

'Buy one get one free,' Sutcliffe said. 'But only to you. Jesus, Dawson, you sound like the fucking Childcatcher.'

'Where's the harm?' Dawson said. 'Did you see their little faces?'

'I wanted to slap their little faces.'

'Don't be tight. We just made their day.'

'You know what would make my day? Shooting you for calling me Mr. Creamy. That would make my day.'

'I reckon we should do it,' Dawson said, ignoring the threat.

'Do what?'

'Sell ice creams.'

'No.'

'Just for a couple of days.'

'No.'

'Just until the gig.'

'No.'

'Why not? It'll pass the time.'

'Look, Dawson, I'll do you a deal. You can sell all the ice creams you like to snot-nosed little brats, but do *not* involve me. And if you ever call me Mr. Creamy again, I will shoot you, I promise.'

'Can I be Mr. Creamy then?'

'You can be Mr. Turd on a Stick as far as I'm concerned. Just don't involve me.'

And so, for the next few days, Dawson happily sold cornets and lollies while Sutcliffe hung around in the cab or outside the van, hoping his malignant presence would put the kids off. Nothing, however, puts kids off buying ice cream, a prospect that Sutcliffe found very depressing indeed. There was going to be an obesity crisis on this island before very long. But fortunately, their job would be done, and they would be long gone by then. This was just one more thing Frankie Davies was going to pay for.

50

Frank stood at the front of the stage and looked at the speaker stacks that Mick's roadies were assembling and felt sick. The members of the current incarnation of The Riflemen were milling about, sorting their instruments out, and the ease and confidence with which they moved about the stage made him feel anxious. As soon as they had finished putting the PA system together, he was supposed to be having a sound check. At the moment, he would rather have been literally anywhere else. Any time now, a group of professional musicians would get a good laugh at what a fraud he was. He became aware that Mick was standing next to him but had totally misjudged the mood.

'I couldn't live without this, man,' Mick said. 'No buzz like it. If I didn't have this, you might as well put me in a box.'

'Right now, I think I'd take the box.'

'Don't be like that, Frankie. You'll be fine. You never forget how to do it.'

'You might not, but you've been touring for like twenty years. Last time I did this, John Major was shagging Edwina Currie. Do us a favour, Mick? You guys do a longer set. No one's going to miss me.'

'You're kidding, aren't you? Everyone's coming to see you. You're a legend, dude.'

'You know what the thing is with legends, Mick? They're not true, and they're never what you think. They're always a letdown.'

'Not you, mate. You're not going to let anyone down.' Mick took a battered tobacco tin out of his pocket and started rolling a hefty joint. 'Not like me. I let people down all the time. Especially Nina. I'm always letting her down. Don't know why she puts up with me, really. But she's done it for eighteen years. Anyway, you'll be okay. I've got something coming that'll help you.' He lit the spliff and took a long drag.

'No, Mick. I'm not taking anything. No way.'

'Well, I know *that*. You've always been too straight for your own good. No, this is a different kind of help. Should be here any minute. In fact...' A tinny version of the opening chords of Should I Stay or Should I Go rang out from somewhere about Mick's person. He patted his pockets and pulled out the tobacco tin again, keys, a wallet and eventually his phone. It was one of the flip-top ones that Frank was expecting to see on the Antiques Roadshow any time now, being admired by the expert as a 'retro classic'. He fumbled with it, trying to open it the wrong way, but finally managed to answer the call before The Clash got to the middle eight.

'Where are you?' he asked. 'The sea?' He turned to Frank. 'If they've reached the sea, have they gone too far?'

'Unless they're trying to get to Ireland the hard way.'

'You'll have to turn round and come back,' Mick said into the phone. 'Yeah, back through the village...well, you know that field you passed with all the chairs and a fucking great stage in it? Try there.' He hung up and said 'Dickheads' to no one in particular.

'Who?' Frank asked.

'You'll see in a minute if they don't get bloody lost again.'

They stood there, staring at the gate to the field for a good five minutes, even though Frank felt slightly foolish because he had no idea what he was looking for. It turned out to be a battered black minivan, which nearly took the gatepost off as it tried to turn into the field at a very bad angle. It sorted itself out and managed to get onto the field without causing any further damage. It didn't look like the van could stand any more knocks without falling to bits completely. It stopped inside the field, and the driver's door opened. A man got out and stretched. He was around Frank's age and dressed in the sort of fringed suede jacket that nobody over the age of thirty should attempt to wear. His jeans looked like they had seen better days, probably some time round about 2003, and he had a black baseball cap pulled down over his eyes, which were hidden behind aviator shades. There was something familiar about him, but Frank couldn't quite put his finger on it. It was only when he took off the cap and the shades that Frank realised what it was. The once jet-black hair was now half-silver, and the forehead was rather more lined than it once had been, but there was no mistaking the face.

'Jesus, Frank,' he said. 'I heard you'd gone off the map, but I didn't realise it was literally true. Doesn't this island have road signs?'

'Yes, but they're in Welsh, you ignorant bugger. How are you doing, Sean? And more to the point, what the hell are you doing here?'

'Heard you were having a comeback without us,' Sean said, wrapping Frank in a hug. 'Can't have you keeping all the groupies to yourself.'

'As if. We never had groupies when we were young. No chance now.'

'Speak for yourself. Hang on a minute.'

He went back over to the minivan and thumped hard on its side.

'Come 'head, bollocks!' he shouted. 'We're here.'

There was a pause, during which Frank could hear movement from inside the van, and then the side door slid open, and Darren, one-time Leisure Decree drummer, climbed out, clutching a case of beer. Where he had once had a full head of hair, which flew when he drummed, his head was now shaved, and it was obvious from the stubble that this was to disguise encroaching baldness, but his face was exactly the same. Even though he was a year older than Sean, he had always been the baby-faced one of the group. He put the beer down on the grass and hugged Frank.

'You all right, lad?' he asked. 'How come you never write anymore?'

'Because you can't bloody read. Good to see you, Daz. Both of you. But come on, really. What are you doing here?'

'Mick told us about this gig, and we thought, why not?' Sean said. 'Let's have one last go.'

'I haven't got a bass, though,' Frank pointed out.

'You don't need one. You were always shit at it anyway. No,

we're the backing band, mate. You're the frontman for tonight. Have you got a set list?'

'Up here,' Frank tapped his forehead. 'I didn't think I'd need to share it.'

'You'd better write it down then,' Darren said. 'We need to get the kit out of the van. Then I need a beer.'

***

An hour later, and it was like they'd never been apart. They had started tentatively, messing up the first number completely. Sean forgot at first that he was only doing backing vocals and kept trying to steal the melody, while Darren seemed to be having difficulty telling one end of a drumstick from the other. They stopped, did their best to laugh it off, then regrouped and started again. This time it was better. They still sounded like a fairly bad tribute band, but it was beginning to come together. By the third time through the same song, their instincts kicked in, and the old trust, forged over countless gigs of all sizes, was there again. Suddenly they were playing as a group, not as three very rusty individuals and Frank remembered how good it felt to be on stage. By the time they reached the end of the song, Frank felt like the years had fallen away, and he was twenty-five again.

'What next?' Sean called as the last chord faded away.

'Fancy having a go at You'll Be Mine?' Frank said. 'You remember that one?'

'I'm sure it'll come back to me,' Sean replied with a grin. Darren beat them in, and they were off. The Leisure Decree, performing the nearest thing they had to a hit, the song that only needed to go up the charts another five places, and they would have been on Top of the Pops, except that it went down three instead, and some other band got their shot at fame. It was, Frank reflected, a good song. He and Sean had written it over two days, and it had amused them when a review in a small-press magazine had praised the lyrics for being 'literate'. When all that had happened was that Frank and Sean constantly challenged each other to come up with obscure words to try and rhyme. Looking back, some of those words weren't even used correctly but sounded good, so they kept them. They thought they were so clever. They were so young and so full of bravado. They thought they were writing songs that would last forever. Maybe, Frank thought, as Sean launched into the lead break note perfect, that even after all this time, as long as there's one guy on a beach somewhere who remembers the songs, maybe they can live forever.

As they played, Frank looked out across the field. Mick and the rest of the Riflemen had stopped what they were doing and were standing listening. Huw, the old guy who owned the field, was leaning on his walking stick with his dog at his feet. It was hard to read what Huw thought, but the dog was wagging its tail, apparently enjoying itself. And at the edge of the field, by the gate, were the two men Kate had introduced him to the other day, the ones who had the ice cream van. They were watching the stage intently. The one in the stupid T-shirt and shorts looked like he was quite enjoying the music, but the other bothered Frank. He was not smiling, not moving.

51

Gemma had one of the best seats, of course. Kate and Frank had made sure of that. She was right at the front, near the middle, and, although the stage was set back from the seating, it was almost as if she could reach out and touch it. She hoped that her presence wouldn't put Frank off, but he seemed glad of it. The field was rapidly filling up, and music was booming from the speakers. It was quite the event, and Gemma hoped that Frank wasn't feeling as nervous as she was. She had been to see him in what she supposed you'd call the backstage area, which in reality was a bunch of deckchairs someone had put out behind the bands' vans. He hadn't been sitting down, though. He was pacing backwards and forwards, with his guitar slung across his back, looking like a busker who had been moved on from his pitch by the authorities and was looking for somewhere else to play. He had stopped pacing when he saw her and come over.

'How are you feeling?' she asked.

'Like I want to find a bucket and a quiet corner. My stomach feels like a washing machine on spin. I'd forgotten what this was like.'

'Are you going to be okay?'

'I'm not going to puke on stage if that's what you mean. I hope.'

'You'd better not.'

'I'll be fine. I've got to be, haven't I? I owe it to Kate.'

'What, for giving you a job?'

'I got more than a job, though, didn't I?'

She snaked a hand around the back of his head and pulled him in for a kiss.

'I'd better get my seat before someone nicks it,' she said. 'You're going to smash this, Frank. I'll be cheering you on all the way. Love you.'

The words had slipped out before she had realised they were coming. Frank looked like he had been hit on the head with a baseball bat.

'Love you too,' he said.

She gave him another quick kiss and a wave and headed back to her seat. She didn't want the conversation to get any heavier before the gig, but there was also a look on Frank's face she couldn't quite read, a distance in his eyes and a touch of sadness in his voice as he said the words, and it disturbed her. There would be time to find out what that was all about later.

She fingered the strap of her satchel, which was tucked away under her chair and, despite the music, heard a reassuring clink of glass. Time was, she would have heard that sound at a gig and been reassured that her bag contained a bottle or two. This time the noise came from quite a different source. She wasn't quite sure why she had brought the Moondancers with her. It was partly for their own safety. There were a lot of strangers around the bay today, and while she didn't seriously think anyone was going to break into her workshop while she was away from it, she didn't want to take that risk. It was also, she thought, for her own security too. She felt better when they were around, as if they had become talismans of some kind. They were certainly inextricably linked to her feelings for Frank, and those feelings were stronger and warmer when they were near the strange spheres. It had occurred to her more than once that the Moondancers had pushed her and Frank along a little bit. Would it have happened without them? Probably. Maybe. But did that matter? It had happened, and she was glad. She tried not to think about the fact that she had told a man she loved him and meant it for the first time in a very long time and that he had replied in kind. The trouble was, she wasn't at all sure he had meant it as much as she had, or if he was saying it because he was supposed to. What *did* that look mean? But before she could wonder any more, the music faded, and Ruth came onto the stage. She was casually dressed in jeans and a Riflemen T-shirt (presumably donated by the band)

and didn't look overawed by the crowd. She walked straight up to the microphone and tapped it twice. Then she shouted, 'Hello Chapel Bay!' like she was at Wembley and whooped at the top of her voice. The audience responded with a cheer, especially the rows of her pupils and their parents at the front, and Gemma knew Ruth would be fine. Her speech was short but funny, and she thanked everyone she was supposed to. Then she called Kate onto the stage. Kate looked about as comfortable as a rabbit staring at an oncoming lorry but managed to get her thank yous out. She got off the stage as fast as she could and hurried back to the coffee van, looking flushed. Gemma was glad to see that Briony enfolded her in a huge hug when she arrived. It warmed her heart to see how good for each other they were.

'And now the moment you've been waiting for,' Ruth said. 'Chapel Bay, please go absolutely crazy for Frank Davies and the Leisure Decree!'

The crowd did indeed go reasonably crazy, even though, judging by the proliferation of T-shirts like the one Ruth was wearing, a large number of them had come to see the Riflemen. But they were here to have a good time and showed it. Sean and Darren bounded onto the stage and took up their positions. Frank hung back, and it appeared to Gemma he was trying to sneak onstage unnoticed. It was obvious that he wasn't used to being the frontman and took his place at the microphone in front of the band almost apologetically as if he had ended up there by mistake. He cleared his throat, coughed once, which caused a howl of feedback to erupt from the speakers, then counted the band in for the first number.

It was a shambles. The lack of rehearsal and Frank's nerves at being thrust into the spotlight showed. He was either too far back from the microphone to be heard clearly or too close for his voice not to be distorted. He also seemed to have no idea as to the beat Darren was keeping. The drummer kept adjusting his tempo but struggled to keep up. Around her, Gemma could sense how uncomfortable the audience was, and her heart went out to Frank. He had needed a good opener to settle his nerves, and this was definitely not it. He was dying on his arse on stage, and there was nothing she could do about it. Just as she wondered whether Frank would do a second song at all, something thumped hard against her leg. She looked down and saw that her satchel was moving backwards and forwards as if something (and there were no prizes for guessing *what*) was struggling to get out. A green light from inside the bag was clearly visible through the canvas. She glanced around to see if anyone on the adjacent seats had noticed, but they were all transfixed, and not in a good way, on the spectacle unfolding on the stage in front of them. She bent down and cautiously opened the satchel with the intention of trying to placate the Moondancers, but before she could do anything about it, the bag had toppled over, and the spheres had rolled off through the grass towards the stage. Gemma was torn between wanting to run after them and hoping nobody else saw, but her indecision made her freeze. She could only watch in horror as the Moondancers reached the stage and rose gently up, landing on the boards in front of Frank's feet. There, they started to pulse turquoise in time with the beat of Darren's drum. Frank looked down, noticed them and caught Gemma's eye. All she could do was shrug. The chaotic first song ended with a polite smatter of applause. Frank gave a sheepish smile and addressed the crowd.

'That was crap, wasn't it?' he said, and Gemma was relieved that this was greeted with warm laughter. 'You'll have to excuse us. We haven't done this for a very long time, and I was usually hiding at the back. Anyway, thanks for coming and those of you with long memories or a copy of Now That's What I Call Music 38, I think it was, might recognise this. I'm playing this for Gemma.'

He counted in, and the band ripped into You'll Be Mine. A roar of recognition went up from the crowd. Frank glanced back at Sean and Darren and grinned, and Gemma caught a glimpse of what he must have looked like all those years ago. The years fell away, and she could picture the three floppy-haired young men just starting out and hoping they would be massive. And just like that, the band found their feet and their unity. By the time they reached the first chorus, sections of the audience were up on their feet and singing along. All of a sudden, Gemma knew it was going to be all right. The Moondancers, which were continuing to provide a rhythmic light show at the front of the stage, had somehow provided Frank with the reassurance and courage he needed. Free of anxiety, he really began to play, and he was good. But more than that, he looked more alive than she had ever seen him.

From that moment, until the end of the set, the Leisure Decree had the audience in the palm of their hand, and Gemma could have wept with relief. They played six of their old songs (or at least Gemma assumed they were, since, much as she enjoyed them, she only vaguely recognised them from the CDs) and followed them with cover versions of The Killing Moon and All You Need Is Love, which had the whole audience dancing and singing. With the applause still surrounding them, they left the stage, only to be summoned back by cries of, 'Encore!' and Gemma shouted louder than anyone. She could see Frank consulting with Mick Rogers by the vans, and after much head nodding, the Leisure Decree returned to the stage.

'Thank you!' Frank called over the applause. 'We'll have to make this quick, though, because the Riflemen want to get home in time to watch Mary Berry later. But have a go of this. See what you think.'

The audience reaction showed that they thought the Leisure Decree covering Wonderwall was a great idea, particularly when Frank started playing up his Scouse accent as a clear dig at the song's Mancunian origins. They all stood up, swaying, singing and waving their arms in the air. Gemma was amused to see that at the back of the field, old Huw, who had taken up residence near the coffee van, was joining in, even though he was waving completely out of time with everyone else. The song ended and, after Frank had shouted his thanks once more and blown kisses into the audience, the band finally left the stage again. This time, the set was over, and despite some more calls from the audience, the Riflemen hurried onto the stage to start organising their own instruments. Gemma gave Frank five minutes or so to enjoy the moment before she got up and headed towards the vans to go and see him. As she approached the vans, she could see Sean and Darren sharing a beer and a smoke and were laughing together, but she couldn't see Frank straight away. It was only when she suddenly remembered that the Moondancers were still on the stage and hopped up to retrieve them, that she spotted him. Bizarrely, he was standing away from the vans, but he was not on his own. He seemed to be deep in conversation with the two men from the ice cream van, of all things. The conversation looked quite intense, too. They were standing close together, and the one in the shirt and jeans was leaning in, talking in Frank's face. The other, the one dressed like everyone's embarrassing dad on holiday, looked like he had hold of Frank's arm with one hand. There was something in his other hand, but Gemma couldn't make out what it was. There was something about the picture that definitely wasn't right. As she watched, the three men began to walk off, away from the vans, and round the back of the speaker stacks on the stage, where she lost sight of them. She rushed back to the front of the stage to grab the Moondancers, but as she got close to them, they abruptly shot up high into the air. With the sun in her eyes, it was hard to see where they had gone at first, but then she saw them, flying towards the back of the field at a speed she didn't know they were capable of. She could see Frank, still accompanied by the two ice cream men, walking briskly along the side of the audience area towards the ice cream van. She tried to follow, but there were people everywhere, some standing by their seats, some taking the opportunity to stretch their legs in the interval. She pushed and excused herself through the crowd, but only arrived in time to see the door of the ice cream van slam shut and the van, with Frank and the two men in it, drive out of the field into the lane. She ran after it, but even a battered ice cream van was too fast for her.

She stood in the middle of the lane with her hands on her hips, breathing hard and feeling completely out of condition.

She had no idea what to do next. She considered telling Kate and Briony and maybe calling the police, but she knew the local officers would take forever to get here. She knew that she didn't have that kind of time. Then something caught her eye—a glint, no, two *green* glints in the sky high above the fields. With no better plan, she hurried off down the lane, glancing upwards frequently, following the Moondancers, hoping they were leading her in the right direction.

52

In the end, the takedown went rather quicker and easier than Sutcliffe had expected. He and Dawson had hung around, waited until Davies and his band had gone on stage and started performing, then walked the length of the field until they were in the backstage area. If the members of the other band weren't too busy getting stoned to notice them at all, they didn't question it. It probably seemed perfectly reasonable that the two guys from the ice cream van would take advantage of their position by getting themselves a good vantage point backstage. They waited there while the Davies's band ran through their set and, although it wasn't the sort of music Sutcliffe normally listened to, he had to admit that, after the mess they made of the first song, they were pretty good. Apart from the encore. That was one song that Sutcliffe absolutely loathed and made him want to put a brick through the radio every time it came on. They held back after the first encore in case there was a second. But once it seemed apparent that the set was finished, Sutcliffe nodded to Dawson and then called over to Frank Davies.

'Excuse me! Frank? You got a minute?'

Davies looked round with a bewildered *Who, me?* look on his face, but Sutcliffe forced a smile and beckoned him over.

'Could we get your autograph?' Sutcliffe asked. 'Any chance?'

'Yeah, we're big fans of the Leisure Degree,' Dawson joined in.

'Decree,' Sutcliffe corrected. 'Big fans?'

'Well, yes, okay,' Davies said, coming to meet them. 'The other guys did all the work, really, but...'

'No,' Sutcliffe said. 'It's you we want. You're our...er... favourite.'

'We're not exactly Take That,' Davies said and laughed.

'What did you want signing?'

Sutcliffe took a marker pen out of his pocket, handed it to Davies and pointed at Dawson.

'His arm.'

'His arm?'

'You must have been asked to sign stranger things than that by all your female fans.'

'Once or twice. That's why I wanted to make sure I hadn't misheard. Okay, the arm it is.' He popped the lid off the marker pen and waited for Dawson to hold his arm out. He looked understandably surprised when Dawson lifted his arm and had a gun at the end of it. Sutcliffe glanced over his shoulder to make sure he was obscuring the view of the gun from anyone by the vans.

'You're coming with us, Davies,' he said.

It was then that Davies gave him the first of what would turn out to be several surprises that day. He didn't argue, didn't protest. He raised his hands, palms out and shrugged.

'I wondered how long it would take,' he said.

'You weren't that easy to find,' Sutcliffe said. 'But we've found you now, haven't we?'

'Yes. You have.'

Sutcliffe was a bit disappointed. He preferred it when they offered at least token resistance, so he could flex his muscles and get a bit of exercise. Contrary to popular belief, he didn't enjoy hurting people and killing them. It only made him feel hollow inside, but he did like having the opportunity to exert his dominance in any given situation. He liked having the chance, at least, to be cuttingly sarcastic, but Davies wasn't even giving him that. It made Sutcliffe want to blow his kneecaps off for making him come to this shitty little town, if nothing else. But for the moment, that would have to wait. There were too many witnesses on the field, but the fact that everyone was here, meant that there were plenty of places they could go with no prying eyes. With the gun concealed under his jacket, Dawson led Davies by the arm to around the back of the speakers and down past the crowds. They simply looked like two mates going for a nice stroll. Plenty of people were moving around during the break between the two bands, and they were able to get to the ice cream van without anyone bothering them. Once they reached the van, Dawson opened the back door, and Sutcliffe pushed Davies in and climbed in after him. Dawson went around to the driver's cab and started the engine. There was a lurch, but Sutcliffe steadied himself against one of the freezers. It was then that Davies said the second strange thing.

'This is about Tim, isn't it? Tim Barnes?'

'Who?' Sutcliffe asked, but Davies didn't seem to be listening.

'I knew someone would come for me some time since his brother spat at me outside the court. I knew there'd be someone. It wasn't my fault, you know. The court said that. There wasn't anything I could do. If I could take it back, I would. I'm sorry.'

'What the fuck are you talking about?' Sutcliffe asked.

'Tim Barnes,' Davies answered.

'Yes, you keep saying that name like it's supposed to mean something to me. I don't know who you're talking about.'

'The boy on the bike. The boy I killed.'

'You killed someone?' Sutcliffe was almost impressed. 'You?'

'It was an accident. But if you're not here about him, who...?'

'I'm here about Mr. James,' Sutcliffe said. 'Mr. James and the money you nicked.'

'What? What money? I haven't taken any money. What are you talking about?'

'Mr. James's money. Don't come the innocent with me, Davies. The money Deano Ashcroft stole. You know perfectly well what I'm talking about.'

'I haven't got any money! I'm practically skint! Why do you think I'm working in a bloody café? I don't like the job that much, you know.'

Sutcliffe pulled the gun out from under his jacket, but before he could say anything, a bright green flash lit up the interior, and something hit the side of the van with a bang.

From inside the cab, Dawson swore loudly, the van tilted for one long moment and then fell on its side, showering Sutcliffe and Davies with wafer cones and cans of drink. Sutcliffe regained his footing in time to see Davies kick the van's back door open and scramble out. Something caught his foot, though, and Davies fell out of the door and onto his knees on the road. Sutcliffe jumped out of the van, grabbed the back of Davies's jacket, and jabbed the barrel of the gun into his neck at the base of his skull.

'I don't know what the fuck you just did...'

'I didn't do anything!'

'Whatever. I suppose here will do as well as anywhere. Mr. James said if you haven't got his money, then we've got to sort you.'

'He doesn't know anything about Derry James's money,' a voice said. Sutcliffe turned his head and saw a dark-haired woman, who he recognised as Davies's girlfriend, come around the van. She was red in the face and out of breath from running.

'Who the fuck are you, then?'

'I go by Gemma round here,' the woman said. 'But that's not my real name. My real name is Francesca Davis. *Frankie* Davis.'

53

Gemma followed the Moondancers as best she could. She was lucky that the geography of Chapel Bay wasn't complicated. From Huw's field, you could either go left down the lane which led to the bay itself or take a right and keep going through the village, up to the main road and away. The gleaming spheres were high in the sky and moving, but the direction was unmistakable. Left it was.

She didn't know who those men were or why they had taken Frank, but it certainly had nothing whatsoever to do with ice cream. Maybe he owed them money. It wouldn't be uncommon for moneylenders to turn nasty, and Frank was clearly not well off, or he wouldn't need to work for Kate. Perhaps he had got himself into financial difficulties after the accident and had tried to borrow his way out of it. It only emphasised how little she knew about him. But she did know how she felt about him or at least thought she did, and that was enough to make her want to help him if she could. Why she had taken off on her own rather than getting help was another matter. Kate and Briony would definitely have helped, as would Ruth and Phil. There was a whole rock band of Frank's mates, for God's sake, but independent, spontaneous Gemma had decided to go it alone and was now jogging down a country lane in hot pursuit of an ice cream van. No one over the age of six was supposed to run after ice cream vans. It was ridiculous. It was also just her luck that she had wanted to look nice for Frank's gig, and so was running down a road full of potholes in a summer dress and the only pair of unsuitable shoes she owned. She lived her life in trainers and espadrilles and never had to run anywhere. Now, on the only occasion when she was going somewhere at anything other than a stroll, she was wearing heels (not big heels, she hated them, but big enough) that would have been risky to walk in on this surface. That she was running made the possibility of twisting an ankle far greater, but she was doing it for Frank, so on she ran.

Up ahead, the lane bent around to the right, and she knew that once round that bend, it was a straight run downhill to the bay. Once she hit the straight bit, she should be able to see exactly where the ice cream van was. Before she could get around the corner, however, her eye was caught by a glint in the sky, and she could see the Moondancers, clear as anything, swooping down fast. They disappeared behind the tall roadside hedge, and then a green flash lit the sky, like the one that Gemma's dad had told her appeared on the horizon at the precise moment the sun goes down. There was a bang from somewhere around the bend, the sound of scraping metal, then silence. Gemma stopped and listened. All she could hear was her heart pounding in her chest, the angry twitter of birds in the hedgerow and the now distant thump of the Riflemen's bass. Then she heard a clang and voices and hurried on around the corner.

The sight that greeted her would have been surreal enough to be funny were it not so serious. The ice cream van was leaning at an angle; its passenger side wheels caught deep in a ditch at the side of the road. It would undoubtedly have been on its side had it not fallen on the thicket of brambles and hawthorn that made up the hedge. Frank was on his knees in the road, unharmed by the looks of things, thank God. But the guy from the ice cream van was standing over him, pointing something at his head and *Jesus Christ, was that a gun*? His mate was struggling to get out of the cab, but he looked like he was caught in his seatbelt. He also had quite a nasty cut on his forehead. Then the ice cream guy said something that struck Gemma like a bout of vertigo, and it felt like the ground had fallen away from beneath her feet.

'Mr. James said if you haven't got his money, then we've got to sort you,' he said.

As soon as she heard that name, she knew what this was all about and, much as all her instincts were screaming at her to turn and run, she stepped forward and spoke.

'He doesn't know anything about Derry James's money,' she said. The ice cream guy, who Gemma now knew had never sold an ice cream in his life, looked up.

'Who the fuck are you, then?'

'I go by Gemma round here,' she said. 'But that's not my real name. My real name is Francesca Davis. *Frankie* Davis.'

'Gemma, no!' Frank said. 'Go. Get out of here.'

'No, Frank. I can't. This isn't your problem. It's mine.'

'Go on,' said the man with the gun. 'Explain.'

So Gemma did.

'I'm sorry, Frank,' she said. 'You shouldn't have been mixed up in all of this. A little while ago, I did something very stupid, and I always wondered if it would catch up with me. It was when I lived for a bit in Liverpool. Yes, I know what I said, but this is kind of why I treated you like I did. The shop I was working at had closed down, and I was out of work and bored, so...'

'Yeah, now I'm bored too,' the man with the gun said.

'I could do with some help here,' called out the other man, who was still half hanging out of the ice cream van cab, the seatbelt wrapped tightly around his ankle.

'Shut up, Dawson,' the man with the gun said, then turned back to Gemma. 'Is there a point to all this?'

'Yes, there is. The point is I got involved with this guy. I don't know why. I didn't really like him that much. He never told me what he did, but I guessed it was a bit sketchy, so I didn't ask. He always had plenty of money, and he treated me quite well for a bit. His name was Dean Ashcroft.'

'Dean Ashcroft?' the gunman echoed. 'Deano?'

'That's what people called him, yes, but I guess everyone called Dean gets that. Anyway, he got bored too and started staying away for days at a time. I figured there were other women. There usually are. I should have dumped him there and then, but I didn't. I got curious instead. One night, when he'd been around for a couple of days, he'd gone out, on business, he said, wouldn't be back 'til late. So I had a good poke around his flat and hidden away, right at the back of his wardrobe, was a bag, you know, the sort of holdall you take to the gym. Only Dean didn't go to the gym. It was full of cash. And there was a notebook. He didn't like computers very much, old Dean, so he had everything written down. It was a list of businesses and amounts of money.'

'So you stole the money.'

'Who's telling this story, you or me?'

'Well, hurry up. We're standing in the middle of the road next to a fucking ice cream van in a hedge, and that gig will be letting out soon.'

'I think it's cutting my circulation off!' shouted the other man from the cab.

'Hang on a minute,' the gunman said, and Gemma was treated to the sight of him hurrying over and disentangling his colleague from the seatbelt. He let the other man drop to the floor, smacked him across the back of the head and came back.

'Let's get this over,' he said.

'Stop interrupting then. There's not much more to tell. Next time Dean went out, I followed him. He and this other lad were calling into chippies and restaurants. Didn't take a genius to work out what was going on. He was running some sort of protection racket, probably for the guy he was always talking about on the phone. Guy called Derry James. I guess he's your boss too.'

'Right. So you took the money. Give it back, and we'll be on our way.'

'I haven't got it.'

'Yes, you have. Where is it? Look, do I have to shoot your boyfriend first? I don't mind. His songs are shit.'

'No, I haven't got it. The next time Dean went off shagging, I took the bag and went round the businesses in his notebook. It took all night, but I gave them all a chunk of money back apart from a grand or so that I kept for expenses, packed a bag and got the hell out. Long story short, I ended up here. There might be a couple of hundred left if you let me go to a cashpoint, but that's it.'

In the distance, a clamour of applause went up, and someone shouted something indistinct over a microphone.

'Sounds like the band are done,' the man with the gun said. 'Assuming they were good enough to get an encore, that's how long we've got to get out of here.'

He raised his hand and brought the gun sharply down on Frank's head, sending him sprawling on the ground, then advanced on Gemma.

'Come on, Dawson,' he called. 'Stop fucking about. We need to finish this and go.'

54

Frank had seen plenty of films in which someone was hit over the head and knocked unconscious. They usually stayed out cold for whatever length of time suited the plot. He'd never wondered if it worked in real life. It wasn't one of those things you ever thought about. Now it had happened to him and it was almost certainly one of the most painful things that had ever happened to him. Yes, he'd bumped his head on things on a number of occasions. He remembered one time when he was out on the road with the band, and he had been putting a guitar in the boot of Sean's car. Sean hadn't been looking and had assumed Frank had moved out of the way when he closed the boot. He had brought the boot down on his friend's head instead. The protruding latch had caught Frank right on the top of his head. But apart from giving him a cut on his scalp and knocking him sick, it hadn't had any long-lasting effects. The crack with the gun felt similar to that, but worse. He suspected he'd find blood if he touched it but was reluctant to check. It was entirely possible he had blacked out and might be slightly concussed because, for a moment or two, he wasn't sure where he was. It tasted like there was soil in his mouth, and there seemed to be something hard nudging his shoulder. Then he remembered. *Gemma!*

He pushed himself up from the floor into a kneeling position, trying to ignore the sharp jag of pain searing through his head and looked around. The ice cream van was still there where it had been abandoned, but there was no sign of Gemma or the two men. It was also apparent what it was that had been nudging him while he lay on the ground. Under the current circumstances, it made perfect sense that two glass spheres would be hovering around him, glowing with a dark blue light and making urgent noises that could probably best be described as chirrups. It was quite evident that they wanted him to follow them and that, during the brief time that he had been stunned, his day had turned into Skippy the Bush Kangaroo, directed by James Cameron. He brushed some of the gravel from his trousers and the palms of his hands, and without questioning any further, followed where the Moondancers led.

They took him down the lane to the bay. When they reached the steps that led down to Kate's café, they paused, as if trying to get their bearings, then led him down the steps to the beach. It was eerily quiet; there were no people. They were presumably all still at the gig, and the café was, of course, closed. The squawking of the seagulls and the whisper of the waves on the shoreline shingle were the only sounds that broke the silence. Then the Moondancers moved off again, towards the path that Frank had taken virtually every lunchtime, the path which led up the cliffs. He could still recall how it felt to follow that path, knowing that he would find the place at the top where he could sit in peace and watch the beach (and often Gemma) below. And there was Gemma now, halfway up the path, struggling against the two men who were not ice cream sellers, as they led her upwards. Despite the ache in his head, Frank broke into a run and went after them.

Most of the path up the cliff was enclosed on either side by foliage or rocks, and he lost sight of Gemma part of the way up. He kept going, though, following the Moondancers, who were hovering above with a much better view than he had. They had to be going up to the cliffs. It was the only logical place the men could be taking Gemma, but he dreaded the reason why and forced himself on. He had to get there in time. The alternative didn't bear thinking about.

When he first emerged onto the cliff top, he thought he was already too late. All he could see was the backs of the two men. Then one of them moved a little, and his heart leapt as he saw Gemma, alive and well, but standing at the cliff edge with her back to a sheer drop into the sea below. The man with the gun had his hand raised and was pointing the pistol at her. Frank needed no second thoughts. He shouted Gemma's name and ran as fast as he could across the turf towards the men. Above him, he was aware that the Moondancers had dropped down low and were shooting through the air in the same direction. He grabbed Gemma and threw her onto the grass, away from the cliff edge.

Then there was a deafening bang, and everything turned blue.

Part Five

55

Every time Kate went out of the café to collect cups and plates from the outside tables and saw Gemma sitting outside her workshop, her heart broke a little for her friend. Today was no different. As Kate loaded her tray, she could see Gemma on her deckchair, gazing out to sea. She looked small and alone and had done for several weeks now, ever since Frank. She pretended to be okay, still calling in most days for a cup of tea (she seemed to have gone off lattes for some reason) and chatting, but there was a spark missing, and Kate feared that before very long, they would lose Gemma too.

'She still there?' Briony asked when Kate came back inside. Bri was loading the dishwasher and took the tray to add its contents to this load.

'I wish I knew what to say,' Kate said. 'I can't help feeling this is all my fault.'

'What do you mean, your fault?' Briony closed the dishwasher door, started the programme. She then stripped off her rather unflattering rubber gloves, came over to Kate and put her arms around her. 'Of course, it's not your fault, you tool. They're grown adults. You're not responsible for them.'

'I know, but I introduced them. I gave Frank the job here. If I'd known what was going to happen....'

'You'd have given him a job anyway. Because you've got the kindest heart of anyone I know, and he was good for this place. You've got nothing to reproach yourself for.'

'But it was the gig, wasn't it? That was when it happened. If I hadn't agreed to do that bloody gig...'

'...we wouldn't have raised all that money. And Ruth wouldn't be spending half her time talking to roofing contractors. If it wasn't for you, the school would be closing, Katie. That's something to be proud of, isn't it?'

'I suppose. It's certainly put a smile on Ruth's face, that's for sure.'

Kate knew that the prospect of a new school roof wasn't the only thing that was putting a smile on Ruth's face. Only yesterday, she had taken Kate to one side and told her in strictest confidence that there was something that hadn't happened since Phil had gone back—something that usually happened with brutal accuracy. There was a strong possibility that Phil had left something rather special behind and that a school roof wasn't the only new thing coming into her life. She couldn't tell Bri or anyone else yet, though. Ruth had told her that she had miscarried once before and had no intention of jinxing it until she was absolutely sure.

'Be proud, Katie,' Briony said again. 'You did a good thing. Anything else that happened had nothing to do with you. And yes, he could have given you a bit more warning, the little shitbag, but, you know, every cloud. At least it created a vacancy and brought our plans forward a bit.'

'Well, I suppose it does mean we're going to find out if we can work together rather sooner than we expected.'

'It'll be fine. You know I'm loving it already, don't you? Honestly, Kate, I wouldn't be anywhere else. Yes, sure, we're going to have our ups and downs. Yes, there are going to be times when we get on each other's tits, and we'll argue over stuff. But I think we're strong enough to get through that. I think we'll find ways of talking about it and sorting it out. It's a bit like a marriage in some ways. There'll be good days and bad days, but there will be a lot more good than bad.'

'Like a marriage? You think so? I hadn't thought of it like that. Is that a good thing?'

'I think so. I've never had one, so I'm only guessing. But yes, I think it would be a very good thing. In fact, hang on.' Briony broke off, went to the back of the café and delved into the pockets of her coat. When she returned, she had something concealed in her hand. 'I was going to wait until we were home tonight to do this, but now seems as good a time as any.'

'Bri, no...!'

'Yes. But please don't ask me to go down on one knee. I'm not sure I could get up, and it would be my luck that we'd get a bunch of customers. Do you want me to spell it out?'

'Yes, please.'

'You asked for it. Right then. Kate Wilde, will you marry me?'

'Yes, please,' Kate said again, but this time she held her fiancée in her arms when she said it and kissed her afterwards. Old Geraint came in at that rather inopportune moment, and for that day only, he was kept waiting for his teacake.

56

Gemma sat on her deckchair staring out to sea and wondered if he was out there somewhere. He was, of course, he was. But at this moment, she had no idea where. Her satchel was on the ground by her side, and the Moondancers were nestled inside. Since she had picked them up from the grass that day on the cliffs, they had been more or less inert, just two pretty spheres of green glass. She had put them in her satchel there and then, and that was where they had remained ever since. She hadn't used the satchel for beachcombing much over the past few weeks. She hadn't felt like it. She kept remembering the time she had shown Frank what she did and doing it on her own made her feel sad right now. Every now and then, she opened the bag in the privacy of her flat and talked to the Moondancers. There was never any reply, but it made her feel better to talk to them about what had happened because there was no way she could ever talk to anyone else.

She talked to them about how Frank had pushed her out of the way, standing where she had stood and faced the man with the gun as he pulled the trigger. She talked about the bang that had left her ears ringing and the dazzling deep blue flash which had blinded her for a few minutes and made her see stars for the rest of the day, a flash which was still imprinted on her vision whenever she shut her eyes. She talked about how, when she could see again, the Moondancers were lying on the grass by her side, and Frank and the two men Derry James had sent were gone. Where the men had stood, there was a crater burnt into the still-smoking turf, and the only sign that anyone had stood there was one incongruous, scorched sandal. It looked for all the world as though someone had lit a bonfire or a barbecue there and forgotten to put it out. Where Frank had stood at the cliff edge, there was nothing at all. She had gathered the Moondancers up, got to her feet and called Frank's name, knowing deep in her heart that he would not answer.

She talked to the Moondancers some nights about how badly Derry James's men had miscalculated, how they had assumed that the edge of the cliff went straight down to the rocks and the sea but hadn't bothered to look and hadn't seen that there was another shelf of turf below. That was where Frank had landed when the gunshot had made him stumble backwards. Where the bullet had ended up, nobody would ever know, but it had missed Frank completely. She told them, as best she could because there really weren't words, of the relief she felt when he appeared over the edge of the cliff, put his arm around her and told her it was over. She didn't know then it was over in more ways than one.

They had walked back to the field where the gig had just finished virtually in silence. Frank seemed dazed, bewildered as to what he was doing on the cliff in the first place. He remembered coming off stage and talking to Sean and Daz, but after that, it got a bit hazy. He seemed to have no recollection of the two men from the ice cream van at all, even when they walked past the van, which was still slumped against the hedge. Gemma told him that he had wandered off after the gig, and she had come after him because he didn't seem himself, and wasn't that lucky? She didn't tell him that as far as she could see, the Moondancers had apparently killed two men, obliterating them totally, apart from one item of footwear. Frank had already been involved in one death, and she wasn't sure he could cope with any more. Perhaps that was why his mind wasn't letting him remember, or maybe the Moondancers had wiped out that memory when they wiped out the two men. At least it saved her having to explain why Gemma wasn't her real name, and that she had picked it largely at random when she left Francesca behind, because it seemed to fit with what she did. It was best if Frank just knew her as Gemma.

Back at the field, Gemma made small talk with Kate, Briony and Ruth while Frank went off to chat with his old musician mates and that was that. But it wasn't, not really. Something had changed. Frank seemed distracted, with her but not with her, and two days later, she found out why.

She woke up that morning and found herself alone in the bed. She put a fleece on and went down the fire escape, and sure enough, there was Frank sitting on the wall watching the waves. She sat down next to him and watched too for a while.

'What is it?' she asked eventually. 'Is it what happened?'

'What happened?' he echoed, frowning. He obviously still didn't remember, and she wasn't going to push it. There was a long pause. 'It's Sean and Darren. Seems like they had such a good time it's given them ideas. They're talking about putting the band back together and doing a bit of a tour, maybe even recording some new stuff. They asked me to join them.'

'And you're going, aren't you?'

'I don't know. I thought I might.'

'So when were you going to tell me?'

'Today probably. I said I'd let them know by the end of the week.'

'What about us?'

'Now there's the thing,' Frank said and turned to look at her for the first time since she had sat down. 'I'm not sure what this 'us' *is*. I can't help but think they did something to us.'

'Who?'

'Them. The Moondancers. I can't help thinking they did something to our heads. We did talk about it. We said they were grateful.'

'That's daft. I know how I feel about you, Frank.'

'Do you? It's been a strange time. How much of it was circumstance? I know we're friends, and I do love you. I think we always will, but everything else? I'm not sure.'

'We're a bit old for holiday romances, Frank.'

'It's a bit more than that. But I think we need a chance to find out, and I'm not sure we can do that while I'm here. Not right now. Not with them around.'

'Do you remember that night when we saw the shooting star? Maybe we got what we wished for. Maybe that's all it is.

Yes, it was circumstance, but that doesn't mean it's wrong. Everyone's got to meet somehow, and it's usually a coincidence of some kind. Perhaps these things really are written in the stars.'

'I'm sorry, but that's almost certainly bollocks.'

They laughed and then went silent again.

'Are you coming back?' she asked. 'You know, once you've made your fortune?'

'I doubt that's going to happen. We probably won't even get a gig or find out that we actually hate each other.'

'You didn't answer the question.'

'I'd like to think so.' Frank let that hang for a moment. Then said, 'You could always come with me.'

'Really?' Gemma laughed. 'You don't need a Yoko hanging round at this stage. Anyway, thanks, but I belong here, by the beach. Are you planning on writing to me?'

'Well, I thought we might do it the modern way. Texting. The occasional phone call. That sort of thing.'

Gemma turned away.

'I know how that'll go. We'll talk every day at first. Then one time, we'll skip a day. Then two. Then we might go a week without getting round to it because, you know, we're so busy. Then before we know where we are, we'll be like a couple of mates who text when they have some news, not for the sake of it. Then one day...'

'That won't happen.'

'It happens all the time.'

'I'm not like that, though.'

'Frank, your phone's so ancient I'm surprised you can text at all. And you're so ancient I'm not sure you'd know how. I don't think I've seen you text anyone in all the time I've known you.'

'I'm not too old to learn.'

'We'll see. I've always been of the opinion that relationships need work, and to put the work in, you've usually got to be present.'

Neither of them quite knew how to follow that. After a bit, Gemma sniffed and said, 'I'm being daft. Go on. Go play your music. You're so good, Frank. You're wasted here.'

She talked to the Moondancers, those nights when she wanted someone to talk to, about how he left three days after that conversation, how Kate had said she was sorry to see him go but had moved Briony into his place very quickly afterwards. She told them how Frank had refused to let her come and see him off and hadn't cried when he left. She told them that he did text most days, and his texts were short but often funny. But he didn't talk about them, and he didn't talk about the future. She was starting to think that talking to the Moondancers was driving her batshit crazy. That was why she knew what she had to do.

***

She did it two nights later. She wanted to wait for a clear sky, and the last couple of days had been cloudy. Today had been sunny, though, and the sky was a patchwork of stars. She went down to the beach barefoot because somehow that seemed right. When she reached the water's edge, she put her satchel on the sand at her feet and took the Moondancers out. She held one in each hand and raised them to the sky.

'Go on,' she said. 'Go home.'

The spheres did not move, but she thought that perhaps they felt a little warmer than they had when she first took them out of the bag.

'Go on,' she said again. Was it her imagination, or had they begun to glow? It was soft, barely discernible, but there was something. She waited, but nothing else happened.

'I'll be okay,' she said. 'Thank you. For everything. But I'll be okay. Go on. You belong together out there.'

And there it was. The glow was stronger, and she felt it. The pressure lifted from her palms, and suddenly they were hovering above her hands, and they were singing.

'Go,' she said once more. 'I'll never forget you, but you have to go.'

They did. They hovered above her head briefly, bathing her in a turquoise light that made her feel at once strong and serene, then shot up into the sky and out of sight. She watched them go, wiped away the tears she hadn't even known she had been crying, and then walked back up the beach towards her home.

57

Jonathan Liddell walked out of the hospital and down the path. He walked away from the pyjama-clad and drip-fed smokers who congregated around the main door, ignoring the recorded voice that periodically blurted out of concealed speakers and told them not to do so. Once he was a safe distance away, he took his cigarettes out of his pocket and lit one. He didn't smoke all that often and preferred to be as considerate as possible when he did so. There were occasions, however, when only a cigarette would do, and this was definitely one.

Ever since Sutcliffe and Dawson had dropped off the map, he'd had people monitoring the hospital intake, on the off-chance that they might show up there, but up until now, their whereabouts had remained a mystery. Either they had failed to find and deal with their target, or they had absconded with the money themselves, but whichever it was, Mr. James wanted a word. One thing was for sure, nothing untoward had happened at any charity gigs on Anglesey. Not unless the North Wales Press had so much else to report that it didn't think such a thing warranted any attention. The ice cream van had been found abandoned in a ditch, with a large dent in the side. The compensation that had to be paid to its furious owner was yet another thing Sutcliffe was going to have to account for, assuming he and his idiot partner ever turned up.

After several weeks, Liddell was starting to believe that Sutcliffe and Dawson were gone for good, which was bad news because Derry James was running out of cat videos to watch; that meant trouble for someone, and Liddell suspected it might be him. He was surprised and relieved, then, to get a call from his contact in A&E to tell him that two men had been brought in who might possibly match the description of the men he was looking for. They were apparently under police guard in the hospital, waiting for a psychiatric evaluation. It seemed that they had attempted to hijack the van of an ice cream vendor who had been innocently going about his business until these two characters appeared in the middle of the road. Luckily, a passer-by had seen what was happening, called the police, who, for once, arrived quickly before the ice cream seller could be harmed. The two men refused to surrender at first, yelling something about how the ice cream van was their destiny. When one of them announced that 'Mr. Creamy and Mr. Sprinkles have to make the children smile', they were rapidly tazered, sedated, then taken to hospital, where it seemed extremely likely that they were going to be sectioned. Liddell headed straight for the hospital to make sure.

He was only allowed a glimpse of the two men and barely recognised them. Their clothes were ripped and scorched, one of them was missing a sandal, and their skin was covered in grime and what appeared to be soot. To Liddell, they looked for all the world like two koalas that had barely survived a bush fire. Even though they were sedated, they were rambling about Cornettos and Fab lollies, and it was obvious that whatever their bodies had survived, their minds had not been so lucky. Liddell apologised to the nurse whom he paid for this information, explained that they were not the men he was seeking, and left.

He finished his cigarette and conscientiously disposed of the butt in the nearest bin. He decided it might be a good idea to go for a cup of coffee and a sandwich somewhere before going back to break the news to Derry James that, in all likelihood, he wasn't going to get his money back now. That was not a conversation that would go particularly well, and Liddell thought he might need a holiday after that. He wasn't very good with heat. He generally avoided going abroad, preferring instead to take his holidays in Britain. This year, however, he thought that perhaps Cornwall might be nice. Anywhere, in fact, but Anglesey. For some reason, the North Wales coast just didn't appeal anymore.

58

Gemma was used to finding unexpected things in the alleyway at the side of the workshop, but she hadn't anticipated what she would find there that night.

He was sitting on the steps of the fire escape and was so concealed by the shadows that she only recognised him by the guitar case at his feet.

'They've gone, then,' he said. 'I saw them go.'

'Yes, they've gone. But you seem to have come back.'

'Yes, I have. Though, God knows what I'm going to do. I haven't exactly got a job anymore.'

'What about the band?' she asked.

'It was a very bad idea. As soon as we all sat down together, I realised that. None of us are the same people anymore. We had one rehearsal, laughed and then quit. I'd have come back sooner, but I wasn't sure you'd want me to. But I missed this place. I missed the beach and the cliffs. I missed you.

'And are you planning on staying this time? I'm not going to start anything that isn't going anywhere, Frank. I think I'm worth a bit more than that.'

'You're worth far more than that. You asked me once what I wished for that night the Moondancers came down. I didn't wish for anything because I already had what I wanted, right here. I was just a bit too stupid to see it.'

'That's very poetic, Frank. You should write a song. And what about that? You were so alive on stage that day. Aren't you going to miss the music?'

'Sod the music,' Frank said, getting up and coming towards her. 'You gave me the stars.'

The End

Author's Note

Anglesey is a real place. Have a look – it's there on the map. Better still, go and visit. It's lovely there. Letting the Stars Go, however, is a work of fiction and so I have taken considerable liberties with the geography of the island. Chapel Bay and its environs are entirely fictitious. Any errors or inconsistencies in how long it takes to get from one place to another on Anglesey are wholly my responsibility.

I never intended to write this book. Sometimes you get an idea and it won't go away and you have to write it down. This wasn't one of those times. That you have been able to read it at all (which I hope has been a pleasant experience) is down to one person.

A couple of years ago, I hit a brick wall. I'd finished writing a Young Adult trilogy and discovered I had no other good ideas. I was starting to think of the popular expression *Everyone has a book in them* and that maybe I'd written mine and that was it. In my desperation to write something –*anything*- I asked a very good friend of mine to set me a challenge, to give me a brief for a short story. She did and I wrote a story called Letting the Stars Go. We both thought it was okay and that was that. There was something about that story, though, and I wondered about expanding it to see if it could fill a novel. I introduced a much bigger cast of characters and filled out their back-stories and here it is. All the way along, that same friend encouraged and pushed me when needed and consequently was the first person to read it. She didn't just read it, she did a thorough job of editing it, too and her input has made it a better book. It also now contains substantially fewer instances of the word 'really' (sorry about that!) Any remaining errors in the book are, I must add, purely down to me.

That friend is Estelle Maher, the Estelle to whom the book is dedicated. She is my writing buddy, my editing mate and one of my greatest sources of support. She is also a very fine writer herself and I urge you to check her books out immediately. You'll be very glad you did. So thank you Estelle. From the bottom of my heart.

In the original draft of this book, only one of the love stories had a happy ending. I'm not saying which. But before I committed to the planned ending of the book, I celebrated my Silver Wedding Anniversary to my lovely, patient wife Wendy, and it got me thinking that maybe, just maybe, if the stars are in the right place, happy endings are possible, so one couple in this book has Wendy to thank for theirs.

The stunning cover is by a hugely talented artist by the name of Gemma Dolan. She really is amazing and I suggest you have a look at her work on Instagram.

The title of the book is lifted from one of the wonderful songs Paddy McAloon wrote for Prefab Sprout. Thanks for the music, Paddy.

Keep looking up and watching the stars. If you see one fall, make a wish. But keep it to yourself or it won't come true.

B.S.
September 2021

Also by Bob Stone

A Bushy Tale (illustrated by Holly Bushnell)
A Bushy Tale: The Brush Off (illustrated by Holly Bushnell)

Published by Beaten Track Publishing

Missing Beat
Beat Surrender
Perfect Beat
Out of Season
Faith's Fairy House (illustrated by Gemma Dolan)

Find me on Facebook, Twitter and Instagram